Ragged Robin

CW00468444

Other Books by Sherrie Hansen

Night and Day
Daybreak

Maple Valley Trilogy:
Book 1: Stormy Weather
Book 2: Water Lily
Book 3: Merry Go Round

Love Notes

Wildflowers of Scotland Novels:
Thistle Down *(Prequel Novella)*
Book 1: Wild Rose
Book 2: Blue Belle
Book 3: Shy Violet
Book 4: Sweet William
Book 5: Golden Rod

Wildflowers of Ireland Mystery:
Seaside Daisy

Wildflowers of Bohemia Mystery:
Plum Tart Iris

Ragged Robin
A Wildflowers of Scotland Mystery

To believing;
Sherrie Hansen

By

Sherrie Hansen

Published by Blue Belle Books

St. Ansgar, IA

Sherrie Hansen

Blue Belle Books

www.BlueBelleBooks.com

PO Box 205, St. Ansgar, Iowa 50472

Cover Design: Sherrie Hansen

Cover Photo: Nataliya Hora

Manufactured in the United States of America

ISBN: 9798504040509

DEDICATION

To Ang Andrew, my sweet friend from Scotland, who introduced me to the Selkie legend one day while walking on the beach near the Moray Firth. The mist and fog were so atmospheric, the sea so shrouded in mystery, that my imagination ran away with me... xoxo

Sherrie Hansen

CHAPTER 1

Rebecca Ronan focused on the scent of lavender, lemon and blueberry scones wafting through the restaurant and tried to block the odor of bleach that was slowly overtaking her nostrils.

"Keep looking up! The world is full of promise!" The Queen had made it clear that the frightening days of the pandemic were over and what happened next was only limited by their own collective imaginations, energy, and hard work.

Last year's virus scare still seemed like a bad dream. But it was far more than a mere hallucination. She'd lost her grandmother, her stepfather, and several lifelong friends of the family who lived in London. Dreams weren't supposed to hurt, and she definitely had been. Last year had been a nightmare. But while thousands of restaurants in the UK had closed, at least her business was still plodding along. She was eking by.

She grabbed a mitt from the counter and reached into the oven to take out the scones. The edges were a perfect golden brown. At least something was as it should be.

She sprinkled a little sugar infused with lavender buds on top of some of the scones and left the rest to be frosted. The need to regroup, move on, and start anew was unanimous.

Scotland, the UK, the world – they'd all been so optimistic about reopening. She'd been beyond excited when the announcement was made that they could allow tourists back onto Skye. She'd felt so motivated, so enthusiastic about getting back to normal.

Now, here she was again, less than a year later, wiping down every surface in the restaurant with sanitizer and wondering how she was supposed to catch up on her mortgage payments when she'd barely had six months of piddling receipts before the prime minister announced the new shut down order.

She set her timer and waited for the bleach to do its job. The whole procedure was a necessary evil, but at least this time, she knew the drill.

She heard a quiet knock on the back door and glanced up to see a silhouette outlined in the lamplight from the garden. The light shone off a head of hair that was thick, long, and reddish blond. It looked like Robin. What was he doing in Portree on a Wednesday? He should be docked in Lochmaddy by now, ready to leave North Uist and come home on the morrow.

Then it dawned on her. The second travel ban. No customers. It would hit him even harder this time, with a new boat and a new loan to pay off. Her stomach clenched. It wasn't fair. Not when they were all just getting back on their feet.

She unlocked the door. Robin came through along with a gust of cool air.

Robin gave her a lopsided half-smile. "I saw the light and figured you were baking."

"They're still letting me do take-out orders. It breaks my heart to have to bag things up and hand them out the window so my customers can freeze to death eating on the pier when I've got a warm, cozy, freshly-painted dining room waiting to be used."

Robin's stomach rumbled. "At least you have customers. People have to eat."

"I know. I shouldn't complain. I'm making enough off the to-go orders to stay afloat."

Rob laughed.

"Sorry. Poor choice of words." She looked at his waterproof jacket and fisherman's cap and was tempted to lean in for a hug. Darn social distancing.

She smiled instead and hoped he could see her eyes crinkling above her mask. "So how are you handling things? My heart breaks to think about that beautiful boat bobbing around on the water empty as a message-less bottle."

"It's not empty. I gave up my apartment and moved into the boat last weekend."

Well, her stupid mask was good for something anyway. At least, she hoped it was hiding her shock. She finally eked out "Because you wanted to?"

"I didn't have a choice."

"Oh, Rob."

"Even without a rent payment, I'm not sure I'll make it."

"Of course you will! This new shut down can't last for long. Not after last year. I mean, the medical experts are all so experienced by now, aren't they? They'll have the mystery wrapped up in no time after learning everything they did with COVID." Her caretaker instincts revved into high gear. "How are you managing without a kitchen?"

"I have a microwave that I can use when I'm in dock." His stomach rumbled again. "When the sun stays out for several hours at a time, the deck sometimes gets hot enough to fry an egg."

"Right. When does that happen? Even on the best of days you'd be lucky to have one cooked enough to call it sunny side up."

"Right. My mum always flipped ours and cooked 'em all the way through. But Dad liked his a bit runny. If he could do it, I can, too."

She swiped a still warm scone with a swirl of cinnamon frosting and handed it to him on a napkin.

He looked at it, took a deep breath, and looked like he

3

could melt right along with the frosting. "I don't have any money."

"I can't sell it to anyone else now you've breathed on it. You know the regs."

"Fine." His voice sounded wistful, full of longing and – she supposed, joy.

Her scones did that to people.

"No worries." She slid the rest of the scones onto a cooling rack on the other side of the convection oven. "Robin?"

He licked his lips and swallowed. "Yes?"

"You're not still eating fish, are you?"

"I live on a boat. On the sea. I'm broke. Of course, I'm eating fish."

"Well, you need to stop it. They think this virus is transmitting to the human population through infected fish."

"What?" His facial features turned from blissful to annoyed. "You're serious?"

She nodded. "They've forbidden us to make anything with whitefish, cod, salmon or herring. Even smoked haddock is suspect."

Robin's face fell. "So the smoking process doesn't kill the virus, the bacteria, whatever it is this time?"

"No. I can't even make my famous fisherman's pie with smashed tatties and Mull cheddar on top. Not until they know what's going on."

"So much for chartering any more fishing expeditions." He took a step back until his heels were touching the threshold. "I shouldn't have come. Sorry. I mean, I didn't know."

"Because you've eaten a little fish?"

"More than a little. I love haddock. Cod. North Atlantic salmon. I follow the seals to their secret fishing spots. Most of my diet consists of whitefish."

"You mentioned that you like to swim with the seals."

"I share their beaches. Their whole diet is fish. I could be a carrier and not even know it."

4

Her mind went into overdrive. "Have the seals been getting sick? I mean, have you seen any evidence of their being more tired, less frisky, coughing – barking – more than usual, looking peaked?"

"No." He looked thoughtful. "Why?"

"I was just thinking out loud. Maybe the seals have some sort of immunity."

Robin's face turned stony. "They didn't last year. Thousands of them died of COVID. Dolphins and whales, too. Infected by human waste water." He set the last bite of his scone on the counter. "You have to promise me you won't say anything to anyone about this theory of yours until I—."

"I was just—"

"You know what will happen if they latch on to the idea of seals being immune. They'll capture and dissect the whole lot of them in the name of science."

"Calm down. I was just thinking out loud. I wasn't suggesting that—"

"Just promise me."

"I will." She meant it. She'd given her word. But still – she wondered why Rob was reacting so intensely. She had forgotten how devastating COVID was to the marine mammal population in 2020, but still, what was going on? Wouldn't Robin be happy if the seals weren't meant to suffer through this ordeal like they had the last one?

She handed him a meat pie she'd made some hours ago. It was still under the heat lamp, but it was too old to sell.

"It's on the house."

"Thank you." Robin turned and left as fast as he had come, the ragged edges of his hair hanging well below his tattered collar. Poor man probably hadn't had a decent haircut in months just like the rest of them. The wind and salt water were hard on clothes. Robin had been a schnazzy dresser before he'd purchased his boat. He'd never worn a suit as far as she knew, but he'd loved hand-dyed and knitted lamb's wool sweaters. He'd always made it a point to support the local artisans and weavers on Skye who grazed and sheered their own sheep and earned a living selling handmade woolens. But that was the old days. If Robin looked a little ragged around the edges after what he'd been through in the last year—what they'd all been through—one could hardly blame him.

#

Robin Murphy felt his ankles tilting with the slant of the pavement as he walked down the hill to Portree Harbor where his boat was docked. He'd tried to keep his trips to town at a minimum but he had to refill his fresh water tank and come close enough to get a signal long enough to retrieve his phone messages and check his email at least once a week. In the old days, he'd have stocked up on supplies for his excursions and placed his catering order with Rebecca. His customers loved her boxed lunches and the homemade goodies she packed them with. He'd sent her a lot of business when things were good. But the ugly truth – his new reality – was no customers, no commerce. These days, he couldn't afford even one serving of restaurant food say nothing about the hundreds of orders he'd typically placed in an average week.

The twinkling lights of Portree reflected in the sea along the pier, rippling across waves that bore the slight tint of each of the colorful buildings that lined the water front.

He was just starting to relax – the gentle lull of the sea affected him that way – when he heard an outburst of raucous laughter.

He wasn't normally one of those people who was nosy enough to want to gawk while other people flaunted their dramas—in fact, he tried his best not to get caught up in it— but this time, his instincts were screaming at him to see what the hell was going on.

A commercial fishing boat docked two boats down from his was bobbing around on the surface of the water. He knew the boat, and the handful of hefty fisherman that manned the rig. They were a bawdy bunch even when they were happy and sober, which granted, didn't often occur at the same time. But tonight, they looked to be mad and drunk. Not a good combination.

He could tell by the way the boat listed in the water that its hatches were fully loaded with freshly caught fish. The crew typically stayed out at sea for a few days, then came into Portree loaded to capacity with crab, salmon, haddock, North Atlantic cod, and more, which they sold to the restaurants to use for their Catch of the Day and other fresh seafood dishes. It was a system that had worked for years. Rebecca got at least part of her supply from them.

By the time he got close enough to actually see and not just hear what was happening, the men were staggering across the deck, swearing like the proverbial sailors, dumping their catch overboard. Poor gents must not have heard the news that the shipment they'd thought would be in high demand couldn't be unloaded because of the new virus. He felt a moment of pity as he watched them dump basketful after basketful of their load over the side of the ship. What a waste of a lot of backbreaking effort. It was no small feat to catch that big of a haul but no one was going to pay for fish they couldn't use.

It was heartbreaking, that's what it was. Such a waste.

And then, he saw the seals gathered around the perimeter of the boat, snatching and gulping down the fish as fast as they were being thrown into the water. For a second, he felt relief that at least someone was benefiting from the rejected shipment. But if the fish really were contaminated...

He was trying to decide what to do when he caught the glint of shiny metal flying through the air. The men were spearing the seals! His sympathy turned to rage. One of the crew was shining a bright light on the water and joking about seal skin coats, hats, boots, and sporrans, while the other threw one spear after another into the water. The poor seals were so intent on their supper – so unaccustomed to be hunted—that they probably didn't even realize they were in danger. The fact that the men were drunk and mostly incapable of getting off a decent shot was a blessing.

Robin found himself running toward the boat before he even consciously realized his feet were moving. "Stop!"

"Oh, yeah? Gonna make me, ye numpty?"

"I'm ringing up the harbormaster and the police right now. Seals are a protected species and you know it full well. Or maybe you don't mind doing time." The thought of spending time incarcerated in a small cell with no windows or fresh air would certainly make him sober up and stop messing with the seals.

"Yer bum's out the windae if ye think that will stop us, ya crazy bawbag. The whole kit and caboodle are in hospital, sicker than dogs from eating fish."

Robin was not a small man. His neck and shoulders were thick and muscular from wresting with the boat, anchors, and gangplanks, loading and unloading gear, swimming in the ocean. He was well over two meters tall and his legs and arms were strong. But he wasn't a fighter. He was in fairly good shape, but he knew he'd be no match for five burly fishermen looking for a fight.

"What have the seals ever done to hurt you? Leave them alone, ye blathering eejits," Robin yelled. "Being bloody bullies isn't going to get you paid for your catch. Let them be."

"They're gonna die from the virus anyway. Eejit seals aren't going to give up seafood and switch to eating grunters or mutton until fish is safe again. Might as well let us have our fun, ya sleekit diddy."

"How can you take pleasure in killing an innocent family of seals?"

"I'll get plenty of pleasure when I pocket a few thousand selling sealskins.

"Not after I report you to the British Wildlife Commission for violating the Conservation of Seals Act and hunting a priority species."

"Shut yer geggie, ya numpty, tree-hugging pansy," one of the crew yelled.

"I'd rather be a tree hugger living in the wild than a seal killer locked up in a prison cell."

It was time for action. Much as he was cringing at the thought of how badly he was going to get beaten taking on the five fishermen, he had to do this. He had to make them stop.

He was chomping at the bit to do what needed to be done, when someone grabbed his arm.

.

CHAPTER 2

Rebecca was just putting the last of the scones under a glass dome when she heard the buzzer. She threw in a few sprigs of fresh lavender. It was only a few minutes before closing time, but instead of resenting the last minute business, she was thrilled that her cash receipts for the day would be ten or twenty pounds greater – maybe more if it was a big order.

She tightened her mask, squirted her hands with sanitizer, gloved up, and slid open the outer glass take-away window. She recognized Nancy, a journalist from Glasgow immediately. She'd been stopping by every night for over two weeks. At first, she'd been tasked with writing an article about the recovery efforts on Skye and what it was like to welcome the tourists back.

"Hi, Rebecca. If you have time to make me a chicken salad croissant, it would be much appreciated."

"Sure." She smiled from habit even though her mask covered her lips. At least she wouldn't have to reheat the grill or the convection ovens. "I'd be happy to." She turned and took a croissant from the cooler, grabbed a serrated knife, and sliced it in two. "Hope things are going well for you."

The other woman's sigh was audible. "No new news, I'm sorry to say. We're at a complete standstill, a total dead end." Another sigh.

Rebecca held her breath. If she could only tell the researchers her theory about the seals. They could test her premise. If she was right, they could save millions of lives.

"If only we could find out exactly how the virus is being transmitted, we could begin to look for a cure."

"I thought it came from eating fish."

"That's how it jumped from species to species. But now that it's taken hold, it's adapted. It's gone airborne, just like COVID did. It can live on surfaces and transfer through a sneeze or a cough. It's not only wreaking havoc on people's digestive systems, it's destroying other organs. It's a vicious virus and we have to stop it. We're desperate to find a cure."

Rebecca's hands shook as she tried to spread the chicken salad on the croissant, then reached into the bag of Parmesan and Asiago cheese flakes and gave the sandwich a sprinkle. The journalist seemed like a nice woman—unlike the one a few months ago who had called her a "greedy restaurant owner who only cared about profit." Still, it made her nervous even serving her from behind her plastic shield. The woman had been at a laboratory watching scientists work with contaminated tissue all day. Why did she have to take a fancy to her restaurant?

"So many thousands of people are already sick. If they all die, what will happen to places like Skye?"

Rebecca garnished the croissant with a generous bit of flat-leafed parsley and a nasturtium blossom, some carrot sticks and a few fresh pea pods, and stuffed it into a cardboard take-away container. She was itching to tell her about the seals. How could Robin expect her to keep her idea to herself when hundreds of people were dying, when thousands of lives could be saved?

"I truly hope you find a cure," she said. She wanted to be a loyal friend, and she had promised Robin. But Scotland could be wiped from the map. Obliterated. "Whoever solves the mystery will be lauded as a hero."

"True," Nancy said.

It would feel so good. Not that she wanted to save the world for a moment of glory. But it would feel good to do something for the common good, something more important than providing people with food. She'd hated being painted as a villain in the press. She'd just been trying to generate enough business to pay the bills. Her mortgage, insurance, utilities, payroll. Money didn't make itself. Was that so wrong?

Even with her efforts to keep things afloat, she'd had to cut her chef down to half-time, then a quarter.

"One theory is that the virus entered the food chain through any one of the bugs that hover near the surface of the water, since at least some of the fish come to the surface to nibble on insects," her journalist friend continued. "And then there are crabs – since they can live on land or in the water, they're suspect as being a link between marine life and mammals."

Rebecca froze. Seals were mammals. It was just a matter of time before someone else made the same connection she had. Why shouldn't it be her? Maybe the government would even pay for a suggestion that led to a cure. She could use the money. If anyone had asked her to keep her idea to herself except Robin, she'd be contacting the authorities or researchers right now.

"The government has sent plenty of researchers to investigate the situation, but it seems to me what they need is a team of marine biologists."

She felt like she was playing a game of Hide the Thimble. She almost whispered, "You're getting hotter. You're getting so hot you might burn up if you get any closer." But she didn't. She owed Robin at least that much.

"It's got to be hard on you, what with just getting out from under the havoc the last pandemic caused," the journalist said. "Especially the way Scots love their fish."

She got a bottle of ice water from the cooler. "If I tell you a secret, will you promise you won't say anything to anyone?" The words slipped from her mouth with no conscious thought from her brain. No! Now she had to think of a fake secret to share, something to put the reporter off the real secret. What was she thinking?

"I promise."

Exactly what she'd said to Rob.

Her mind scrambled for something that would sound halfway plausible. "It may sound silly—I certainly don't want to be quoted in the press for ever having said such a thing. But the truth is, sometimes I long for the good old days when all I had to worry about was salmonella, E. coli, listeria, and cross contamination when handling raw meat – or dirty toilet seats and employees who didn't wash their hands properly after using the loo."

The journalist picked up her takeaway food and laughed. "What a great line! I love your attitude! Are you sure I can't use it if I don't name you as my source?"

"You promised." Rebecca could feel the stain of a deep red blush spreading across her face and down her neck. Darn pale, freckly skin.

"Fine. You think about it and let me know if you change your mind. I'd love to use it in a story."

Rebecca nodded and pulled the glass window closed. She'd think about it all right.

#

"Emma?" Rob felt someone grab him from behind. Rebecca's mother latched onto his arm like a barnacle on a ship. "What are you doing here?"

Emma patted his arm. "Making sure ye're still alive at the end of the day. Ye're nay thinking of taking on those eejit fishermen are ye? Not that ye're not a completely able specimen of a man, capable of great feats of strength, but…"

He laughed. Emma could always make him laugh.

"There are five of them and only one of ye, just in case ye hadnae noticed."

"But the seals are—they're in trouble. I can't just stand by and let them…"

Emma squinted her eyes. "They friends of yers?" She paused. "Selkies?"

"No. I don't think so." Adrenalin cascaded from his brain to every taut muscle in his body. He was in attack mode. At the same time, he could feel his bravado starting to fade. If he ended up in hospital, beaten to a pulp, he wouldn't be able to help any of the seals.

And then her comment finally sank in.

"Selkies, eh?" He laughed—not that there was anything funny about his feelings aboot Selkies, but making light of their existence was a good smoke screen, a safeguard to cover his tracks in case she'd been teasing him.

Emma eyed him warily, like she was deciding whether or not she could trust him. "I've always stuck to the belief that it was better nay to mention my experience with the Selkies, but I'm going to make an exception because they're in danger."

He strained to see what was happening in the harbor, feeling like a race horse ready to run, restrained by the starting gate. He gulped and tried to focus on Emma. "You can trust me."

Emma spiraled around as though trying to assess their surroundings. He followed her eyes with his. The hubbub down at the dock had died down. Whether or not due to his warning didn't matter as long as the seals weren't being slaughtered. He didn't see any more spears being hurled. The fishing boat was blocking his view of the bay, so he could only hope the seals had eaten their fill and were safely back at sea, heading home to some sandy beach where they'd be safe.

"I would feel a little safer if we had a more private place to talk."

"My boat is two doors down. Or, if you'd rather, I'm sure Rebecca would let us in the back door of the café so we could talk there."

"Are ye kidding?" Emma looked aghast. "Rebecca can ne'er hear what I'm aboot to tell ye. I dinnae even want ye mentioning that I was down at the harbor or that ye saw me.

I'm supposed to be home in bed, keeping out of trouble and staying safe."

"Aye. The boat it is." He didn't want to come between Rebecca and her mother, but he wanted to know what Emma knew about the Selkies. If a little white lie is what it took to find out what was on Emma's mind, it was a price he would have to pay.

He turned, making sure to keep Emma on the inside, just in case Rebecca was outside, battening down her takeaway window shutters. Something bumped against his leg and when he looked down, he saw that Emma was carrying a reusable tote bag, stuffed to the gills. Quite literally.

"Quite a haul of fish you've got there, Emma. You have heard the news aboot seafood, haven't you?"

"Bunch o' malarkey if ye ask me. Even if it's not, I've got immunity because of my—um—unique—um—somewhat intimate connection to the Selkies."

She had his attention now.

"Follow me." A few minutes later, they were bridging the gap between the dock and his boat. The water beneath them was inky and black, reflecting the lights from Portree.

"So how many days are ye going to stay put this time, Rob?" Emma stepped on board and looked around. "Do ye by chance have a refrigerator on board? If I could stash my fish here, I'd split my catch with ye. I could stop by every afternoon to get enough to cook us dinner. Or do ye have a galley?"

"Only a mini and it's full. How are you going to keep Rebecca in the dark about the seafood you're consuming if she comes home to a house that smells like fish every night? You are still living with her, right?"

"It's her that's living with me."

He hid a smile. "You really think you're immune to this virus?" He wanted to hear what she had to say. He'd always admired Emma. She was a wild child, a free spirit, very open minded—the exact opposite of sweet, serious, sincere, solid Rebecca.

"Ye've met the Selkies, haven't ye?" Emma eyed him confidently. "I can see it in yer eyes, in the way ye looked when the seals were in danger."

He felt a surge of hope. Maybe he hadn't just been dreaming. Maybe he had been swimming with the Selkies. Maybe Soren and Shelagh were real and not simply figments of his imagination. "Tell me what you know."

"I was a young woman when I met Shawn. I'm sure ye've heard the legends—when "seal folk" use therianthropy to shed their skin and change from seal to human form, the result is a male who is extremely handsome and alluring to human women. The myths always say that Selkies seek out women who are unhappy or dissatisfied with their life, which was certainly true of me at the time."

Emma stretched nonchalantly, like she wasn't completely and unequivocally challenging his whole belief system. "At the time, I was engaged to a charmer of a man, very wealthy and well-placed in society. I knew he was cheating on me, knew he really dinnae love me, but I was afraid to confront him or call off the wedding. For starters, my parents would have killed me." She laughed.

"From there, my experience was Classic Mythology 101. A couple of weeks prior to my, shall we say, encounter, I had gone through a pregnancy scare, visited my doctor, and learned it was unlikely that I would e'er bear a child."

He nodded. "I've heard that part of the myth – that a male Selkie can give a barren woman a child."

"Then ye also probably know that if an ordinary mortal sees a Selkie in human form, they will inevitably fall in love." She sighed wistfully. "And so it was, and so I did. The lovemaking was simply surreal. I was so desperate nay to lose my lover that I woke up early one morning and hid Shawn's seal skin in a place I thought he'd ne'er find. Eventually, he discovered my hiding place." She wiped a tear from her eye. "My heart still breaks when I think of the day my love slid back into his seal skin and left me and my child behind. But I cannae blame him. Like all of his kind, Shawn was powerless to resist the call of the sea."

His mind reeled with confusion. Her child? To the best of his knowledge, Rebecca was an only child. Was Emma actually claiming that Rebecca's father was a Selkie? His brain jumped to the only logical conclusion. Rebecca had never mentioned that her mother had dementia or Alzheimer's. She'd told him on more than one occasion that living in the same house as her mother was irritating her no end, but he'd gotten the feeling that it was because her mother was too clever rather than not clever enough, or that Emma was headstrong, or overly independent rather than gullible or easily deluded.

If it wasn't for his nocturnal dreams, Rob might have been ringing Rebecca up right now. But as things stood…

Emma looked at him. He saw a wave of trepidation pass over her eyes, gauging his response, wondering if she'd told him too much. "Ye can ne'er tell Rebecca that I've told ye. She would be mortified. She's made me swear ne'er to tell a soul, on threat of death."

He tried to swallow and finally managed it. His throat was thick with glumpy, stress-induced saliva. "So you've never tried to talk to Rebecca aboot any of this?"

He thought of another tidbit from his studies after he'd started dreaming of the Selkies. The line in almost every account that read, *The Selkie legend has several variations but never ends happily.*

Emma looked a little chagrinned. "Oh, I've told her awright, but she's nay a believer, and she gets insanely mad when I try to convince her of the truth – that her real da was a Selkie. It doesn't help that she has no memories of her real da—either that, or she's buried them so deeply that they'll nay ever surface. I met Rebecca's stepfather when she was just a year and a half, not quite two years old."

"Maybe she thinks it's a dream." He didn't know how much or what to share about his own experiences – assuming they had been real and not just incredibly sensual dreams.

"A dream, eh? Is that what ye think it to be?"

Was Emma testing him, throwing out a little bait to see what his response would be, or was she really sincere? He certainly didn't want to be the one who got carted off to the loony bin. If Emma was edging her way toward forgetfulness, he didn't want her to be privy to private information that she might inadvertently reveal at some point down the road. Or didn't people pay attention to the mad ravings of someone with dementia?

Besides, Emma seemed perfectly lucid to him. She wasn't even that old – early to mid-fifties maybe?

"Well?" Emma looked irritated.

He breathed deeply. "I've only ever experienced the world of Selkies when I've been asleep, in a dreamlike state. When I wake up, I have memories of names, faces, sensations, sights and sounds." He hesitated. "The scenario is that I fall asleep tucked up tight in my boat, anchored just offshore, or in an old sea shanty that I fixed up where the beach meets firm ground. I wake up naked, on the beach, soaked to the bone, with wet hair."

"Aye." Emma's face lit up with a knowing glow. "It's the Selkies, awright."

"Or I could be sleepwalking."

"Or sleep swimming?" She smiled and rubbed his arm. "No need to deny it to me, lad. I promise ye, it's a blessing, nay a curse. Ye're one of a few chosen ones. Most likely, one of the female Selkies has taken a shine to ye. That's the way it is when ye've tickled the fancy of one of the seal folk."

"I've wondered about Shelagh." He felt himself blushing.

"Have ye any memories of the lovemaking?"

"No." He realized he'd probably aroused suspicions when he spoke so quickly, but he wasn't ready to share that part of himself with anyone, least of all Rebecca's mother. He'd always had feelings for Rebecca. How the whole Selkie thing figured into that was a discussion for another place and time—and with someone other than Emma.

He pushed Selkies and being naked on the beach and even Rebecca out of his mind. "We have to stay focused on saving the seals."

"Aye, Captain Rob. I'm at yer service. Now what can I do to help?"

He knew Rebecca and her mother had been struggling to make ends meet ever since the first pandemic had hit and the tourist business on Skye had crashed. "What we need is money. And people we can trust. My main fear for the seals isn't a few drunk, morally degenerate fishermen with spears. It's that they'll be killed in droves by researchers in the name of science if anyone figures out that the seals eat seafood all the time yet haven't gotten sick."

"Agreed. We have to be very discreet. If we go public with the fact that the seals need protection, we may as well announce to the whole world that seals are likely immune to the virus."

Rob looked out at the sea. "The news would go viral in minutes—which is the last thing we want."

And then, something even worse occurred to him. Assuming Emma's story was true, and Rebecca's father was a Selkie, it was probable she was also immune. If so, what would happen to her if anyone found out? He wondered how many people Emma had shared her story with over the years, and which of them would be the first to sell her little secret for a great big wad of money.

CHAPTER 3

Rebecca locked down the takeaway window, and then the back door to the restaurant. Robin was the only one who ever dropped by, and he'd already been in. It was unlikely anyone else would come round given the late hour, but she wanted to be sure. She lowered the shades and turned the lamp low, then reached inside her cooler and brought out her secret stash of fresh seafood.

She looked over her shoulder before she added a half stick of butter to her best skillet, lit the flame, then threw in several sprigs of thyme, some freshly snipped garlic chives and green onion shoots, and a rounded teaspoon of minced garlic. When the savories were starting to sauté, she added a half pound of sliced mushrooms and kept the flame just high enough to brown them on both sides.

She used a slotted spoon to remove most of the seasonings from the pan, then dropped in peeled, deveined shrimp, bite-sized bits of cod, some locally-smoked haddock, and crab meat fresh from the shell. When the fish was just cooked and still moist, she filled two individual casseroles with the mixture, then added her homemade alfredo sauce to the frying pan, to which she added a half a can of clam juice and a little garlic pepper. She grabbed a spoon, tasted the sauce to make sure the seasoning was right, and then, even though it had tasted fine the first time, took a second clean spoon and tasted it again, savoring the delicate flavors.

When she was satisfied, she poured the sauce over the fish in the casseroles, then topped them both with homemade mashed potatoes she'd made earlier. She sprinkled a few chives on top, then a light layer of her favorite white cheddar from the Isle of Mull. She took a deep breath and drank in the scents. Divine.

She popped the fish pie into the countertop convection oven on medium heat. By the time she was finished scrubbing down the kitchen, it would be piping hot and ready to eat.

Did she feel a tinge of guilt about eating fish pie when she'd forbidden her mother to eat fish and warned Rob not to touch the stuff? Sure. But Rob wouldn't listen to her anyway, probably not her mother either. She'd just accepted delivery of a week's supply of fresh fish before the order came down to remove it from the menu, and there was no way she was going to let it all go to waste if she had to eat it three times a day.

Somehow—she wasn't sure how—but she knew eating fish wasn't going to hurt her. Call it instinct, call it intuition, call it whatever you like…she trusted her body not to lead her astray, and she knew the fish was safe to eat.

Forty-five minutes later, she licked the last drop of the first fisherman's pie and got up to wrap the second one for the morning. She'd likely have to eat it cold so her mother wouldn't find out she had it, but that was fine. She was used to eating cool leftovers at the end of the business day because she was too hungry and tired to spend two minutes reheating her dinner in the micro. And she loved fish pie just that much. Truth be told, the casserole would probably be gone by morning. It might not even make it up the hill to her house.

She was just aboot to turn off the exhaust fan over the oven when she changed her mind—better to let the kitchen air out overnight to get completely rid of the smell of shrimp and smoked haddock.

She was just ready to lock up when her mobile cheerfully jangled in her pocket. She took it out and glanced at the number hurriedly. Not many people would call her at this time of night.

"Rebecca?" It was her friend, Judy.

"Hi. You're up late."

"Going through a stack of paperwork over two feet high. It's been a crazy few days."

"Here, too. I'm just leaving for home."

"I hate to bother you about business at this late hour, but a complaint's come in and I'd like to sort things out before it escalates any further."

"What?" She was shocked. Judy was one of several food service inspectors on Skye, a fact that had never impacted their friendship. Rebecca had always done perfectly when the department had checked her out for infractions. The inspectors from the Health Department had always said places like hers made their jobs easy.

Judy's voice took on a serious tone. "There's an older woman in hospital with the virus who claims she must have caught it at your place. Says she hadn't eaten seafood for a month prior to coming to your establishment so it had to have been your fish pie."

"But I took it off the menu immediately when I received your notice."

"Well, that's the thing. She dined at the café the same day the seafood ban took effect."

Rebecca's mind went into overdrive. She'd checked her email first thing that morning, as was her habit, then come into the café to get her prep work done, opened, and served a good crowd for lunch. She'd been on her own, rushing to keep up with the flood of takeaway orders as well as the usual lunch bunch. She hadn't checked her email again until late that afternoon, when there had been a little break before the dinner crowd started in. That's when she'd found the notice.

Her first instinct was to try to explain what had happened,

but then she thought better of the plan. Yes, Judy was her friend, but anything she said could probably be used against her in an investigation. Her heart started to pound and she began to feel clammy. Oh, Lord. An investigation? Could it come to that? And what if the woman died? Could she be held liable?

"You did get the public service announcement we sent out to all food service establishments on your mobile, didn't you?" Judy's voice sounded anxious. "It came out a couple of hours after the email—still early in the day."

"I'm sure I did—at some point. With the coolers going and the exhaust fans and the ovens and the faucets and the dishwasher, I don't always hear it over the din. But I stopped serving all seafood dishes the second I saw the message."

"Well, nothing we can do aboot it this time of night anyway. I just wanted to give you a head's up. I probably shouldn't even be mentioning this, but the woman in hospital is the mother of that reporter who got after you for being greedy last winter when you first reopened."

"You're kidding. That Aggie something? The one who told all of Glasgow and the world that I was a greedy restaurant owner who only cared about profit?"

"Yes." Judy barely whispered the word.

"Cripes. Well, we know I'll be getting a good night's sleep now."

"I'm so sorry, Rebecca. I really am."

"No worries," she said staunchly. But of course she was worried.

Judy spoke again. "The good news is, Aggie's mother loves Café Fish and adores you. It's only her daughter who seems to want to make a fuss. Something aboot a letter to the editor that you wrote after her article came out?"

"Well, someone had to say something after she treated me and nearly every other merchant on the Isle of Skye like rubbish! I was only trying to defend our honor."

Judy sighed loudly. "Well she hasn't forgotten whatever it was that you said to refute her article. But thankfully, her mother—"

"Wait a minute. Is her mother a regular? Have you met
her? What does she look like?"

"Little old lady, a wee thing with curly hair so white that
it's purple."

"The one who always wears argyle knee highs and
Birkenstocks with a skirt?"

"One in the same."

Rebecca leaned against the cooler for support. "That sweet
thing is Aggie's mother? I've always wished my mother could
be like her. You've got to be making this up."

Judy said, "I wish I were."

"Well, no worries. I'll pray she makes a full recovery. And
if she doesn't, my attorney will have to handle it. He loves my
fisherman's pie. Do you think he'd take the case on trade if I
promise him an unlimited supply once the scare is over?"

"It's more than just a scare, sweetie. It's another
pandemic."

"That's right. It's gone airborne, correct? How can the
woman possibly know for certain that she caught the virus
here and not from her own daughter, or her neighbor, or the
shopkeeper down the street?"

"I guess that's the question." Judy sighed. "So sorry it had
to be you."

"I guess I'll talk to you tomorrow."

"Rebecca?"

"Yes?"

Judy hesitated. "If I were you, I'd make sure there's no
trace of seafood anywhere on the premises come tomorrow
morning. I mean, I'm sure you've already disposed of
whatever supply you had on hand, but just in case."

"I understand." She frowned. "Thanks for the heads up,
Judy. Please know that I won't say a word about the fact that
we've spoken."

"I appreciate it. Good night then."

"Have a good sleep." One of them might as well.

She spent the next hour packing up what was left of her

last seafood shipment. She'd walked down the hill to work that morning, and knew there was no way she had the energy to make her way back up the steep hill carrying forty or fifty pounds of seafood. She hiked up the hill to get her auto and drove back to retrieve the seafood.

She was bone tired by the time she got home and carried the seafood inside the house. That was when she opened the refrigerator and found it full of fish.

Where on earth...?

"Mother!"

#

Robin left at daybreak the next morning. Dawn came early this time of year on Skye. He would have liked to sleep in after spending a restless night mulling over everything he had seen and learned, but he felt an urgency aboot getting to the island and checking on Soren and Shelagh and the others.

Emma had tried to talk him into taking her with him, but he refused. He needed to find the seals and hope that he could communicate with them, something he'd never tried to do, at least in his waking, cognizant hours. It was complicated enough without introducing a stranger to a colony that had come to trust him.

He adjusted his settings as he wove his way through the Outer Hebrides islands. The sun shone strong and clear at his back, illuminating the east side of each mass of land, shining deep into their nooks and crannies, making the white sand of the beaches shine as though illuminated by a spotlight.

He pushed the boat as hard as he could. Thank goodness the wind was minimal and the sea, calm. When he could finally see the island in the distance, he felt a surge of hope that everything was going to work out.

The island where he had his shanty was remote and uninhabited. The seals weren't always there, but it was one of their regular hunting grounds and they seemed to love the beach.

His enthusiasm mounted as he grew closer and closer. He could see the forms of seals on the beach. Yes! They were there. When nighttime came, he would swim with them and try to communicate the danger they were in, encourage them to spread the word to other sea folk and find an even more remote island.

As he grew closer, he noticed that there was no detectable movement amongst the seals. Was he still too far out to see what would be faint shifts at this point? He scanned the mounds, looking for the flip of a tail, the flap of a fin, a head lifting. Anything. His heart started to pound. He never put in this early in the day. The seals were nocturnal after all. They slept during the day. Maybe this was the time of day they spent in deep sleep.

He grew closer and closer. Still no signs of movement.

He ran below deck and got his binoculars. His heart thundered in his chest as he lifted the eyepiece to his face. Blood. It stained the sand. It ran from their mouths. He could see chunks of flesh missing from each seal. He counted six or seven total. His ship eased even closer. The seal's skins were intact. Thank goodness it wasn't more. Although who knew what he would find on other beaches or adjacent islands.

Rage flared within every fiber of his being. Rebecca must have called the research facility or the newspapers or both before he'd gotten halfway to the pier. How could she do this to him?

He couldn't bear to put ashore. The seals had obviously gotten the message he had intended to deliver before any of them died. He had no way to render medical assistance. What was done was done.

When he turned to head back to Portree, he was facing full on into the sun. He put his sun glasses on and tried to get the images of the dead seals out of his mind. He could barely contain the fury he felt for Rebecca. It had to have been her who told someone. He tried to concentrate on the friendship they shared, the attraction he'd always felt for her, the few times they'd shared a kiss. But deep in his heart, he knew he could never forgive her.

CHAPTER 4

The first thing Rebecca saw when she woke up and checked her phone was an article about research being done on seals, who, according to the news, seemed to have a natural immunity to the virus. She flicked through the news sources she followed and found it slathered across the internet. Another article she found claimed that the virus had seeped into their drinking water supply, contaminating their taps, but that story was definitely on the far back burner. It made her gut twist and her insides churn to think that people were willing to kill a herd of seals to do research on a theory before they even found the source of the problem. But even if she'd known how she could help, she didn't have time. She showered, dressed and rushed down the hill to the café, making sure she used lavender scented soap and minty fresh mouthwash to wash away any remnant of her seafood feast the night before.

Speaking of, what was with her and the sudden craving for seafood? She'd always loved fish of any kind. She'd never thought it unusual that it was her favorite food—she did live on Skye after all, one of the seafood capitals of the world—and usually had at least one serving a day. But ever since the authorities had said they shouldn't—couldn't—eat fish, it was all she wanted. She didn't know what was wrong with her.

She unlocked the back door of the café and slipped in, sniffing the air for any trace of buttery, sautéed shrimp, boiled crab legs, or smoked haddock.

"Thank you, Lord." She could detect a lingering hint of garlic, green onions, and thyme, but those were ingredients in many of the dishes she prepared. She seemed to be in the clear. She started her lunch preparations, which would create a whole host of delectable new scents, just to be on the safe side.

She was aboot a half hour away from opening when she heard the knock on the door. Please, God, don't let it be the health department. She couldn't bear the thought of the food she'd just prepared going to waste should they shut her down – not on top of all the seafood she'd thrown away the night before. Even if they didn't bolt the takeaway window, she couldn't talk to an inspector and serve customers at the same time.

She grabbed the doorknob and pulled it open, ready for a fight. She was not going to lose her business due to some technicality in timing.

"Robin? What are you doing here?" Was she imagining things or did he look angry?

"I'm here to thank you for keeping your theory about the seals a secret until I could warn the colony on the island where I dock the boat." His voice oozed sarcasm.

What on earth was going on? "Warn them? Just how were you going to do that? Have a set down and chat up the dangers posed by seal hunters?"

At least he had the good grace to blush. "You're missing the point. You promised me you wouldn't say anything!"

"I didn't say a word! Believe me or not, I don't care anymore. I don't have time to argue with someone who is supposed to be on my side. I have far bigger problems." Tears were sliding down her face. She couldn't bear Robin being mad at her. Not on top of everything else."

"Then how did they find out? Did someone overhear us?"

"Oh, good grief, Robin. Skye is ground zero in the new

pandemic. The whole island is crawling with geniuses from all over the world, all trying to solve the mystery before someone else does—investigative reporters, scientists, immune specialists, doctors, pharmaceutical companies hoping to be the first to come up with a vaccine. They're at it like a pack of wild dogs fighting over a piece of meat. As they should be! Millions of people could die. We have a responsibility to act quickly before any more people get sick."

"There it is. People are more important to you than seals. In my mind, the loss of any life is equally tragic."

"It's not as though I don't care about the seals. You know me better than that." The tears continued to flow. "I feel terrible about what's happening, but I am not responsible." She felt horrible about one of her customers being in hospital, but she refused to take the blame for that either.

Rob still looked hurt. Hurt and dubious. "I know. It's just that—"

"You had to have known that someone else would come up with the same idea we had. I hoped it wouldn't be so soon, but what can I say. Brilliant minds. They think alike."

"You're sure you didn't drop a clue?"

"I told you I didn't say anything, Robin. But I will say, I was tempted. After the treatment I've gotten today, I probably will say something next time unless you help me understand." She looked him straight in the eyes. "I think we'd all prefer that not a single seal need die in the process of finding a cure for this horrible plague, but I have to wonder how you can live with yourself, knowing that millions upon millions of people could die, when sacrificing a handful of seals in the name of research could be the answer to the mystery of what's causing this pandemic and lead us to a way to stop it."

For a second, Robin looked like he wanted to hug away her tears. And then he scowled. "I can see we're never going to agree on the subject, so I'll go."

"Fine! Go!" She was sick of being unfairly judged. Sick of feeling responsible for the woes of the whole world. "Just go!

Take your fishy smelling clothes and go!" She held the door open until he'd gone through and slammed it shut behind him.

Lord, help me!

Wasn't there anyone in the world she could depend on for a little support? He mother was off in her own little world and had been for years. Her staff was scattered or gone. Now Rob. She'd thought he was a friend she could count on no matter what.

She went to the sink to wash away her tears, re-sanitized her hands and went to open her take-away window to the world once again.

#

Robin stood on the bridge of Sea Worthy, feeling droplets of water spraying his face, the sun warming his back, the wind tousling his hair. He may have only owned Sea Worthy for a year, but he loved the old girl nonetheless. The last thing he wanted to do was give up his dream, his link to the sea, the lifestyle he'd chosen, and sell the boat. But at the moment, it was the only way he could think of to raise enough money to save the seals.

He eased the boat through the narrow channel that led to Loch Carron and scanned the shoreline for the spires of Lachlan Castle that were tall enough to show above the trees. Assuming the trees hadn't grown tall enough to hide them. About the time he gained his bearing, he spotted a golden eagle's nest. It was almost hidden from view, but then, it was his job to spot almost hidden nests for his customers.

He felt a small sense of satisfaction. He may not have any customers, he might soon be without a boat, but at least he could say he was good at leading wildlife expeditions. Someday, he hoped he would be able to restart his career.

A short time later, he was putting in at the dock closest to Lachlan and hiking up and over the wooded banks of Loch Carron to meet Rod and Katelyn MacKenzie. Rod was waiting for him where the trail met the garden. From the looks of things, the garden had been expanded to include seating or even tents for a few hundred people on grassed areas surrounded by flower beds and bushes. He'd heard the castle had become quite the wedding destination.

"Katelyn sends her greetings," Rod said. "She had hoped to be here, but this was the only time she could sneak away to Inverness to do a little shopping. There are still some things she can't get at our local grocery."

Robin smiled. "So she's finally taken to cooking? Last I knew, she was having none of it."

"I still do most of the savories, but she bakes a little, and does a fine job keeping the pantry stocked and maintaining the inventory. With her business and budgeting expertise and my love of the kitchen, we make a good team and attempt to keep our heads above water."

"There's a lot more to running a successful food service establishment than most people realize. I've learned that much watching my friend, Rebecca, do everything from start to finish when she had to let her staff go."

"She runs a tight ship awright. We've eaten at Café Fish several times and the food has always been excellent. Her fisherman's pie is to die for."

All Robin could say about that was that if she would fix him one, right now, he would gladly eat it, pandemic or not.

Rod scanned his face as though he knew exactly what he was about. "So speaking aboot tight ships, what's this about wanting to sell Sea Worthy? You haven't been late on a single payment. I assume you've been eking by at the very least."

"It's been rough with no tourists allowed in, but I've managed. I made a little profit when they started allowing in-country travel again. Gave up my apartment so I only had one payment to worry aboot."

"You living with Rebecca then? Or your brother's family?"

"I would never impose on my brother's family. He offered, but only out of guilt. And Rebecca—well, our relationship hasn't progressed to that state, and she'd have none of it anyway unless we were married. And, well, what can I say? Penniless men don't propose."

Rod smiled. "I get that. Am I remembering right that Rebecca's mother moved in with her after her husband died?"

"Yes. But her mother's not the issue. She's much more the free spirit than her daughter. Rebecca is a strong Christian, and what the Bible says is what she does. It's one of the things I admire aboot her, although sometimes it gets in the way of– well, you know."

"Ye need say no more. I've strong beliefs myself when it comes to my faith. Finding balance can be a real struggle." Rod shrugged and they were both silent for a few seconds.

Rod said, "Ye didn't say why ye want to sell the boat then."

"Right." It was easier to talk about other things, that was for sure, but he had to say what he'd come to say. "Since I gave up my apartment, I've been camping on the beaches of some of the more remote isles. I've seen how the seals live— how intelligent they are, how harmless and gentle they are. Now, they're in danger because it's believed they hold a natural immunity to the virus. Many of them have already been killed to get the tissues the pharmaceutical companies need to do their dirty work."

A fast succession of expressions washed over Rod's face while Robin waited for his reaction.

Rod finally spoke. "You must be pretty attached to these seals to be willing to give up your entire livelihood to protect them." He hesitated. "There are legends about seals interacting with humans." He waited a few more seconds. "You do know that there are government agencies designated with the task of looking after seals and other protected species, using taxpayer pounds and donated funds, correct?"

"Of course I do. But they'll take forever to act, and even then, they're known for being reactive rather than proactive. Prosecuting and fining offenders is not going to save my seals from being caged or butchered." He paced a circular walking area around a fountain. "The seals need help now. With the right amount of money, I could hire security teams to protect the major beaches where the seals sun. We can't just wait until they're all dead to do something!"

"So you want me and Katelyn to buy back the boat so you can afford to hire harbor patrols to protect the seals?"

"Yes. Or if you can't, please help me think of someone who can. Was there a second highest bidder when I bought the boat? Katelyn have any rich American friends?"

"I'm sorry, Robin. I'm not able to help. The money you paid down is gone. If you're friends with the owner of a restaurant, you have to know how rough the last two years have been. I'd like to be able to help, but Lachlan is in the same predicament everyone is. We thought we were in the clear after things finally opened up at the beginning of the year, but now that we're locked down again, we have to find a way to keep the business going when all of our reservations for special events – weddings in the garden, business retreats, family gatherings – have been banned to contain the virus."

"I understand." Robin sighed. He would have liked the boat to go back to Rod, first because he loved it, and second, because he'd hoped Rod would hang on to it until he could buy it back from him.

"How aboot this? Rod asked. "If it would help, I can grant you a loan deferment so you don't have to make any more payments until at least the end of the year."

Robin gulped. "That's pure generous of you."

"If our business weren't rubbish right now, I would do more."

"No. No. This is more than I deserve."

Rod started pinching dead heads off the plants he was standing next to. "Never think yourself unworthy, Robin. It defeats the whole point of Sea Worthy."

Robin stood a little taller. "Yes, sir, Captain."

"Robin, I have a great deal of admiration for the difficulties you've overcome and the huge strides you've made in your relatively short lifetime. Well, done." Rod pinched off a geranium head that was past its prime. "I am going to give you one small piece of advice though."

Robin froze. He'd always liked Rod MacKenzie, but the whole advice thing made him feel like he was back in Portree dealing with James. His older brother was by and large the reason he felt unworthy. And his advice always came with a catch.

Rod cleared his throat. "Before I met Katelyn, I thought the old legends were just like fairytales—no truth in them, stories made up for the entertainment of wee ones and adults alike. There were legends of ghosts trapped at Lachlan and a curse that said the eldest son would never inherit. I didnae believe a word of it. Brownies? Fairies? Peter Pan?" He paused. "Selkies? All figments of wild imaginations. Nothing more."

Robin looked down. He knew. How could he?

"And then I met Laird Valan and Rosemary, better known as the Blue Lady of Lachlan. Over 500 years old, and as real to me as my lovely wife."

Robin felt his eyes open wider and wider.

"Suffice it to say that I nay longer discount the old legends. I'm a believer. But I'm also here to warn ye. If the Selkies have bewitched ye—if you hear their siren song—so be it. But never turn down the likes of a good woman—a real woman like Rebecca—for the allure of the sea, no matter how enticing it may be."

"I understand." And he did. "Thank you." He nodded at Rod and turned to leave.

"Something else just occurred to me," Rod said. "There's no way to patrol every single beach on each and every island in the Hebrides. But if you find out who's killing the seals and put a stop to it, the battle could be won fairly easily."

Robin's mind flashed to a headline he'd caught a glimpse of on his phone as he neared Lachlan and picked up on their WiFi. Something about a German Pharmaceutical Company that was claiming to already be working on a prototype for a vaccine. He could almost guarantee what they were researching.

He looked at Rod. "Things are never easy when you're dealing with governments and political factions and even pharmaceutical companies who stand to gain millions if they get their way."

"Especially when all that's standing between them and their goals is a few dead seals."

Robin wanted to cry. "Aye."

"Be careful, Robin. And good luck saving your seals. It's been a long time since anyone posed a threat to my eagles, but I guess if it ever came to it, I'd do the same for them."

Robin watched as Rod lifted his eyes to the sky just in time to see a pair of sea eagles soaring high above the gardens.

CHAPTER 5

"Mom? Are you almost done in there?" Rebecca stood outside the bathroom door listening to the sound of running water and trying in vain to convince herself that she didn't have to use the bathroom as badly as she thought she did. She and her mother rarely crossed paths on weekdays since her mother liked to sleep in and Rebecca was up at dawn. But on Sunday mornings, when Rebecca could relax and get ready for kirk at a more leisurely pace, they could have used two bathrooms.

"I'll be out in just a second or two, love."

What? Was that her mother? Oh, Lord! She'd heard the virus could constrict a person's bronchial tubes and make their throats gruff, but her mother's voice sounded as low as a man's.

A few seconds later—as promised—the door swung open. But instead of her mother, the door frame was filled with a bare-chested man whose shoulders were covered with thick salt and pepper hair.

"Who are you and what are you doing in my house?"

She clutched at her robe to tighten the belt and realized she wasn't wearing it, which meant her nipples were probably straining against the sheer fabric of her camisole – the camisole that floated two or three inches above her waist, and a good six inches above the skimpy little panties that went with it. What could she say? She'd always liked sexy underthings, especially ones made from slippery fabric. It had never mattered because she'd had her own home, her own, private home where she could sleep in whatever she wanted to, or not.

At the risk of flashing the stranger with her scantily covered bottom, she turned and beat it back to her bedroom as fast as she could, screaming. "Mother! If he's not gone in 5 minutes, I'm calling the police!"

"Ha!" Her mother came charging out of the guestroom in a teddy that made Rebecca's look downright prudish.

"Lot of good that will do you—from what I hear, the whole police department is in hospital with the virus."

For a second, Rebecca thought she was going to faint. Oh, my Lord – it couldn't be—but it was—her mother's teddy was—crotchless.

She took a deep breath and prayed for strength. "Who is this man and what is he doing in my house?" Being as her mother was dressed for a party, he was obviously here at her invitation.

"His name is Henry. And I have just as much right as you do to have friends spend the night."

"I never have friends—I would never—"

"And whose fault is that, Rebecca?" Her mother was just getting wound up. "Robin is a perfectly wonderful specimen of a man and anyone with eyes can see he's into you. The man is sleeping on a flimsy little cot on his boat for heaven's sake. He has no kitchen. He loves your food. I'm sure he'd love to share your bed."

Rebecca's head started to reel, whether from the thought of Robin in her bed, or the dread of having to listen to her infuriating mother for one more minute. "My relationship with Robin is no concern of yours! Now get Henry out of here, right now! In case you've forgotten, we are in the middle of a pandemic. We're on lock down. We've been ordered to stay at home with only our immediate family members except in the case of work, doctor visits, or buying essentials."

"Sex is essential!" Her mother slid past her and reached for Henry's hand.

At least, that's what she hoped she was groping for.

Her mother glared at her. "Tell her, Henry! Sex is necessary to our well-being and peace of mind. Which you would know full well if you'd ever tried it."

Again, the feeling like she was going to faint. Yesterday had been absolutely grueling between visits from food inspectors and health department officials and phone calls with her solicitor—all she wanted to do was to go to the bathroom, take a nice, long shower, and go to kirk. Was that asking too much?"

"I have to use the ladies room." She felt ill. Who knew what kind of bodily fluids or germs or filth her mother's friend had left behind when he used her bathroom? If she didn't have to go so desperately, she would have demanded that her mother completely sanitize it before either of them used it. Trying not to think of how many ways this man's presence violated the restrictions, she passed down the narrow hallways, squeezed past the love birds and re-claimed the bathroom. Her bathroom.

She used the privy, knowing they could hear every move she made. By the time she was done, she wasn't just mad, she was furious. When she reopened the door, they were waiting for her, cozied up like a pair of pigeons in a roost.

"This is completely unacceptable, Mother. You know the rules."

Her mother looked at her defiantly. "Fine. We'll sleep at his place next time. The only reason we're here in the first place is because his son invited a woman he met at one of the bars to spend the night and they wanted some privacy."

"Oh great. That makes me feel better. Henry's son deserves privacy, but I don't even get a warning that there's a half naked man roaming the halls of my house. Worse yet, it's clear neither Henry nor his son are practicing social distancing which means the likelihood that they're carrying germs increases exponentially. Who knows what disease you might bring home from Henry's place? Do you realize the predicament you're putting me in?"

"Excuse my daughter, Henry. Not only is she jealous, she thinks she's always right. So there's no use trying to get anything through her thick skull."

So now this whole sorry episode was her fault? This was so typical of her mother. When her stepdad was still alive, he'd kept her mother in check. Without his calming, stabilizing influence, her mother was completely out of control.

Tears welled into her eyes as the loss of her stepfather swept over her in fresh waves of grief. Her stepdad had understood her so well. They'd been able to talk about anything, and he'd almost always been on her side. When they'd disagreed aboot something, he'd helped her understand why he held his opinion, and they'd talked about it—quietly and reasonably—until they had it figured out. She couldn't talk to her mother about anything without getting into a fight.

"Mother, you and I will talk about this later, when I'm back from kirk and you are alone and fully clothed." What was wrong with her mother? Her stepdad hadn't even been gone for a full year. Certainly someone of her mother's age ought to be able to do without sex for a year or two while they were in mourning? Shouldn't they?

She retreated to the bathroom, locked the door and stepped in the shower. She couldn't wait to get out of the house and walk to the kirk, where she could kneel in her isolated little corner of the sanctuary and pray to the Lord of Lords for wisdom, guidance, and deliverance from her latest set of woes.

#

Robin rapped on the back door of Café Fish and waited

for Rebecca to answer. He didn't want to seem like some
loser who was using her, but she always seemed happy to see
him. He counted her as his best friend. The fact that she
usually had uneaten leftovers this time of night didn't hurt
things either.

He knocked a second time, a little louder. They hadn't
exactly parted on good terms last time they'd seen each other.
Maybe she didn't want to talk to him. Hmm. He could see
light peeking out from behind the blind, so she had to be in.
She was too thrifty to leave the lights on when she wasn't
there. Maybe she was in the restroom. He knocked again. He
didn't want to disturb her, but he really needed to talk.

He waited. Finally. The door inched open and he heard
Rebecca say, "Yes?"

"Hi Rebecca. Can I come in?"

"Maybe." Silence.

"Is something wrong?"

"I got into a big fight with my mother last night because
she's refusing to social distance. I guess if I'm going to call
her out for breaking the rules, I need to be consistent."

He smiled in spite of himself. Knowing Emma—and
Rebecca—he could only imagine. He reached inside his
pocket. "I have a mask."

"Okay. But only if you wear it and don't breathe on any of
my food, and stay six feet away. And only if you promise to
be nice to me. I'm already involved in so many disputes that I
can hardly stand it."

"I promise." He could see a shadow indicating that she
was retreating. He entered and closed the door behind him,
staying just inside the door.

"So what's changed since I was here last time? Not your
mother, I suspect. She's driven you crazy for years."

"True."

He couldn't see if she was smiling or not. He hoped he
could help her relax a little.

Becca slammed a drawer shut. "I know it's only been a
few days since the new lockdown began, but it feels like a

month. To start with, I've been interrogated by health department officials and food service inspectors and their solicitors, and my solicitors and reporters until I'm aboot to lose my mind."

Rebecca wasn't one to be overly dramatic. He could tell by her voice that she was entirely sincere. "Are you in some sort of trouble?"

"I served a fisherman's pie to a woman about an hour after the lockdown went into effect because I had the volume on my mobile turned down and I missed the announcement. Now she's in hospital and her daughter is the reporter who called me a greedy restaurateur during the first pandemic."

He looked at her over his mask and hoped his eyes were communicating the tenderness he felt toward her. "Are you sure you want me to stay six feet from you? Because I'd sure like to give you a hug."

"Oh, Robin. I want to, but I shouldn't."

"Okay." He thought for a second. "Do you want to talk aboot it? Tell me all the gory details and hash it over?" He paused. "Or would it help to think on something else for awhile?"

Her voice quavered. "What's been going on with you?"

"I don't want to add to your troubles. But I do need someone with a sharp mind and objective reasoning."

"And you think I'm that person?"

"I know you are. Listen, Rebecca. I know the sea and the creatures in it are not exactly your thing."

"Not unless I'm sautéing something from the sea in garlic butter or making a fricassee for my fisherman's pie."

"Right." He smiled and hoped she could tell what he was thinking by looking at his eyes. "But you have to admit that seals are more like dogs than fish. First of all, they're mammals, and secondly, once you get to know them, you discover that they each have their personalities. And they have cute faces, and adorable whiskers, and…"

"You know I don't feel comfortable with the sea, or sea mammals. It's just so foreign to me. It's like an alien world."

"Well, then, for the sake of this conversation, if you can imagine that you have several dogs as pets and that scientists were killing them to gain tissue samples to use for research."

"Why would they be taking my pets? Wouldn't they just go to an animal shelter and get a few unclaimed dogs who were going to be put down anyway? Not that my scenario is any less repulsive, but at least they wouldn't be using personal pets."

Robin tried to take a deep, calming breath, but his mask made it hard. "Okay. Here's the thing. I need to figure out who's killing the seals so I can try to stop them. Whether or not you agree with my goals, I'm hoping you will help me find out who's killing them."

"I'd be happy to."

"Great. The only lead I have is that there's a German pharmaceutical company named Die Droge that put out some publicity that would indicate that they're close to beginning to test a prototype for a new vaccine."

"Wow. That seems fast."

He nodded. "I thought the same thing, but with all the research facilities in high gear after the last pandemic, I suppose they've been able to respond more quickly this time."

Rebecca said, "Yes, but—Let me think for a minute." She took a scrub brush from her dishwashing sink and scoured the inside of a pot until the stainless steel gleamed. She finally looked up. "This may be way out there, but what if the pharmaceutical company intentionally introduced the virus into the food chain, intending in advance to make and release a vaccine that would rake in billions like the companies that found a vaccine for COVID-19?"

His mind started to race. "I can't imagine anyone..."

Rebecca started in on another pot. "Lust for money. The thirst for power. Greed. And I'm not talking about restaurant owners who are working their butts off trying to make enough money to survive."

"It makes sense. I should have anticipated this new

pandemic wasn't a chance occurrence."

"Aye. After listening to all of the twisted political rhetoric that went on between the Chinese and the Americans last year, and knowing what kind of money and power was at stake, you can certainly understand where someone would get the idea."

He frowned. Inside his mask. What was the point of a good facial expression when no one could see it? He tried to relax so he could think more clearly. "So what do we do now? Take our theory to the police? Try to get some proof? If these people are truly evil enough to purposely infect the world's food supply, they're capable of doing anything to get what they want."

Rebecca's scrubbing turned to gentle rubbing on a well-seasoned cast iron sauté pan that he knew was her favorite. "Think, Rob. You're out on the water more than the harbor patrols are. Did you see anything suspicious? Overhear any conversations at the docks? Notice any unusual activity? We're at ground zero. If something went down, it was probably right here in Portree."

The image of a dark, completely unmarked boat slid from his memory bank to the forefront of his mind. "I did!" He struggled to remember details along with the vague impressions that were slowly unveiling themselves.

"I remember seeing an unmarked boat dumping something into the sea near the beach where I often stay. It was dusk so I wasn't able to see well. I might not have remembered it at all or thought anything of it, but as I said, the boat was completely unmarked, which is not only suspicious, but illegal. And, I remembered seeing the same boat at a Skye fish farm, also at nightfall, I was taking some tourists on a stargazing expedition. Again, it was just odd enough to catch my eye. Any authorized boat would have been branded with the fish farm logo."

"Good! What else do you remember? Did the boat have any distinguishing characteristics? A particular shape? How many crew were aboard?"

"I'm not remembering any details, but I do remember one of the tourists asking me if I would take a video of them with some of the more distant islands in the background. The sun was shining low in the west and the hills were overlapping each other in different shades of blue and navy and purple."

"I love the way the sun sets behind the isles. Do you think the boat might have been in any of the photos?"

"It's possible. We were in the general vicinity of the fish farms because I remember thinking we needed to get away from the lights on the fish pens if we were going to see the Milky Way."

"Perfect. Do you have records? Names and contact information for your passengers?"

"Yes, if I can remember what the date was and which group they were."

"Sounds like a good place to start."

"I'll get on it first thing in the morning." He paused. "Rebecca?"

"Yes?" She turned and the light shined on her hair, illuminating her forehead. His knees suddenly felt weak.

"You look pretty standing there in the light," he blurted without thinking.

"Yeah. Well." She laughed. "Incandescent light doesn't bring out my features quite like sunshine does, but this time of night, what you see is what you get."

He smiled again, then realized once again that she couldn't see his lips. And then he knew what he had to do. "Becca?"

"Yes?" The light was still pooling around her shoulders. They were sagging just a little. She looked tired and more than a little discouraged. One more reason that he had to say what needed saying. "I just want you to know that you're pure important to me, that I value your opinion, and think the world of you."

Her eyes filled with tears.

"I try to show you how I feel aboot you in little ways – you know, flash you a quick smile, put on the old charm, give you a look that's loaded with meaning."

45

She fumbled with a tissue box and finally grabbed a paper towel.

"The thing is," he continued, "right now you can't even see me smile, so I thought it was time to go beyond expressions and actually say the words. You're so precious to me."

"Oh. Robin." She put down her scrub cloth and eased into his arms.

He could feel her mask and the side of her face, and her ears and hair snuggling against his whiskers. Her hair was so soft. He probably should have ripped his mask off and kissed her, but she seemed pretty fragile tonight and he didn't want to push his luck. It felt good to hug her, and it eased his mind to know that if anything happened to him because he was nosing around in a big pharmaceutical company's business, she knew how he felt. Well, except for the part about suspecting he was falling in love with her.

"It's weird," she was saying, "but I feel so sapped of energy by the end of these long days I'm putting in, that I don't seem to have the time for emotions, or caring, or thoughtful gestures or even love—not even self-love. I mean, I haven't been taking very good care of myself. I haven't slept well in weeks."

"I know," he said. "It's been the same for me." He rubbed her back. "We don't need to talk aboot it anymore right now. I just wanted to say what was on my mind."

"I'm glad you did." She backed slowly out of his embrace. "I tried something new today—Chicken Mornay. It doesn't taste quite as good as my Haddock Mornay, but it's the best I can do under the circumstances. I'd really appreciate it if you would give it a try and tell me what you think. And honestly. Don't be afraid you'll hurt my feelings. I need to hear the truth."

"Gotcha. I'd love to give it a go."

An hour later, he was full and satisfied. Becca was talked out and seemed more relaxed than she had when he came. The pots and pans were all sanitized, dry, and put away in their various cubbies. And he had a plan.

He walked her up the hill after she'd locked up the café.

"I'll be in touch," he promised.

"Thanks for helping with the dishes." She blew him a kiss through her mask and slipped through the door to her cottage.

He turned and started the trek back down to the harbor.

CHAPTER 6

The next day, Rebecca was so busy dishing up food and filling takeaway orders that she didn't get a break until it was almost time to close. Now that her famous Fisherman's Pie was off the menu, different dishes were taking up the slack, but she wasn't as accustomed to preparing them on the go. It caused all kinds of chaos. She was running herself ragged.

It took a lot more effort and mental concentration to prepare Welsh Rarebit over Toast Squares and Sliced Ham, which all had to be made fresh immediately before serving than it did to heat up a pre-assembled pie, top it with already made mashed potatoes and pop it in the convection oven just long enough to brown the cheddar.

Many of her customers and the few tourists who were in town had just assumed with a name like Café Fish, she would be closed— she'd heard through the grapevine. Having to spend money on advertising to inform them otherwise would only add injury to insult at this point, so she could only hope and pray the word got out that she was still in the kitchen cooking up chicken, pork, mutton, and mince to perfection. She'd just taken delivery on 100 pounds of potatoes the day before the new pandemic, so she'd decided to add Cottage Pie with a Thatched Roof to the menu, which was also topped with mash and Mull cheddar. She'd always been fond of the recipe, and her customers were slowly catching on. She'd even toyed with ordering in some venison, but thought it made more sense to wait until her indoor dining room could be reopened. Whenever that might be.

When she locked the takeaway window, she'd been hopeful that Robin would stop by again. When he didn't, and she'd finished cleaning up, she decided to do her own bit to help and do a little research.

She started by Googling fish farms in the Skye area. Robin hadn't specifically mentioned that the contaminated fish had originated at the local salmon farm, but it seemed logical to start there. The salmon at the farms were known to be disease ridden. That's why she'd always used fresh caught fish from the local fishermen for the restaurant.

But the sad thing was, every time the farm-grown fish managed to escape, they interbred with the wild population. In the past year, there had been more than one ecological disaster when farmed salmon had escaped after a storm damaged the pens and cages. No surprise that fish farms were not well-liked. If things continued on as they were going, in a few years, there would be no such thing as a truly wild salmon.

Her mobile started to chirp annoyingly. The thing sounded like it was half dead or out of synch with time. What was wrong with it? She grabbed it, put it on speaker phone, and glanced at the caller ID.

"Judy?" Lord, she hoped it wasn't more bad news. She wanted to ask if the reason for Judy's call was business or personal, but she squelched the impulse. She'd find out soon enough.

"Hi Rebecca. I just thought I'd update you on your case."

Crap. "They're calling it a case?"

"It even has a number. Case number 52754."

Her heart sank. "It all sounds so official. How serious is this? Am I going to lose the restaurant over something so, so…" She didn't know what to say. It wasn't silly. A woman was in hospital. But it was all so crazy. She'd been 30 lousy minutes late seeing a text, and now her whole life was on the line.

"They know it wasn't intentional. Honestly, I think if the woman's daughter weren't so blatantly aggressive about pressing charges, the whole thing would have been dropped."

"Maybe it's her I should be offering free meat pies for the rest of her life instead of my solicitor."

Judy laughed. "Yes. I don't think she'll have much of a hankering for fisherman's pie anytime soon."

"Oh, I don't know. If my fish pie ends up making her a millionaire, it might become her favorite food. Oh, Judy! What am I going to do?"

"You have insurance, don't you? Just let the solicitors handle it. Don't give it another thought."

"I raised my deductible to 5000 pounds and reduced my coverage to lower my monthly premiums. With business as slow as it's been, that alone is enough to bankrupt me."

There was silence on the other end of the connection. "I'm really sorry, Rebecca. There's got to be something we can do. Hey—she's a reporter isn't she? Maybe if you were to deliver the latest, greatest scoop, she'd take the story and run."

"Hmm. Leave the money and take the story?"

Judy laughed. "It's a thought. Got any ideas?"

"Not really." But she did. If she and Robin could figure out how the fish had gotten infected, who had wanted to bring Scotland and the world to its knees in the first place, they'd have the story of the decade, maybe the century.

She went back to her research as soon as she could get rid of Judy. The next article she found gave her a little more insight into why the Scots hated fish farms. Fish feces were a major problem. She was surprised to learn that fish feces from a single farm contain nitrogen and phosphorous equivalents to that produced by millions of humans. Ew. And Rob wondered why she didn't like to swim in the ocean.

She read on. In addition to destroying the natural beauty of an area and increasing fish waste, the diseases, lowered fitness, and depression introduced in the wild by farm-raised fish created a regular extinction vortex which severely affected vulnerable wild salmon and whitefish populations. She shuddered. She'd been told that sea lice were one of the things the farmed fish had been known to spread to the wild-caught fish in the harbor. It made her sick to think about it. Based on what she had learned, if someone had wanted to infect Skye's seafood supply with a disease-producing contaminant or virus, all it would probably have taken was a few bucketsful of infected sea lice.

Story indeed.

#

Robin rummaged through the papers on his desk, looking at the registration cards his guests were required to fill out, and trying to match the names and itineraries with the many faces in his mind's memory banks.

He finally found the records from the tourists he'd been thinking of and rang them up at their contact numbers. Bridget, the woman he spoke to, promised she would search through her photos and videos and see what she could find as soon as she got off work. But she warned him that she took hundreds of photos every month, so it would take her awhile. She also mentioned that she routinely deleted extraneous photos to make room for new ones. He ended the call feeling less than hopeful.

He spent the rest of the day wandering around the harbor, asking the crews of every ship in port if they remembered seeing a dark, unmarked ship around the fish farms or known fishing grounds around Skye or the other nearby islands.

"Sure, I remember seeing it. They would put in here occasionally but they always left as soon as they were resupplied."

"Not sure who the owner is."

"Isn't that the boat that's drifting off Raasay? If it's the one I'm thinking of, it's been deserted. I asked one of my crew members if he knew why it was adrift. He said he'd heard the whole crew had been taken to hospital with the virus."

A chill ran down Robin's spine. There was still plenty of light—the sun didn't set in the summertime until almost ten, and the moon was almost full. If he could get Rebecca to go with him to Raasay, she could hold Sea Worthy steady while he boarded the unmarked boat to see if he could find out who it belonged to and what it had been up to before the crew got sick—assuming the rumors were true. If they found the boat and its crew was still onboard, they would be more likely to believe he was on a pleasure cruise instead of a fact-finding mission if Rebecca was with him.

The thought that the boat itself might be infected niggled at the back of his brain, but he cast the thought away. He had to do this, no matter the risk. He made his way from the dock to the café. He hoped Rebecca agreed that it was worth the risk.

All he knew was that he had to do something. He toyed with the idea of going back to the island to see if any more of his seals were missing or murdered, but he simply did not feel equipped to deal with the devastation until he had some idea of how to stop what was going on.

He hoped, by morning, he might have word from Bridget about any photos or videos she might have found on her camera. He could testify that the unidentified boat had been near the beach but there was no crime in that. If he could place them at the fish farm, he would really have something. His whole body shivered with anticipation. If he could find and interview even one member of the crew, he could move up the food chain from the small minnows to the big fish and bring them to justice. He thought back to the dead seals lining the beach and wanted nothing more than to take these people down.

The lights were off at Café Fish. He made his way to the alley and saw a crack of light shining through the kitchen window. For now, the best he could do was to try and talk

Rebecca into going for a ride on Sea Worthy.

A few minutes later, he was standing in the kitchen with his mask over his nose, eating an open-faced sandwich featuring meatloaf made from ground chicken, sausage, and spinach topped with a tomato basil spread.

"I hate this," Rebecca said gloomily. "But what else can I do? I have to replace the seafood items on the menu with something."

"I like it. It's really quite tasty."

"Thanks. My mother isn't a fan."

He smiled and took another bite. "Well, Emma doesn't know everything."

"She doesn't know anything. I didn't think she knew diddlysquat when I was a teenager, and then, I came round to her way of thinking aboot some things – you know, learned to respect a bit of her wisdom. But now, I'm becoming more and more convinced that she's lost it. Utterly and completely lost it."

He thought aboot Emma's claim that Rebecca's father was a Selkie and didn't say a word. Maybe Rebecca was right.

He smiled again, took another bite and said, "Yum."

Rebecca seemed to relax, like she almost believed him. "Do you like the crushed tomato spread on top?"

"It's delicious. Although a sprinkle of Parmesan might be a nice touch. I love the focaccia bread. It's the perfect touch. Is that rosemary I taste?"

"Thanks. Rosemary garlic."

"Well, you did good." He used the napkin she'd given him to wipe his lips, squelched a burp, and smiled again. "If we leave right now, we could still make it to Raasay before dark."

"No. There's no way I'm going out to some remote bay looking for who knows what in the middle of the night. The weatherman said the waves were going to be choppy tonight and you know I don't do well on boats even on smooth seas."

He wasn't sure there was any hope for Rebecca when it came to boats and the sea. From what he could tell, Emma had ruined her by instilling a fear of water in her from the time she was a babe.

"How aboot early tomorrow morning?" Becca surprised him by saying. "The sun is up by aboot five isn't it? If we left at first light, you could have me back at the café in time to do my prep work and be open at the regular time."

"You'll do it?"

"I want to solve this mystery as badly as you do."

He ignored social distancing and gave her a ten second hug. He wanted to do a happy dance but he didn't want to appear overly enthusiastic for fear of scaring her off. She was a skittish one, Rebecca was.

"At first light then, at the boat?"

"Yes. It's a plan."

He watched as she rinsed off his plate.

"If you're done, I'll walk you up the hill."

She nodded. He imagined he could see her smile. It had to be there, hiding behind her mask like the sun peeking out from behind a bank of clouds, right?

CHAPTER 7

The morning sky over Portree dawned clear and bright. Before she'd come down the hill, Rebecca had seen a long, low, bank of clouds to the west, lying on the horizon like a distant threat. She'd wanted to mention it to Robin to make sure it was nothing to be concerned about, but she didn't want him to know how afraid she was. She was trying to act as confident—even cocky—as she could be so he wouldn't realize how uncomfortable she was on his prized boat.

"Sleep well?" Robin asked. He had his mask on for now, but he'd already let her know that the second they were out on the open seas, it was coming off.

"I don't know. I tossed and turned a bit until my mother came home. She's got a new boyfriend and they've been keeping pretty late nights. The night before last she didn't come home at all."

Rob looked sympathetic, but that was probably her reading into her wish that he would understand her feelings. He'd always liked her mother—maybe he would take her side.

"That's got to be hard to take—I mean, seeing as your da hasn't been gone all that long."

She hesitated. She didn't want Robin to get the impression that she was itching to talk about sex. "I think it would be easier to deal with if she wasn't always gushing on and on aboot their wild sexual escapades." She gulped. "Last night, they made love under the stars. It was all I could do to listen to her swooning aboot it."

She paid close attention as Robin prepared to launch Sea Worthy, starting up the engine and easing the boat away from the dock and out to open water. He moved with ease. It didn't matter that she didn't like the boat or the sea – she loved watching him work.

"So, speaking of your mother," Robin said.

Her jaw clenched. She certainly hoped he wasn't going to lecture her on her relationship with her mother. She grabbed hold of the railing on the deck as Robin sped up. A fine mist of water sprayed them both. It might have felt good later in the afternoon, when the temperature had warmed up.

"I saw Emma down at the dock last week and she started talking aboot when you were a baby."

"Oh, no." Rebecca tried to laugh in what she hoped was a nonchalant way, but it sounded nervous even to her own ears. "She didn't tell you that my father was a Selkie, did she?"

Robin stared at her like he was shocked. "Well, yes, but I promised her I wouldn't tell you that she told me. She said you'd be furious."

She sighed. "She's spun an entire fantasy aboot some handsome Selkie she met on the beach whom she believes to be my father. The truth is, she was already pregnant with me when my birth father ditched her, and she thought— dreamed—imagined—she had an affair with a Selkie. It was a romantic tale, and the story she made up was considerably less humiliating than having to admit that she was expecting a child with a man who had dumped her for a prettier, richer woman that his family approved of."

Rob looked absolutely flummoxed. "So you don't even think she might have met a handsome man on the beach who she believed to be a Selkie? You really think she made the whole thing up?"

"If you're asking if I think Selkies are real, the answer is no. My mother is delusional if she honestly thinks Selkies exist. The story that I'm the child of a mythical, half-seal, half-human creature is pure nonsense. Surely you can see that."

Robin was silent. The sea was so still that the only motion from where he stood on the deck was the slight movement of his hand on the rudder every once in awhile as he guided the ship toward their destination.

He turned to her. "Does Emma know that you think she's lying aboot the Selkie? Because when she told me, I got the impression that it was some big secret that no one was supposed to know and that it would devastate you if you found out she told me."

"Oh, please. She's told almost everyone we know at one point or another. She thinks I've never heard her talk aboot it, when in fact, I overheard her telling a friend when I was six or seven years old." She sucked in her frustration. She could almost laugh about her mother's idiosyncrasies now that she was a grown woman, but when she thought about all the nightmares she'd had as a child on account of her mother's deceptions, it made her so angry she could hardly stand to look at her.

"Come on, Rebecca. Surely you have to extend her a little grace. She was obviously going through a hard time. Maybe she was already pregnant with you when her boyfriend dumped her, but how can you be sure of the precise timing? How can you possibly know what really happened?"

"Well, it doesn't surprise me that you're taking her side."

"I'm not taking anyone's side. I'm just saying you should talk to her aboot it. Get to the bottom if it. Hear her out."

"You wouldn't say that if you knew what it's been like for me."

Robin stared ahead toward Raasay. "You can talk to me."

She gulped. "I was a championship swimmer in my younger years. My coaches thought I could go all the way to the Olympics if I worked hard. Everything was good until they suggested I participate in a triathlon. When my mother found out I would be swimming in the ocean, she completely freaked, and I heard her telling her friend that if I went swimming in the ocean she was afraid my father would come for me. I already had a dread of the sea—my mother feigned a fear of open waters for years so I would acquire a phobia about the ocean. Well, I fell for it as a child but when I grew up, it didn't take long to get sick of her manipulating me."

She watched as the shadow of a sea gull passed over Robin's face. His mask was off, but that didn't mean she could tell what he was thinking. She hated this. Why had she spilled her guts to him? She didn't want him knowing her secrets. Maybe once they were closer. She just wasn't ready. But then, as usual, her mother had taken that choice away from her.

"Come here." Robin was holding an arm out to her.

She went to him. Maybe she shouldn't have, but she did.

"Becca? I need to tell you that I love you just the way you are. Crazy mother or sane mother. Selkie father or rich jerk father. Rich restaurant owner or closed-for-good, former business owner. Scared to death of boats or lover of the high seas. None of it makes any difference to me. Do you understand?"

She nodded. Smiled. Hugged him tight. "Thank you."

Robin kept one arm around her and one on the rudder. "I have one question for you though."

"Yes? What's that?" As long as he had his arm around her, she could handle anything.

Robin gently massaged her arm. She felt safe. She felt wanted. She felt wonderful.

"Why don't you try to find out who your father is? Join one of the DNA sites and try to build your family tree. See if you get any matches."

"Sure. Why not?" She pulled away from him and laughed. "I can see my DNA report now—25% Scot, 25% Scandinavian, and 50% Selkie?"

"If you knew the truth—if you're right—"

"If I'm right?"

Robins eyes were fixed on a dark spot up ahead. He turned and looked at her like he was actually serious. "Who are you to say the legends aren't true? Stranger things have happened."

"You've got to be kidding."

He shrugged. "If you found out the truth, it would force your mother to stop telling stories."

"And open a real can of worms where my birth father is concerned."

He turned the rudder just a little. "Do you think Emma ever told him aboot you?"

"No. Why would she when she doesn't believe he's my father?"

Robin scanned the horizon. "Okay. Well, it's something to think aboot."

Of course it was. She had thought about it ad nauseam over the years.

Robin pointed. "There she is."

She shielded her eyes from the sun and a ripple of fear shivered down her spine. A small, dark boat was bobbing on the waves caused by Sea Worthy's approach. She didn't see signs of anyone on board.

"If you'll hold the boat in place, I'll go aboard and see what I can find."

She felt a sudden surge of panic. "Sure."

Robin nudged Sea Worthy's bow to the small boat's stern, gave her the controls, climbed down a ladder and jumped from one ship to the other. She watched as he overturned life jackets, looked inside a pail, and opened something not unlike a glove compartment. He took a few papers from the stash and stopped to skim them. He took out his mobile and snapped a couple of photos, then checked below. When he popped back on deck, he yelled, "No one home." He looked at the pail again. Set it down, picked it up and held onto it as he climbed back onto Sea Worthy.

"You're bringing it along?"

"If it's the pail they used to dump the contaminant into

the fish cages, it could be evidence."

"And what if there's residue that's still contaminated? You might have just exposed both of us to the virus."

Robin's face grew pale. Without saying a word, he hopped back over to the unmarked dinghy and returned the pail to the deck. "Sorry." He came back aboard and used a bottle of sanitizer to clean his hands, then squirted a dollop on hers. "I'll phone the police as soon as I can get a signal and let them know aboot the boat."

"Did you find out who the owner is?"

"I took a photo of the registration. Nobody I know, and the address listed was on the Isle of Arran."

"I went to Arran on a cheese tasting tour a couple of years ago. I still use a certain white cheddar on my Haddock Mornay that's as soft and smooth as butter."

He laughed. "I love it when you get passionate."

She smiled. It was nice not be wearing a mask for once. "Robin?"

"Yes?"

"Promise me you won't get involved in anything dangerous. It's one thing to lose a few seals, but if anything were to happen to you, I don't know what I'd do."

He eased up on the throttle. "I'll do my best. But there's a lot at stake here. I feel like I have to follow through on this— for the seals, for me, for you—for everyone."

"I understand." And she did. She wouldn't say anything more about the seals as long as there was no more mention of Selkies.

#

Robin's plan for the next day included tracking down the owner of the mystery boat and locating any crew members so he could interview them about what had happened aboard the dinghy and find out why it had been abandoned.

He was as worried as Rebecca about what he might be stumbling into, but it had to be done. He wished he had never touched the pail he found on its deck – rumour had it that the boat's crew members were all either dead or in critical care in hospital. He'd never be able to forgive himself if he was inadvertently the cause of Rebecca getting infected.

He was in dock in Portree, ready to start out on his mission when his mobile rang. The number wasn't in his memory and looked to be an Edinburgh prefix.

"Aye. Sea Worthy Expeditions here."

"Hallo. Cameron Allanach here. Wondering if you might have a booking available for later today – say noontime or just past?"

Did he have bookings? He attempted to wipe the shock from his voice before he said, "Let me check my calendar just to be certain." Right. He knew full well that he had nothing booked, not only for the summer, but through the end of the year. Be cool. "Looks like this afternoon would work fine."

The man laughed. "I thought you might be able to squeeze us in, what with the new restrictions in place."

Rob froze. Was this a trick? Someone from the Scottish Maritime Licensing Department calling to make sure he wasn't taking illegal bookings? Or the police? Had they traced his number last night when he'd called in to report an abandoned dinghy? Had someone heard that he'd been asking around?

Again, he reminded himself to stay cool. "How many of you will there be? Have you visited our website or Facebook page and are you familiar with our pricing structure? If so, and assuming you'd like to proceed, I'll need your name, address, contact information, and a credit card to hold the booking. Assuming you're local so I'm allowed to take you out."

"My primary address is in Edinburgh, but I've a summer home on Skye and it's where I am at present."

Well, at least the man was honest. During the last pandemic, things had gotten so bad that the Highlanders and Islanders had refused access not only to tourists from the mainland and the world in general, but anyone from

Glasgow, Edinburgh and most particularly, the likes of London, Manchester and the lot. Didn't want big city folks bringing the virus into the remote areas, which had fared fairly well. Now that Skye was ground zero, things were a little different. He couldn't imagine anyone from off island wanting to expose themselves. Certainly no one would be seeking sanctuary on the Isle of Skye during this go round.

"Can I ask what area of the Isles or what kind of wildlife you're hoping to see while you're out on the boat?"

There was a long pause, during which he heard some indistinguishable words being muttered and a wee bit of laughter. Not that there was anything wrong with that. The men and women who came onboard were his guests and it was part of his job to ensure they enjoyed the journey. If a group entertained themselves and got on famously without any help from him, all the better. It only made his job easier.

"We're hoping to see at least one sea eagle. I suppose everyone is. Sharks, whales, a few puffins—whatever areas you think most scenic." The man finished giving his details for the log. "Would we be able to get some lunch while we're out? I don't think we'll have time to eat before we board."

"I'll call the caterer I work with and see if she's able to accommodate your request on such short notice. I don't anticipate a problem but I need to make sure." He hadn't placed an official order with Becca in weeks, and she wouldn't be preparing Fisherman's Pie like she used to, so he thought he'd better ring her up before he made any rash promises.

"Darn shame we can't have seafood, but Shepherd's Pie, Sausage Rolls—even Coronation Sandwiches would be fine. Whatever she's got. If she's good, I'm sure we'll love whatever she fixes."

"I highly recommend her. Her restaurant, Café Fish, is one of the best on Skye." His first impressions were that the man was not only honest, but understanding and generous. Many of the clients he took out who were from Edinburgh and points beyond the Isle of Skye were pretentious and demanding, traits he had no time for, but tolerated because of the money such passengers brought in.

"I've heard of the place. Throw in some soft drinks and desserts if you can. Surprise us. I'm sure it will be wonderful."

"Thanks." He loved being able to throw some business Becca's way so they could both make a little money. If he called right away, she should be able to cobble something together. He hurriedly ironed out the rest of the details with Mr. Allanach and told him he'd see him at the dock.

"Becca?" He phoned her, filled her in on Cameron's request and was relieved when she said she could accommodate him.

"Did they say what's bringing them up from Edinburgh? I would think anyone who wasn't already here would be staying as far away as possible right now."

"Maybe they were already here when the restrictions came down. Maybe Edinburgh won't let them back in."

Rebecca laughed. "That would be quite a turn around, eh? But seriously—six men? Sounds like a business meeting of some sort to me. Did this Cameron mention what company he works for?"

"I didn't ask for those details. I'm sure I'll find out more once we're out. I always seem to overhear at least some of the conversations that take place onboard – whether I want to or not."

"Well, with everything that's going on, I'd keep my ears open and take advantage of every opportunity to get an inside scoop."

"No worries. I'm still in sleuth mode. I was going to work on the case all day today, but now that I have a booking, I'm going to have to spend this morning cleaning and sanitizing Sea Worthy to get her all spiffed up before we head out."

"The case, is it? That's what we're calling it now? Like the Case of the Nefarious Seafood Affair?"

He thought for a second. "Or maybe the Case of the Villainous Seafood Virus?"

"No. I love the word nefarious," Rebecca insisted.

Sherrie Hansen

"Sounds good." He loved it when she put her foot down and showed her little stubborn streak.

"I'll see you a few minutes before twelve then? I'll have the food bundled up in insulated carriers just like before. You can return them to me when you get back."

"It'll be my pleasure."

They were both silent.

"Robin? Be careful, aye? I'm not sure what's going on on this island but I'm convinced there are nefarious people aboot, and I don't want you to come to any harm."

He smiled. "There's that word again. They seem completely on the up and up." He didn't tell her about the funny feeling he'd gotten when they hesitated at his question about what they wanted to see on their expedition.

Rebecca added, "If you ask me, there's something fishy aboot an expedition that comes out of the blue like this, only a few hours before they're to board. No pun intended." When he didn't say anything, she said, "When you go out on these expeditions, do you file some sort of flight plan—I mean, intended course map—stating your intentions for the day's travels?"

"No, and there's no sea traffic controller to radio if I get off course or lost should a heavy fog set in." Part of him wanted to laugh, and the bigger part of him, to cry. Poor Becca. Her mother really had done a number on her when it came to frightening her off the sea. "That's what lighthouses are for. And buoys. And Her Majesty's Coastguard. And if all else fails, Search and Rescue."

"I'm serious, Robin."

"So am I, sweetheart."

"But what if some sort of squall blows in? Or what they call a perfect storm? I've heard the seas around Skye can get pretty rough."

"I know what I'm doing, Rebecca." He'd never known her to be so skittish. But then, the pandemic—a second so close after the first—really had them all on edge, and about things they wouldn't have given a second thought to before. He cleared his throat. "We'd best each get on with our day before the morning's suddenly gone and I've got an ill-prepared ship and you've got nothing to serve your hungry customers." This virus had turned them into a bunch of paranoid namby-pambies.

CHAPTER 8

Rebecca knew she was going to have to step it up a notch if she was going to get Robin's takeaway order ready and be set to open the Café at the regular time. It wasn't as though she was going to have a long line winding down the pavement if she was a few minutes late in opening the window, but the sense of normalcy she longed for demanded that she stick to her schedule as closely as possible.

She needed to shower and get a move on. She grabbed the doorknob to the bathroom, intending to rush in and get started. It was locked.

"Mother? Are you almost done?"

"Be out in just a second." The voice was not overly loud, but it was firm and pure male.

Not again! "Henry? Is that you? Mother? I thought we'd agreed that Henry-"

The door to the bathroom opened and a man stepped out. "Jack McDonald. Pleased to meet you."

"Jack? What happened to Henry?" She could only hope this Jack wasn't going to say, "Oh, he's here, too." At this point, she wouldn't put anything past her mother. She wrapped her arms around her bosom and backed up a step so Jack could get by her. At least he was fully clothed. He didn't seem bothered by the reference to Henry. Did he not care that the woman he had just slept with was a floozy, or had her mother already made up some story about Henry so the possible mention of his name wouldn't alarm him? Maybe in her mother's circle of friends, sleeping with two different men in the same week was nothing to worry about.

Her head started to spin. Her mother was no where in sight and Rebecca had no time for her nonsense. She returned to her bedroom and grabbed her clothes so she wouldn't have to risk running into Jack with only a towel wrapped around her. Ridiculous as Emma was acting, Rebecca tried her best not to let her mother steal her joy.

Forty-five minutes later, she was unlocking the door to Café Fish when she heard a car door slam. The only people who were allowed to park behind the buildings were the other owners, and none of them were usually in when she started work.

A sense of unease washed over her. Her skin flushed. The hairs on the back of her head stood on end. What on earth? She turned and saw a man approaching her. She didn't recognize him, but there was something familiar about him that caught her attention.

"Is there something I can help you with?"

He was not wearing a mask, so she could see his smile. The man certainly knew how to pour on the charm. The way he carried himself, even the way he stood and cocked his head, was mesmerizing. He was probably twice her age, and looked like a young Sean Connery.

"You the owner?"

She hesitated. "Yes."

"I hear you're catering our lunch on the Sea Worthy today."

"Um. Yes. I'm just coming in to get started. If you want to go around to the front window and have a look at the takeaway menu, I can still switch the order from *Whatever* to *Exactly What You'd Like*." She was hoping he'd take the hint and not try to follow her into her kitchen when she opened the back door. He might be charming, but he was still a stranger, and she wasn't entirely comfortable being alone with him.

"Actually, I was hoping to take my colleagues something for breakfast. They're huge fans of sausage rolls, but quiche would be nice, or even some scones." He must have seen the look that passed over her face because he added, "You come highly recommended. The Captain of the Sea Worthy gave you rave reviews."

"I made a batch of apple scones with cinnamon, sage, and candied bacon last night before I left. Anything else would be nearly an hour since I'm just getting in. I don't normally open until half eleven."

His eyes never left her face. She wasn't wearing her mask either. It was on a hook just inside the door. Maybe that was why she felt so vulnerable. He was standing just a little too close. Other than that, she didn't know why she was so nervous. When the inside seating at the café was open, she was alone with strangers all the time. People from all over the world. And she'd never once felt like this. She wasn't exactly scared. Just flustered.

"I'll take a dozen scones if you have that many, and an assortment of any other baked goods you have on hand. Just something to tide us over until lunch. Oh, and add thirty pounds to the bill for service above and beyond."

"Thanks." She could feel herself blushing. Again, why? What was wrong with her? What was with the weak knees and the quavering voice? Why was she reacting this way? "If you'll wait here, I'll package everything up and be out with your order shortly."

"Thank you, Miss-?"

"Rebecca."

"Thank you, Rebecca." He smiled again – a smile to melt hearts – or break hearts. She wasn't sure. Maybe both. "Allanach here. I'm Cameron Allanach."

When he had paid and gone, she locked the door, leaned against the wall, and took a deep breath. She wasn't even two hours into her day and she was already hot, sweaty and exhausted. All symptoms of the virus, but more likely the end result of an absolutely crazy morning. She just couldn't deal with all this unpredictable, unexpected, different-lover-every-day behavior of her mother's. Which was probably why she was still alone, or as alone as one could be when they'd had to take in their mother.

The world was going crazy all around her. She just wanted a little stability.

#

"Been busy?" Cameron Allanach looked around the boat, paying attention to every last detail. He seemed more interested in Sea Worthy than he did sea eagles, or even the other men who had boarded.

"No. For the most part, I'm just biding time while everyone waits to see what's going to happen next and when tourists will finally be allowed back in."

"No use trying to predict anything with everything that's been going on. I hope you make it. The lass from the Café as well. Seems very nice."

He wanted to ask when he'd met Rebecca, but didn't know how to say anything without seeming inappropriate.

"I suppose you normally see a lot of Americans. I've heard from other merchants that they're sorely missed."

"Yes, and the usual crowd from the mainland. They spend a lot of money on Skye." Rob scanned the sky for threatening cloud formations, hoisted the anchor, revved the engines, and headed out to sea. He adjusted his heading to follow the coastline. Once they got past Kilt Rock, he planned to head north toward the outer islands.

Mr. Allanach left to rejoin his friends, colleagues, whatever they were.

Portree's colorful harbor grew smaller and smaller in the distance. Once he was clear of the small crafts that bobbed haphazardly around the harbor, he turned the wheel to starboard and revved the throttle to full speed. The boat responded so powerfully that his passengers reached for the side rails to steady themselves.

The sea spray misted his face gently. How he loved this feeling. Providing he'd had the money for petrol, there'd never been a time when he couldn't take his boat out on the water, and for that, he was thankful. Rebecca's restaurant had been on total lockdown for months during the first pandemic and he could only imagine how hard it must have been for her not to be able to open the doors.

He didn't do his job for the money he was paid – certainly there were more lucrative jobs with steadier, more predictable income and a much smaller investment required to get into the trade. He spent his time on the high seas because he loved the water, everything that lived in it, and the living creatures that soared above it. Despite what his brother, the priggish pastor, thought, using his inheritance from his late father's estate as a down payment on Rod MacKenzie's expedition boat was the best decision he'd ever made. That said, today he was particularly thankful that he was being granted the honor of getting paid for doing what he loved. It was gratifying. It was affirming. It made him feel worthy of the title Captain, and proud to be an entrepreneur. It was satisfying on a completely different level. It made him want to sing.

He was reveling in the joy of it when the wind carried a snippet of conversation to his end of the boat.

"So you knew this Emma might be pregnant with your child when you broke up with her and you never followed through to see if it was so?"

His mind reeled. Had they said Emma? Or Selma? Or Ella, or Emily, or Anna? He eased back on a throttle just a wee bit so he could hear more clearly.

Cameron said, "My parents had forbidden me to ever see her again or to have any contact with her. I was tempted to go behind their backs and look her up, but I never did, mostly out of respect to Julia. Our family never went to our summer house on Skye after that summer and eventually, they rented it to year round tenants."

"But a kid. Weren't you curious?"

"Of course."

There was a slight pause, as if someone was looking his way to make sure he couldn't hear them. Robin looked out to sea and didn't move, as though he was completely focused on their route and hadn't heard a thing.

Cameron continued in a hushed voice that he could only hear due to the generosity of the wind. "I kept in touch with a handful of mutual friends and found out that Emma had a baby girl exactly nine months and three weeks from the last time we were together. But these same friends told me that Emma practically lived on the beach after I left and was sleeping with anything that had two legs. Then, they told me she was going around telling people that the baby's father was a Selkie, which just confirmed everything my parents claimed—that Emma was completely daft."

"It does sound like she was off with the fairies. And the time frame is a bit inconclusive."

"It's quite common for first time mothers to go a couple of weeks past their due date."

"Thank you, Dr. Gordon."

"Just telling you what I know," the one who was evidently some sort of a doctor said.

Rob's heart raced with theories. Cameron could be Becca's father? If Emma had been rejected and found herself pregnant, it might have been less painful for her to concoct a romantic tale about a Selkie than to admit that she'd been dumped for a more socially respectable woman. He could imagine Emma conjuring up a handsome Selkie lover who had left her with a child because he couldn't bear to be away from the sea.

The sun was in his eyes, so bright against the blue droplets in the air that it blinded him. He eased up on the throttle a bit more and lifted his hand to his brow to shield his face, but the wind must have shifted slightly because he still missed out on the next bits of the conversation.

He straightened the wheel and looked at the sky to make sure they weren't missing any eagles. Kilt Rock was just ahead. He was just ready to call it to the men's attention when another few words wafted into hearing range.

"The seals we've already tested don't seem to have ingested any of the contaminated fish."

"How are we supposed to determine if they have a natural immunity if they won't eat bad fish?"

"So what are we supposed to do?"

"You're the scientist. You'd better figure something out. There's a damn pandemic going on out there. People are dying."

"I told you the timing had to be just right."

"Calm down, gentlemen." It sounded like Cameron. "How could we have known that the seals wouldn't take the bait?"

"It's like they have some sort of sixth sense about not eating bad fish."

"Persnickety cows."

"What if we were to capture some of them and feed them nothing for several days? When they get hungry enough, they'll have to eat infected fish."

The wind stopped blowing just like that, and he could no longer hear a word of what they were saying.

Robin's blood felt like it was about to boil. Not only had the seals he loved died—they had died for nothing. The evil scientist's plan had backfired. There was no ready cure for the virus. How many people would die before a cure was found?

"Here's a theory we haven't considered."

Robin froze. The wind was in his favor again. He gazed off into the horizon and tried to act nonchalant.

"Could it be that the seals not only have natural immunities, but the power to eradicate the infection from their bodies?"

"You mean, after they ingest the toxin, the virus is destroyed so effectively that it's simply erased from their system? Gone without a trace?"

"That's exactly what I mean."

Much as Robin hated to do it, he had to point out Kilt Rock now, or it would be obvious he'd been listening to the men's conversation. He waited until Cameron was in the middle of a sentence, then said in a loud voice, "On the left, you can see the horizontal layers and vertical marking that form a tartan-looking plaid on one of Skye's most famous bits of shoreline."

That was when he made the decision to take them to his beach. He'd say he knew of a nice, sandy beach where they could picnic and enjoy their lunch. When they arrived, he'd act surprised at what they encountered so they could see for themselves the gory aftereffects of the research their diabolical plan had necessitated.

If they were too sickened at the sight of slaughtered seals left to die on the beach to enjoy the delicious meal Rebecca had prepared, so be it. It was the least of the agonies they deserved for their reprehensible behavior.

CHAPTER 9

Rebecca was exhausted by the time she closed up shop that night. She had hoped Robin would stop by and fill her in on how the expedition had gone. She was still curious about this Cameron, and wondered if Rob had discovered what the group was up to.

When the evening was mostly gone, and he still hadn't come, she started up the hill. Her dragging feet were a telltale sign of how much she was looking forward to seeing her mother—NOT. No matter how much she dreaded the encounter, they had to talk about Jack. Henry. Whoever else her mother had invited into her bedroom. Her bedroom in Becca's home.

She could see the harbor even better from her vantage point at the top of the hill, and Robin's boat was not in the bay. Had he dropped off his passengers and gone back out or was he still out with Cameron's group? Worry flooded her mind. The amount of food she'd packed for them was certainly adequate to serve as both a late lunch and an early dinner, but she'd still have thought the men would be back by now.

She could see that the lights were on in her parlor and her mother's bedroom as she neared her cottage. Thoughts of Robin left her mind as her mother's irresponsible behaviors flooded in.

She used her key to go through. Her mother was sitting in an overstuffed chair by the fireplace, where a log was old enough to be white ash on one side and red embers on the other. She was holding a book, her shoulders were stooped, and for the first time, Rebecca noticed how old she looked. Her mother wasn't ancient by any means, but the years had definitely taken a toll.

No surprise there. She steeled her heart from a rush of empathy and reminded herself that her mother was toxic. That's what poison did to a person—it wore them out, and left them riddled with diseases of the mind, spirit, and body. That's what her mother's lies and deceptions had done to her.

For another fraction of a second, she felt sorry for her.

"Hi, Mom."

Her mother looked up. Rebecca had known her mother's hearing was a little off, but had she really not heard her come in?

"Hello, Rebecca." Her voice sounded defensive.

Rebecca put her purse in the bin and hung her sweater on its hook.

Her mother looked at her defiantly. "I suppose you want to talk about Jack."

"Well, at least you remember his name. It must get confusing when you're entertaining so many different men in such a short time span. At least I assume they've all been men." Okay, so the last bit was uncalled for. That's what her mother did to her. She'd put up with so much over the years that all it took was a word or two from her mother to make her lose her temper.

Besides, her mother knew how to egg her on. She was plenty adept at delivering her own zingers. "Well, darling, if you weren't still a virgin, you'd understand that each man has a unique kind of expertise when it comes to pleasing a woman. Maybe someday I'll meet a man who can satisfy all of my needs, but until then…"

"I am not going to listen to this again. Part of the reason

I'm a virgin is because I don't want to be anything like you!"

"If you knew what you were missing, you wouldn't be so—"

"You know what, mother? Ever since I heard you telling your friends that I was the love child that was the result of a torrid affair with your Selkie lover, I've dreamed that my father would come and take me away to live in the sea with him and others of my kind. It was my favorite fantasy when I was little, an escape from reality when I got mad at you. But I'm an adult now, and I refuse to let your warped perceptions of the world define who I am, or who you think I should be."

Her mother's face registered shock. "I thought you liked knowing your da was a Selkie. It was our little secret, and it set you apart. It made you unique. I meant for you to feel special."

"If you imagined for one moment that I liked being told that my father was a Selkie, you are even more delusional than I thought. As for feeling special, well, you've told me often enough that I'm 'just like my father' for me to realize it for the insult it was. The only thing you made me feel is confusion and, as I got older, shame. I know that I don't believe in Selkies. The only thing I don't know is whether my father was your former fiancé or one of your many lovers."

"You're nothing like Cam." Her mother spit out the words, seemingly without thinking, then recoiled as if she'd been slapped.

"Cam? Is that my father's name?" In all these years, she'd never been given so much as a first name. And now, when she'd just met a Cameron—a Cameron who had aroused feelings in her that she couldn't explain. What kind of coincidence was that? Could the two men be one in the same?

"Cam is not your father."

"Right. My father is a Selkie."

"His name is—was—Stephan. I don't know if he's still living. The average life span of a harbor seal is only 20 to 30 years, but no one seems to know if being a Selkie increases or decreases expected life spans."

Becca put her hands on her hips and hoped her face reflected as much disgust as she felt inside.

"This is why I disconnected from you emotionally years ago, Mother. When I was ten I had a couple of friends who imagined that they were adopted because they couldn't believe they were actually born from the people who claimed to be their parents. I knew exactly how they felt."

"Why are you being so cruel to me?"

Her head started to spin. Why indeed? Whether her mother had gotten pregnant having sex with a fiancé whom she thought loved her, or a lover who she imagined to be a Selkie, she'd been spurned and rejected and left to raise a baby on her own.

She felt her brave exterior crumbling. She couldn't do this anymore. Like it or not, she lived with her mother, and she couldn't endure this kind of stress—the constant bickering—in her own home, the place that should be her sanctuary, her quiet place, the one spot she could relax and be herself.

Becca said, "Just forget it. I shouldn't have said anything. It's just... I only know how I felt when—but it's okay. We don't need to talk aboot it anymore."

Her mother didn't say a word. Rebecca went to her room and closed the door. She needed to think, read her Bible, pray for wisdom and patience. She needed to get some sleep. She slipped down the hall to use the bathroom and peeked into the living room on her way back. Her mother's bedroom door was open. The room was empty. She checked the living room again, and then the kitchen.

Her mother was gone.

#

Robin spent a fitful night trying to sleep and not meeting with success. After dropping off his passengers, he'd gone back to the beach to drag the bodies of the dead seals out to sea. There was something obscene about allowing their bloated bodies to be eaten away by blowfly larvae. He knew it would do no good to bury them in the ever shifting sand. Returning them to the sea was not only the sole option, it was the right thing to do. He should have thought of it before.

The sea would lull their bodies to rest in its sweet, fluid embrace.

One by one, he'd used a shovel to roll their bodies onto a tarp that he'd then dragged to the shoreline. The tide had done the rest. He'd left the deceased creatures bobbing on the surface of the sea, rocked by the waves, the waters gently eroding each cavity of their worn carcasses. His heart was broken.

He might have found out if any of the seals he felt like he knew personally were still alive if he'd spent the night on the beach, but he couldn't believe they'd be frequenting the site where so many had met such a tragic end. He had no desire to stay there either. The island had always called to him in a siren song. Now its shores sang a death dirge.

He tried to shake away his feelings. He had work to do and he couldn't do it when he felt so morose. He'd lost a whole day taking out Cameron and his doctor and scientist friends on their teambuilding excursion. While they'd bonded by participating in ridiculously inane brainstorming exercises, he'd accomplished very little.

Today, he intended to track down the crew of the abandoned ship. After he'd found out what had become of them, he hoped to interview them and find some answers.

He needed to stop by the café and pay Rebecca from the proceeds of his tour, but he preferred to do that later, when he might actually have some conclusive news to share with her. If he had time, he also intended to do some research on Cameron Allanach—what company he worked for, what his roll was in all of this mess, and if he indeed could be Rebecca's father.

He started by phoning the hospital.

The receptionist seemed to be wired with a very short fuse. "I already told the policeman who called that anyone who was part of that boat's crew is dead except for the Captain."

Robin sucked in his breath. Had they died from the virus itself, or had whoever hired them to do their dirty work murdered them to make sure they couldn't be implicated? What kind of madness had he stumbled into?

He hesitated. "Is it possible to speak to the Captain? I have information about the whereabouts of his boat, and if I could speak to him aboot securing it, I would be happy to make sure it—"

"We are enforcing a very strict visitation policy until the threat of transmission is past."

He thought for a second. May I have his room number so I can send him a card?"

"Room 14. But that could change if he's transferred to critical care."

He thanked the receptionist and hung up the phone, mulling over what to do with the information. He could hardly break in to hospital… Or could he?

For the first and very probably last time in his life, Robin wished he was his brother. He was so over his pious brother, Pastor James, that he wanted nothing to do with him, but in this case, his brother might be his only hope. If he could talk James into visiting the ship's captain and then phoning him on his mobile so he could talk to the man, perhaps he could find out what he needed to know.

He thought about the situation—tried to figure out a way to do this without involving James—before finally deciding to walk up the hill to pay his brother, the good reverend, a visit.

Twenty minutes later, he was knocking on his brother's door. The rectory was made of the same stone as the kirk, and just as austere and lifeless as it was. Sarah had placed a pot filled with a perfectly manicured boxwood tree on either side of the door. He could hear a telly blaring out the latest numbers, casualties, and new cases, so he knew someone must be home somewhere. James was as tight as a drum. He would never waste a dime of the kirk's electric by leaving on a telly when no one was around to watch.

He knocked once again. "James? Sarah? Anyone home?"

"Robin. How good to see you." Sarah's voice was stiff and formal. Like always, she looked like she was dressed for a worship service. He supposed after years of living right beside the sanctuary, with people dropping in at all hours, she'd learned not to lounge around in her pajamas. But there didn't seem to be any happy medium with Sarah.

"You're looking well."

"Thank you." Sarah blushed in a demure, pastor's wifely sort of way.

"Is James here?"

"He's speaking to a parishioner. He should be finished in a minute or two." She hesitated. "Would you like a cuppa?"

"No thank you. But I do need to speak to him as soon as possible. Do you mind if I wait in the garden?"

"No. Of course not. Such a lovely day. I'd join you if I weren't busy with the laundry."

"I understand." He didn't know anyone else who wore heels, a fancy dress, and jewelry to do the laundry, but that was Sarah.

"I'll be outside then." He ducked out the door, rounded the corner to the left, then turned right and let himself in the gate to the garden.

Sarah wasn't kidding when she said she was doing laundry. There were clothes strung out along a vast network of clotheslines, some hanging from hangers and some stretched out with clothespins. James' shirts and Sarah's skirts fluttered in the wind, soaking up the sunshine. It made him feel at home in a soothing sort of way. He had a seat and waited.

James appeared momentarily. His brother didn't appear happy to see him, but that was no surprise. Maybe if he'd called to set up an appointment—no. James considered the people of his parish who paid his salary to be his family. Blood relatives who didn't attend services or put money in the offering plate were a low priority.

"James." He tried to sound warm and forgiving without

being too obvious. James would pick up on the fact that he was there because he wanted something soon enough.

"Robin. What brings you here today?"

See? James was already suspicious.

"I need a favor."

"If this is aboot money—if you had listened when I told you that buying the boat was a mistake, you wouldn't be—"

"It's not aboot the boat. The pandemic is making things a little tough, but I'm getting along just fine."

"If you call sleeping on the beach or on a boat with no proper living quarters getting along—"

"I said I'm fine." They glared at each other for a full minute.

Robin finally spoke. "What I'm aboot to tell you is confidential. Can we agree on that much, Pastor James?"

"You have my word."

"Fine. There's a man in hospital who captains a small boat. I believe he and his crew are responsible for infecting the fish in the bay with a virus that started the pandemic. His entire crew is dead. I need to talk to him before he dies, too, and if I can, find out who's behind the operation, who paid him to contaminate our food chain."

James looked shaken. "What do you expect me to do?"

"I'm not allowed in hospital to visit. You are. If you went to his room, then called me on your mobile so I could talk to him—"

"Why aren't you letting the police handle this?"

"Most of them are in hospital, too. I'm involving myself because I'm not only pure eager to see the pandemic end, I'm highly motivated to find out who's messing with our aquatic life and put a stop to it."

James sneered. "I should have known. This is aboot the seals again, isn't it? Don't even try to deny it."

Robin opened his mouth to protest and closed it again. A few months earlier, he'd given his nephews a children's picture book about the Selkie legend for their birthdays. James had torn the book in two, denounced it as akin to witchcraft, and told him he'd had enough of Robin's rubbish, seafaring lifestyle.

His brother quickly took up the slack. "Don't even try. I saw the article aboot seals being captured and killed so their flesh can be tested for antibodies or natural immunities to aid in a cure or development of a vaccine. This is aboot saving your Selkie friends, isn't it? Well, I'll have none of it."

James turned on his heels and headed for the house. He turned when he got to the door. "I offered you a place to live when you lost your apartment. I asked you to take your meals with us until the economy turned around. You rejected my help then, so you'll not have it now." He shook his head, effectively letting Robin know that he thought he was a hopeless cause. "The next time I see you, I pray to God it will be at the altar, with you on your knees, asking forgiveness."

What his brother thought of him hadn't mattered to Robin for a long time, but that didn't mean the words didn't hurt.

James went inside the house and slammed the door closed behind him.

That was when Robin spied his brother's shirts beckoning to him from the clothesline. If he temporarily borrowed one of his brother's clergy shirts, he could fashion a clerical collar and pretend to be a pastor just long enough to gain admittance to hospital. Without any further thought, he loosened the clothespins from the hem of the shirt, grabbed it and ran.

CHAPTER 10

Rebecca was at the café frying up a package of mince and trying not to worry about her mother when she heard a knock on the back door. "Come through!" She had just given her hands a good sanitizing wash and if she were to have touched the doorknob, she would have had to repeat the whole process.

Robin cracked the door and rushed in, flushed and looking in a hurry. "I have your payment for the catering job yesterday." He set down the two large insulated food carriers he was holding. "Sorry I didn't come round last night. Thanks again for the generous portions and for pulling it together on such late notice." He spread out the money on the counter where she set her purse, an area which was not sanitized.

Smart man. She smiled and counted the money with her eyes. "That's way too much. You need to take your cut. You sent the business my way."

"A finder's fee after all the free food you've been slipping me?"

"But that's all leftovers. It would just go to waste if you didn't eat it."

"No worries. Cameron left a big tip for each of us. He was pure generous."

She tried to act nonchalant. "So what did you find out

aboot him? Is he going to be in the area for awhile? Do you think he'll be bringing in more business? Did you find out what company these men work for?"

Robin looked hesitant.

She noticed he was holding a black shirt under his arm.

Robin shifted so the shirt was blocked from her view. "Well, they were a pure interesting lot. At least one was a doctor, and another a scientist. Obviously here to investigate the pandemic in some capacity. Cameron owns a summer home on Skye that's been in his family for at least two generations." Robin hesitated again. "he talked aboot spending summers here when he was a teenager and young adult. Knew a few locals."

She stirred some finely diced onion into the mince. "Any one we know?"

Robin blinked a few times, swallowed hard and looked uncomfortable.

"Sorry aboot the onions, but I need to stay on task. I've a busy day ahead, an appointment with my attorney, and on top of everything else, my mother's gone missing."

"Missing?"

"We had a bit of a row last night and when I went looking for her a few minutes later, she was gone. Still wasn't around this morning." She wiped a tear from her eye. And it wasn't the onions.

Robin eyed her cautiously. "Cameron mentioned a couple of things that happened on Skye when he was young that made me think he might have been a friend of your mother's."

"Really?" Her heart leaped in her chest. "After two and a half decades of not knowing anything aboot my lineage, my mother let slip last night that I was nothing like my father. And she called him by name. Cam."

"Really?" Robin looked like he knew something – something that he didn't want her to know. He looked guilty as sin, and vastly uncomfortable.

"Okay. So I did overhear a little bit of their conversation

and we should talk aboot it when we have the time." Robin opened the door a crack and peered out into the parking lot. "But right now, I need to get over to hospital to take care of some business. Do you by chance have some white card stock and a scissors I could use?"

She pointed to her desk. "The scissors is in the top right drawer. No card stock though." She thought. "I might have some old tagboard that was used for signs a decade ago. I have no idea where it might be."

"How aboot that empty sour cream container?" He pointed to the plastic container she'd just used up. "Can I have it?"

"I guess. It's only white on the one side."

He went to the sink and rinsed out the container with hot, soapy water,   took the scissors from her desk, and used it to cut out a strip aboot five inches long and an inch wide in the center.

"I need to go," Robin said. "I'll explain everything later. I promise."

"But what aboot Cameron?" She tried to convey the urgency of her emotions with her eyes. "If you know anything more…I'm wondering if he could be my father."

"We'll talk aboot it later, sweetheart. I really have to do this, now, before my brother…"

"Pastor James?"

"Yes. And if he should call or come by looking for me, please don't tell him I was here or that I said I was going to hospital."

"Aye."

Robin headed for the door and she caught another glimpse of what looked to be a black shirt.

"Rebecca? Please promise me you won't go getting your hopes up aboot having any sort of relationship with this Cameron. He seems like a nice enough man, but I believe the group that he was with are part of the nefarious people that we were talking aboot yesterday."

She smiled behind her mask. She wanted to cry. "As in

The Case of the Nefarious Seafood Affair?"

Robin's eyes were filled with empathy. "Yes. Now stay safe until I get back. I'll come by tonight and we can talk more."

She sniffled. Had she finally found the man who could be her father, only to discover he had somehow participated in causing a pandemic?

She added her own secret seasonings to the mince mixture and tasted it to make sure it was right, then added a little more pepper. She was glad Robin had stopped by, even if only for few minutes, but distractions when she was cooking were dangerous.

Another knock on the door. She frowned. She needed to get her mini pie crusts rolled out and filled with mince before the meat mixture entered the dreaded danger zone of no longer hot enough but not nearly cool enough. "Come through!"

The door opened a crack. It was her mother.

Rebecca kept doing what she was doing and waited for her mother to speak.

"Just wanted to pop in and let you know I'm still alive."

"Well, I'm happy to know it."

"I'm sorry I taunted you aboot being a virgin. I know your faith is important to you, and I respect that."

Okay. Rebecca supposed she should respond by saying that she respected her mother's right to sleep with whomever she wanted, whenever she wanted, and wherever she wanted, but she simply couldn't say the words. She had to say something, but she couldn't say that. Her brain felt as mush as the mince in the pan.

"The only reason I'm sleeping with so many different men is that I'm scared I'm going to die. I know, I know. I act like I'm not afraid of anything. But honestly, I'm at a vulnerable age, and if I don't have that long to live, why should I forego having a little fun?"

Rebecca tried to keep her thoughts to herself. Tried. "Because you could catch a disease or bring the virus home to me, because you might not die, and then, you'll be forever known as a floozy, and men will be sniffing around our house for the rest of my life."

Her mother's nostrils flared. "Is it any wonder I turn to strangers for a little affection? All I want is to be loved. All I feel from you is disapproval."

Right. Well, you give disapproval, you get disapproval, she wanted to say. That's the way it works, mother. Rebecca wanted to be the bigger person, but-

She heard another knock at the door. "Come through!" Thank you, God, was her first thought, saved by the bell – until she saw who it was. "Cameron."

"Good morning, Rebecca." He smiled in his charming way. "Anything I can buy off you to feed the boys for breakfast?"

She glanced frantically to the left to see how her mother was reacting. That first facial expression upon seeing Cameron Allanach could be very revealing.

But her mother had disappeared. There was no other way out, so she must have gone through to the dining room or hidden in the bathroom.

She looked back at Cameron and tried to steady her emotions so a quavering voice wouldn't give her away. "I just made several loaves of homemade zucchini bread with blueberries and cinnamon. It's moist and tasty. Today's scones are blackberry apple with fresh mint and a ginger glaze."

Cameron smiled once again. "The zucchini bread sounds divine. You're very creative. Are the ideas your own?"

"Yes. I let my fresh herbs and whatever's on hand at the farmers market inspire me. I have a few small fruit trees in the back yard of the house where my mother and I..."

There was an awkward silence.

"Let me get the bread sliced for you. It's still a little warm. I'll put some butter pats in the box in case anyone likes it that way."

"Thanks." He leaned against the counter and watched her

work. "So I take it you're not married – because you mentioned living with your mother. Any kids?"

"Well, actually, she lives with me, and only since my stepfather died a few months ago, during the first pandemic. And no, I don't have any children. Hopefully, one day, I will."

"I hope so too. It would be a shame if someone as beautiful and talented as you are didn't get a chance to pass along their genes to a new generation."

She could feel her cheeks blushing as she handed him his order. "Anything else I can get for you?"

He handed her a large wad of cash and waved at her to stop when she reached for the cash drawer to make change. "Not unless you have some sausage rolls hiding somewhere."

She handed him a business card. "If you want sausage rolls, call me the night before and tell me what time you'd like to pick them up so I can have some ready. I won't start making them on a regular basis again until the pandemic has passed, but I can do a special order anytime as long as I know a little in advance."

"Will do." He grinned. "Just so you know, I meant what I said aboot being beautiful and talented. Look in the mirror next time you have a second. You've got it all, girl."

"Thank you."

"See you another time." Cameron exited the kitchen with a wave.

Rebecca silently counted to ten. "Mother?"

"Is he gone?"

"Yes. What was that aboot?"

"I thought it was the food inspector. I didn't want to get you in trouble. I know I shouldn't be here, not since I've not been social distancing." Her mother looked profoundly uncomfortable.

That was her mother awright. The exact opposite of social distancing. But that didn't mean she had fallen for her flimsy excuse about the food inspector.

Her mother rattled on for the next ten minutes about

nothing in particular—the weather, the rising prices at the grocery, how slow the mail had been of late, what the lack of tourists was doing to the economy – nothing that pertained to their relationship, their argument, Cameron, or Henry or Hank or Jake or Jack or whatever the names of the various men she was involved with—or not.

Her mother finally took a breath. "Well, I guess I'd better get going."

And Rebecca breathed a sigh of relief. "Yes, I need to get back to work." She never had worked well when she kept getting interrupted, and today had been one continuous doozy of a distraction.

#

Pretending to be a pastor visiting a patient on his death bed was more complicated than Robin had anticipated. Thankfully, Portree Community Hospital was small, with few rules, and even fewer security personnel. Of course, who would want to sneak into a hospital that was ground zero in a pandemic? Even the news had recommended staying away from hospitals unless you were in the middle of a dire medical crisis and had to be seen. And because no one wanted to go near the place unless they had to, there were no guards watching for people trying to sneak in.

But being in a small town had its disadvantages as well as its advantages. Everyone working in hospital knew James, and a good half of them probably attended his kirk and got a good look at him every Sunday.

He was glad he had thought to run home and grab a hat after he left Rebecca's. James was going bald, and Robin still had a full head of hair. According to the tabloids, women noticed that kind of thing. It made no sense to risk drawing attention to himself. He tried to slouch like James. They were about the same height. His mask covered half of his face, and he and James both had green eyes and reddish blond sideburns. For added effect, he hummed *Amazing Grace* as he walked through the corridors of hospital, just as James was prone to do, following the signs to Room 14.

He faltered for a minute when he saw the symbol for poison outside the room and a sign indicating the room was part of a quarantined area. No visitors allowed. He sighed. He had to do this. He owed it to his friends. He owed it to Scotland. He owed it to the world.

He made sure his mask was tight, opened the door slowly, and quietly slipped in. James probably would have said it was God looking out for him when he found Room 14 empty except for the good Captain. There was not a nurse in sight. Robin chalked it up to a stroke of good luck. One couldn't expect God's blessings to rain down on him when he was impersonating one of God's own calling—if that's what it was. Robin didn't understand why he had to accept James' job to be some sort of divine intention whereas his purchasing Sea Worthy had been viewed by his family as some sort of devilish scheme concocted by a madman. But that was a problem for another day.

The Captain's skin was a sickly shade of yellowish gray, but he was wide awake and seemed as cognitively aware as anyone Robin knew, probably more so than the generally clueless James and Sarah.

Never one to waste a perfectly timed opportunity, Robin jumped right in to the questions he had prepared. He found the Captain eager to talk, even confess his wrongdoings. It never occurred to him to explain who he really was, but once he discovered how eager the man was to spill his guts to a "priest" he just sat back and listened while the whole tale came pouring out.

"Forgive me, Father, for accepting a large sum of money from the Germans. I knew it was wrong to let the insects, um, sea lice, into the fish hatchery and fish farms around Skye and in random spots across the isles for wild fish populations to ingest. But I swear I didn't know they were infested with a virus. I mean, I know I shouldn't swear, but I specifically asked them what the drop was aboot and they told me it was a growth enhancement supplement that they were experimenting with that would help fish to grow faster and mature more quickly, thus increasing the food availability to meet growing demands – so they could lower the price to the groceries. Being a good man, and wanting to help, that's all I'm really guilty of. Please believe me, Father."

Robin thought about correcting him—the Captain believing he was some sort of priest was an unexpected advantage. And then he thought again. "Bless you, son. I do believe you. Please go on—as your heart prompts you. But the more you confess, the more I'll be able to advocate for you."

"I understand, Father. I mean, I guess I knew deep down that something was wrong. I got a lot of money from them. But I had to promise to be discreet, you know? In the beginning, the only reason I even suspected that something illegal was going on was because they insisted I use my unmarked boat, and that I make the drop when it was almost dark, and that I approach the fish farm from the exact coordinates they gave me. I thought it was some sort of a steroid for fish. I didn't see any harm in it. I mean, they use genetics to make corn grow faster and tomatoes grow bigger. Everyone's doing it, right?"

Robin didn't know what to say so he made the sign of the cross. God forgive him. He hadn't told the man he was a priest—the Captain had assumed it. He couldn't be held liable for that, could he?

The Captain continued. "So we made many trips and drop-offs. I was paid, and I thought everything came out pretty well. But then, when the first of my crew fell ill. I was worried, you know? Then one of them died, and I really felt guilty."

"Go on, my child."

The Captain had a coughing fit so severe that Robin almost left the room. He hoped his mask was good.

"I talked to the men from Edinburgh who had contacted me to begin with but got nowhere. So I called the Germans and demanded to speak to whoever was in charge. Lot of good it did me. I didn't know what to do. Then another of my crew died. Thank goodness I made a photocopy of the check I received from them before I cashed it. It's still in the top drawer in my desk in my office. What do you think I should do, Father? Assuming I don't die like the rest of my mates."

Robin swallowed. He'd been trying not to breathe, but he could only do that for so long. Oh, that he had the skills and physiology of his friends, the seals. "Do you remember hearing any names? Any indication of the company that was involved? I'm sure it would please the Lord greatly if you were to help bring these men to justice." Robin started to sweat under his white plastic, sour cream container collar. Lord, forgive me.

"I remember hearing the words 'die droge' a few times, but I thought it was in reference to a drug, not a company—you know, the growth enhancement drug they paid us to give to the fish."

He asked a few more questions, but the Captain seemed to be getting tired.

"Thank you so much for coming, Father." The Captain's voice was growing weaker and weaker. "They tell me my chances of surviving this aren't very good. I'm glad I could confess my part in this and get it off my chest in case the worst happens. I can't stand the thought of taking what I did to my grave."

Robin started to panic. He had no idea how to absolve someone of their sins, which said something about how often he went to Sunday services.

The Captain coughed once again, on and on and on. He finally eked out, "Bless me, Father."

Robin had no idea how to respond, so he made the sign of the cross once more and said, "Bless you for trying to help."

The Captain's eyes were closed and he was snoring gently when Robin glanced out to the hallway, found the corridor empty, and left after squirting his hands with sanitizer.

He exited the hospital as quickly as he could. His fake collar came off the second he was out of the building. He gulped down as much fresh air as he could get into his lungs. He didn't recall ever wearing a black dress shirt but if he did see someone he knew, they probably wouldn't think anything of it without the telltale white strip.

Of course, if Sarah or James had gone to take in the clothes from the drying line, they'd surely notice it was gone. He made a beeline to the boat to shower and change into his own clothes.

He hated what he'd done and the deception he'd perpetrated, but at least he'd gotten more information to go on. What he needed now was proof. He still hadn't heard from the client he'd had on the boat to see if she'd found any video or even photos of the boat actually dumping their toxic cargo into the bay. The second he got back to his boat, he checked his email. There it was. Perfect timing. The proof he needed to go to the police. She'd sent a copy of the video and a couple of photos from the same cruise.

Now, he just needed to decide what to do next, who he should talk to, who he could trust. Should he speak to the local police or go directly to the government officials in Edinburgh, assuming they'd let him anywhere near Edinburgh? The locals on Skye had called the first tourists to return to the island after the initial pandemic *Plague Rats*. Now, anyone from Skye who attempted to travel was regarded the same way.

He thought about Becca while he showered and wondered if it would help her if he went to press. If he gave the story to the woman whose mother had gotten ill at Café Fish, perhaps the situation could be resolved.

His desire to speak to Rebecca grew so intense that he couldn't stand to be away from her for one more minute. Without another thought, because all he could think about was her, he dried off, pulled on one of his own shirts and sprinted toward Café Fish.

He got halfway down the pier and realized he didn't have

his mask. Where was it? He raced back to Sea Worthy and searched the deck, searched below deck, and checked every surface where he could have laid it down. It wasn't tangled up in the clothes he'd stripped off when he'd returned from hospital. It wasn't in the pocket of James' shirt. It wasn't anywhere to be found. Which meant it was probably just outside the hospital, that he'd lost it when he'd removed the sour cream container tab he'd used for a clergy collar. In fact, the tab was missing, too.

He washed his hands one more time and grabbed another mask while his mind raced with probable repercussions to losing the first one. Upon thinking about the situation, he realized he shouldn't be using the same mask he'd worn in hospital anyway. But if anyone had seen him coming or going, if he'd been caught on a security camera, they would certainly speak to James, who would deny having been at hospital. An investigation would ensue. Robin's DNA would be slathered all over his mask. What if the Captain died? Would they think he'd killed him? Oh, Lord. What had he done?

CHAPTER 11

Rebecca was doing dishes when she heard a soft knock. She instantly knew it was Robin. "You're back!"

He held out his hands, motioning her to back off. "No hugs tonight. I visited the Captain of the unmarked boat in hospital and he was pretty bad. I showered and changed, but we should err on the safe side. If you want me to leave…"

"No! I need to talk to you aboot Cameron. I just can't shake the feeling that he might be my father. He stopped by this morning after you left to get breakfast goodies for his friends and my mother was here, but she ducked out of the room before he saw her. I tried to get a reaction out of her, but she was being even more tight-lipped than usual."

She looked at Robin and found his eyes to be soft and caring. "Well, he definitely knows Emma—or did, back in the day. And they did have sex. But according to him, you weren't born until nine months and three weeks after they last had contact, so he thinks someone else is your father."

"He told you that?"

"No. I overheard bits and pieces of a conversation that would have meant nothing to me if I didn't know you and Emma."

Her head spun with the implications of what Robin was saying. "So, if Cameron doesn't think he's my father, who?

The Selkie my mother took as a lover?" She laughed. "Fat chance."

Robin's face paled a shade. "I know you don't believe in Selkies and I understand that you don't like to think aboot the possibility, but we need to talk aboot every possible option. Could we just stay open to the idea of Selkies for the sake of discussion?"

"What? Don't tell me you believe Selkies really exist?" Waves of incredulousness washed over her.

Robin looked defeated before he said a word. But his stubborn streak was peeking through and his voice gained confidence as he spoke. "I don't know what I believe aboot Selkies. If you want the truth, I feel like I've met a few. But it's always been in a sleep-induced, dream-like state – never in my waking hours – so I can't know if it really happened or if I dreamed it all."

"You really think there might be – that my father might really be…"

"The main thing is that I can accept you either way— Selkie father, human father. Because I believe in you. Because I love you just the way you are." He grasped her hands in his. "The question is, can you accept me saying that I believe in Selkies, that I've known a few, and hope to swim with my friends again one day when this has all passed? Or are you only willing to accept me if I agree with you and deny their existence?"

It was a good question, and she respected him for asking it. She was flattered that he trusted her enough to be vulnerable with her.

She searched her heart and did her best to find an honest answer. She had a great deal of respect for Robin. In all honesty, a good part of why she didn't believe in Selkies— had never even entertained the idea that Selkies could exist— was because her mother thought they did.

Robin finally spoke again. "I've done a lot of research on Selkie lore and legends. Can we please just set our emotions aside and examine my findings?"

"I suppose that's a good place to start."

"Thank you." Robin took a deep breath. She could tell because his mask plastered itself to his face until he exhaled. "First of all, there's a possibility that Emma was drunk or high and only thought she slept with a Selkie. Many of the legends aboot Selkies seem to have come aboot because of a mistaken identity."

"I can see that happening." No insult intended, but she could definitely imagine that happening, especially if her mother had just had her heart broken by someone as steamy as Cameron Allanach.

"Just one example, but I found a book aboot seal people by Gaelic historian John MacAulay that starts on the premise that the Selkie legend arose from sightings of Eskimo-type kayakers in sealskin canoes who traveled down to Scotland from remote Arctic Norway or Finland. There's a documented tribe of nomadic hunter-gatherers called the Sea Sami who used Eskimo kayaks and technology to hunt and fish."

Rob continued in his soft, but strong voice. "Imagine how such a kayaker must have looked to someone who had never seen one before. A sealskin kayak becomes waterlogged after eight hours and so lies just below the surface of the water. All you would see from the shore would be the top half of a man and below the water, the shape of a long tail wavering in the refracted light. It must have looked remarkably like a creature that was half man, half seal. And imagine the islander's shock if that creature came ashore, took off its sealskins and became entirely human."

"I suppose that makes sense. Do you think that's also the case when people think they've seen a mermaid?"

"Could be. Sealskin kayaks have to haul out onto a rock every so often to dry out. If a kayaker took the chance to comb out their hair while sunning themselves on the rock, and then, when they saw they were being observed and launched their kayak back into the water, it could appear that a long-tailed creature had dived back into the sea."

"I can definitely accept that theory, but it doesn't account for my mother thinking she had sex with one of them." She felt her skin blushing. "I actually did a report on Selkies when I was in primary school, and I remember another theory about Spaniards being shipwrecked at sea and being washed ashore. Their dark hair reminded the people of seals."

"Yes. And there are a lot more complex theories, like that Selkies are fallen angels that dropped into the sea and transformed, and that after Christianity swept through the British Isles, the seal people became representative of those perceived to be in purgatory, caught between two worlds. One of the most popular theories is that Selkies are formed from the souls of drowned people who were granted one night each year to return to their human form and dance upon the shore of the sea."

"Okay," she said. "But all of these theories explain how legends came aboot from people who just thought they were seeing Selkies. So they're basically refuting the existence of actual Selkies. Right?"

Rob nodded. "Yes. So now, let's talk aboot the actual belief that Selkies are more than a mythical being. That theory would indicate that seal folk are capable of therianthropy, and that they are able to change from seal to human form by shedding their skin."

"Right – which is much harder for me to accept. Although I've heard the stereotypical folk-tale where a man finds a naked woman on the sea shore and steals her Selkie skin. She becomes his wife, and bears him children, but spends her time in captivity longing for the sea, her true home, and is often seen gazing longingly at the ocean. As soon as she finds her seal skin, she goes back to the sea, abandoning her husband and children."

"So if your mother's claims are true, she met a male Selkie, who like their female counterparts, are described as being very handsome in their human form, and having great seductive powers over human women. They typically seek those who are dissatisfied with their life, such as married women waiting for their fishermen husbands."

"Or a poor, heartbroken woman who's just been dumped by her rich fiancé because she wasn't good enough for his family."

"Exactly. The legend goes that Selkie men often give children to barren women."

Rebecca nodded. "Or needy, recently devastated women like my mother."

"Meeting a Selkie would be a fairy tale come to life except that Selkie legends never end happily."

Rebecca sighed. "What a conundrum. I've read that if an ordinary mortal sees a Selkie in human form, they will inevitably fall in love. So while he or she is powerless to resist the allure of life with a Selkie, the Selkie is powerless to resist the call of the sea."

"So can you warm up to idea that Emma might actually have had an encounter with a Selkie?"

For a second, she almost wished she could believe. But she couldn't. She just couldn't.

Rob's voice sounded so endearing and hopeful. "There are several families from the Outer Hebrides who claim to be direct descendants of sea people. The famous poet MacOdrum was said to be one. It was claimed he got his skill in song writing from the seal's gift of singing. Don't you have a beautiful singing voice?"

"Aye. And I was a championship swimmer." She rolled her eyes, a form of communication she was glad could be utilized even when wearing a mask. "So if I'm half Selkie, at least I'm not alone."

Rob said, "That's the theory."

"Theory schmeory. Can we talk aboot Cameron now? Please?"

"That's fair. Thank you for at least considering the Selkie possibility."

"You're welcome – only because I have so much respect for you. But now I want you to tell me what you know aboot Cameron. What else did he say?"

Robin told her everything he knew—what the men on the boat had discussed, what he'd learned at hospital. She tried to digest the information, but it was going to take time. It was a relief to know certain things, and it was disappointing, and it was confusing.

When he was done talking, she felt like she had more questions than answers. But there was time to find all of that out, time to pump her mother for answers, time to make up her own mind about what she believed and what she didn't. But there was one question that she needed answering now. In a strange sort of way, her future—and Robin's—hung on his answer, unfair as that might be.

She looked him in the eyes and asked, "Have you ever made love to a Selkie?"

She could accept that she and Robin might not agree on politics or religion or even Selkies. She could deal with the fact that when you entered into a relationship with someone, you were never going to think exactly the same way. But there were some things that were triggers for her, some things she just couldn't deal with, at least right now. She rubbed the upper edge of her mask and discovered it was wet, either from sweat or tears.

"Do you have a Selkie who waits for you to come back to your island? If so, is there any possibility she's pregnant with your child?"

Please say no, her mind cried. *Please.*

#

Robin knew he and Rebecca needed to have this conversation, but he'd been hoping they could schedule it for a time when they were both well-rested and free from everyday stresses. With emotions and fear and tension running amuck, he was fearful one or the other of them was going to say something unforgiveable.

He looked at Rebecca. Her eyes were teary and she looked exhausted. But if this was what she wanted, when she needed it…he could only explain it as best he could and hope she accepted what he had to say.

"You've heard the story aboot the elephant, haven't you?"

"You mean the one where six blind men each touch an elephant—one the ears, one the tusks, one the tail, one the legs, one the side, and one the trunk—and each gives a completely different description of what the elephant was like."

"Yes. Each based on their own perspective." Robin looked straight into her eyes. "What I'm aboot to tell you is based on my own, unique experiences."

Rebecca nodded faintly. "So my perspective is going to be different because I haven't experienced the same things you have."

"Aye." He started to pace as much as the tight quarters in the kitchen allowed. But then, he was used to his boat, the deck of which wasn't much bigger.

"You know how it's been. Almost a year of shutdowns, and then a soft opening to see how things went, and then another huge spike in the numbers, and another shutdown. It was hard, but I managed. I spent a lot of time alone, working on the boat and visiting different islands, scouting out places where I could take my clients once the pandemic was over."

"Believe me, I know. Some days I counted having my mother with me as a blessing, and other days, a bane."

"At least you had someone to talk to."

"Argue with," Rebecca said without skipping a beat.

"Well, I had no one. I thought aboot getting a dog, but I periodically get clients who are allergic to them, or scared, so I didn't think it would be a good idea going forward. There were always seals around the area where I would camp, and eventually built a little sea shanty. At first, I tried to stay as far away from them as I could. I'd heard the males could be aggressive, especially when protecting their cows, and the females, when they perceived their babies to be in danger."

Rebecca said, "I've heard they can carry diseases, so it's not wise to swim in waters near their nesting grounds."

"Who told you that? Your mother?"

"Yes." She giggled.

"Figures." At least she could laugh about it.

"Go on," she said.

"Well, I told you there was a particular island that I especially liked, with a beautiful beach where the seals seemed to like to congregate. The harbor seals seemed to take to me. They became like pets. Their faces kind of have a dog-like profile, and with the whiskers—don't you think there's some resemblance? Anyway, I welcomed the distraction and they were good companions. I could tell them apart because of their markings and variations in colour. Some are blonde, some black, but the cutest and most common of them are generally grey with dark spots. Not only did each of the seals have a distinctive look, they had unique personalities, also like dogs, I suppose."

"You mean, like some are nervous and bark a lot?"

"Yes, and others were sweet and cuddly. And some had a lot of energy and some liked to lie in the sun and do nothing all day long."

"Okay. That makes sense. I can accept that."

"So eventually, I gave them names to fit their looks or personalities."

"Okay. Got it." Rebecca looked a little wary, but she seemed to be doing fine with the whole concept – so far.

"Eventually, a couple of them became my favorites. Shelagh, one of the cows, would always bat her eyelashes at me and do this cute little thing with her tail when she saw me. And Soren, one of the bulls, always seemed to listen so intently when I talked that I truly felt like I had a friend and a confidant in him."

"So they were your friends." Rebecca looked thoughtful. "I guess it's not all that different to having a dog or a cat that you're really attached to."

"Exactly. Maybe it's what social distancing drove me to. Maybe it would have happened anyway. I always had a dog or two when I was a boy and they were more like family to me than my human family ever was. And they understood me better, too."

"I can relate." Rebecca was looking at him like she really did get it. Hopefully she did. She had never mentioned having a pet, but maybe somewhere along the way, she had. And then she said, "Everything you've said so far has been aboot seals. No one ever disputed the fact that seals are cute and entertaining and playful or that they can be trained to interact with humans. But there's a vast difference between having seals whose company you enjoy and believing in Selkies."

He felt his cheeks heating up inside his mask. He didn't speak right away.

"It started one night when I couldn't sleep. The moon was full, or nearly so, and I was just wide awake. It was near midsummer's eve, and the days were so long that I knew dawn would come in just a few hours. Eventually, I dozed off and started dreaming. Shelagh and Soren were walking and then dancing in the moonlight. They wanted me to join them. We were singing and doing a dance similar to dancing around a Maypole. It was so vivid it seemed real. It was one of the most enjoyable, completely fun times I've ever had in my life."

Rebecca smiled. "Is it wrong of me to feel a touch jealous?"

"There's more." He looked away from her. "When I woke up the next morning, I was lying on the beach, stark naked. My hair was wet and I felt like I'd been swimming. I never did find my clothes. Shelagh and Soren were nowhere to be found – probably hunting for food. Later on, when they reappeared, they were seals again."

He bowed his head, sure she was going to laugh at him or mock him or tell him he was insane.

"And this has happened more than once?" She asked.

"Yes. Many times since, but only in my dreams."

"It's almost as though you can't accept what happened with your conscious mind, so you enjoy it in a dream form."

"I guess that's a reasonable theory."

She seemed thoughtful, like she was really trying to understand what he experienced. "Seals are nocturnal, so the fact that this happens at night makes perfect sense."

"Thanks, Rebecca."

"Do you ever remember sleepwalking when you were a boy?"

"I don't. But I could ask my mom if I used to—or James, once he's forgiven me for borrowing his clergy shirt and impersonating a priest."

"Oh, Robin." She hugged him and he almost melted when he felt how warm and soft she felt, molded against his frame.

She kissed his cheek. "We're both exhausted. It's been a long day and we've got a lot to process. Let's sleep on it and see what tomorrow brings."

"I'll walk you up the hill."

He watched while she checked to make sure her gas burners and ovens were turned off, checked to make sure the faucets weren't dripping, or a cooler door cracked open a notch. None of it was as exciting as dancing in the moonlight with Shelagh and Soren, but it was classic Becca, and he loved her for it.

He kissed her when they got to the top of the hill. "I wanted to talk to you aboot where we should go from here. I mean, as far as the information we've gathered aboot the unmarked boat and Die Droge."

She leaned closer and this time, it was she who kissed him. "Meet me first thing in the morning at the boat? Cameron has stopped by the Café twice in the last week, so I don't think we should talk there, just in case he shows up again. I mean, since it involves him."

"Sounds like something else to contemplate while we try to sleep," he said. He stroked her shoulders. "After what I've told you aboot Selkies and what you've learned aboot Cameron today, do you still hope he's your father, or do you prefer the theory that you're part Selkie?"

"I think I'll choose Option C. Neither."

They laughed quietly. "If only we could choose our

parents…" They said it at the same time, and laughed again. "Until morning."

CHAPTER 12

Rebecca's emotions warred within her mind for most of the night. She finally fell into a deep slumber what seemed like minutes before her alarm went off.

Robin's words replayed in her dreams over and over again. The main question that was unsettling to her was this: In his despair and loneliness, would Robin eventually listen to the siren song of the Selkies and choose them over real, live flesh and blood people—namely her? All the legends agreed that once a human man or woman met a Selkie, they couldn't help falling in love with them. How was she, a mere mortal, supposed to compete with the Selkie allure?

Robin had said more than once that his primary goal for the pandemic was to protect the seals, or Selkies, as the case might be, who were his friends. They were obviously near and dear to him no matter what form they assumed. In a way, he'd already chosen them over humans when he'd declared their safety to be paramount.

Whereas she could justify sacrificing a handful of seals for experimental purposes if it meant finding a cure for the virus and saving hundreds of thousands of human lives, Robin would hear none of it. If that were his priority, would she ever really be able to trust him, or at some point, when their relationship had deepened, would she awake one morning to find him gone, called back to the Selkies he loved more than anything, including her?

She slipped from her bedroom as quietly as she could and was gratified to find the bathroom empty. Of course, that didn't mean her mother hadn't invited a man to share her bed again last night. This one, if there was one, could be a late sleeper. Or, perhaps he'd already been up and gone back to bed to go at it one more time.

She pulled the straps of her teddy from her shoulders, forced the thought of her mother's sexually active lifestyle from her mind, and stepped into the shower.

There was another bothersome thought in her brain that she couldn't seem to get rid of. If Robin was so enamored with the carefree pursuits, fun and frivolity of singing and dancing on the beach with Selkies, would he ever be content to share her mundane, workaday, constantly-at-it lifestyle as a business owner and restaurateur? Café Fish was everything to her – her dreams, her family, her life calling, her passion. No matter how much she cared for Robin, she wasn't about to give it all up to live on a beach, sailing the high seas by day and frolicking with Selkies by night.

She was in front of the mirror, getting ready to fasten her bra and slip into her panties when she had another thought. What if Robin had made love with a Selkie? He might not have conscious memories of having sex, but if he was waking up naked, fresh from a swim, there was at least a possibility that something more than frisking around had gone on in the water, or even on the beach.

She looked at her body and tried to see through the faint mist of steam still clouding the mirror. She raised her hands and cupped her breasts. Not to be vain, but they seemed to be a good size. Not too big. Not too small. Her areolas were a nice brown color and well-defined. Her nipples were fairly long—big enough to tease or pinch or even latch on to if a person was so inclined. The mirror stopped short of letting her see her pubic area, so she ran her fingers over her mound and tried to imagine how it would appear to Robin. It felt good. She assumed it would feel even better—much better—if Robin were in charge of the exploration. It was getting wet in the center. That had to be a good thing, didn't it? Sometimes a pain from her perspective, but if a man was going to… the juiciness between her legs would have to be an asset.

The thing was, she was a virgin. Assuming she had assets, she didn't have a clue how to use them to their best advantage. She had no skills, no expertise, no experience with which to lure a man. How was she supposed to compete with some sexy, sultry sea creature who could slip and slide through the water at whim and dance under the moonlight with naked abandon on land? If Robin had experienced any of the above, he'd be bored with plain, simple, virginal Rebecca in two seconds.

Hopeless! She grabbed her clothes and got into them as quickly as she could.

Robin was not the type to steal a Selkie's seal skin after dancing with her in the moonlight and hide them under lock and key so said legendary Selkie would be bound to stay and be his wife. But that didn't mean he wouldn't give in to his lust and share a night of passion with the cow. Isn't that what female seals were called?

A short time later, she was still preoccupied with thoughts of sand and Selkies, but dressed and ready to report to work nonetheless.

When she'd walked down the hill as far as the café, she decided to stop and set some butter out to soften before she went to Robin's boat. When she went to open the door to the café and heard a voice calling out to her from the parking lot, she thought Cameron right off. But this time, it was an inspector—and not Judy.

"Just a quick stop by to make sure there's no seafood in your cooler," he explained. "And a quick peek at your dining room to make sure it's not been in use since the new quarantine orders came down."

"No worries," she said. "I've been a good girl."

"Yes. You're one of the best. Such a shame it had to be your place where someone got sick."

Rebecca looked at the inspector. "I'm really hoping it will blow over."

A dark cloud scudded over the inspector's eyes. "They've filed papers. I had to fill out a fact-finding sheet yesterday afternoon. I want ye to know I did my best for ye, lass. I even took on some liability for the department. At the very least, we should have sent out a text message right at the start, or gone round to each business personally when we issued the order to stop serving seafood immediately. At the time, we were looking at it as more of a precautionary measure than an edict. No one really thought anything would come of it."

"I do try to check my email at least once during the course of the day in case someone has emailed in a takeaway order. But never until after the lunch rush is over. I just don't have time."

"And we know that. We should have sent the text right away instead of later. By then, we knew more aboot what we were dealing with and how serious it was. Not that it's made any difference in the long run. The second the virus went airborne and began to transfer from person to person, it was not even aboot seafood anymore."

She nodded. "Anything on the news this morning aboot the possibility of treatment or a new vaccine? I get home so late that I don't see it most nights and things are too rushed in the mornings."

"The only news is how fast it's spreading. Because it's not only airborne, but in the food supply, it's going round even faster than last time. The whole world is impacted."

"Right." She sighed. "And there you have the other reason I don't watch the news. Too depressing."

"Don't give in to it, lass. Worry and doubt have the power to destroy ye like none else."

"Yes. I agree."

The inspector's eyes were full of concern. "It would be a

shame to have seen ye survive the first pandemic and well on yer way to making it through the second only to have a nasty reporter and her overly pious solicitor take ye down."

"Is there anything I can do to make this better, short of an expensive court scuffle? I can't afford to do battle over this. I could lose the café, and my home. Mother and I would have no where to go."

"It's the daughter that's spearheading the legal end of things. Her mother is holding her own in hospital and more worried aboot staying alive than suing anybody. Perhaps ye should check with yer attorney first, but I don't see how ye could make things any worse by trying to work things out with the daughter in hopes of finding a way to settle yer differences."

The inspector walked around her kitchen, checking things off on his clipboard while he spoke.

"Thank you," she said when he was done. "I'll do my best."

"Ye always do, deary. That's what we all love aboot the Fish."

She was teary-eyed as she watched him exit, and it only grew worse when she saw Robin coming up the walk.

He slipped in the door while she held it open.

"I was just coming up the hill to walk with you down to the boat."

"I stopped off to put some butter out to soften and the inspector dropped by."

"Thought you might have gotten sidetracked when I got to the house and you were already gone – your mom answered the door and told me you'd left."

"Was she alone?"

"As far as I know. No half-clothed strangers sitting down to eat breakfast that I could see."

"Yes. Well. The world would have to come to an end before she'd cook anything for anybody."

"Really? I always assumed you learned your culinary skills from watching her."

She relocked the café and followed Robin toward the harbor.

Robin said, "I've seen her down at the docks numerous times buying seafood—just assumed she knew what to do with it."

Poor, naïve Robin. "She's been known to roll sushi IF I cook the rice for her, make the sheets of seaweed, devein the shrimp, shuck the oysters, crack and clean the lobsters and crab legs, and filet the fish."

"I get the picture."

"Let's not talk about her."

"Fine by me. What did the inspector know?"

"He was just making a routine check to make sure I'm compliant, but then we got to talking about that reporter's mother who supposedly got sick from eating my Fisherman's Pie the day the pandemic broke. He thinks I should talk to her and try to smooth things over."

"Maybe if you did something nice for her, like letting her have an exclusive on The Case of the Nefarious Seafood Affair. And Die Droge's involvement."

Her eyes teared up again. "Would you really do that for me?"

"I would if she was willing to drop the case against you."

"I've worked with this woman before, and I don't think being nice to her is going to get me anywhere. But a big story like this—I think she might be willing to make a deal."

"Then let's do it." Robin leaned toward her and grabbed her around the waist in an ecstatic, celebratory hug.

"Let's do this," he said again, sounding excited and jubilant. And Lord, help her, she thought he meant, Do IT.

"Oh, Robin." She lifted her mouth to his and whipped aside her mask. It didn't take long for him to follow suit and find her lips. Soft moist lips met hers, his tongue nudging her mouth open with such tenderness she wanted to cry. For a second, all she could think about was how splendiferous his lips would feel on her nipples, and the soft spot under her breasts, and sipping on the moisture she had between her legs. And then…

And then, she came to her senses. They were not ready for this. They'd made no commitment. She hadn't figured out the whole Selkie thing. She didn't know what to think about any of it. Yes, she was attracted to Robin, but if she gave in to her passions on a whim, she'd be no better than her mother.

Robin was caressing her neck and kissing her ear lobes when she finally eked out the words, "We have to stop."

"Right," Robin said. His breath was ragged and uneven.

She felt terrible—horribly disappointed, and mean-spirited for leading him on and making him think she wanted to… She never should have looked at herself in the mirror, never entertained thoughts of being naked with Robin on the sand or in the sea or anywhere else for that matter.

"One day soon, I hope the moment will come when the time is right," she whispered.

"Me, too," Robin said.

#

"It's done." Robin stood outside the back door of the Fish. He never should have gone inside or even been in close contact with Rebecca after being exposed to the virus at hospital. At the time, he'd been more concerned about being caught than being exposed to a deadly virus. Now that the Captain was dead, he realized his error.

"Are you sure you don't want to come through?"

"Two wrongs don't make a right."

"I guess it's for the best. But you'll have to talk fast. I've got all day if you want to talk to me while I work, but only a few minutes if I'm standing here doing nothing."

That was his Rebecca. He smiled. "Fine. I talked to your reporter and told her we wanted to get together and talk aboot a possibility to right the situation between the two of you before things get out of hand."

He watched as Rebecca turned white and then a light shade of green.

"I'm so scared, Robin. If this goes to court, I could lose everything—even if I win!"

"That's why we're trying to stop this now."

"So what did Aggie say?"

"She seemed interested when I told her about the deal we were proposing, but she wouldn't agree to it until she has more information."

"But if you tell her what we know—our ideas, our theory—she'll basically already have the story. And then what motivation will she have to drop the charges against me and Café Fish?"

"That's the fine line we have to walk. I set up a meeting for tomorrow morning at half eight at Scorrybreac Walk. It takes about 45 minutes to hike the trail. Hopefully by the time we've circled around, we'll have tantalized her enough to agree to our terms."

"It's sounding a little like blackmail. I don't want to get into worse trouble than I already am."

"We already are." He corrected her. "I'm the one who sneaked into hospital and let a dying man think I was a priest."

"Yes, well, God heard the man's confession. I can guarantee you that. And God is the only one who can forgive us our sins. It doesn't take some priest to grant absolution."

"I hope you're right." He glanced around the parking lot to make sure they were still alone. "There's one other thing I want you to do as soon as possible, Rebecca. Please agree to have your DNA tested. I know you have concerns aboot the validity of the findings, but I think it could be important."

"Is this aboot the possibility that I'm half Selkie?"

"Well, if you are the result of a tryst with a Selkie, and Selkies really are the human personification of seals, you yourself could have immunity or a genetic marker of some sort that could be used to fight the virus. If not, it would still be interesting to see if you share any DNA with the families from the Outer Hebrides who claim to be direct descendants of sea people."

"Assuming any of them have been tested."

"True." He adjusted his mask. "But all of that would just be bonus information. Because what I'd really like to determine is if Cameron Allanach is your father."

"I'm not sure I want to know." She looked a bit gob smacked. "Why is it important? What do you hope to do with the information once we find out? And how will we ever know unless Cameron has also been tested? It's not likely that someone who's rich, who has possible love children floating around, would willingly put their DNA on file in a public forum like ancestry.com."

"That's what's so perfect aboot the timing. I found a short gray hair that I think is Cameron's on Sea Worthy. I also have a beer bottle that I'm almost sure was his. If you can find a short gray hair in the Fish, I think we could be sure it was his unless the inspector has hair of the same length and color."

"No. His is dark, reddish brown and longish."

"Good, because there was another man with hair similar to Cameron's on the boat."

Rebecca looked uncertain if the question marks in her eyes were any indication. "Wouldn't it be better just to ask him for a sample? I feel a little guilty going behind his back."

"That would work perfectly fine if he's agreeable. For all I know, he wants to find out if you two are related just as badly as you do."

"But I don't. At least part of me doesn't."

"Just trust me then. My gut is telling me that we need to know, and that we shouldn't show him our cards until the time is right."

Rebecca had tears in her eyes. "I don't want my lineage to be used as some sort of bargaining chip."

He felt for her, he really did. But it had to be said. "Even if it means saving millions of people?"

"Sure, I mean, if it came to that."

"I understand, Rebecca. I do." He paused for a moment. Should he tell her? "Promise you won't tell anyone?"

"Aboot Cameron, you mean?"

"No. Aboot what I'm aboot to tell you."

"My lips are sealed."

"Okay. I'm adopted. Until the pandemics started up, I was actively looking for my birth parents. I've had to put things on hold for now, but every once in awhile I get a lead, and I'm convinced I'll find them eventually."

"Oh, Robin!"

"Explains a lot doesn't it?" He could tell she wanted to hug him, so he stepped back a couple of feet to put a little more space between them.

"I always did have trouble imagining that you and James were cut from the same cloth." Her eyes sparkled. "And your family really are the quintessential landlubbers. And you love the sea."

"True."

She blew him a kiss. "So when we were all kids, dreaming that we were adopted, you really were."

"Yes. But I wasn't happy aboot it. When I was younger, I wanted to be like them. But I just wasn't. I didn't understand why, and it made me pure sad."

"You felt like the Ugly Duckling."

"Pretty much."

"Well I'm glad you're you."

She started toward him and he motioned for her to back off.

She stopped, but he could tell she didn't want to. "Because I like you just the way you are."

"Even if I find out I'm the son of a marauding pirate or a nefarious criminal?"

"Hey—maybe your mother was a Selkie, but when she found her Selkie skins, gave in to the lure of the sea and abandoned you and your father, he just couldn't manage caring for you on his own."

"Well, there's a twist I hadn't thought of." He smiled and looked at his watch. "It's been a lot longer than a few minutes."

"Oh my goodness."

"I'll let you get back to work then. I have to figure out a way to get my hands on the photocopy of the check that Die Droge made out to the captain of the unmarked boat."

"Be careful." She blew him a kiss.

"I'll do my best."

CHAPTER 13

Rebecca worried about the meeting with Aggie up until the time she fell asleep and immediately again when she awoke. Her mother appeared to have spent another night alone. Rebecca hoped her words had sunk in and that there would be no more incidents of random men showing up unannounced in their bathroom.

Robin's timing was perfect and she stepped outside the door to meet him, mask in hand. They walked down the hill just far enough to intercept the trail head at Scorrybreac and waited for Aggie to appear.

"Probably short for Agnes," Rob said.

"Probably," she agreed. They were both nervous. So much hinged on this meeting and whatever words were exchanged. How she wished she could be sure they were doing the right thing. The feeling that they should be going directly to the police kept niggling at the back of her brain.

"Did you find the photocopy of the check Die Droge wrote to pay the captain?"

"No. It was gone. But I found a bank deposit receipt for an extremely large sum of money. I've done a little research on the captain and if my estimates are right, this deposit was for more money than he would make in the course of eight or ten years, maybe even twenty—if he was lucky."

"Wow. Kind of scary that the photocopy was gone, but a good find when all is said and done. How on earth did—"

"You don't want to know." She waited for his laugh, but evidently he was not joking.

She checked to see that they were still alone. "Are you sure we shouldn't be handling this some other way? Every day, the numbers of people who have died from this virus grow higher and higher. I just want to put an end to it right now!"

Rob's face was grave, but he didn't waver. "It's not going to end until they have a vaccine, and they don't. Their efforts have failed. In fact, it occurred to me last night when I was—well—if we move on the information we've got, too soon, their efforts may be curtailed before they find a cure, and millions more could die. My instincts are telling me to let the story ferment a little until they have a breakthrough. Now, if there's a way to do that without the lives of more seals being sacrificed, I'll be pure happy."

She thought about what he'd said. "There would be some sort of poetic justice in letting them think they're going to get off scot-free and then arrest them and send them to prison the second they release their vaccine."

"Exactly—throw them in jail before they see a penny of the profit."

She hated to think about Cameron ending up in jail just as she and he were finally getting a chance to know one another. He seemed like such a nice man. But even nice men could be lured to their downfall by greed and the desire to manipulate events for profit. If that's the trap he had fallen into, then he would have to pay the price along with the rest of Die Droge's henchmen.

She looked down at the beautiful view before her. Because of the lockdown and stay-at-home order the Scottish government had imposed on the islands, Portree had been sheltered from most of the sickness and death that had occurred during the first pandemic. Now, their tiny population was being ravaged by the virus, and they were being blamed for its spread to the rest of the world. Sadly, rightfully so.

Their eyes locked on Aggie at exactly the same moment.

"Hello, Aggie," Rob said.

"Aggie."

Rob swept his arm in the direction of the trail. "The views are beautiful. Would you like to hike while we talk?"

"No thank you." Aggie's voice sounded suspicious, almost hostile. "The sooner we get this over with, the better."

This didn't bode well. What did she think they were going to do? Shove her over the edge of the cliff? Kick her in the knees and laugh with glee as she toppled off the edge of the trail and rolled down the hill toward the harbor, then leave her to the wild animals?

"I guess this is as fine a place to talk as any as long as we're the only ones here," Rob said scanning the empty carpark.

"Do you mind if I record our conversation?" Aggie said abruptly, whipping out a recording device, her finger hovering over a button on the right side.

"I certainly do," Robin said. "This is not an interview. It's a discussion of a pure personal matter and you do not have my permission to record anything I say."

"Nor mine." Rebecca said.

Aggie went to put the device back in her pocket.

"I'd like to make sure the device is off," Robin said.

Rebecca felt a surge of pride. Robin was letting Aggie know that he was in charge, and that he meant business, which in turn, made her feel safe and protected.

Aggie handed Robin the device. She could only assume Aggie was scowling behind her mask.

Her eyes looked extremely hostile. "Fine. Let's get down to business. You said you were prepared to give me a story that would make headlines around the world."

"Aye," Robin said. "We know for a fact that this pandemic is not a phenomenon that occurred naturally. We also know how it started, who started it, and why. If you're interested in an exclusive, then we'd like to have your assurance, in writing, that you're not going to sue Rebecca or Café Fish over the incident involving your mother."

Aggie laughed. "I'd be daft to agree to your little proposal when my solicitor assures me that the settlement from my lawsuit could be in the hundreds of thousands.

Rebecca cringed. "I will not be bullied into giving you a cash settlement for something that was not my fault. Bad timing is the only thing at fault here, and my solicitor tells me that since you have the burden of proof that your mother got the virus at my establishment when none of my other customers got sick, it's unlikely that you will get a pence."

Rob spoke slowly and succinctly. "If your case even makes it out of the fact finding stage to go to trial, you have at least a fifty percent chance of getting nothing. Zero. Zilch. Our story could make you a world famous journalist, and very possibly a millionaire. But the choice is yours. If you insist on pursuing your law suit, then Rebecca and I will be forced to sell our story to the highest bidder, whether that be The Scotsman, BBC News, or the New York Times."

Aggie's face paled. Her eyes glinted.

Rebecca's heart pumped harder and harder. She hadn't stopped to think that the story they were sitting on could be worth millions. She looked at Robin with fresh respect – and a whole lot of chagrin. Rob was doing this for her – because he knew she'd need the money to pay her solicitor's fees, perhaps even a humongous settlement, if Aggie won her case.

It was her that broke the stalemate. "Robin, I can't let you do this. If you sell the story to the highest bidder, or to a major news source like you said, you could pay off your loan, buy an island where you can make a safe refuge for your seals, and never have to work a day in your life. It's not fair for you to give it all up so I have the money to pay a solicitor in some bogus, trumped up excuse for a lawsuit. And it's not fair that Aggie should benefit from all the research you've done to get this story. Any profit that comes from this story should go to you. The payment should be yours."

Robin looked at her. His eyes were shiny. "If that's the

way you feel, Becca. If you're absolutely sure she doesn't have a case—"

Aggie butted in just as Rebecca was ready to reassure him. "But it would be nice to know for certain, wouldn't it? There's no sense in letting the only ones who benefit be our solicitors. Not if we can work something out between the three of us."

Robin turned to her and said, "Rebecca?"

She turned to Aggie. "Would you be willing to sign an agreement not to sue, so we have it all in writing?"

The sun shifted under a cloud and the wind tapered off to nothing. "Wait," Aggie said, her eagerness fading to cynicism in the second it took the sun to reappear. "How do I know the story is actually as big as you say it is? What kind of proof do you have? Can I verify your so called facts? Interview your sources?"

Robin looked at Aggie, and then at Rebecca. "I'm not going to lie to you, Aggie. Our prime source recently passed away from the virus—which is exactly why this story has to come out."

"Then the deal's off. I don't need names, and I don't need to reveal names, but I do need assurance that this story of yours is more than hearsay. I can't go to press unless I have confirmed sources."

"I have a small but significant piece of evidence that links the deceased person to a large payoff from the perpetrators." Robin's face was stony.

"I need to be able to interview someone who has firsthand knowledge of the crime, assuming there is one."

"Oh, this is criminal, awright." Robin traced a ring in the dirt with his shoe.

Aggie spoke in her aggressive voice. "You'll get the same answer from any of the big networks. They'll all need to be able to verify your sources. Without it, your story is worthless."

Robin still looked pure confident. She had to give him that much. She felt like she was about to faint.

"Let me see what I can do," he said. "Can we meet here again tomorrow, same time?"

Aggie looked skeptical, but not as hostile as when she'd first arrived. "I'll be here."

#

Robin had talked with Becca at length about which of them should approach Cameron, and in what way. They needed someone willing to grant an interview with Aggie so she could have affirmation that the story they were pitching to her was true. There was no way that a random Die Droge spokesperson was going to tell an outsider anything about their operation, but the hope was that Cameron would.

It all came down to whether or not Cameron Allanach believed that Becca was his daughter. If he did, he might go out on a limb to protect her—give them just enough to convince Aggie that the story they were trying to sell her was solid and verifiable.

He tried to talk her out of it, but Becca insisted it had to be her. She could be pure stubborn when she felt strongly about something.

So he'd decided to head for Sea Worthy, go to his beach, spend the night in his shanty, hope to see a few old friends. It was time to find out if Shelagh and Soren were still alive. His gut clenched at the thought that their bloated, decomposing bodies could have been among the dead seals he'd found on his previous visit. By the time he'd returned and lugged the carcasses out to sea, they had been unrecognizable.

He pushed his tenderhearted sensibilities aside and steered the boat into the deep channel closest to the shore. When he reached the island, he put down the gangplank and used it to get as close to the beach as he could, then waded through the clear blue waters until the sand turned from wet to dry, clinging to his soles, wedging between his toes.

The shanty came into view, sheltered behind a dune about a hundred feet off shore. The sun was warm, and a few seals were scattered around the sandy shoreline, sleeping, some in the classic banana formation, others dozing, flipping wet sand over their backs every few minutes.

Not one single seal raised their head to greet him. No one clapped their flippers or loped over to get closer. Was this a new herd? One that hadn't witnessed the carnage? One for whom there were no bad memories entrenched in the shoreline?

Regardless, he would stay until nightfall and see what the darkness brought. He wanted to think that Shelagh and Soren would be happy to see him, that they thought of him as not just a human being, but as a friend who was different than others of his species. He hoped they knew that he cared for them, and would do anything to protect them.

He wandered the length of the beach, looking for familiar faces, markings, or spots. The seals ignored him. He supposed he should be thankful that he hadn't come back only to discover hostile or aggressive behaviors directed toward him.

He went to bed as soon as darkness came, hoping he would dream of Shelagh and Soren, walk with them, dance with them, swim with them.

He slept fitfully at first – waking up to a state of semi-awareness every hour or so, then falling back into slumber. Whether he'd finally fallen into a deep sleep or whether he was still half-awake wasn't clear when he heard voices.

It was Shelagh's voice that spoke to his heart, his mind, whatever part of him they engaged to communicate with him. His body reeled with the wonder of it.

"I'm here," he whispered from his dreams. "Just like always." He was usually greeted with joy, but this time he sensed tension and wariness.

Robin wouldn't hurt us for the world.

I hope you're right. The world is exactly what humans are using as their latest excuse to kill seals.

The knowledge that the seals were aware of man's use – and often, abuse—of other species shocked him. But of course, they were right. In the old days, seals had been hunted for their meat and oil, but only when the remote settlers' crops had failed and their young were in danger of starving. Robin had heard of the superstitions since he was a boy. The islanders of the Outer Hebrides believed that killing a seal would bring bad luck, so it was only during extremely hard times that the people of the Scottish Isles made use of their skin and blubber. Rob supposed that if they had to resort to killing a seal to put food on the table, it made sense not to waste the oil that they could use to light their lamps.

Rod felt a sense of compassion and forgiveness floating through his mind.

Just as it is with the fish we eat. Nothing goes to waste. But Shelagh's voice sounded so vulnerable that it made him want to cry.

Sadly, there had also been a time when seals were hunted because their fur was fashionable for coats and sporrans. Robin tried to push the thought from his head.

The Creator endowed us with wondrously desirable waterproofing. Whereas Soren radiated cynical thoughts, Shelagh sounded so sincere it hurt him to listen. *Our skins kept them warm and dry.*

The Creator seems to favor humans above His other creations.

A God who had favorites? Rob's heart clenched with the unfairness of a supreme being he wasn't even sure he believed in. He preferred to think that if there was a God, he gave each species the exact gifts they needed to survive in their own unique environment. But of course, humans were never satisfied with anything. They wanted to live in environments of their own choosing, even if the climate or the landscape was ill-suited for their survival. People wanted more and more and more. It hadn't changed in centuries.

And it never will.

Robin thought about an article he'd once read that talked about hunters in Asia killing male seals so they could harvest their penises to use as an aphrodisiac.

He heard a grunt from the water that was so loud it startled him.

When had he left his bed and walked to the shoreline? He was ashamed to be part of a species so arrogant as to think their sexual satisfaction was more important than seals' lives?"

Robin tried to get his bearings. Had Shelagh and Soren come to the shanty or could he hear their thoughts this clearly from afar? It was pitch dark except for a sliver of a moon and millions of stars. He reached out to them with his mind, hoping he could communicate that he was not like the men who had come to club them to death and extract their tissue.

His heart ached for the Selkie community. What if they suspected that he had conned them into trusting humans only to laugh at them as they were lured to their deaths?

The voices stopped and he must have fallen deeper into the sleep cycle.

When he awoke once more, he was dancing with the Selkies. It was not a carefree dance like the others he'd experienced. The women had scarves – long, sheer gauzy scarves that floated on the wind, slowly twirling to the music. He watched their bodies dip and bow. Mourning music at sunrise. Again, he wanted to weep with them, to purge his soul of the guilt he felt just for belonging to the human race.

When he woke next, he was lying naked on the beach, soaked to the skin, his wet hair plastered to his face, his backside covered with sand. The clothes he'd been wearing had disappeared.

He took a moment to assess his feelings and try to remember the conversations he'd overheard. He felt a deep sense of contentment. Was it because he was back on the beach, in the only real home he had at the moment, or was it something more?

The more he recalled of his experiences the night before, the more he became convinced that he had been able to communicate his love for the Selkies, more importantly, that Shelagh and Soren knew he'd had nothing to do with the murders that had occurred. He also sensed a deep rift within the Selkie community between those who liked humans and encouraged contact with Robin versus those who considered humans to be evil polluters of creation. Some of the Selkies were glad the new virus was hurting the humans. Those Selkies said it was time to rise up and break the stranglehold Robin and other humans had over all of creation.

Robin stood and walked around naked until the damp sand clinging to his skin dried in the wind. He brushed himself off with a cloth he kept in the shanty and put on a spare set of clothing. It was then that he felt a strong premonition that he needed to return to the unmarked boat and search the Captain's vessel. It made no sense. He'd looked everywhere when he was there the first time and hadn't found anything more than the boat's registration.

When he rounded the sandbar the tall sea grasses parted. The first thing he saw was Sea Worthy, the second, a small, unmarked black boat bobbing alongside his craft. He started to run. Because he didn't have a mask, he took a deep breath before he boarded in hopes he could do a glance around while he held his breath.

He saw the black, leather-bound book on a wood box just beside the captain's wheel. He was sure it hadn't been there before, and it was as dry as kindling even though it was setting out in the open, and it had rained at least ten times since he'd first been there.

He glanced around to make sure he didn't see anything else and left the boat. Only when he was a safe distance away, he picked it up. The captain's log! He flipped through the pages to the end and checked out the logs for the last month. It had details of every phone call, the times and dates and exact coordinates of every drop they made for Die Droge, even minute details like the check number and amount the Captain was paid.

Rebecca would say it was a God thing, but his response was to wonder if the ghost of the sea captain had brought his log to the boat, and his boat to the exact island where Robin always docked. His other thought was even more unsettling.

What if the Selkies knew what the sea captain had done and wanted Robin to make sure he was brought to justice?

His final thought before he boarded Sea Worthy and revved up the engines was, now that they had the captain's log, they should have enough evidence to satisfy Aggie without having to beg for help from Cameron Allanach. If he went directly to Portree, perhaps he could catch Rebecca before she showed Cameron their hand.

The closer he got to Portree, the more he wished he had never entertained the idea of Becca talking to Cameron. It was far too dangerous. Of course, that was easy to say now that he had the captain's logbook. At the time, trying to make a deal with Cameron had seemed to be their only option. In retrospect, the whole idea seemed downright foolhardy.

His head filled with all the things that were wrong about their plan. What if Cameron went to Die Droge and told them what he and Becca were up to? These people weren't afraid to kill. They'd already proved they were willing to sacrifice millions of people and as many seals as needed to accomplish their goal. What were two more?

He gunned the engine and thrust through the water full throttle ahead, not knowing what he would find when he reached home.

CHAPTER 14

Rebecca had known in her heart from the start that she should be the one to talk to Cameron. Part of it was about getting the proof they needed to persuade Aggie not to sue her, but a big part of it was also finding out who her father was. One way or another, she was ready to know. Emma had had over two decades to tell her the truth and she still hadn't done it. It was time to find out for herself.

She felt like a primary school student who was too nervous to give the boy she liked a Valentine. But this had to be done, and it had to be done now. Cameron was the only chance they had of getting the proof that Aggie needed.

She practiced what she was going to say several times. Her voice was shaking so badly that in the end, she texted Cameron instead of calling to request a meeting. His response, also texted, reeked of curiosity and perhaps a little dread. The charm he'd oozed at their previous encounters had disappeared.

She tried not to judge. Maybe he was just a poor texter.

It was his suggestion to meet at the Lump so they could enjoy the harbor views and get a little fresh air while they talked.

She tried to calm herself as she walked toward the watchtower. She whispered to herself while she walked, rehearsed what she was going to say. She felt horribly awkward.

"Rebecca." Cameron was leaning against a tree, his arms crossed over his chest, one leg crossing the other.

"Thanks for meeting me." Her voice sounded stiff even to her own ears.

"What can I do for you?" His eyes were cautious and half a shade darker than she remembered them being.

"I need to ask a favor of you."

He smiled. That dazzling smile. "I'd be happy to write a review of the Fish, if that's what this is aboot—let the world know that it's a wonderful place to eat even though the Fisherman's Pie is temporarily off the menu."

"Well, in a round aboot way, I do need to speak to you about fish—not Café Fish though. Just plain fish."

"Awright." He looked confused.

"A friend of mine—the two of us have been trying to solve a mystery regarding the pandemic. We've spoken to the captain of a ship that apparently got paid a large sum of money by a company called Die Droge to make some deliveries at various drop off points around the Isles."

Cameron winced as though he'd been slapped.

Be cool. She told herself. Don't tell him too much. Tell him just enough. "We're just trying to connect the dots at this point, but if you have any information that might help us, it would be much appreciated."

His face turned a sickly shade of gray. It took him only a few seconds to recover. He cleared his throat and took a sip from his water bottle. "And why would you think I have anything to do with this?"

She stared into his eyes. "Let's be honest, shall we?"

He cleared his throat, then laughed with a thick, nervous jolt of the throat. "I have no reason to feel obligated to help you, Rebecca. But because I think you're a nice girl and an exceptional cook, I am going to be honest with you."

He leaned away from the tree and started to pace back and forth. "Here's the thing. Your little mystery investigation sounds dangerous. Something like this should be turned over to the police so they can deal with it. It's simply not worth the risk you're taking when this is probably all one big misunderstanding."

She continued to stare at him. "I thought you were going to be honest."

He made an overt show of shrugging. "So let's suppose just for the fun of it, that whatever theories you've come up with are correct. Still a bad idea. A very bad idea. You have no idea what sort of people you could be dealing with here, or what they might do to you if they found out what you're up to."

"That's why we need your help."

He laughed again, more quietly this time. "Supposing I did have information pertinent to your investigation. It's bad enough you're involved with something so dangerous. Why on earth would I want to risk my life to get the information you need?"

She took a deep breath. "Because I believe you may be my father. Because there's every probability that I'm your daughter."

The blood drained from his face, and the pure athletic, pure smooth, pure polished man who stood before her began to crumble.

And then, before her eyes, the cockiness, the confidence, the charm came back. And he said, "I am not your father."

"Why not?" She stammered. "How can you be sure? Did you have me tested when I was a baby? When I was too young to remember?"

"You were never tested—which is exactly why I'm sure you're not my daughter." He looked smug, arrogant, horrible.

"I'm not sure what the reasoning is behind your deduction, but—"

"When my father first learned about the messy break-up I'd had with your mother, he sat me down and we had a long talk. I still remember what he told me. Number one, he said that if Emma thought there was any chance that I was the father of her baby, she'd demand a paternity test to prove it so she could use it to milk me for as much money as she possibly could."

Rebecca's mouth dropped open. "So you assumed that because she never asked for a test, you were not my father?"

"Well, that and the fact that she evidently slept with several men after I broke up with her, and then went around telling everyone that she had a torrid affair with a male Selkie which resulted in her pregnancy."

"So you don't think it's possible that she was so mad at you and so disillusioned that she didn't want anything from you? Or that she was doing her best to protect me from you and your family because she didn't want me to be anything like you? Or that she simply didn't want to share her baby with someone like you, or that she was extremely stubborn and independent, or—"

"Okay. Enough. I get your gist." He cut her off.

At least she knew what kind of parenting style her dear dad subscribed to. And maybe he was right. Maybe he was the one with the right idea about her. Maybe she was just a fool who wanted to have a daddy who loved her so badly that she had to make up fantasies about every man who could be her father.

When she said nothing, he spoke again. "Fine, so I suppose there's a chance—a very small chance that you were the result of Emma and me having sex."

So it was sex. He couldn't have called it lovemaking? Cameron and her mother had been engaged. Her mother had never been willing to speak about their relationship but it went without saying that people don't usually get engaged unless they're in love. And Emma had been devastated when Cameron had broken up with her. Why would she have cared unless they'd been in love?

"Can you at least consider the possibility?" She choked out the words.

He looked out toward the harbor and sighed. "Even if you are my daughter, why on earth would you think that I would

131

want to help you?"

"Oh, I don't know. Maybe because I thought you might care. Maybe because one way or another, your involvement is going to come out, and if you help us, it would go better for you, and you'd be less likely to go to jail."

She looked up and said a prayer to God, the Father, about the earthly father she'd always wanted. "And because if you don't, I may lose my café and my home."

"You could lose a lot more than that."

She gulped for air. "We can promise you anonymity. The person we're working with doesn't have to name names, but she has to be able to interview someone with direct knowledge of what transpired. We can't proceed based on hearsay."

She rambled on for a few more seconds and finally shut up.

There was silence between them for some time until Cameron finally spoke. "I'm divorced. You probably know that."

"No! I don't know anything about you."

"Okay. Here it is. You wanted me to be honest." He laughed, a hollow, bitter sounding cackle filled by cynicism. "I never had children with my wife. I've always wished I had a family—but a perfect family, on my terms, with no problems. Not a daughter that I have to sacrifice everything for, lose my job for, possibly go to jail for."

"I understand. I don't know you very well, but it makes me sad that you're involved with these people, that you would do something that would hurt so many people. I always wished I had a father, too. I dreamed that he would be a good person, a man that everyone admired and respected. A man that I could look up to. A man who would be there for me."

Tears were streaming down her face, and his. The breeze blowing off the sea was drying and abrasive, soothing and comforting at the same time. The wind cradled her in its arms.

"It's your choice, Cameron. I'd be forever grateful if you

agree to give the reporter what she needs so she will drop the charges against me, or, you can do what you're doing and hope things work out for you. I'll probably lose everything. But I'll survive."

He was listening pretty intently. She had to credit him for that. The sun went under a cloud and she looked up to see what was happening.

When Cameron spoke, his voice was as ominous as the cloud that happened to be moving in from the west. "What makes you think I won't tell Die Droge what you're accusing them of? What makes you think they won't find a way to infect you with the virus, or hire a hit man to kill you before you can tell anyone else what you know? You can't possibly realize what's at stake here. These men will do anything to keep this project moving forward. They will get what they want. They do not care who they have to step on to get there."

Her blood felt like it was freezing in her veins. How could she and Robin have been so naïve to think that they could go up against such evil? How could she have believed that a man who had trampled on her mother's soul and ignored her and her daughter's very existence for almost three decades would help her, say nothing about going to jail for her?

"The choice is yours," she said. Her voice sounded meek. And pure sad. And a little scared. She wished she'd let Robin come with her. But what if she had, and something had happened to both of them, and there was no one left to tell the truth?

"You need to leave. Now." Cameron's voice was no longer charming in any way. His hand grazed his pocket. "I know what I should do. But for whatever eejit reason, I can't seem to make myself do it. Now run! I told you to get out of here right now! Now! Before I change my mind!"

She tore her eyes from him and ran. Her heart was breaking. She was three fourths of the way down the trail to the carpark when her foot snagged on an exposed tree root. She flew through the air, her mind going a million places while her body thudded to a halt at the base of a Douglas fir whose trunk was at least three of her. She heard her neck crack, and then, everything went black.

#

Robin went to Café Fish first. When he found the doors locked and no note informing people why the takeaway window wasn't open, he began to panic. He was huffing by the time he got to the top of the hill imagining all the awful things that could have happened.

"Becca? Becca! Emma? Is anybody home?" He pounded on the door, then waited, pounded some more and listened for any sound that might indicate that someone was home. All that met his ears was silence.

He didn't know what to do, where to start looking. Becca hadn't told him where she and Cameron were meeting. He wasn't sure she'd known last time they spoke.

He ran partway down the hill to James' kirk. Why he thought they might have met there was beyond him, except that Becca's faith was pure important to her, and she might have thought of it as a safe place.

The kirk was empty. It occurred to him that she might have suggested they go to Scorrybreac Trail since it was fresh in her mind. He raced back up the hill to the parking lot. No cars, no voices in the distance, no fresh footprints in the mud. He had never been so frustrated. Where could she be?

If they'd been at the harbor, he would have seen them when he docked. If they were anywhere downtown, she would have doubled back to leave a note on the door of the café.

He looked up and let his eyes follow the curve of the harbor. They caught on the Lump. There was a nice trail to the old watchtower. Townspeople went to enjoy the harbor view. Teenagers went there to party and enjoy a little privacy, What went on there most of the time didn't exactly fit Becca's style, but Cameron had spent summers in Portree. He'd know the place.

He wished he wasn't on foot, but it was faster at this point than finding a car. He had to find a street that wound around the town, parallel to the harbor that connected the two trailheads.

Why, oh why had he let her meet Cameron alone? How would he live with himself if anything had happened to her?

CHAPTER 15

Emma pressed her body to the stone wall of the watchtower and prayed there weren't any spider nests nearby. She had waited and waited, listening to the tail end of the conversation between Becca and Cameron until she was sure Becca was out of ear range. It had taken every ounce of restraint she possessed not to lay into him the second he'd uttered his shameful words.

If she hadn't hated him before, and she had, she hated him all the more for the way he'd shattered Becca. And those off-the-cuff threats he'd made were reprehensible – so unfeeling, so grossly insensitive. Didn't he realize the girl sincerely thought he was her father?

She listened and waited. Cameron was fiddling with his mobile. Good luck with that, she thought to herself. Fool thought he could get reception with that watchtower deflecting the signals. Fat chance.

She waited one second longer, then stepped from the shadows.

"Emma?" Cameron gasped.

"It's been a long time."

He smiled the same dreamy smile she'd been in love with as a girl. And sadly, she felt herself falling for it just like she had all those years ago. The nasty threats he'd been uttering seemed completely out of character for this charming, sexy man. She knew him so well, and yet she didn't know him at all.

"You're—you're just as beautiful as the day I last saw you."

"Aye. The day ye made wild, passionate love to me and then trounced on my heart and sailed off into the sunset."

He had the decency to look a little chagrinned. "Listen, Emma—" He ran his fingers through his hair, which was still its original color and extremely lush. Just one of the many reasons she didn't believe in God. If He did exist, if there were any kind of justice in the world, Cameron Allanach would be fat, bald, and have skin cancer on the top of his head.

"Nay." She said, from a place deep inside her heart. "I listened to ye once. I hung on yer every word. Now it's yer turn. Ye listen."

Cameron looked shocked. No wonder – she'd never stood up to him in all the time they'd been together.

"Ye will not speak that way to my daughter ever again. Ye will nae only nae be rude and insensitive to her, ye will nae harm her in any way."

The charming smile was gone. "Then you need to tell her—"

"I will do nothing of the sort. Because she's ne'er going to know that ye and I spoke. Ye're going to leave her alone because she's my daughter, and ye owe me. And because, for all we know, she could be yer daughter, too, and males dinnae eat their children—unless you're a wild boar. I hear boars eat their young."

"You're being ridiculous, Emma. Your daughter crossed the line when she—"

"Not one word. Not one finger laid on her. Do ye understand me, Cameron?"

"You don't understand. When these people find out what's going on, there will be no stopping them. They won't listen to me. They won't listen to anyone."

"But that willnae be a problem, will it? Because they're nae going to find out—are they?"

For a few seconds, Cameron didn't say a word. "I guess not."

She took his hand. "Sealed with a kiss." She sang the words just like they'd done back in the day when they'd made a promise to each other, and every time they'd said good-bye.

He grinned. "We always did love the oldies but goodies."

She laughed. "Never thought I'd be one."

"Or I." He smiled again, more thoughtfully. His mood had changed again. He'd always been as changeable as the weather over the Western Isles.

"So are we?" He squeezed her hand.

"What? Sealing it with a kiss?"

He pulled her arm, firmly but gently, reeling her in like a sea bass on a rod. She could have refused to take the bait, tugged herself free – but she remembered those kisses of his. Remembered them well.

He leaned toward her, nibbled on the corner of her lips, and used his tongue to gently open her mouth.

What harm could one little kiss do? For old times sake?

"Ye promise me ye're not going to do or say anything that will harm our daughter?"

"You have my word. But if she and that friend of hers keep going on aboot Die Droge, they're still going to be in danger."

"So ye'll do everything ye can to make sure that does nay happen, correct?"

He kissed her again, deeper this time. She didn't have to fake her response. She'd spent almost three decades hating the man, but seeing him again… It was hard not to remember the old magic, impossible not to feel the passion they'd always shared.

His tongue probed her mouth. It didn't help that she knew what was coming. Cam knew exactly how and what she liked. She was a genie unleashed when it came to knowing not only what he liked, but exactly when, in what sequence, and at what stage. She knew she shouldn't indulge, but she'd been doing it with complete strangers just for the pleasure. If she could do that, she could certainly engage in a little homecoming sex with someone with whom she had a long history.

"Are ye still married?" She knew it could kill the mood, but she didn't care. Even she had her standards.

"No. Not for twenty years." He continued to kiss her, now focusing on her neck, her shoulder.

What a waste. She'd known even back then that the woman Cameron's father had picked out for him was not a good match.

She shuddered as his lips grazed the soft skin behind her ears. It felt exquisite. Pure magic.

It was all so tragic. Why hadn't Cameron come and found her? Tried to undo the wrong and make it right? Two decades, and he'd never once sought her out? Not even for an occasional romp?

He found her lips again, which did nothing to turn off the objections, the confusion she felt in her mind. The feelings were so intense. She'd loved this man. A part of her still did.

He touched her breast. Even with clothing separating them, feelings of pleasure and well-being and passion flooded her body from head to toe. Perhaps it was her confession of love, even if only to herself, that allowed her to give in to him. She was helping Becca, after all, wasn't she? Her usual sexual pursuits were all about the pleasure, all about her. Sometimes, they hurt her daughter. But this time, she was performing a heroic deed. She was saving her daughter's life!

That was all the permission she needed. She pulled Cam into the shadows of the watchtower onto a soft bed of pine needles. She was going to make love to Cameron Allanach. She had loved him enough to agree to marry him. Now, she was completing the circle of life they'd begun before Becca was born. It not only felt good, it felt right.

#

Robin checked his mobile for messages, texts and missed calls. Nothing. He dialed Becca's number one more time while he was walking / running and got her voice mail again. His mind was frantic with possibilities. If she was at the watchtower or even hiking the Lump, she should have reception, shouldn't she? The tree cover was a little dense, but there should be a clear line from the tower that served Portree.

Where else could she be? His mind flew back and forth from all the places she could possibly be to the dreams he'd experienced the night before, the Selkie conversations he'd overheard, and the Captain's log he held in his hands.

He had to find her before it was too late!

He jogged by a row of stone houses with brightly colored front doors and flower gardens so expansive that they filled the entirety of their front yards. He relaxed and took a deep breath. For a second he felt a sense of well-being. Becca had a deep faith. He hoped God would protect her in return for her faithfulness. Maybe that wasn't the way it worked. He didn't know.

A second later, his brain jerked to attention as he thought of another possibility. What if she'd gone to Cameron's summer house? How many of his friends were still there? She could be outnumbered as much as six or even eight to one if Cameron had any staff or security guards watching over the place. He sadly knew who would win in a struggle between Cameron and Becca—add even one more person to the equation and she'd be overpowered in seconds.

He looked up to see where the watchtower was in relation to his current location. He wasn't familiar with the small streets in this part of town and everything looked different on foot. He struggled to figure out which of the lanes went through, which ones led to higher ground and which went back down into town. He'd been using the watchtower as a guide, but he was close enough now that it was barely visible. One more turn and another climb in altitude and the trees would completely hide it from view.

He was debating which way to turn when he heard the wail of an ambulance. His heart sank. He knew, knew instantly that it was Becca. He made his way to the side of the street and a few seconds later, it passed him, lights flashing, siren blaring, heading up the hill to the Lump. He was high enough that there wasn't much else between here and there except trees and the watchtower.

Oh, Lord, he prayed. Please let her be okay. But even though he tried to invoke what little faith he had, he still had a bad feeling. He started to run even faster, his legs spurred on by the adrenalin coursing through his veins. All he knew for sure was that if anything had happened to Becca, he was going to kill Cameron Allanach.

#

Becca could hear voices, so she knew her ears were working just fine, but nothing else seemed to be. She tried to figure out who was talking, but her brain was so muddled she couldn't seem to figure it out. She tried to tell them she could hear them talking, but her mouth didn't seem able to form the words.

"Shouldn't they be here by now? The ambulance bay can't be more than ten or twelve furlongs from here. What's taking them so long?" The man's voice was familiar, but she couldn't quite place it.

He sounded impatient. Irritated. It wasn't Robin. That much she was sure of.

"Maybe we should call the police. They man the first response unit, don't they?" Her mother!

She was sure that was her mother talking. What was she doing here? And where was here? Where was she and why couldn't she talk, or move her legs for that matter? What was going on? And what time was it? Shouldn't she be at the Fish? She had visions of customers lined up outside the takeaway window, waiting for the orders she'd promised to have ready by a certain time, wondering where their food was, wondering where she was!

"I feel so guilty," her mother said. "If we hadnae made love, we would have found her thirty minutes ago. If she has a brain hemorrhage, or a brain bleed, that 30 minutes could mean the difference between life and death."

Oh no! Not this again. She waited for the man to speak again. Now that she had a point of reference, she should be able to figure out if it was Jack or Henry or whatever the heck their names were. All she knew for certain was that if she ended up being brain dead because her mother was too busy shagging her lover to pay a mind to her own daughter, she would never forgive her.

"Don't look at me," the man said. "I'm not the one who insisted she needed to have multiple orgasms to achieve satisfaction."

Oh, no! Was it Cameron? It couldn't be. She wouldn't.

"Ye enjoyed every second of it." Her mother rubbed her arm absently, like she was still only paying her half a mind because she was too preoccupied with thinking about her recent romp with Cameron.

What was wrong with the woman? And more importantly, was it possible to pass out because you were so completely and utterly mortified by your mother's behavior when you were already unconscious or comatose or whatever?

"I feel awful that I didn't make an effort to find out if Becca was mine. I barely know her. Now, I may never have the chance." It was definitely Cameron. "She probably tripped because she was rushing to get away from me. I was—I was pretty rough on her back there.'

At least Cameron sounded halfway sincere. She could almost be persuaded to forgive him if he hadn't just engaged in sexual intercourse with her mother.

She heard her mother's quiet sobs.

"I never should have gotten involved with Die Droge in the first place. I just wanted to prove to my father that I was capable of charting my own course and making my own money. But now – my actions have jeopardized the well being of the young woman who could be my daughter, my wonderful Emma, my first love—"

"Along with a good half of the world." Emma quipped sarcastically.

"It didn't seem to bother you a few minutes ago when you were begging me to touch you in all your secret places."

Becca wanted to gag, but she knew enough not to. Being out cold and throwing up were not a good match. You could choke and die.

"I've always been so critical of Becca. And for what reason? She's been a wonderful daughter. She's ne'er gotten into any trouble. She's such a hard worker. Why, look at the success she's made of Café Fish! I couldnae ask for a better daughter." Emma's voice grew as quiet as a whisper. "Just last week, I taunted her because she was still a virgin and got after her because she wasnae more supportive of my, my need to—well, none of that matters now. If she makes it, I swear I will turn over a new leaf, and try harder to respect Becca's wishes."

"At least you've had her in your life all these years, I've missed out on so much." Cameron sounded truly remorseful.

Her mother butted in again, when really, all Becca wanted to hear were the words Cameron was speaking as he lamented that he barely knew her.

Her mother again. "At least ye can rest assured that if Becca dies, she will go to heaven to be with Jesus—her faith is very strong."

"Please don't even suggest such a thing. I couldn't live with myself."

A shadow fell over her as her mother and maybe-father leaned over her, holding hands, and whispering love words to her and each other. It was truly mind blowing and at the same time, rather grotesque, given their history and their age.

Whether she fell asleep or drifted off for a second, she couldn't remember, but when her mind awakened once again, it was to the wail of a siren coming closer and closer. Her first instinct was to move to the side of the road as quickly as possible. And then she remembered they were coming for her.

She was aware of most of what happened after the first responders took charge and began to care for her. Her mother was designated her "plus one" and allowed to ride in the ambulance with her. Cameron was told he would have to find his own way down the hill.

It seemed only fair to her situation, although she got the distinct feeling that it was breaking her mother's heart to be torn from the arms of her newly rekindled love.

Her head started to pound, in part because the paramedics chose that moment to slide her onto a backboard, move her to a gurney and lift her into the ambulance, and in part because of the realization that her mother was so full of herself already, she honestly couldn't imagine a world with a more confident, more cocky, Emma Gibson.

#

Robin was running so fast that his side was cramping when he heard the ambulance coming down the hill. He supposed that was a good sign—that Becca was alive and being taken to hospital instead of carted off to the mortuary.

Honestly, he didn't know that he had another lap around town in him. But of course, he would find the strength. He had to know what had happened to Becca. He was about to turn before catching his breath and heading back down—thank God that after reaching the top of the hill, there was a downhill path to the harbor—when he saw something—someone – out of the corner of his eye.

Lo and behold, there was Cameron jogging down the path. Surprise, surprise.

Robin stayed put until Cameron caught up to him.

"Is Rebecca in that ambulance?

"Yes, but—"

Robin slammed his fist into Cameron's jaw.

CHAPTER 16

Robin put Emma's car in park and jumped out to hold the door open while Rebecca slid gingerly into the passenger seat. Once Rebecca was settled, Emma got in the back seat. When he heard her door close, he eased the car into reverse and slowly backed out of the hospital carpark.

"I'm surprised they're sending you home so soon." Robin shifted into first gear and slowly accelerated.

"It's just a light concussion," Emma said. "She'll be fine in nay time."

"I have a lot of bruising and contusions. They said the bruises will get worse before they get better." Rebecca's voice was so soft he could barely hear her.

He reached over and touched her leg as gently as he could. She winced.

Emma coughed.

Becca sneezed. "Ouch. That hurt.' She clutched her side as she sneezed again. "They said they were sending me home so I don't catch the virus."

He hoped she didn't already have it. She sounded horrible. He hated knowing how much pain she was in. Robin shifted into second, and then third, being careful not to lurch from one gear to the next.

Becca winced or whimpered every time he so much as

drove over a crack in the road. He tried his best to avoid potholes for fear of killing her. He felt awful about what had happened to her. He hoped once she was at home and tucked into her own bed, she could rest more comfortably until she was healed.

He was also scared. Becca hadn't said anything – and they'd not had a minute alone—but his senses told him that she was worried and scared about something.

They finally had a chance to speak once she was snuggled up in her bed.

"You can pull up that chair."

He did as she suggested. Her bedroom wasn't large, but there was enough room to maneuver. The walls were the color of the bachelor buttons that his grandma had grown in her garden, cousins of the ragged robin wildflowers he was named after. "How do you feel now?"

"Fine as long as I don't move."

He took her hand and rubbed it gently. "Do you want to talk about your meeting with Cameron?"

"I feel so bad that I ever drew you into this mess."

"You didn't draw me in. I'm here because I want to be."

"We could end up dead, Robin. Is it worth our lives to save the Fish? I mean, the café is pure important to me, but I can't run the place if I'm dead!"

"The fact that we could die is the very reason we need to keep fighting." He tried to choose his words with care. Becca was clearly traumatized. "Sure they could kill us if Cameron won't cooperate, but the fact that they're threatening us is just added proof that this is bigger than both of us. We have to keep fighting. It's not just aboot the Fish anymore, it's aboot millions of people's lives and Scotland's economy and the future of the world. We can't let them get away with this!"

"I'm just so scared. For a second, I thought Cameron was going to shoot me."

"I hate to say it, but you should be. It's bad enough that pandemics can occur naturally, but if deceitful companies are allowed to create viruses with the ultimate goal of creating a vaccine and making millions of dollars, we're all doomed. Every single one of us." He took a deep breath and tried to keep his voice from shaking. "If we have to die, wouldn't you rather go down fighting for what's right than to succumb to this virus, or the next, or the next? Because if Die Droge gets away with this, it will never end."

They fell quiet for a few minutes. The house was still except for the faint sound of Emma coughing.

"Does Emma suffer from allergies, or should we be worried?"

"It's because she was out in the woods. Being in the forest always sets her off. She's much more comfortable at the beach."

They heard a sneeze echoing down the hallway.

Becca clutched her side. "If I were to sneeze that hard, it could be the end of me."

"I should go and let you sleep."

"I like having you here.' She changed positions and a moan escaped her lips.

"You need rest." He stayed for a little while longer, then said good night and let himself out, making sure he wasn't followed.

But later that night, he got a text from Becca, saying that her mother was wracked with chills, and feeling feverish. So her mother was starting to exhibit symptoms. She'd been at hospital with Becca for several hours. If she had the virus, was that where she'd contracted it?

At two a.m., he got dressed, put on his mask, and hiked back up the hill to drive Emma back to hospital. Two orderlies in hazmat suits met them outside. They tested Emma and then tented a cart to roll her into the hospital.

"Heal quickly, Emma." How he hoped Becca's plus one didn't become a minus one.

#

Becca paced the floor near her front door while she waited

for Robin to appear. Café Fish had been closed for two weeks. Besides being battered and bruised, she'd been quarantined. She'd had no choice but to shut it down.

The regret that plagued her even more than having to close Café Fish was the realization that if she had self-quarantined from the beginning instead of trying to keep the restaurant going, her mother would probably be okay. Why hadn't she taken the safer choice and just stayed closed? So she'd made a few extra hundreds of pounds and kept her regulars happy. Was it worth it now?

She felt so guilty! Her mother hadn't been careful. She hadn't worn her mask. She'd eaten seafood that might have been contaminated. She'd slept with multiple partners, blowing social distancing to the wind. But even so, she had to accept that her mother most likely got the virus because of her. How could she ever forgive herself when her mother could die?

At least she hadn't any reason to heap a second helping of guilt on her already fragile ego. Thank goodness Robin hadn't tested positive.

Cameron had not spoken to her since she'd called to tell him Emma had the virus. He'd been cold and noncommittal. She hadn't liked hearing that Cameron and her mother had made love when she was unconscious, but looking back, she was thankful she'd gotten to hear and see a glimpse of Cameron acting like the concerned and loving father she'd always longed for. Judging from his recent behavior, it was likely the first and last dose of fatherly love she was going to get from Cameron.

And her mother. She wasn't getting any better. That was the crux of it. She was getting weaker and weaker by the day.

Her mother's illness had changed everything for her.

She watched as Robin walked up the drive. She opened the door, slipped outside, and locked it behind her.

"Hi." Robin reached for her hand and helped her down the walkway. "Starting to feel a little stronger?"

"It's amazing how weak a person can get after two weeks

of sitting around the house doing nothing."

"I'm just relieved that the test came back negative." Robin tightened his jacket around his neck.

"I am, too. But this whole time of worrying and waiting has really messed with my mind. I'm getting more and more nervous. We don't know if Cameron has told his business partners that we know what they're up to, and we haven't been to the police, and it's like we're in a stand-off. The eye of the hurricane. And now that I'm back in circulation, I'm worried that the flood gate is going to break and all hell is going to break loose."

Robin kept his head down. The wind was so strong that there were white caps cresting in the normally calm bay. "Maybe they were waiting to see if we died."

"Yeah, save them having to kill us to keep us quiet."

"Like the captain and crew of the vessel that delivered the virus to the fish farm." Robin's face was wreathed in a grimace.

"Exactly." She knew she sounded cynical, but it wasn't as though she didn't have good reason. "That worked out perfectly for Die Droge, didn't it? The eye witnesses died of the virus before anyone even thought to investigate or question them."

"So what are we going to do next?" Robin asked.

It was a valid question, and one for which she didn't have an answer.

She hesitated. "I want to see Die Droge brought to justice, but now that my mother has the virus, my first concern is finding a cure. If we go to the police now, we could end up inadvertently thwarting Die Droge's efforts to finish the vaccine or find a treatment."

"We know they're close. But if we wait until they come out with their treatment, won't we be duplicitous in their lies? And if they're still killing seals to test them for natural antibodies to the virus—well, that's something I can't live with. Can't the police subpoena the research they've already done so other scientists can pick up the ball and find a cure? I feel that the sooner they're stopped, the better for everyone."

She stopped walking and turned to face Robin. "Listen. I sympathize with the seals, and with you, because I know how much you adore them, but all I want is for my mother to get well. I'm so desperate to find a cure that I don't care how many seals have to be sacrificed." She gulped and tried not to cry. "Robin, please know how much I care aboot you, and how much I appreciate all that you've done to try to help me, but if your priority is to continue to protect the seals at any cost, then this is where we part company."

She watched as Robin's face drained of its color.

"If you're implying that I don't care aboot Emma, you're wrong. You're dead wrong."

"I'm not trying to offend you. I just... I just... I just can't think aboot the seals when my mother is dying. I care about their fate. I care very deeply. But I love my mother, and I will do whatever I have to do to save her life."

Robin's face was a mask. "So where do we go from here?"

"Try to get an experimental drug from Die Droge?"

They walked in silence for another block or two before Rob answered.

"Here's the thing. If Cameron hasn't already told Die Droge that we have proof that they started the pandemic for their own gain, then we're risking your mother's life and our lives if we go to them now."

"Because if they know we know, it's all over."

Robin grabbed her hand again. "But if we don't say anything, we have no chance of getting a drug for your mother."

"We have to try." She held her breath for a second. "Should I contact Cameron?"

"I guess so. We don't really have a choice, do we?"

She stumbled on an uneven rock in the path and Robin caught her arm. "I'm starting to get tired. I just hate this! I'm so worried and depressed aboot Mom that I just can't get my act together. My brain feels like mush."

They turned around and started to head toward home.

Robin squeezed her hand. "Any thoughts on when you'll reopen the Fish now that you're out of quarantine and in the clear?"

"I'm just so tired."

"No need to rush things."

"If I don't do something soon, my regulars will have found a new favorite place and I'll be done for."

"We all have to stay positive."

"I'm so sorry, Robin. Here I am complaining about losing two weeks of business – and the bigger problem, which is my loss of momentum—when your business has been slower than slow for months."

"It's frustrating," Rob said. "More importantly, I have to wonder what the long-term damage will be to the ecosystem. Will we ever be able to enjoy seafood again?"

"Well, I'm counting on it. But then, I seem to be blessed with a natural immunity."

"Right. It's the Selkie in you."

She just smiled. It had become their private joke. "I think it's you who's descended from Selkies. It would explain your passion for protecting them."

Robin shrugged, but she saw a smile flit across his face.

They walked in silence until her house appeared in the distance.

"Robin?"

"Yes?"

"Will you stay with me tonight?"

He squeezed her fingers.

"I just need someone to hold me."

"I understand."

#

Robin could almost hear the human part of his heart singing. The part of his heart that increasingly belonged to the Selkies was whooshing through the air, breaking the water's surface with a spray of droplets, every one of which shimmered in the sunlight in a rainbow of colors.

A few minutes ago, he'd thought he was losing her. Becca and he disagreed on the logistics of how to handle Die Droge, but their goal was the same.

He waited while Becca used her key to open the heavy wood door.

He wanted to make love to Becca more than he'd ever wanted anything. But he would take holding her. He would take lying next to her. He would take walking by her side. He would take whatever she was ready to give.

Becca put a pot of tea on when they got inside. She had several kinds of tea. He chose Apple Spice and soon, the scent of fresh-from-the-tree apples, cinnamon and cloves filled the sunny conservatory off her kitchen. She waved at a round table with a floral cloth on top while she poured her cuppa. It felt cozy, like home. Not that he didn't love his boat, but he missed having a house. He'd made the right choice when the pandemic started – it had been necessary to cut costs however he could. But after living on the boat 24 by 7 for the last few months, he'd gained a new appreciation for hearth and home—especially a home that had a woman's touch, even more especially when that woman was Rebecca.

"I'm going to call Cameron," Becca said resolutely. "There may be repercussions, so I'll apologize to you in advance. Please know that I'm praying no harm will come to either of us over what's aboot to happen."

"I'll take all the help I can get. James used to tell me he prayed for me, but I think he gave up on me some time ago."

She smiled. "You mustn't give up. We mustn't give up. I prayed a lot when I was quarantined and God promised me that the best is yet to come."

"Sounds good to me." He didn't want to put a damper on her faith – and probably couldn't even if he set out to – and that was a good thing. But he didn't feel as confident about things working out in their favor as Becca did.

She picked up her mobile and touched Cameron's name.

He held his breath while they waited. She must have

turned on the speaker phone because a Celtic ringback tone bounced off the glass walls and ceiling. It was cheery sounding, with a lilting melody that didn't begin to match his feelings about talking to Cameron. Perhaps a death dirge would have suited him better. Perhaps some Tchaikovsky. Or a little Gilbert & Sullivan—"Ah, Leave Me Not To Pine Alone and Desolate."

"Hello." Cameron's voice was terse and impatient sounding—and somewhat hoarse and craggy. No doubt he knew who was calling. He sounded sick. His stomach lurched at the thought of what Cameron's wheezy voice, now coughing meant.

He caught Becca's eye and raised his eyebrows. Had she noticed how terrible Cameron sounded?

"Are you okay?" She stared at the phone, like it was starting to sink in.

"I'm not feeling well, as you can probably tell."

"Have you been tested?"

"What good would it do as long as there's no cure?" He coughed. "It's probably just allergies."

Or the broken nose I gave you, Robin thought, trying not to look smug.

But Becca wasn't even looking at him. "Allergies? How can you even say that? You were with Emma just a few hours before she got sick."

"I didn't start feeling bad until a couple of days ago. Probably just a mild case. I'll be fine," Cameron insisted.

Becca looked as determined as Robin had ever seen her. "Well, you might have a mild case, but my mother is slipping a little more every day, and nothing the doctors do seems to be helping. I swear—if she dies—I will bring Die Droge down. I will tell the police everything I know, and I know enough to ruin them. If they have an antidote—even an experimental or early version that they're still working on—I demand that my mother be given a dose. I'm convinced that she doesn't have a chance unless she gets treatment."

There was dead silence on the phone. After a few very

long seconds had gone by, Cameron coughed.

"IF they have a treatment, it would be dangerous to administer it to your mother without further testing, especially in her already weakened state."

"I don't care." Becca's voice was staunch and filled with conviction.

"IF Die Droge has a treatment and IF they would agree to give it to your mother, I feel sure they would only agree to help you IF you and Robin agree to keep your mouths shut and stay quiet about Die Droge's roll in the pandemic."

"Done." Rebecca's voice was still resolute. He tried to get her attention, to indicate to her that he wasn't sure what the best course of action might be, that he didn't like ultimatums, that she had no right to be making such a promise on his behalf. She wouldn't look at him.

"I'll talk to Die Droge then—if you're sure that's what you want me to do." Cameron had a coughing fit before he finally proceeded. "As I've warned you before, once Die Droge knows that you have information that could harm them, I have no idea what they'll do, and I can make no promises when it comes to your safety—or your mother's—or Robin's."

"I understand," Becca said, still refusing to look at him.

"I don't think you do," Cameron said, after another bout of coughing. "If you did, you wouldn't be so quick to agree."

"I'll do anything to give my mother a chance."

"Your mother knows what you and Robin know?"

"I'd rather not say."

"And by not saying, you've told me what I need to know. Besides, once they find out that you and Robin know, they will assume she does just to be on the safe side."

"I have to try."

"To save her?" Cameron choked. "You think your mother will want to live if she knows that you forfeited your life and Robin's to save hers?"

Robin had to think about that one. He loved Emma, but she was pretty self-centered, stubborn, pretty determined to live her life the way she wanted to live it no matter how much her choices hurt or upset Becca. Becca, on the other hand, was pure selfless and giving, and her actions proved it.

Becca didn't answer Cameron's question directly, but she did say, "My mother's will to live is very strong. So is mine. I will do whatever it takes to save my mother. And I promise you that I fully intend to be alive when this is all over, and when the moment is right, I will do whatever it takes to bring Die Droge down for what they have done to her, to Scotland's aquatic life, economy, and well-being, and to people around the world. And if you care anything for her or your daughter, you will find a way to get any treatment they might have for my mother without letting them know that Robin and I have information implicating them in the cause of the pandemic."

Whoa. Robin still didn't agree with or approve of everything Becca said, but she'd certainly delivered a powerful message. He wanted to chime in with the suggestion that Cameron simply tell Die Droge that the woman he was in love with was probably infected and that he most likely was, too, and just leave him and Becca out of it.

By the time he'd formulated the words to express himself, Becca had ended the call.

She turned to him with a cold look on her face. "I know what you're thinking."

CHAPTER 17

Becca plopped down on the window seat that bordered one side of her kitchen table and glared at Robin. So much for a nice quiet evening of snuggling and holding hands. So much for supporting one another through the stress of Emma's fragile condition and the ensuing decisions that needed to be made.

What Becca needed right now was an impartial friend, someone who would listen and help her decide what to do about reopening Café Fish, and how to handle her feelings about everything that was happening with Emma. But Robin had his own agenda, and it wasn't likely to change just because she wanted him to see things from her point of view.

Robin looked completely mystified.

He finally spoke. "Whatever it is that you think I'm thinking—well, I hope you're going to tell me what it is so I can tell you if you're right or wrong."

"Oh, I'm sure I'll be wrong. I always am."

"Becca. I'm your friend. I know you and your mother have a lot of differences, but you and I see eye to eye on most things. And if we don't—"

"Don't you dare! Don't you ever say anything critical aboot my mother ever again. She's in hospital dying. You are not allowed to bring up her bad points. I can. Although it's unlikely I'll want to at a time like this. But you! You cannot, will not, speak ill of her at a time like this."

"Okay." Robin looked flummoxed.

And no wonder, the way she'd lit into him. "I'm sorry. I'm just a bit touchy."

Robin's face said she was more than a bit touchy. "So tell me," he said. "What am I supposedly thinking? And more importantly, what do you want me to think?"

"I don't know. IDK. I told you this morning my brain was mush. All this sitting around and thinking aboot things while I've been quarantined has not been good for me. I'm exhausted, yet I've accomplished nothing." She stood and started to pace the perimeter of the kitchen. "I've got to get the Fish open again. I'll go down there tomorrow and give the place a good cleaning, throw away all the veg and other perishables that have gone bad and check my inventory. If I'm over there first thing in the morning, I can shop for supplies tomorrow afternoon and call in an order with my wholesaler. I have to do something. I don't care if it's dangerous. I have to have something to do!"

"Here's what I'm thinking." Rob's voice was gentle and calm. "I understand why you told Cameron what you did. And you did a lovely job by the way. You made your point unequivocally. There's just one qualification I need to make."

"And what is that?" She narrowed her eyes and glared while she waited for him to finish.

"We are not doing this alone. We've got nothing to lose and everything to gain by calling in Scotland Yard. They'll be discreet. They'll provide protection and surveillance if we need it. And when the time comes, they're equipped to catch the bad guys. We are not."

"Don't you understand what's at stake here?"

"I do. And I understand that we don't know if we can trust Cameron or not. We do know that he's a liar whose first priority is to save his own skin, and that of his colleagues."

"But my mother…"

"Your mother would be completely appalled if she

thought for one minute that you were going to make a deal with the devil on her behalf, with no regard for your own safety or mine." Robin glowered back at her.

He was right. She hated it when he was right.

"The time to contact them is now," Robin said. "Right now. If we wait until Die Droge knows what we know, it may be too late. If we let Scotland Yard know now, they can be on the lookout for trouble. And, if anything happens to us, what we know aboot Die Droge will already be in their hands."

She could feel her lip quivering. "Do you think Scotland Yard will go along with the plan to give Mother the experimental drug?"

"If they don't agree to it, we won't tell them anything."

"And if they lock us up?"

"Better to be behind bars for a time than to end up in a body bag in the harbor with a load of stones."

She gulped; "Right once again. Who would take care of Mom if something happened to me?"

"We're not going to worry about what ifs. We're going to think positively. Should we use my mobile or yours?"

"Yours. I think it would be better since mine is the one Die Droge's going to be using to contact us."

She watched as Robin did a search and then put his mobile to his ear. She motioned to him to switch to speaker phone and listened as he jumped through a million hoops and finally got transferred to the department in charge of investigating any problems related to the pandemic. How she wished she could have seen the man's eyes as Robin spelled out their terms and told him what they knew. She and Robin conferred briefly after they were offered a safe house. When they declined, the officer told her that she should set up a bed inside Café Fish so she could sleep downtown, and that Robin would be issued a special permit to dock his boat in the harbor right in front of the Fish. The longer she thought about it, the more she realized that it would be the safest place for them. The dining room wasn't being used anyway since they were still on lockdown for anything but takeaway food. She had a small bathroom with a shower sprayer in the back room in addition to the guest bathroom. Officially speaking, it was the men's room, the important thing was that it was unlikely Die Droge would try anything in the heart of town, where someone was always up and about. Her cottage was secluded and on a quiet street where she would be much more vulnerable—even if Robin was there with her.

Despite their growing sense of urgency to get to safer ground, they spent a few minutes trying to figure out how they were going to pay their bills when neither of them had any income, and what they needed to take from the house to the Fish so they wouldn't have to come back, and what she was going to sleep on. Robin offered the air mattress and memory foam pad he slept on in the boat. There was a built-in berth he could sleep on even if it wasn't quite as comfortable. She remembered that her mother had a foam pad in her closet. Doubled over, it would suffice. They packed a set of sheets, the clothes she would need, and her toiletries. Her home refrigerator and icebox were pretty cleared out after two weeks of being quarantined.

The whole thing was an inconvenience, but better that than dead. And if it meant saving her mother and putting the corrupt Die Droge people in jail, it was so worth it.

They talked about spending one last night at the cottage, but the sun was setting over the harbor by the time they finished with their plans, and they decided it would be better to make the move under the cover of darkness.

Robin was helping her lock up and secure the house when he went back to her mother's room to make sure the lights were out.

"What's your mother doing with a clerical shirt and collar in her closet?"

She heard him from the hall and joined him in her mother's room. "Who knows?" She shrugged. "She probably slept with a vicar. Or maybe she made one of her lovers put it on so she could pretend she was sleeping with a vicar. Who knows what the woman has done in her lifetime? I certainly don't. All I do know is that I don't want to."

"I thought we weren't going to say anything bad about your mother."

"First of all, she wouldn't think it was bad. She's proud of her exploits. Second, it's you that can't say anything bad aboot her. I can say anything I want. She's me mum."

"Well, I'd like to borrow her clerical shirt," Robin said. "I stole one of James' when I snuck into hospital to see the sea captain, but he won't fall for my ruse a second time. If I'm the one who gets to take Emma her present from Die Droge, I'd like to be prepared."

So that's what he did. She wished she'd had time to launder it after—well—whatever it had been used for, but there was no time. And that's the way it was.

#

Robin collapsed onto the berth in Sea Worthy's lower deck. So much for a nice, relaxing evening cozying up to Becca. After getting Becca settled in Café Fish, hiking out to his boat, and maneuvering into the city center harbor to take his place in his newly designated, high-rent docking spot, he was pretty wiped out. At least he was finally out of quarantine and able to do something about the mess the pandemic had made of his life. Who knew if the results of speaking to Scotland Yard would be immediate or long term, but at least it was a start.

He eased his body onto the thin mat that covered the berth in the bowels of his boat. The air was stale and stuffy, but he didn't feel comfortable falling asleep with the hatch open like he normally did. He wasn't really afraid, but caution was certainly warranted.

What he really wanted to do was to head to his secret isle and spend time with the seals. Maybe it sounded crazy, but they felt like family to him, and he missed them after two weeks of not seeing them. When he'd been told he had to quarantine, he'd toyed with the idea of trolling out to sea and not coming back for two weeks, but he'd wanted to be close by in case Becca needed him. Mobile reception was poor to non-existent out at the island, and the thought that Becca might become symptomatic when he wasn't around to help her had kept him tethered to Portree.

He decided to sleep for a few hours and then head out to the island. Knowing that Scotland Yard was aware of their situation and keeping an eye on things – Becca in particular – was reassuring enough to make him feel like he could be gone for a few hours. He was glad he had a place to dock so close to the Fish, but no one had said he had to stay anchored 24 by 7.

The second the sky started to light up in the east, he was off. There was no way to quietly start a boat's engine, but he tried anyway, hoping not to wake Becca as he headed out to sea.

As the waters churned into a frothy wake that followed his boat and the sea mist started to waft over his body, he resolved that it would be the last he thought of Becca for at least two or three hours. No offense intended, but he needed a break.

His mobile jingled cheerily.

"Robin?" It was Becca.

He smiled, grimaced, stifled a groan. "Did I wake you up?"

"I was already awake. Couldn't sleep."

No surprise there. "I decided to visit the island, see how the seals are doing. Go back to sleep. The last thing either of us needs is to get run down. We need strong immune systems to fight this thing now that it's airborne."

"Easier said than done."

He was going to lose his signal soon, if past experience was any indication. "I'll sing you a song before you lose me."

"A lullaby?"

"Aye." He thought for a minute and started to string together the words that were floating around in his head.

"There once was a lass named Rebecca.
A sweeter lass no man could find.
The call of the sea was a strong one,
But her man, he felt love, knew his mind.

The wind blew the ship to an island,
Full of seal folk and those of their kind,
But the man bade farewell to the Selkies
And sailed back to the lass that he pined.

By the time he finished, his signal was gone.

The sky was streaked with color when he finally reached the island. Soon after, the sun rose behind him and illuminated the view before him in sunbeams. He watched as a dozen or two seal heads poked up from the water, all looking in his direction, their whiskers skimming the opalescent ripples of the water as their eyes focused on him. The shallow waters reflected the dappled grey and white of their coats. One, with a lighter, grayish brown coat, threw his head back and called out to the other. Or perhaps he was just admiring the sunrise.

He could see the shoreline now, and with it, the sight of seals napping onshore. He held his breath until a white and grey seal lifted her head to see who was coming. He'd been afraid he would find more dead. More lifeless bodies. More carcasses left to rot after Die Droge's troops had extracted whatever flesh or organs they needed for their experimentation.

Joy flooded over him to see that things appeared to be back to normal. As if to confirm his assumptions, a seal's big, expressive eyes took in the sight of him, and then, paid him the greatest compliment—with her flippers still curled together, she lay her head down and went back to sleep.

He scanned the faces of the circle of seals gathered around him, looking for Shelagh or Soren. He was always amazed at the variety of expressions. One male hovered underwater, with only his nose showing, his wise eyes sad and disheartened. A younger seal, with eyes opened wide, moved her pretty head in one direction and then the other, clearly curious about what was going on.

He put down his anchor, hoisted the ladder off the side of the boat, and climbed into the water. The deeper water was chilly, but it warmed by the time he reached the shallow waters near the shore.

How could anyone hurt these innocent creatures?

"A good question." He heard Soren's voice speaking in his head instead of through his ears. He knew it made no sense, and never would to anyone who hadn't experienced the phenomenon, but he simply accepted it. Why try to analyze what was clearly illogical, maybe even magic of a sort? It didn't matter how he could communicate with Soren and Shelagh, only that he could.

"Have you been able to stop the evil ones from exploiting more seals?" Shelagh's voice was so quiet it was almost a whisper. Or was he simply imagining that she had spoken?

"They are not in custody. We have proof, but it can't be verified since the man who wrote of what he saw is dead."

He hoped there had been no more killings. He imagined Soren organizing patrols to guard the waters night and day, watching, waiting, awakening the colony so they could dive into the sea and escape if trouble arose. He wondered about the fate of other colonies, and if they also had ways of communicating impending danger. Most wild animals did, didn't they?

"I'm so sorry for what you've had to endure." Robin let empathy flow from his soul until he could almost feel the Selkies acknowledging and accepting his offering of emotion.

He'd heard rumors around Portree that there were foreign ships hovering around the Outer Hebrides, most likely searching for seals and conducting their own tests. All anyone knew was that they spoke in foreign languages and looked like they were from the east. Robin's heart sank faster than a dropped anchor as he considered the possibilities. He'd feared it wouldn't take long for other drug companies around the world to realize that the seal population, whose diet mainstay was fish, weren't succumbing to the virus. Experimenting with seal tissue wasn't an automatic solution to the problem of creating a vaccine or finding a cure, but it was someplace to start, and with millions of people in danger of dying, it was worth grasping on to. It was something instead of nothing.

"I know, my brother," Soren's mystical response surprised him, as did his seeming ability to tap into Robin's thoughts. It spooked him a little, but it also explained why the Selkies trusted him and absolutely believed in his sincerity and honest desire to help.

He spoke aloud and hoped they would understand his words, at least on some level. "I can continue to try to stop Die Droge, but I'm not equipped to mount an international manhunt. I want to help, but it will take Scotland Yard and very probably a multinational task force to halt the killings. Countries all over the world are desperate to find a cure. If I bring it to the attention of the media, it would most likely make things worse before they got better."

He immediately knew that the seals understood his reasons for wanting to keep the connection between seals and possible immunity as quiet as they possibly could. He felt both Soren's and Shelagh's presence just as he had before, when they'd danced in the waves.

"I'm hoping—" He spoke with a quiet reverence, his words catching in the wind, and hopefully, somehow magically ending on ears that could hear and understand. "I'm hoping the companies competitiveness and the desire to beat one another out of millions of pounds will work in our favor in this case – as long as too many do not catch on."

One of the smaller seals flicked their tail in the water, as if inviting him to play in the waves. Shelagh? The morning was still fresh and clear. He longed to let the sea wash away the tension in his shoulders and the restless energy in his soul.

He shucked his clothes just out of reach of the tide and waded into the water until it was deep enough to support his weight. Two seals approached him, one on either side, and escorted him into deeper waters. The seal he believed to be Soren had a face that was kindly, with almond shaped eyes, long, distinct whiskers, and a coat of mottled grey and brown. Shelagh was more petite, although still large for a female. Her eyes had long lashes, her nose pert and a little upturned, and she was grey and cream colored. She swam with a lithe grace that mimicked her gentle spirit. He had seen them both in human form, although only in his dreams, and the funny thing was that, unless he thought about it very succinctly, their faces were the same—they looked like themselves in whichever form they took.

But that was a mystery to be solved at another time. Today, they were here to swim, frolic, reconnect, relax. Today, they would enjoy each other and focus on the hope that no more of them—in either of their worlds—would became casualties of the virus.

CHAPTER 18

As soon as Rebecca said goodbye to Cameron, she leaned back and let the soothing aura she felt surround her. A few seconds later, she rolled onto her side and scrunched her legs to get up from her makeshift foam bed on the dining room floor of Café Fish. Her arms and legs still ached from the deep bruising she'd sustained when she fell.

She'd dreaded the thought of any further contact with Cameron, but she felt a real lift in her anxiety levels and a tremendous boost to her spirits after talking to him again.

What Robin would think of her and Cameron's new plan worried her a bit, but she had already decided that if Robin didn't like what she had agreed to, it was his own fault for leaving her and running off to see his seals.

Cameron still sounded terrible. He didn't want to draw attention to himself by testing, but based on his symptoms, she felt sure he had the virus. The good news was that being sick gave him the perfect reason to call Die Droge and demand that they give him an antidote.

She could certainly understand why he wanted treatment even though it was probably still in the experimental stages of testing. Cameron intended to take one dose of it himself, and smuggle the remaining dose to Emma in hospital.

Becca could only hope that a half dose for each of them

would be enough to defeat the virus. Cameron felt confident in his own strength, but they were both still worried about Emma. The doctor he'd spoken to at Die Droge had warned him that the drug was most effective when administered as soon as possible after contracting the illness.

It took Becca longer to shower and dress without the ease of being in her own bathroom and having everything in its place. The water came out of the pipes a bit rusty and the water heater must have been half the size of hers at home because it was gone in what seemed like no time.

She was barely dressed when Robin texted and said he was at the back door.

She hurried to let him in and asked him straight off if he'd had fun.

"Fun might not be the best word. We were very conscious of the fact that we're all in danger. It kind of hangs over you like a shroud. It's hard to forget the horror even when you're relaxing and enjoying the water."

"Well, at least you got to go for a swim, spend some time in the sun…"

"You sound like you're jealous."

"Maybe I am," she said. "But that's beside the point. I heard from Cameron. We talked for a long time, and we finally struck a deal."

Robin looked dubious. "So, what happened? What did you talk aboot?"

"He's angry that Emma engaged in high risk behavior and then infected him." She could tell Robin was reacting badly, so she let him jump in.

"Like we're supposed to feel sorry for him? I certainly can't muster any sympathy knowing he's the one who is responsible for the pandemic, and destroying who knows how many seals' lives. Emma could die because of him!"

She frowned. "You have to give Cameron a chance, Robin. I think he really does care for Mom—and for me."

"Well, that's the big question, isn't it? Sorry to be so cynical, but how do we know he's telling the truth? Does he really love Emma—or you—or is he just pretending so we won't turn him in to the police?"

"I talked to him. You didn't. And after speaking to him today, I feel like he's a different man. He's contrite and apologetic. Frustrated as he is with Emma, I think her being sick and the thought that he might lose her made a great impact on him. I wish you could have heard him."

She watched as Robin started to talk, then stopped, then started again.

"So you're saying that you've forgotten all the horrid things that Cameron said to you two weeks ago and even just yesterday, and that you now trust him wholeheartedly."

"You don't need to mock me."

"I'm not mocking you. I completely understand why you want to believe that Cameron is being sincere. I honestly hope you're right and that he's changed. There's nothing I would love more than for Cameron to realize how precious you and your mother are. But you can't blame me for being suspicious that he would have such an abrupt turn around, especially when the stakes are so high."

"But I'm the one who heard his voice. I know you think Cameron is probably manipulating me or double crossing us so he won't have to go to jail, but I believe him." It hurt her terribly that Robin didn't trust her to be an accurate judge of Cameron's true intentions. She'd always been a good judge of people. She was cautious. That was why she was still a virgin. She didn't leap into bed with any man who threw her a bone like her mother did. She was careful. She weighed the facts before she made a decision. Why couldn't Robin understand that?

The silence in the room was charged with an uncomfortable energy. She hated it.

Robin finally spoke. "You have to remember that I've heard Cameron speak, too. It's only been a few weeks since he and his Die Droge cronies were out on the boat with me. There was nothing at stake at that point – they were speaking candidly, not knowing that I had any knowledge of you or your mother or the situation with the pandemic. Becca, they were completely unapologetic. They showed no remorse."

"Yes, well, people can change!"

"Be reasonable. If Cameron still loved Emma or thought you might be his daughter, then why didn't he search out Emma the second he came to the island, and why did he say the things he said about Emma and you when he was on the boat with the other men?"

"Because he didn't know me."

"Then what aboot the things he said to you the day you got hurt? He knew you pretty well by then, yet he threatened you and scared you so badly that you practically got killed trying to get to safety."

"I was quarantined for two weeks. I've had a lot of time to think."

Robin clenched his fists. "Please don't let him came between us. I don't want to argue aboot it. I just want you to be careful, to think aboot what's motivating his words before you accept everything he says as the God honest truth."

"I am trying my best to be objective. If you will please do the same, we'll get along just fine. But if you've already made up your mind aboot him and refuse to consider the fact that he might be telling the truth, then I don't think we have anything more to say to one another."

Robin looked shocked and hurt. He stared at her for onwards of a minute. "Seriously? You're giving more credence to a man whom you've just met, a man who associates with known criminals, a man whose actions have already resulted in thousands of deaths and the decimation of Scotland's economy, a man who nearly killed you, than you do me, who you know and hopefully respect and love? If that's really the way you feel, then maybe this is the end of our conversation."

"Of course, I respect you!" At that moment, she was so upset that she wasn't sure if she did love him. Nor was she entirely convinced that Robin loved her as much as he said he did. "Why can't you understand? My first priority has to be saving my mother. And right now, Cameron is the only one who can do that."

"No, no, no! If we stop trying to protect Cameron, we could take this to the media, and give Scotland Yard the evidence they need to shut down Die Droge and confiscate their research. In the hands of an honest scientist, the cure might be available in half the time. Emma could still be given any experimental drugs they've been working on, and millions of lives could be saved. Die Droge knows that the more people die, the more valuable their cure will be. If they're not exposed, people will keep getting sick, and in a few more months, the world will be so desperate to stop the dying that whatever cure or vaccine they've come up with will be worth hundreds of billions of pounds."

She felt her eyes narrowing and her blood pressure rising. "Just because you don't have a good relationship with your family doesn't mean that I can't be thankful for a mother who loves me and a father who cares very deeply for both of us. Admit it, Robin. You don't want me to be close to Cameron because you're jealous."

But deep down, she wondered if Robin was right, and later, as she thought about what he'd said and reflected back on the expression Robin had on his face when he left, she felt bad. She didn't exactly regret what she'd said to him – but it made her sad that the father she'd dreamed of for years was coming between her and Robin. She wanted both men in her life – not one or the other.

#

Robin sat on the deck of Sea Worthy and watched as the line of people waiting to pick up takeaway food from the front window of Café Fish inched along. He felt a wee bit guilty thinking about Becca being there by herself, knowing that she didn't feel the best, hadn't been sleeping well, and wasn't fully recovered from her fall. But she'd made it clear that she didn't want his help or his advice.

At the moment, he felt more empathy from Soren and Shelagh than he did from Becca. The kinship he felt with them felt deeper and more simpatico than what he felt with Becca, too.

What was wrong with her? He just didn't get it. How could she put more trust in Die Droge than in him? He loved Becca, but he considered what she'd done a betrayal of the worst kind.

There was still a line in front of the takeaway window when the sun started to sink into the sea. He went below to open a can of tuna—hopefully canned before the contamination occurred. He wondered what the price would be if he tried to buy a can today? Or maybe it was just him who craved seafood. Maybe the masses were so scared and freaked out by what was happening that they didn't want to touch anything from the sea. He sure hadn't been getting any calls for fishing expeditions, but one would think someone out there would miss the feel of the wind in their hair, the warmth of the sun bouncing off the waves, the feel of the sea's mist teasing their faces. It was as though the seas of Scotland had been turned red by a horrible plague.

He had dozed off when his mobile rang.

"Robin? It's my mom. She's taken a turn for the worse. Cameron had the drug she needs, but he's horribly sick himself, so he had someone drop it off so I could deliver it. I've spoken to every one with any authority at hospital in hopes of getting permission to see her, but no one will agree to it even though I've cited the fact that she may not survive and I should be allowed an end-of-life visit to say goodbye." Becca stifled a sob. "And they all know what I look like, since I was just in hospital myself, so I can't imagine that I could sneak past security."

"I'll be right there," he told Becca. He went to his closet and pulled out the clerical shirt and collar Becca had found in Emma's closet. He put on a light jacket so no one – especially not their new protectors from Scotland Yard – would see a "pastor" leaving his boat or entering and exiting the Fish.

When he got close to hospital, he would leave his jacket in a bush so only a "pastor" would be seen entering hospital. It was a tricky business, and once again, he found himself praying to a God he wasn't quite sure even existed for good luck while he committed a crime.

The whole world was so mixed up that he could barely begin to figure it out. He was at wit's end.

He quickly trimmed and combed his hair on the sides like James wore his, and donned a hat to cover the top of his head. He trolled the boat close enough to the seawall to jump on shore and head to the Fish. He wanted to stay and talk to Becca but she was adamant that the medicine had to be delivered and administered to Emma without any delays.

He jogged to hospital – taxi drivers had eyes and he didn't dare risk one of them tattling on him if the police got involved. Parking lots had security cameras and if "James" was seen getting out of his brother's auto, it wouldn't bode well for Robin. He stopped running, stripped off his jacket, hid it in some bushes and walked the last block or two so he wouldn't be winded when he arrived.

Once again, he walked past security with a nod. Thank God he looked enough like James to gain access. Because the hour was rather late, he met only a handful of people in the halls. He sailed into Emma's room without a glitch, found the security camera, blocked the sightline with his body, and gave her a shot in her right arm just as Becca had specified while making an obvious show for the camera of making the sign of the cross over her. She didn't cry out, which had been his biggest fear. Conversely, she didn't even seem to know he was there, which was an even bigger fear. It was hard to see her in such an awful state.

But better he than Becca. He'd find a way to put a positive twist on things if he got out of the building without getting caught. No need to get Becca more worried than she already was.

A wave of relief washed over him. Such a tense business. He walked away from the hospital in the direction of the kirk and James' rectory just as he had come. He'd tried to think of everything. Now, all they could do was to wait and see if Emma responded to Die Droge's treatment.

#

Becca pulled down the window covers and locked the bottom of the window covering to the counter. Closed at last. She'd never been more exhausted. But then, what did she expect? She was not on good terms with Robin, who'd been her rock until now. Her mother was not improving, Cameron was all over the map, Scotland Yard was hovering around but not really doing anything to help, her business was faltering, and Die Droge was a huge unknown, and dangerous besides. Preparing one little takeaway order after another all day long was going to be the death of her. There couldn't possibly be a harder way to make money—takeaway was so labor intensive, and the least economical way she could think of to run a café. What she wouldn't give to host a well-organized business event, a rehearsal dinner with a three-choice menu, or a bridal shower where everyone was served the same meal. She actually made money doing large parties, which meant that the normal business she did was the icing on the cake. Takeaway was such hard work and so stressful, yet there wasn't enough business to warrant having her staff to help her.

She groped her head. Something had to give, and soon.

She missed her mother. She missed the rejuvenating effects of being away from the Fish and resting at her own, cozy little cottage up the hill. And she missed Robin. Oh, she still saw him every once in awhile, but their conversations were stilted and she felt more tense when he left than before he'd come.

There was a quiet knock on the back door. She peeked out the newly installed peephole and slid the deadbolt aside to let him in.

"How's your mom doing?" Robin looked over his

shoulder, then stepped inside and re-latched the door.

"No change. Maybe even a little worse from what I'm told." She sighed.

"Have you spoken to Cameron? Has he improved?"

"He said he felt a little better, but that was yesterday. Today when I called, he didn't pick up. Maybe I should be worried."

"Probably just sleeping." Robin rolled his eyes. "Or maybe he's not even sick. Maybe the whole thing was just a ploy to gain our sympathy so we wouldn't turn him in. Or maybe he took all of the real drug himself and sent your mother a vial filled with saline solution."

"He wouldn't do that."

"We have no idea what he would do. We know very little aboot him. But what I do know is what I heard him say, and how I saw him acting when he was on my boat – before he knew who I was, and before he met you, and before he had his little rendezvous with Emma. So that's what I believe aboot him. I know you've had a couple of conversations with him that I haven't been in on, but nothing I've heard so far has changed my mind aboot Cameron Allanach."

"We just have to be patient. He said it might take a few days or even a week for the medicine to take effect."

"Which is pure convenient. It gives Die Droge more time to cover their tracks, create false documents, and destroy the evidence that they started the pandemic."

"I just can't go there, Robin. I have to believe they're going to help me and that my mother is going to recover."

"Well, I'm sorry, but I think we've been had. I hope I'm wrong, but I would bet money—if I had a pence to my name—that Emma was given a placebo, or some drug that they'd already tested and proved ineffective, to buy them time."

"Please, can we talk aboot something else?"

Robin didn't say a word, but he did go to the sink and grabbed a scouring pad. He had scrubbed out two large kettles and a roasting pan by the time she'd wiped down the countertops and restocked the plastic utensils, napkins, individually portioned condiments and takeaway containers.

He rinsed off the pans he'd scoured and dried them with a paper towel.

"What's this?" He pointed to an envelope in a stack with her purse. He stepped closer. "It looks like it's from Ancestry. Have you looked at it?"

She shrugged. "No. It came yesterday, and I just didn't feel up to learning that I'm half Selkie, so I didn't open it. And then I kind of forgot aboot it in all the commotion."

"You really don't want to know?"

"Not really. Maybe. I don't know. I guess so." She picked up the envelope and slowly eased it open, pulled the folds apart and started to read. "Well, there you have it. Or not. The results are inconclusive, most likely because we sent in a strand of hair for Cam's sample instead of saliva."

"Does it mention anything aboot ancient Nordic bloodlines found on a remote seafaring island?"

"Robin. Please. I'm just not in the mood."

He picked up a dishtowel and dried the pans. "Do you think Cameron will agree to be tested now that you have a relationship?"

"Just leave it alone. Please."

"Fine. I need to be getting to bed anyway. Keep me posted if your mother shows any improvement."

"Sure." She watched as Robin unlatched the door, peered out the slit after opening it a crack, and stepped out. She immediately dead bolted it as soon as he was gone.

More disappointment. How she hated that their difference of opinion over Cameron was driving a wedge between her and Robin. Maybe if Cameron had been her dad – if she'd been able to prove it – maybe Robin would have started to accept him.

CHAPTER 19

Robin wanted to scream. And he would have if he'd been out to sea. He'd started to think of Becca as family. Emma, too. That's what he'd wanted for a long time—a connection to someone who liked and appreciated the same things he did, and wanted the same things out of life. It's not like he and Becca were identical twins, but he felt a kinship with her that he'd never felt with anyone before, especially not his own family.

But suddenly, it was like she was a different person. And all it had taken was one or two conversations with Cameron – conversations that he hadn't been part of. Cameron was pure charismatic. He got that. And Cameron had the added bonus of possibly being Becca's blood relation. On the other hand, Robin had been there for Becca for years, and Cameron had done nothing for her except reject and abandon her for her entire childhood.

There was one other thing that bothered Robin. Didn't Becca want to grow up and move on, as in away from her parent – parents if Cameron turned out to be her father – and have a romantic relationship with a man and a family of her own? What was holding her back? What was she afraid of? What was she waiting for?

One of the things he'd always admired about Becca was

her independent, self-sufficient personality. It was the reason she was such a good businessperson. She was motivated. She knew what she wanted, and she wasn't afraid to follow her dreams, even reach for the stars. She'd accomplished something huge when she'd bought the Fish, made it her own, and made a success of it. Not many people as young as she could have accomplished as much in such a short time. Becca was amazing.

So why, all of the sudden, had she become so gullible? It was like Cameron had brainwashed her.

He hoped it was just a phase she was going through, because he wanted the old Becca back. In the meantime, all he could do was try to identify with what she was going through—to be considerate of her feelings—a hard task when he didn't begin to understand.

His mobile rang just as he was headed for his berth.

"Robin, please."

"This is he."

"This is Mac, the one who's handling your case at Scotland Yard."

For a fleeting second, he worried that Die Droge had found out they'd gone to Scotland Yard, that they were trying to trip him up, get him to admit it, before they killed him. And Becca. His adrenalin surged until he felt feverish. His imagination flowed at lightning speed until he felt totally exhausted, and all in the span of a few seconds.

"I just wondered if you would be willing to answer a few questions."

"I'm happy to help if I can." His heartbeat slowed down a bit.

"You named Die Droge in your affidavit and spoke about the men who were on your boat, but you didn't give us the names of the specific individuals who were involved."

So here it was. Did he give Cameron to the police, or did he continue to protect him? Would more lives be saved if he gave them the names from his expedition roster? Or would it only serve to shut down the whole vaccine effort before a cure was found? Would the government allow him to withhold what he knew without consequence or would he be charged with collusion if he didn't give them what they wanted?

He was about to say that he guessed he had better contact his solicitor, but then he thought better. First of all, he didn't have a solicitor. Second, he barely had enough money left to buy fuel for Sea Worthy, pay his insurance bill, and put food on his table, except that since he gave up his apartment and started sleeping on the boat, he really had no table. He hadn't asked to be involved in this mess and it shouldn't be him who had to come up with money to defend himself when he hadn't done anything wrong. He was just trying to help!

"Do you have the names?" The agent's tone was still polite, but had taken on a firm, no nonsense tone.

He didn't want to lie, couldn't lie and say he wasn't on the ship and would call later when he had his roster in front of him—not when Scotland Yard had agents in the area, keeping an eye on him and Becca for their protection.

He reached for the ship's log. Becca would probably never speak to him again once she found out what he'd done – assuming he gave them what they wanted. He didn't know what to do.

"Are you sure this line is secure?" He was trying to figure out a way to stall a little longer until he came up with a plan. Like he was smarter than Scotland Yard. Like he could try to pull one over on their agent and get away with it.

A new thought prickled at his conscience. If he withheld the names, they would certainly issue a search warrant— maybe already had for all he knew. He didn't want to destroy his log—couldn't legally even if he wanted to. When the time was right, he fully intended to turn over the names of each of the people involved in the cruel plot to start a pandemic for their own, selfish, financial gain. He couldn't wait until the day the smug grins and nonchalant attitudes were stricken from their faces so they could be prosecuted and punished to the full extent of the law. He wanted them to be brought to justice now, before they disappeared, took their obscene profits and scampered off to hide on some secluded island in the Mediterranean or even the Caribbean.

"I've tried to be nice aboot this, Robin. But there will soon come a point that if you and Becca are not willing to divulge the names of the men involved with Die Droge's operation, you will risk being charged with collusion."

His brain started to buzz. "Have you spoken to Becca?"

"I phoned her first. She said I should contact you."

Thank you, Becca.

"And what if I say that you need to contact her?

"Then I will be forced to issue a search warrant, and to tell my supervisors that you are both being uncooperative. If that's the way you want to play this, I'm sure charges will be pending. I hate to see a good man prosecuted for something evil men have done, but there are too many lives at stake here to slow up the investigation any further."

"I just need time. There's more going on than you know." He said the words, but even as they came out of his mouth, he realized how unacceptable it was to withhold the names in hope of saving Emma's life, or soothing Becca's sensibilities when every hour, thousands of people around the world died of the disease Die Droge had purposely introduced into the food supply.

The agent spoke, this time, his tone a wee bit more understanding. "If you're worried aboot privacy, why don't I book an expedition for tomorrow afternoon at half two and we can talk while we're at sea."

Robin breathed a sigh of relief. It bought him a little time. Everything was better when he was at sea—even divulging your friend's possible father in a criminal investigation, if it came to it.

"A real booking? Because I'm very short on funds and I'll need to fill the boat with fuel before we head out." He shouldn't have gone to the island the other day. He'd known that intellectually, but he'd let his heart dictate his behavior, not his head. He'd needed to see the seals, talk to them, be with them. Sometimes he thought it was more likely he who had Selkie blood than Becca.

"A real booking. Charge your usual rates. There will be two of us."

"Thank you. I'll see you tomorrow at half two."

#

Becca had never felt so lonely. Her mother was alternately non-responsive or off with the fairies because of her fever. Cameron wouldn't speak to her except to answer the phone to say, "I'm still alive," and hang up again. Her relationship with Robin was in the crapper. She couldn't do anything else to help her mother other than praying, hoping the medicine Die Droge had sent would eventually work, and be patient. She had no idea where things stood with Cameron or where they would ultimately go. Maybe the whole thing was a big dead end and she was just not able to admit it. Her relationship with Robin was the one thing she did have some control over—at least she hoped it wasn't too late to repair things. She had to find a way.

What was she thinking when she alienated Robin and let Cameron come between them? In the beginning, she'd done everything she could to save Café Fish, but what had she gained? If she lost her mother and doomed her relationship with Robin, what did it matter if she had the Fish? She felt so horrible that she was questioning her very reasons for living.

She finally got up enough courage to call Robin. Maybe it was a mistake. Maybe she should have done it sooner. How was she supposed to know?

"Hello? It's Becca. I was wondering if you'd like to come to dinner tonight. I miss you." She held her breath until Rob answered.

"Aye. It's kind of weird that we're suddenly next door neighbors, and we see less of each other than when you lived up the hill and I was on the edge of the harbor." Robin sounded sincere, but a little cautious.

"I'm sorry I haven't done more to welcome you to the neighborhood. I'd like to change that if I can."

"What time would you like me to hop across the street? I'd be happy to come early and help with the easy stuff if you want me to."

"That's okay. But let's eat early so we can have a relaxing time of it. Maybe half six?"

"I'll be there."

She knew Robin would love whatever she fixed. As long as it was food, he would be all in. Make it from scratch and he'd be in heaven. She was really starting to miss seafood, but there was no way she could risk violating the health department's ordinance at this point. She'd always been so proud of her locally sourced, pulled straight from the harbor, fresh catch of the day policy, but at the moment, she would have given anything to have a freezer full of Alaskan salmon, Norwegian cod, or tiger shrimp, caught and flash frozen before the pandemic.

She considered several options and finally decided on Tipperary Chicken with a Banger and Mash, Irish Cheddar, and Bread Stuffing topped with Brown Onion Gravy. She'd had a version of the dish a few years back when she'd gone to a cooking class at a restaurant near the Rock of Cashel in Ireland. It was down home cooking, jazzed up a bit, and she felt Robin would like it. It was different and special. If he gave it five stars, she might even add it to her specials board once she opened for dinner—when the pandemic was over.

She suspected a lot of people would continue to be leery of seafood even when the all clear was given. Even she wondered how and if the virus would ever be completely gone from the fish population. How many generations would it take before they could be sure the fish supply, especially that of Scotland, wasn't contaminated? "When the pandemic was over" might be wishful thinking. How she hoped the repercussions to the eco-system wouldn't be as extensive as she feared, but it still seemed wise to develop her repertoire of chicken, pork and beef dishes in the meantime.

She sighed. What had Cameron and his associates done when they unleashed this virus on the world?

She made a salad of chopped cabbage, bananas, salad dressing and a little vanilla to serve as a starter, and a simple mash of potatoes and white cabbage to go with the chicken— Rumpledethumps without the cheese, because she'd already added plenty to the dish. Dessert would be Rob's choice of whatever almost-outdated delicacies she had in the cooler. The problem with being shut down or out of commission for any length of time was that you ended up throwing out massive quantities of food that was expired or past its prime. She was used to the ups and downs of the restaurant business, but now, instead of having the usual momentum to make it up the next steep hill, it was like pausing at the bottom of the hill, and then starting the hard climb back to the top from a dead stop.

She was ready for a rest by the time she heard Robin's secret knock on the door. They'd come up with it the other day – two soft raps followed by one hard rap and a series of quick rat-a-tat-tats. Between it and the new peephole, she could always be sure it was him.

The second Robin was inside and the door relocked, he took her in his arms and hugged her for a long, long time.

"Please, please, let's never fight again." Robin nuzzled his face in her neck. "I want us to be on the same side from now on."

"Me, too." The only reason she broke off the hugs was because she could hear the brown onion gravy simmering on the stovetop and it was a small enough batch that she knew it wouldn't take long to boil dry or scorch.

"Let's eat," she said.

"Can I serve you? I know I won't plate things as beautifully as you do, but you've gone to all the work of making everything. It would make me happy if I could do the rest—even the dishes—if you'll let me."

She was just tired enough to agree. The thought of being pampered was quite appealing. She gave Robin a quick rundown on the different dishes, gave him another quick hug and went and sat down at the intimate table for two she'd set under an arch in the back corner. The archway was dripping with wisteria and tiny white lights. In the center hung a mobile of fairies in different color dresses that appeared to be popping out to sprinkle fairy dust on the guests. It was her favorite table – and everyone else's.

Robin appeared a few minutes later with their cabbage salads. She'd laid them out on two cut glass salad plates and the effect was dazzling if she said so herself.

She looked up at him and smiled. "I meant them for a starter but they'll make a nice side if it means you can finish plating and join me a little sooner."

Robin nodded his head. "As you wish, my lady."

He returned holding two square plates that were bone china—treasures she'd found at a boot sale one day long ago in Wales. The plates were rimmed with delicate English wildflowers—bluebells, violets, buttercups and ragged robin—her favorites. She loved that Robin had noticed them in the cupboard and chosen to use them. He was truly a man after her own heart.

"Dinner is served." Robin set a plate in front of her first, then moved his napkin aside and put down his plate. He'd centered the chicken breast on the left side of each plate, opposite a spray of wildflowers hand-painted on the opposite side. A few rings of HP Sauce, just the right amount of gravy, and a nasturtium blossom alongside a spray of sage leaves standing up in the center, completed the plate.

"It's beautiful!"

"No worries. I washed the plates before using them."

She laughed. Such elegance. Such down home candor.

Robin left the room and returned with a wicker basket lined with a cloth napkin. Ah…he'd found the quick breads and rolls she'd made that morning. He had a seat, then waited until she lifted her fork before he did the same.

"Actually, do you mind if I say grace?" She put her fork down.

"Feel free."

She bowed her head. "Dear Lord, I pray that you would heal my mother." She hesitated. "And Cameron, and all the other people suffering from the virus. I pray that you would keep me and Robin safe, and that those who are responsible for the pandemic would be brought to justice when the time is right."

"Amen," Robin said.

She was surprised, but she continued. "Lord, I pray that you would guide and direct our steps as we deal with everything to do with Die Droge.

"Now bless this meal, our conversation, and our time together on this day. In Jesus' name I pray, Amen."

They ate in near silence. The meal was just that delicious, if she did say so herself. Robin complimented her several times, but his actions spoke just as loudly as his words.

"Would you like dessert now, or later?"

"Later," Robin said, gazing across the candlelit table.

For awhile, they talked about what they wanted to do, and where they wanted to go when the lockdown ended and the travel restrictions were lifted.

"This is going to sound odd," Robin warned her. "But I used to drop by the Eilean Donan Castle Café quite often on my expeditions so my guests could tour the castle. Don't take it personally, but I absolutely love their castle pâté."

She laughed. "It's not like you like their recipe better than mine. I've never even tried to make pâté."

"They wrap it in pastry and shape the top like a castle, with spires and turrets. You'd love it. Anyway, it's the perfect lunch bite. Plus, their millionaire bars are almost as good as yours."

"Isn't it odd? I mean, it's only a few miles away, but we're not even allowed to visit."

Robin's shoulders sagged. "Right. We're not allowed to be more than six miles from home."

"During the first pandemic, I wanted to go to France in the worst way," she said, wistfully. "That's where I'd planned my vacation. Of course, it never happened. Now, I'd be happy if I could spend a day or two in the Kingdom of Fife, visit The Peat Inn, and enjoy a great meal prepared by someone other than me."

Robin's face lit up. "Maybe we should take a trip together when this is over. I've always wanted to see the Callanish Standing Stones on the Isle of Lewis. It's a bit of a trip by boat, and we'd have to get a rental car once we got there, but it would still be cheaper than the ferry."

"That would be perfect! I've dreamed of recovering my seat cushions in a Harris Tweed, and I've heard there are places that stock factory seconds and outdated patterns. It's the only way I could ever afford to do it. And if I brought back a couple of cases of Stornoway Black Pudding, I bet the savings would pay for the whole trip. It would be so exciting!"

Robin beamed at her and took her hand. She loved feeling hopeful. She loved the heady feeling of anticipation that was surging through her body. She loved being able to look forward to doing something, going somewhere, anywhere!

"I'm so glad we're allies again." Robin squeezed her hand and looked into her eyes. He slid around to her side of the table and kissed her deeply and tenderly.

The heightened state of her senses was so great that she almost melted just from his kiss.

Robin leaned back from kissing her and took a deep, contented breath. "I have an expedition planned for tomorrow. My first in weeks. I won't be going far but if you'd like to come along just for a change of scenery, you're welcome to ride along."

"Really," she said. "I thought with the infection rate so high, and the lockdown in place, no one would be booking anything. I mean, locals just don't usually—"

"It's not locals. It's two agents from Scotland Yard."

Her mood plummeted, the euphoria she felt faded as quickly as it had come. "Please don't tease me aboot something so important."

"It's not a joke."

"What's going on? Do they want something? Why didn't you tell me?"

"I just spoke to them a couple of hours ago. And yes, they want names."

She closed her eyes and tried to absorb the implications of what Robin was saying. "This is aboot your log then?"

"I tried to stall them, talk them into giving us more time, but they wouldn't take no for an answer. They threatened me with obstruction of justice and aiding and abetting a criminal. I don't think we have a choice at this point, Becca. They gave us time to work with Cameron to get a drug that we hoped to use to save your mother's life. The time has come and gone, the drug has been administered. They're not willing to delay their investigation any longer."

"But Cameron tried to help us. He did everything he promised, up to and including giving up a dose of a drug that could have saved his own life so my mother could have it."

Robin said nothing but his sad-eyed puppy dog look said it all.

"You can't turn in Cameron after all he's done to help us."

Robin lowered his eyes.

"I won't have it. If my mother keeps getting worse, our only hope is to go back to Cameron and Die Droge and ask them for more help. If we don't have Cameron as a point of contact, we have no hope of getting through to them. Giving Scotland Yard names at this point is—you might as well be signing my mother's death warrant."

"I'll do my best to convince them, Becca. You know I will."

She said nothing.

"Do you trust me to do the right thing, to use my instincts to figure out what our next action should be?"

"You should go."

"As in, I should meet with the agents and go out on the boat with them?"

"No. As in, you should go. Home. Get away from me.

Now."

"Oh, Becca. This isn't how I want our evening to end! Let me help you do the dishes. We can talk aboot it, vent our frustrations, work things out."

She couldn't. She just couldn't. She wanted Robin to hold her. To kiss her in places well south of her lips. She wanted to work with him, not against him.

And then she thought about Cameron, and the fact that there was still every possibility, every probability, that he was her father.

And she just couldn't.

CHAPTER 20

Rob waited until the two agents from Scotland Yard were onboard Sea Worthy, then latched the gate and revved the engines. He wanted to be gone – and inconspicuously so – before Becca was done with the lunch rush. Better not to irk her any more than she already was.

He smiled at his passengers. "Where are you from? Have you ever been to the Inner Hebrides before you were assigned to this case or are you seeing the Isles for the first time?" Might as well be friendly.

"I'm from Glasgow," the taller agent said. "Never been this far north, so I'm looking forward to seeing the sights."

Rob shifted up and slowly guided the boat out of the harbor into open water. "Nothing wrong with combining a little pleasure with business."

The shorter, stockier of the agents said, "Spent my whole life in Edinburgh, but I've traveled a fair bit. My wife is Danish, and she's always had a case of good Viking wanderlust. We were scheduled to go to the Faroe Islands during the first pandemic but the trip was cancelled, just like everything else. Haven't been anywhere since."

"Well, I suppose it's always nice to have a break from the old paperwork grind. Surveillance duty, too. Must get kind of boring."

"Always is until something happens." The men looked at each other.

It was hard to read their faces when they were both wearing masks. They were sure making a lot of eye contact. What was up with that? Must have been an inside joke. The stocky man looked down at his mobile.

A sudden thought occurred to him. "There are more agents still in Portree, right? To keep an eye on Becca?"

"Of course." The tall one responded emphatically, looking down at his mobile.

Not very comforting. Rob thought about asking for specifics. Where were they watching from? How many agents had been assigned to the case? It bothered him that the agents didn't seem more concerned about Becca. And why hadn't they asked him any questions yet? He tried to think of a word that described the way they hit him. Unprofessional? Humdrum? Average? Apathetic? He shifted up to top speed as they rounded the western point of Raasay. Then again, how was he to know what personality traits someone from Scotland Yard was supposed to exhibit? And who was he to call them out? He was out on this expedition in the first place because Scotland Yard didn't trust him.

The tall man glanced at his mobile again. He would have expected a teenaged peon to be fiddling with his mobile non-stop when he was supposed to be working, but not a supposedly top-notch representative of Scotland Yard.

"Wait!" Now the short stocky one was looking at his mobile.

Rob cut the engine. What on earth?

"Aren't we near the spot where you first found the ship that purportedly dumped the contagion in the water?"

"Yes, in the general vicinity." He pointed toward Raasay.

"Can we double back so I can get a picture?"

Both men continued to look at their mobiles.

"Sure." He slowly circled around and eased his way back toward the island. Under normal circumstances, the waters this close to Skye would be dotted with boats – pleasure craft,

sailboats, fishing trawlers, a few yachts, security patrols for
the fish farms. But today, the waters were bare. With
everything shut down, there were no tourists, no locals, and
no workers. There were certainly no fishermen.

"There. That's good," the taller man said, still looking at
his mobile.

"No problem." Rob turned back to the throttle and tried
to keep the boat as still as possible so they could get a good
photo.

"Step away from the helm."

What on earth? He turned to see which one of them was
talking and what was going on. The first thing he saw was a
gun pointed straight at his heart, which started to pump
frantically.

"Who are you people?" But in the same heart that was
doing double time, he already knew. "Die Droge?"

"You're going to call Scotland Yard and tell them you're
retracting your story in regard to the pandemic. We have a
prepared statement for you to read. Don't skip a single line. If
you try to signal them in any way, you will be dead before you
can get the words out." This from the tall one. The short one
handed him a piece of paper.

"What?" He started to read to himself. 'I'm sorry that I
lied but I was desperate to save my business. Both Becca and
I were out of money. The first pandemic almost took us out
and we'd barely had a chance to recover when this one hit us.
When we found out that the man who may be Becca's father
worked for a pharmaceutical company, we saw it as an
opportunity to make some money. Not because we're greedy,
but because we were completely broke and had no where else
to turn.'

"This is ridiculous. There's no way I'm going to read this
to anybody." He could have kicked himself. Why hadn't he
examined their credentials more carefully?

"You don't have a choice."

He waved at the gun. "Go ahead and kill me. Scotland
Yard will have all the more reason to hunt you down and lock

you away."

The tall man removed his mask and sneered at him. "Oh, you will call Scotland Yard and read the statement—very convincingly—if you ever want to see Rebecca again."

He tried to hide his visceral reaction, tried to convince himself that they didn't have Becca, tried to bluff his way out of the corner they'd boxed him into.

"You can't make me do anything. Scotland Yard will sort this out and Die Droge will pay for what they've done to the world."

The tall man motioned at the short man. "Why don't we give Rebecca a ring and let her weigh in on what Robin should do."

"Sounds like a plan," the short one said.

"Does Cameron know you're using his daughter as bait?" But the truth was, these men probably didn't even know who Cameron was. They were hired hit men who'd been given a job to do and told how to manipulate the situation to their advantage. They didn't give a whit for anyone, including but not limited to the world's entire population.

He tried to discreetly look for his mobile. He touched the pocket of his jacket. He always put it away when he was navigating. Salt water and mobiles weren't a good mix, and not far from Raasay, he always lost his signal anyway. His gut wrenched in two. *Please God, if you care anything for your children, don't let anything happen to Becca.*

"If you have to take someone, let it be me."

The shorter man walked toward him with malice written all over his face. On closer introspection, Robin could see that his arms and chest were totally ripped. Great.

The man reached into Robin's pocket and pulled out his mobile. "I'll take this."

"Please leave Becca out of this."

The man ignored him, looked at his recent calls and pressed on Becca's name.

#

Becca wiped off the countertop and misted it with bleach water. Lunch had been twice as crazy as usual because she didn't have her head screwed on straight. Everything that was happening was just too much for her to handle.

She set a timer for the bleach water and started scrubbing out the sinks, then sprayed them with the same sanitizer. That's when she heard Robin's two soft raps followed by one hard rap and a series of quick rat-a-tat-tats. Her heart skipped a beat. She was surprised, that's all—after last night—that he would drop by, not knowing what kind of a reception he would get.

A strand of hair fell over her face when she turned toward the door. She tried to flip it out of her eyes, and failed. Somewhere in the middle of trying to see a paper towel that she could use to get the bleach off of her hands, she reconsidered even going to the door. Did she really want to see Robin so soon after their argument? Maybe it would be better to let both of them – and their tempers – chill a bit.

She tried again to flip the thick strand of hair that was blocking her eyes out of the way. No such luck. Once again, she heard the sound of two soft raps followed by one hard rap and a series of quick rat-a-tat-tats. "Fine." She walked to the door, unbolted the lock, and flung the door open.

What? She saw no sign of Robin. A man and a woman walked into the kitchen and hurriedly closed the door behind them, bolting them in.

"Scotland Yard." The man flashed a shiny badge from its leather case, flipped it shut, and slipped it back into his pocket in one swift movement.

Had something happened to Robin while she was busy with her lunch orders? Had her mother – please God – no! Her mind was so busy trying to figure out how these people had known her and Robin's secret knock, and what was happening that she barely saw their credentials. And – her hands still had bleach on them and the lock of hair was still in her eyes.

She finally found her voice. "Can I help you with something?"

The pair was dressed in black—he in a classic suit and tie, her in a woman's suit with a tight, knee length skirt and matching pumps.

"Yes. We have questions that need to be answered. We understand that your mother is gravely ill, but people all over the world have contracted the virus – hundreds of thousands are already dead. We can't delay the investigation any longer. We have to move on and the only way we can do that is for you to divulge the names of the people from Die Droge who are involved in the crime.

"Robin has the names and their signatures in his ship's log." She looked at the time on her microwave. "The two agents out in the boat with Robin will soon have all of the information we know. There's nothing else I can tell you. I have a lot to do, and I'm not feeling the best. So if you don't mind…"

The two agents looked at each other. "There are no agents out on a boat at this time."

"No. It was set up for half two. Robin told me last night." She walked into the other room and looked through the slats of the window. "His boat is gone. Where else would he be?" Fear sliced through her belly.

The two agents looked at each other once again. She couldn't gauge their expressions because of the masks. But something was going on. She could feel it.

"Your friend may have thought he was going on a boat with two agents of Scotland Yard, but we can assure you that none of our agents are out on das boot."

For the first time, she detected a slight German accent in the woman's voice—and couldn't imagine why. Scotland Yard wouldn't hire foreigners to work in matters of national security, would they? Of course, these days, half of Scotland wasn't Scottish by blood. Despite Brexit, more immigrants poured into the UK daily. What were you supposed to tell them, that you couldn't be employed in certain sensitive areas because they're not trustworthy enough, not Scottish enough?

"From the sound of it," the man said, "your friend has been conned."

"By who? Who would do such a thing?" Die Droge would. The agents didn't say a word, but she knew. She knew. "If he's out there alone with people who want to harm him, then we need to do something aboot it! Now!" She pulled out her mobile and tried to ring him. No answer. Probably no reception. She looked at the agents, her whole body tense with a vile, frantic feeling that something was horribly wrong.

She was shaking. She was so scared for Robin that she felt sick.

She turned on the agents. "What do you need to know?"

But what did it matter now? She couldn't lose her mother and Robin. She was so scared of Die Droge that she wanted to, needed to, did tell them everything she knew.

She was just getting into the intricacies of her conversations with Cameron when her mobile rang.

"Rebecca Ronan?"

"Yes. This is her."

"There's someone here who would like to speak to you."

"Becca?"

"Robin! Where are you?"

"Listen carefully, Becca. I'm out on the boat with two Die Droge operatives and they want me to call Scotland Yard and recant my previous statement about Die Droge's involvement in the pandemic."

"Involvement? They started the whole thing!" She looked at the agents, expecting them to affirm her statement. She could only see their eyes, but she had the strangest feeling that they knew something she didn't.

Rob said, "I told them I wouldn't do it. They said they would hurt you if I didn't cooperate. Please, please, if anyone tries to—"

"I'm safe, Robin. Don't give it another thought. There are two Scotland Yard agents with me right now."

Her statement was met with complete and utter silence. What? Why wasn't Robin acting relieved?

She heard laughter in the background. Both backgrounds. What was so funny? Was this some sort of joke Robin was pulling on her to make her realize they needed to come clean with Scotland Yard and tell them the whole story?

She turned to the agents. They were both holding guns. They were pointed at her.

For a second, she thought she was going to faint.

"Robin? The people that are here have guns, and they're pointed at me." More laughter. She heard a loud crunching noise, a thud, heavy breathing. A moan.

"Let him go!" She screamed into her mobile.

"Stop!" A loud, deep voice split the air. "We need him to sound rational and reasonable when he calls Scotland Yard, not like he's been beaten and coerced."

The woman in her kitchen stepped close to her phone and yelled, "Ja. There will be plenty of time for that later."

Who were these people? They didn't seem like the pharmaceutical type, that was for sure. Die Droge must have hired thugs to intimidate them, hurt them. As her mind grasped the truth, she could feel the hysteria rising in her soul and creeping through her entire body.

"Goodbye, Becca. I love you."

She crumpled to the floor, sobbing. "No!"

The man holding a gun to her grabbed her mobile, dropped it on the floor, and stomped on it with his boot.

CHAPTER 21

Robin's head throbbed with pain as he tried to focus his eyes on the statement Die Droge was forcing him to read to Scotland Yard. He'd already told them he was lying and needed to recant his previous statement. His whole body felt twisted. He was not a good liar.

He took a deep breath, ignored the pain in his ribs, and picked up where he left off. "When we found out that the man who may be Becca's father worked for a pharmaceutical company, we saw it as an opportunity to make some money. Not because we're greedy, but because we were completely broke and had no where else to turn.

"We threatened Die Droge that we would go to the press and release our manufactured evidence unless they paid us off. We know it was blackmail, but like I said, we were desperate. The only reason we named Die Droge was that Cameron Allernach worked for them, and we thought he would tell them to give us the money since Becca may be his daughter. We thought it would be pretty easy to finger them since they manufacture drugs and stand to make money off a possible vaccine just like Pfizer and Moderna did with COVID."

"You do understand that you and Miss Ronan can be prosecuted for attempted extortion, possibly even perjury or slander for making false claims against Die Droge?"

Rob swallowed. Not only did Die Droge's narrative make him a liar. It made him out to be a stupid idiot. "I'm just glad we never went to the media." Lord, how he hated this farce. Why was he even doing this? They were going to kill him anyway. Becca, too, from the sound of it. It broke his heart.

He cast his head down, filled with shame and remorse. He didn't know how they could have handled things any better, or differently, but he felt like the whole mess was his fault. And one thing he knew for sure was that he never ever should have gotten Rebecca involved. So what if she'd lost Café Fish because of that ridiculous reporter's claim that her mother got ill off Becca's fisherman's pie. Becca could end up dead. How could he have thought it was worth the risk to take on Die Droge? What was wrong with him?

There's nothing wrong with you.

He jerked his head up to see which of the men had spoken. He couldn't believe either of them capable of such a soft-spoken, caring comment. They were killers. They were sadistic. They were going to hurt Becca.

Stay calm. Help is on the way.

What? His eyes went to the water instinctively. Circling the boat was an army of seals. Faces he would have normally thought of as cute were bent into vengeful lines, rock solid, their thick necks bulging with resolve, their mouths thrust open to reveal sharp, jagged teeth.

Was he dreaming? How had they known they needed to come to him?

We sensed the evil in their hearts. The voice in his head rang to true and clear that he could have sworn the words were spoken aloud.

He saw the seal he believed to be Soren use his flippers to slap the water, directing the other seals to encircle the boat. If he hadn't known how gentle they were, he would have been terrified.

A sense of calm washed over him. The feeling of peace did not extend to Becca, however.

You cannot save her unless you first save yourself. The minute or so in which he communicated with the seals seemed long and intense. In reality, the time passed in a second. It was the seals who put the idea in his head. His instincts told him that he needed to wait until the time was right, so he did. He was still slouched down, his posture defeated, the only comfortable position given the damage to his ribs.

Now! Go! He didn't stop to think about how he knew the time had come, he just went. He used his head as a battering ram and charged the tall man with the gun. He went for his crotch, battering the man's knees with his fists.

He heard the water around the boat erupting into huge splashes.

The agent doubled over and stumbled backwards, completely caught off guard. The gun skittered across the deck. The agent hit the edge of the deck and almost toppled over the rail. Robin lunged for the gun, but the stocky, short man was closer by a good foot. The short man's hand stretched to reach the gun. Robin jumped like he was at a track and field event and landed squarely on the man's hand. The pain in his chest was so intense that he nearly passed out.

"Ouch!" The short man let go with a string of expletives and drew his hand to his side to nurse his wound. Robin grabbed the gun in a move that couldn't have been more precisely choreographed if he'd tried. If there was a God, he owed him big time for this one.

"Stop. Stay where you are. Do not move," he commanded them, waving the gun like a madman.

"Over there. By the ladder. Do what I say or you can take the easy way out and have a swim with the seals."

Both men looked over the edge of the low side wall. The seals put on quite a show. He couldn't wait to tell Becca about it. If she was still alive.

A crack of thunder split the air.

"What the hell was that?" The stocky one cowered.

Robin wondered the same thing. Random, un-forecasted thunder storms were unusual in Scotland. The wind picked up. The waves suddenly sported whitecaps. The storm had come out of nowhere.

In Robin's mind, he caught a vision of Becca on her knees—crying, begging, praying. For him. Another bolt of lightning struck so close to the ship that he heard it sizzle. Thunder cracked a split second later.

"Lord have mercy," the tall man cried. "I'm not ready to die."

And in that moment, Robin became a believer. A strange calm surrounded him as he inched backwards toward the helm. He always watched the weather closely. He'd never been out in a storm—rain maybe, and plenty of the dreich days Scotland was known for, but nothing wild like this one. Did he stay put, try to outrun it, look for shelter near the shore? Lightning was drawn to and usually struck the highest point on the landscape. He knew that much from playing golf when he was younger. He also knew that as long as he stayed in open waters, Sea Worthy may as well have had a bull's-eye painted on its back.

He opened the throttle with one hand and revved the engine to full speed. If he was destined to die today, he might as well do it trying his best to get to safety.

The tall man lurched when the engine caught and surged forward. A sound—was it the seals? Aye. The sound of angry seals filled the air.

Was it Soren's voice coming to him once more?

No. It was his own thoughts bouncing around in his brain, and no wonder, with everything that had been going on in his life.

Why, he wondered, did there have to be so much evil in the world? What possesses some people to believe they can manipulate other people until their lies enable them to grab power and trample their enemies underfoot? Why do these people believe that they deserve to have more money and more power, and to force the rest of us to pay for their evil deeds? What is wrong with them? Do they hate the rest of us so much that they don't care if there are repercussions to their actions? Do they not care what happens to us? Do they value their own needs and wishes so much more than ours that they think it doesn't matter if they have to kill us to get what they want?

He still had the gun on Die Droge's lackeys, although it was getting harder and harder to steer with only one hand with the seas so choppy and the wind so strong.

He saw the stripe of wake trailing behind the boat before he saw the actual vessel. "Help!" He screamed into the wind. And then, "Thank you, God!" He felt exhilarated. He felt devastated. His hard-fought survival would count for absolutely nothing if Becca wasn't by his side.

It was the harbor police. "Rob? Robin Murphy?"

"Here. I overpowered them and secured their gun. I don't know if they have a second one or not."

A few minutes later, the harbor police boarded Sea Worthy swat team style and handcuffed the Die Droge men.

"An agent from Scotland Yard who was on surveillance duty noticed two unknown men boarding your ship. When you took off, they alerted us. We didn't take the time to pick them up and bring them along, so hopefully you can tell us what's going on."

Robin was in an adrenalin haze the rest of the way home. The storm calmed. The sun came out. There was a rainbow. Becca talked about 'God things' happening. This had to be one of them, didn't it?

He could barely contain his anxiety as he pulled close to the sea wall, gave the controls to one of the harbor police and jumped from Sea Worthy's deck to the cobblestone street in front of Café Fish.

"Mr. Murphy, you need to let us handle the situation inside Café Fish. We didn't rescue you so you could turn around and get killed."

So, the element of surprise was no longer on his side. But it didn't matter anymore. He had to save Becca. Nothing else mattered.

#

"Please, God. Keep Robin safe." Becca tried to keep her mind on the Lord, tried to sing praises for answered prayers even though they really hadn't been answered quite yet. That's what faith was all about, wasn't it? She tried to trade her sorrow, her fears, her anxiety for the joy of the Lord.

But a part of her couldn't let go of the urge to fret and stew, and it was while she was doing just that, biting her lower lip and fending off tears, when she finally realized that the only way Die Droge could have known what she and Robin were up to was if Cameron had ratted on them and told Die Droge what they knew.

Her spirits sunk even lower.

"We must leave now," the woman said, not even trying to hide her German accent.

"Where are we going? I want to stay here." If they took her somewhere, how would Robin find her? No. She wanted to stay here until he or the agents from Scotland Yard found her. Of course, if Robin was dead, and her mother soon to be, who would care? Who would miss her? A few of her customers would no doubt miss her meat pies, her bread pudding with caramel whiskey sauce, and some of the other foods they regularly bought, but they wouldn't miss her. She served them. She tried to keep track of their names and remember their stories so she could ask them about their lives and be friendly, but they weren't really her friends. It wasn't her sitting at their table, relaxing, laughing, and chatting away.

Tears sprung to her eyes. Emma's and her family tree had effectively been cut down, sliced clean through with an ax, never to put forth a new sprout. Never to grow any more branches. The end.

She tried to remember to pray. To have hope. To think positive thoughts.

She was praying when the woman manhandled her shoulder, turned her around, and marched her toward the door. She was puffing on a cigarette. Hadn't she seen the No

Smoking sign? The smell made Becca ill. Just what her lungs needed when she was trying to stay healthy enough to avoid getting the virus.

"No smoking!" What did it matter, really? The new owner would probably be a smoker. They'd probably do a gut job on the whole kitchen, the entire dining room – get rid of the paintings she loved and her handcrafted collection of little lambs, and throw away the heavy chintz table cloths she'd sewn to go with the matching plaid centerpieces and runners on each table.

Who would care if the place had a dingy look or a stale, smoky atmosphere? Some of the customers would probably prefer it, be happy she was gone.

The woman threw her cigarette on the kitchen floor just to the left of the stove. Becca watched it smolder. There it was. Her legacy. The first thing people would see when they walked in the door of the abandoned Fish. How sad. Another casualty of the pandemic, whether it be due to health or finances. No one would care which. They had their own troubles. Who could blame them?

The German woman wrestled her into a car, pushing down on her head to make her fit, then slammed the door and locked it from the outside.

In two or three months, no one would even remember who Rebecca Ronan was. If they thought of her at all, they would recall her as one of those passersby who had come into Portree, tried to make her mark, failed, and moved on. She wasn't the first and she wouldn't be the last.

The car careened around a corner and the driver swore. "Just wanted to make sure we're not being followed."

"Where are you taking me?"

"We're off to see your daddy." The man sung it to the tune from The Wizard of Oz.

Great. A musical thug. And Cameron. Just who she wanted to see right now. The traitor.

#

Rob was frantic by the time he ran around three buildings to the alley where he could get to the back entrance of Café Fish. The door was slightly ajar, which didn't bode well. If Becca was safe inside, the place would be locked and bolted.

He stepped up to the door and looked inside. "Becca!" The Fish was full of smoke. "Fire!" He yelled as loudly as he could. "Get help! Becca could be inside."

One of the other shopkeepers came out the back door of their building and yelled that they would get a wet towel.

Robin hovered just outside the door, yelling for Becca, waiting for a towel. He didn't know what to do. He had his mask. Wouldn't that keep him from inhaling smoke? Becca could be dying inside. And the restaurant – if he could get to a fire extinguisher, maybe he could put the fire out before it did too much damage.

He turned his face away from the door and took a deep breath of somewhat fresh air, slipped his mask on and tightened it around his ears. He thought he knew where the fire extinguisher was, so he headed there first, stepping cautiously in case Becca was on the floor. He still hadn't seen any flames, but the smoke was so thick that he could barely see two inches in front of his face.

He saw a flash of red and grabbed the handle of the extinguisher. Now he just had to find the fire. But before he did that, he had to breathe. He rushed outside and tore off his mask. He coughed and coughed.

The shopkeeper from next door handed him a wet towel. "Use this when you're ready to go back in."

He grabbed the towel and started back toward the Fish. He prayed. He ran.

"Becca? Becca? Can you hear me?" He listened. He heard sirens and yells, but he didn't hear Becca. And then he saw the flames, on the floor by the ovens, licking at the tiles, tiles covered with a thin film of kitchen grease. He emptied the extinguisher. He almost had it now. But he had to breathe.

Still no sight of Becca.

A fireman appeared in the corner of his sight, muffled by the smoke, the surreal reflection of the fire in the windows. The smoke was clearing.

He started to feel faint. He needed air.

"Go!" The fireman pushed him out the door.

A man in a black suit ran to his side. "Robin Murphy?"

Die Droge or Scotland Yard? At least he had witnesses this time.

The man thrust his badge at Robin. "Scotland Yard. We know what happened on the boat and we know where Becca is. We saw a man and a woman force their way inside the Café, so we planted a tracer in their car. Becca has been taken to a Cameron Allanach's home. Google Earth shows it's not accessible due to a massive gate, fence and security system. We can get in, but it's going to take time."

"I know how to get to Cameron's home by boat. There's no security on the beach, at least not usually." Robin wracked his brain. "I've spotted the place when I was on expeditions. I think there's path from the house to the beach and I'm almost sure I know which one it is."

He started to run back to the boat. He could hear the agents in pursuit. All he could think about was Becca. He didn't think Cameron would let anything happen to her, but then, Becca herself had told him Cameron had said he should have killed her while he had the chance. And who knew if the thugs who had taken her had also taken Cameron into custody? It was possible that Die Droge was retaliating against Cameron because he hadn't immediately told them about Robin and Becca's case against them.

If they didn't have Cameron on their side, Becca could be in real trouble.

His heart thudded in his chest as he eased the boat out of the harbor for the second time that day. Thank goodness they hadn't lost their light. The skies were clear and it looked like a beautiful sunset was building in the west as he plowed his way to open waters.

The agents plied him with questions, talking over the engine and the wake. He answered as best he could. Please, Becca, be okay.

He pulled as close as he could to the small stepping off point and cut the engine. He was still quite a way from the shore but he wanted to let the boat drift in as quietly as possible to give them the surprise advantage they needed.

CHAPTER 22

Rebecca rubbed her knees and tried to get Cameron to look at her. The manhandling Die Droge's thugs had given her had not only given her a horrific headache, it had resulted in banged up knees, elbows and hips. She felt like a lorry had run over her.

Cameron had not once looked in her direction. It was like she didn't exist to him, and it made her want to cry. He also didn't look the least bit sick. Had he even had the virus, or had that whole story been just another lie?

"I demand to know why I'm here." She tried to sound forceful, but no one even looked at her even when she repeated her request in a louder voice.

When she couldn't get them to respond to her, she started watching and trying to listen to what they were saying. They were in opposite corners of a very spacious room, so it was hard to hear. She caught words like "kill", "risk", and "serves them right," which were all worrisome. She got a sense that Cameron was trying to defend her and Robin, but it was probably just wishful thinking on her part. After all, he hadn't even acknowledged her presence in the room.

Maybe he hadn't looked at her because he didn't want Die Droge's henchmen to know that she was special to him. Maybe his nonchalance was an act. If they'd known he cared about her, it could have gone worse for her. And then, she thought, how could things possibly have been any worse than Robin probably being dead and her mother being near death, and her father not caring enough to save her, and probably being the one who had ratted her out in the first place. Tears started to stream down her face.

Well, she guessed it could be worse if they raped her, or burned down Café Fish, or tortured her. Whatever. Did it matter if she was going to die anyway?

The man and woman kept talking in the corner, sometimes arguing. Cameron slammed his fist down on the table. They murmured. They swore. They yelled. It was driving her crazy.

And then it occurred to her that maybe Cameron was trying to give her a chance to escape. Maybe he was attempting to distract the thugs, make them forget about her so she could slip out the way she'd come and hide somewhere on the grounds. There were probably sea caves along the coastline. If she could find the path that led down to the beach, she could disappear pretty easily. The tricky part would be getting out of the house, and from the house to the sea grasses to the thick patches of gorse and heather that would camouflage her movements.

She had to try. What did she have to lose?

Cameron was ranting about something. She inched her way toward the door. The hardwood floors were smooth and slippery. She scrabbled along like a crab in sand. Quiet, she told herself. Smooth and steady. Quick movements might catch their eye. She crept backwards, nearer and nearer to the door.

The conversation died down. They were looking at some sort of a document, or a map. She stopped and slumped her shoulders like she was comatose. Hopefully, if they glanced in her direction, they wouldn't realize she'd moved from where they'd left her.

Cameron gestured and flipped the map over. Sea charts? What were they planning now? Which seals they were going to kill next? Or were they going to release an antidote for the infected fish?

"She's no use to us. The only one who cares enough aboot her to be manipulated by the thought of her being in trouble is Robin, and he's dead." Cameron's voice resounded through the room.

"We can't just let her go. She knows too much." Thug number one. The man.

"She could identify both of us. I'm not going to let that happen." The woman.

She inched a few feet closer to the door. She had to get away while they were still just talking about killing her and not actually doing it.

Her rump hit the threshold. Almost there. In a second, she was out of the great room and in the foyer. There was an oriental runner in the entry. It made creeping harder. Once she was out of their sightlines she could make a run for it. If she was quiet, they wouldn't know she was gone until she had disappeared down the side of the bluffs and out of sight.

She stood as quietly as she could, no small feat given her aches and pains. She tiptoed to the door, slipped it open, and closed it behind her with one gentle motion. And then she ran. It hurt like hell, but she ran as though her life depended on it, understanding for the first time what the phrase meant.

Help me, Lord Jesus, she begged. The ground began to drop off under her feet, and she slid in what felt like a combination of loose sand and pebbles. A tall strand of sea grass slit her palm open when she tried to slow her descent, but it didn't matter. She was alive, and she wasn't being followed—yet.

She focused her eyes on the path and hoped it was a direct route to the sea. It was almost dark and the clunk on her head had made her vision blurry. She didn't want to run straight off the edge of a cliff and end up in the sea, or lying on the beach with a broken back.

A sea bird of some sort took off from the grasses and she winced, hoping she hadn't disturbed a nest. Please God, save me. Please! She didn't even know why she wanted to live, but she did.

She slid down another embankment. At a slower speed, the path would have been just lovely, but she was going way too fast to be safe.

That was when she heard voices. Quiet voices. Were they the whispers of someone close at hand, or loud voices, quiet, because they were coming from a distance?

She crept along, step by quiet step. It almost sounded like Robin. She probably had a concussion. Tears started to slip down her cheeks again, the dust and sand turning them to a wet, gritty paste.

She crept, crab style, down the hill to the shore. Cameron probably had security guards posted on the beach. She was getting tired. The boost of adrenalin that had catapulted her out of immediate danger had faded and she could feel herself crashing. Falling. Fast.

And then she saw him. Robin's ghost, calling to her. "Come to me. We'll be together for all eternity. Let me take care of you. It'll be all right."

She heard screams behind her. "She's gone."

"Don't let her get away."

"We're losing our light. Find her! Now!"

She tried to roll from the path to the underbrush on either side of the trail. Spiny thorns from the gorse jabbed into every exposed soft spot and some covered spots, too.

Robin's ghost was with her once again. "Can you walk? Follow me! I'm anchored just offshore. Only a few more feet to go. Come on! You can do it!"

"Robin?"

"Yes, sweetheart."

"I love you. I wish you hadn't died."

"I'm not dead. I'm right here, with you."

She tried to focus her eyes. Everything was cloudy and dim.

Robin's ghost reached down and picked her up. She was being jostled and she hurt. She buried her head in Robin's arm and let the tears flow.

"Faster! They're coming!" A voice she didn't know sounded in her ear.

"You go ahead. We'll hold them off. We're armed. You're not. Just take care of Becca. We can handle Die Droge."

"I don't want to leave you."

"Just get on the boat and get ready to launch. If we're not there in two minutes max, take off. Get Becca to safety. Be safe."

Robin's ghost didn't say anything. She could feel the momentum of running through the sand, if such a thing was possible. She heard gunshots, yelling.

"It's going to be okay. I promise you. We're going to be okay."

#

Robin tried to ignore the gunfire and ease the boat away from the shore as quietly and unobtrusively as possible. The lights remained off, but only because he couldn't risk it. He knew the area fairly well. There were a few rocks he needed to avoid, but there was just enough light glowing in the west that he hoped he could use his instincts to dodge them.

He'd laid Becca on a blanket at his feet. He didn't know the extent of her injuries, but he hadn't felt blood when he ran his hands over her. He hoped she was just sore. She looked like she'd been beat up pretty badly.

He tried to get a grip on the anger that was seething in his heart. He felt the same way he'd felt a few weeks ago when he'd found the slaughtered seals on the beach. He could kill Die Droge's evil decision makers.

That's when he decided he was taking Becca to the island. She wouldn't be safe at hospital. Who knew how deep Die Droge's hands reached? Knowing the damage they'd inflicted on her body, they would assume that's where she'd been taken. And they wouldn't be afraid of contracting the virus, because they probably had an antidote.

He coughed and the smell of burnt wood filled his lungs. He couldn't take her to Café Fish. He wasn't about to spend the night on the boat, a sitting duck, bobbing in the water, No. There was no way he was taking her back to Portree... not until things calmed down. Not until they had somewhere safe to go.

He glanced back at the shoreline and tried to gage how far they were from Cameron's compound. The lights still twinkled brightly, but they were tiny pinpoints, growing smaller by the minute. He thought about circling around and trying to pick up the agents from Scotland Yard, but he had to make Becca's and his safety a first priority. They could call for back-up. There were plenty of other boats and plenty of policemen.

He scanned the sea. They were clear of any hazards now, but it was almost completely dark and he needed light. He switched the first of the lights on and let his eyes adjust. He still didn't want to draw any more attention to him than he needed to. He didn't have a lot of nighttime navigation equipment on Sea Worthy. He didn't do evening excursions. What was the point? You couldn't see dolphins or whales or sea eagles in the dark. His vessel wasn't set up for or meant to be a party boat.

What a mess. He reassessed his location and put the boat on auto pilot so he could check on Becca.

"Robin?" Becca moaned when he touched her. Poor thing. "Where are we?"

"We're on Sea Worthy. You're safe now. Just relax if you can. You need to rest."

"Are we in heaven? All I can see is a blinding light."

"It's the lights on the boat. The sun has gone down." He turned her head as gently as he could so the light wouldn't hit her in the eyes.

"I remember."

She didn't say anything for a few minutes. He rubbed her arm, redirecting his movements when she winced. How could Cameron have stood by and let this happen?

He had no phone, no way of knowing what time it was, but he thought they were getting close. He alternated between trying to navigate through the dark waters and checking Becca, caressing her cheek, even in her confusion, letting her know she wasn't alone.

And then he heard a voice inside his head. *You're almost home.*

He should be used to this by now, but it would never feel commonplace. How did they do it? Could Becca hear them, too?

No. She's not one of us.

"Us?"

You don't know?

"Know what?" He felt a flush wash over him. Was he talking about him or Becca?

You're one of us, Robin. You have Selkie blood.

He stood still and silent as a standing stone. He'd joked about it, thought about it and dismissed it. He'd let Becca tease him about it. He'd never really believed it.

Soren's voice was too clear to exist only in his imagination. It was sincere. *We are brothers by blood.*

"Brothers in spirit," Robin said aloud. "And by blood."

Robin could see the dim outline of the island just to port. The sound of the waves lapping against the hull changed in intensity as the water grew more sheltered, more shallow.

"Robin?" Becca stirred, tried to sit up. "Who are you talking to?"

"Just rest, Becca. We're going to my island. It's safe here." But even as he spoke, he remembered. Death. Carnage. Suffering.

The voice in his head told him he needed to go to a different beach. If the urging came from Soren or Shelagh, it was as though they could read his mind. But my shelter is here, he argued with himself.

His mind supplied a vision of a new shelter. Was he to build it? Was it already waiting for him—them? Robin followed the path of the newly risen moon through the shallow waters as though by instinct. When they reached the shore on the far side of the island, he could see a path rising up from a rocky outcropping that would hide his boat once he'd anchored it.

He went through the motions of preparing the boat for a night of rest. When he returned to the helm, Becca was sitting up and watching him.

"Are you alive?" She looked hopeful, doubtful, very confused.

"Very."

"You're not a ghost?"

"No."

"Is this heaven? It seems so real." Becca looked as dazed as he felt.

"It is real, and it is heaven—but only in an ethereal sense."

"You're confusing me."

"Can you stand?" Robin reached for her hand. "Heaven can wait for another time. We're here on earth, and we've got work to do. But first, we need to make sure you're okay."

"My head hurts, that's all."

He heard her take a deep breath.

"Well, a few other places hurt, too."

"Just go slow. I'll help you."

A few minutes later, they were on the beach. The moonlight illuminated a gauzy tent that looked like it could be a luxury glamping destination. He guided Becca inside, where silky soft blankets and a down comforter awaited. There were clusters of seals sleeping in pockets of sand several yards away, their well-padded bodies quivering with great depths of sleep. The stars were just starting to come out, first in the east, and then, overhead.

Becca gripped his arm. "It's beautiful."

"Yes. Heaven on earth."

CHAPTER 23

Becca opened her eyes and saw blue sky peeking through strips of filmy white fabric. She could feel Robin next to her, hear the soft sounds of his breathing. Everything finally seemed right with the world—until she moved.

"Help me, Jesus."

Robin stirred, rolled over to face her, and snuggled up to her, all with his eyes closed.

She lay still for another few minutes, then tried to move her legs. "Ouch."

She whispered it, but the pain was truly scream-worthy. Her lower back hurt. Her hips and her side were so stiff and sore she could hardly stand it. She felt blissful when she lay still. She would have stayed there forever, basking in the warmth of Robin's body, not moving, except that she had to use the loo.

"How are you?" Robin's voice was soft and smooth, content-sounding.

"I hurt all over when I try to move. I'm not sure what will happen when I actually do."

Robin lifted himself up on one elbow. "I need to use the loo, such as it is. Shall I bring you anything? Food? Water? Something off the boat?"

"I need to go, too. Maybe a stick I can use as a cane?"

"That bad, eh?"

"Sorry."

"Nothing to be sorry aboot. Do you feel like you need to be in hospital?"

"Maybe. No. I'd like to try to tough it out."

"Any signs of internal damages?"

"Not really. It feels like strained muscles and ligaments and tendons for the most part. Maybe some bruised ribs."

Robin ran a hand down her arm. "I'm so sorry you got hurt."

"I'll survive."

"I'll help you find a place to take care of business without having to walk all the way back to the boat."

"Thank you." She watched as Robin got up, then reached out to give her a hand.

"Tell me if I'm hurting you. Or if there's anything I can do to make it less painful."

"I wish I knew what to tell you," she said, taking Robin's hand and trying to stand.

"When we come back, maybe I should spot check you— you know, to assess any possible injuries." She would have taken him seriously if she hadn't seen his wink.

"I suppose I'll have to take my clothes off so you can do a thorough inspection."

"Well, obviously," Robin said. "And, I imagine I'll have to run my hands over certain parts of your body to make sure there aren't any telltale lumps or bumps."

"Of course."

Robin smiled broadly and she managed a wee one, too. The absurdity of the situation helped her through the pain of getting up and first walking. She wondered later if that had been his intent or if Robin really wanted to see her naked.

"I was serious about checking you over," Robin said nonchalantly. Could he read her mind?

"You must hurt almost as badly as I do." She reached over and took his hand.

"Just on the inside." He squeezed her hand—very gently.

"I thought you were dead. It killed me to know that you were in trouble and that there was no way to help you."

"But you did! You rescued me before they could kill me!"

He kissed her, and ripples of well-being, zings of pleasure drifted through her body.

"I thought you were a ghost when I first saw you on the beach. I thought I'd lost you forever, and then, there you were." She shimmied a little closer.

"I really do think I should feel your ribs to see if there are any loose ends."

"Okay." Her voice sounded shy and bashful, but that was okay. It was how she felt. She slowly lifted her shirt until her torso was bare.

She heard Robin take a ragged breath. "You're beautiful. But you've got bruises in every color of the rainbow cropping up." He was silent for a minute, but she could feel his eyes roaming over her chest. "I'll try to be gentle."

"Thank you." The second she felt his fingertips floating over her rib cage she felt such a surge of pleasure that her hips rose from the blanket. She felt like she was going to dissolve.

"Did it hurt?"

"No! It felt good. So good."

"I don't feel anything abnormal. I'm glad I could help to reduce your pain levels. Maybe I should check for injuries in a few other places."

She wanted to say, 'Yes. Maybe you should check my breasts,' but the shy part of her won over any bravado she'd been feeling.

"Maybe here." Robin teased at the bottom of her bra, then ran a single finger up the peak.

"Oh. That feels good." She gulped. "It's amazing how a little pleasure can make the pain go away. It's simply blissful. Of course, I have nothing to compare it to, since this is the first time you've…Oh, Robin!"

"I thought I'd lost you." He ran his finger just beneath her panties, skimming the very top of her mound, working his way down like he was following a crisscross path that wound down a mountain, going lower and lower.

The pleasure was indescribable. She moaned. Why had she wanted to wait for this? Why hadn't she been experiencing this feeling at every opportunity?

Robin took a deep breath. "If I learned anything from what happened yesterday—heck, what I've learned from living in the new world of pandemics—it's that we never know what tomorrow brings, whether or not there will even be a tomorrow."

She gave into the sensations. "This could be our only chance to be together. If I die tomorrow, I want you to have this memory."

"And I want you to know that I love you. I love you, Becca. All I want is to make you happy, keep you safe, be with you." He touched her in ways she'd never imagined, and she knew that no matter what tomorrow held, she would always treasure this moment in time.

#

Robin nursed the fire along until it was hot enough to cook the eggs he'd had in the galley of Sea Worthy. The cast iron frying pan was well-seasoned, but he wished he had some butter or bacon grease for flavor. What he did have was a tin of Stornoway Black Pudding. It was more than a little intimidating cooking for a chef as talented as Becca, but he got the feeling she appreciated everything he was making, even if it wasn't quite up to her usual standards at the Fish.

He flipped the eggs to bring them to the perfect over easy for Becca, and eventually, to well done for him. He'd prepped the black pudding before he started the eggs, so the slices were ready to add to the pan to warm through.

It had been three days since they'd escaped from Die Droge's clutches. The cove was feeling more and more like home. For him, living off the grid was nothing new. Sure, they'd been roughing it a bit, but they weren't exactly shipwrecked with no hope of rescue in sight. The boat had all of life's basic necessities, including a shower.

Sleeping with Becca in the little tent on the beach had been especially idyllic for him—and from all accounts, for Becca, too. The island had been his second home for quite some time—having Becca there made it just right.

He knew it was not quite as perfect for her. Becca was still adjusting to the art of relaxing and having more free time than she knew what to do with. She'd been so stiff and sore the first day that simply going down to the boat and getting showered had occupied her for hours. The second day, they'd made a sand castle, walked along the beach, and made dinner over the open flames. They'd even gone beachcombing and found some bits and bobs for souvenirs. Becca, who was still hurting, would point at the sea glass, pebbles and sea shells she discovered, and let him bend down to retrieve them.

Although her bruises were still pretty colorful, Becca seemed to be feeling more and more spry with every day that went by. He took her being antsy as a good sign.

He slid two eggs and two slices of black pudding on each plate just as Becca was coming out of their tent. She hugged him from behind. "Happy as I've been with you here on the island, you have to remember that I still own a restaurant. I have customers, and bills to pay, and a cooler full of food going bad, and I'm not even sure the back door is locked. I know you said the fire damage isn't bad, but I'm eager to see the place for myself and get on with airing things out and repairing any damages. There's nothing I'd like better than to stay here with you forever, but duty calls."

"Well, winter will be here one day soon, and we'd have to go back to Portree anyway." He smiled. "I know you're right."

Becca's face took on a serious look. "Scotland Yard has probably put out an all points bulletin by now. And I don't know if my mother is dead or alive. I can guarantee the mail is piling up, my food delivery is scheduled to be dropped off tomorrow, and I'm curious to find out what's happening with the investigation. Aren't you?"

"You can take a girl to Paradise, but getting her to forget her troubles and enjoy island life is a whole other thing."

She laughed. How he had grown to love the happy sounds Becca made when they were talking and swimming, and… especially those sounds. He had never felt so content.

"So we'll leave first thing in the morning?" He wasn't looking forward to returning to reality, but he knew there was no escaping it. At least they wouldn't have to deal with Cameron. Now that Scotland Yard was on to him—he was very likely in jail—the man couldn't come between Becca and him anymore.

Becca nodded and took her plate. "One more night of tropical bliss, and then we sail off into the sunrise."

Well, he was going to say, Scotland isn't exactly tropical, although its white sand beaches and aquamarine blue waters made it look like the tropics—until you took a dip in the chilly, north Atlantic waters.

But Becca was still talking and as usual, way ahead of him. "The first thing we need to do is to get new mobiles. If the agents from Scotland Yard were able to retrieve them, I suppose it's possible to transfer the memory cards to new phones, but I've heard sand is not a mobile's friend."

Such a mystery this woman was: so soft and sweet and vulnerable one moment – all business and bluster the next.

He watched as she took a bite of egg and a wedge of black pudding and ate them together. "I'm fully expecting I'll have to repopulate my entire contact list, and in some cases, that's not going to be easy."

"Your suppliers should be easy enough to Google."

"I wish I had written down Cameron's number instead of just punching it in the mobile. Nothing I can do aboot it now." She sighed.

His temper flared. He tried not to make his displeasure known, but she planned to contact Cameron? What the flipping reason for?

"He's probably in jail. Can't you just go see him, or aren't they allowing visitors because of the pandemic?" The pandemic Cameron helped bring about, he wanted to add, but didn't. She could probably detect his cynicism even though he'd not expressed his true thoughts.

She didn't start an argument. Not this time. She just looked at him with sad eyes and said, "He could well be my father. I can't just abandon him."

Why not, Rob wondered? He'd done it with his family. If it weren't for his nieces and nephews, whom he dearly loved, he would have made the break with his brother complete years ago.

"Let's not ruin our last day on paradise talking aboot Cameron. Even when we get back home, our first thoughts need to be to get the Fish cleaned up and reopened, and for me to book some expeditions. Can we at least agree on that much?"

He saw the dashed look on her face. Maybe she'd thought sleeping together would bring their thoughts totally into synch. He wished it had. He supposed it wouldn't hurt him to put his new belief in God to good use and talk to him about forgiveness and how best to achieve it, but to be honest, he wasn't in the mood.

They spent the rest of the day cleaning up the beach, preparing for their departure, and fixing dinner. They'd always worked well together, but today, there was a chill between them that hadn't been there before.

Give her time. After not having had a single Selkie dream or waking up on the beach naked and wet, it was as though Soren's voice popped into his head out of nowhere.

You're the one who's most important to her. You always will be, but she's the kind of woman who wants it all. Was that Shelagh's soft, velvety voice?

He started to think. It was exactly the way he would have described Becca. The way she was was the very reason she's had such success with Café Fish. One day soon, he could see Becca juggling their home, their bairn—or two or three—and a thriving business as well. Because she wanted it all.

And she'll have it, unless you try to rein her in and end up ruining it. Where did that come from? Soren? Or was it God talking to him—like a message from the Holy Spirit? His heart leaped into his throat. Was Becca pregnant? Was that even possible? Could it happen the first time you…?

Just let things be as they will.

"Thank you," he whispered.

"For what?" Becca looked at him, her eyes soft and misty.

He snapped back to reality. "Um, for getting the water on to boil so we could do the dishes."

"Thank you for making breakfast and dinner."

"I love you, Becca."

"And I love you."

That night, as they lay spooned in each others arms, and then, made love, their passion went all the deeper – despite their differences of opinion about certain matters. Because even paradise wasn't perfect, but after his discussion of sorts with Soren and Shelagh, or God, or whomever was in his head convicting and convincing him of certain things, he realized that loving each other despite your problems was probably as close to heaven as this earthly journey ever got.

CHAPTER 24

Becca shielded her eyes as they drew near to Portree Harbor. The sun was bright, and the colorful buildings along the shore, which included Café Fish, were backlit with light as though they had a secret to share that would soon be lit up for all to see.

In the meantime, the storefronts, still shadowed, were mostly shuttered and closed. It had been so wonderful to be on Rob's adopted island for a few days, where everything was right with the world, and the worries and cares of owning and operating a restaurant were as faded and dim as the harbor. Becca hoped and prayed that the investigation of Die Droge would lead to a cure, a vaccine, or both, so things could get back to normal. She prayed that the virus wouldn't mutate or become more aggressive. She prayed for the health and safety of all she knew—her customers, especially the ones who raved about her food and left her big tips, her mother, her and Robin, the doctors and nurses and essential workers who kept the world going around even during pandemics, the agents who were watching out for them, and for her father—if he was her father—but even if he wasn't.

Robin pulled up to the sea wall in front of the Fish. She assumed his reserved spot still stood. He let her step off while he secured the anchor and locked up the boat. They both had masks at the ready for the first time since their island adventure, and she pulled hers over her mouth and nose before she exited the ship. Robin had refueled Sea Worthy before they came into Portree so they'd be ready to go again if some other danger erupted. Lord, how she prayed this was the worst of what would come.

Her plan was to check on the Fish, make sure it was secured, and relieve her curiosity regarding how bad the damage to the interior was. She was halfway to the alley when her least favorite reporter stepped out from the narrow walkway between buildings.

Aggie didn't even attempt to wipe the smirk off her face. "Well, if it isn't the diva of the news media. Where have you been hiding, Little Miss Becca?" She motioned to a camera crew in an auto across the street, presumably waiting to pounce. "How appropriate that it would be me who found you first. Don't forget you owe me big time." She spoke under her breath, in a threatening voice, which Becca was sure would be all sweet and syrupy once the cameras were turned on.

Becca tried to muscle her way past Aggie to get to the Fish, but she was still incredibly sore when push came to shove, and Aggie was stronger than she looked.

Aggie motioned for two of her cohorts to stand on either side of Becca, effectively pinning her to the wall, and nodded at her cameraman to start filming. "The news media is all over the story of Rebecca Ronan and Robin Murphy's daring escape from Cameron Allanach's gated beach house north of Portree. I'm pleased to have Rebecca Ronan here with me today for an exclusive interview and the answers we've been looking for. Rebecca? Can you please tell us what connection Die Droge has to the pandemic, and why you've been withholding this information from the public?"

"I have no comment. I did not grant this interview. I'm being bullied into it."

Aggie's face went livid. She made a motion to cut the tape. When she was assured that filming was stopped, she turned on Becca.

"Don't even think aboot trying to screw me out of this story, Becca Ronan. I'll have your wretched little restaurant closed down in minutes and your sorry butt thrown in jail for murdering my mother."

"Your mother has died?" Becca's insides turned to mush.

"Two days ago, whilst you were hiding from the world doing who knows what – probably having a little love tryst."

"That's enough!" Robin burst onto the scene and took Aggie's microphone from her. "Are you okay, Becca? Do you want to talk to Aggie right now?"

"No. I do not." She needed to find out if her own mother was dead or alive. She needed to see Café Fish, to make sure her brainchild was okay.

"Aggie. I suppose you'll do what you will, but Becca will not be appearing on your broadcast, you will not quote her, and if you hassle her anytime soon, we'll be calling not only the local police, but Scotland Yard to have a chat with you. Do you understand?"

Robin took Becca's arm – gently, he knew how many bruises her shirt was hiding – and made a path through Aggie's vulture-like crew to get to the back door of the Fish. She had a feeling that Aggie was filming their retreat, and walked over the rough cobblestone pathway as fast as she could. The door to Café Fish was closed and locked. Her keys would be inside, in her purse, if it was still there. Thankfully, she'd hid a key some months ago just in case. She retrieved it, no doubt still being filmed, and unlocked the door.

"No worries," Robin said. "We'll find a new hiding place. Or change the locks. Or both."

They slipped inside and bolted the door before Aggie and company could force their way in. Home, Sweet, Sooty, Smelly Home.

"Oh, Robin."

She felt his arms trying to steady her as she started to fall.

"I'm so sorry, Becca."

#

Robin had never felt so conflicted in his life. Becca was hell-bent on seeing Cameron—by herself. It went against every grain of his body to let her walk into the lion's den with no one there to protect her.

"I was afraid he would be in jail by now," Becca admitted.

He'd been hoping Cameron would be in jail by now.

He said, "The agent from Scotland Yard says charges are pending. Cameron evidently claimed he was being held hostage by the thugs from Die Droge just as you were – that he only played along with them to help you get away."

All of that would have been fine if Robin hadn't been so sure that Cameron was lying. He just couldn't trust him. If they could somehow guarantee that Cameron would be alone, it would be one thing, but how could they be sure Die Droge hadn't sent more thugs to hurt Becca? Cameron had a staff – who's to say they weren't Die Droge operatives posing as drivers, cooks, or housekeepers?

"How aboot this?" Becca turned her long-lashed eyes on him. "If we go by boat like we did before, then they can't use the gate to lock us in and we can make a quick getaway if we need to."

She was wrong on so many levels that he couldn't comprehend how oblivious she could be. Becca was one of the smartest, most astute women he knew – except when it came to Cameron.

"No, Becca. It's not safe. For one, they have guns."

She started down another path of equally ridiculous reasoning.

"No," said Robin. "The only way I'll even consider letting you meet Cameron is if it's in an undisclosed location, a safe place. I have to be there. And the authorities will be notified of the meeting in advance."

She straightened her spine and looked at him defiantly. "You won't LET me meet Cameron?"

"Okay. So I shouldn't have used that word."

"I'm glad you care enough aboot me to want to help." Her voice took on a wee bit of warmth.

"How aboot we see if Cameron will meet us at the park again?"

"No. I'm sorry, but I don't want to go to the Lump or see the watchtower ever again."

He tried to think of a neutral space, somewhere where help could be nearby. "What aboot James' kirk?"

"Do you think he'd let us use the sanctuary?"

"It's open to the public. Who says we have to ask?"

Becca's face scrunched up like it did when she was thinking really hard. "Fine. I think I'll feel safer at a kirk than I would anywhere else."

"Good. And we won't tell Cameron where we're meeting until aboot a half hour before."

"Thank you." Becca's eyes were misty again.

Robin found himself reacting in a way that was totally foreign to him. Is this what true love felt like? He'd been thinking a lot about the time they'd spent on the island. It hadn't occurred to him until last night that he hadn't dreamed of being with the Selkies, woken up wet and nude after a moonlight swim, or any of the other things that typically happened when he was on the island. Aside from the brief feeling that he'd somehow been connected to Soren and Shelagh, he'd been totally focused on Becca. He wondered if that's how it would be from now on – and if Becca and he would eventually develop the kind of extra-sensory communication skills that he shared with the Selkies.

"Robin? This isn't aboot Die Droge. I just need to find out once and for all if Cameron is my father."

"And what if he is?" Robin thought it would be a stretch to go from inconclusive to yes, but he certainly didn't understand all the intricacies of genetic testing.

"If he is, and if my mother lives, then I'm going to encourage them to forgive each other and be together."

Robin wasn't sure how he felt about that. Would he be okay sharing family holiday celebrations with Emma and

Cameron?

"And if he isn't your father?"

Becca looked like she wanted to cry. Did she really want Cameron to be her father that intensely? And if she did, was it because she felt that strongly about Cameron, or did she want him to be her father simply because he wasn't a Selkie, the lesser of two evils? He still hadn't told Becca what Soren and Shelagh had told him about his Selkie origins. Maybe he shouldn't.

"You know," Becca said, "I looked at the seals when we were on the beach, and I mean, they're cute. I love their long eyelashes, and their faces have such personality." She hesitated. "But they look more like cocker spaniels than they do humans. I mean, I'd love to have one for a pet, and I know you feel close to them, but I just don't feel a connection. I can't imagine my mother having a relationship with one of them. I can't imagine having a relationship with one of them."

One of them. Well, that answered that question, didn't it? Becca would rather have a creep like Cameron for a father than a Selkie.

#

Robin sat on a hard pew behind a velvet curtain. He was hiding out in the chancel. If he hadn't felt so uncomfortable, he might have been inspired to sing. When he'd sung in the children's choir as a boy, he'd never felt a thing. Now, having opened his heart to God, he at least felt a little joy at being in God's presence. But that didn't mean he was happy. Mostly because Becca's words about Selkies kept echoing in his ears.

He leaned back as far as he could, given the short wooden plank seating, and listened as Cameron greeted Becca, then asked how her mother was doing.

"She's actually doing a little better. For the first time, I feel hope that she might make it."

"I'm sorry," Cameron said. "I never meant for her to get

caught up in this insane mess."

"I'm just sorry she passed it along to you." Becca's voice was soft and quiet. She was probably hoping Robin wouldn't hear her apologizing for Cameron catching a virus that wouldn't exist if it wasn't for him.

Rob stifled his reactions and vowed to give Becca a chance. He didn't understand her reasoning, but he hadn't lived her life, or walked in her shoes, so he knew he shouldn't judge.

"How have things been going with the investigation?" Becca's voice was a little louder now. She knew Robin would approve of this line of questioning.

"I've been treated fairly because I'm cooperating with the police. They've got 24 by 7 protection in place in case my colleagues at Die Droge attempt to do me in, but other than that, no worries."

"It's quite a mess, isn't it?" Becca sounded like she didn't know what to say next.

"So, one of the reasons I agreed to see you," Cameron said, "is that I may need to relocate in a bit of a hurry if things get, um, any more tense."

"I understand."

"Becca, I've heard from the Ancestry people, and it does appear that I'm your father. Which delights me no end – but I'm not going to give you a hug. Let's maintain our two-meter distancing protocols and just say I couldn't be happier. I'm proud to call you my daughter."

Robin tried to peek through the curtains where they came together in the corner, but he didn't dare risk it. He willed himself to stay still, no matter how he would have liked to see Becca's face. He flicked on his mobile and hoped the light didn't shine through the velvet where it was nearly threadbare.

He touched the icon for Ancestry's website and went to Becca's Family Tree. He'd set up her family tree as a subcategory on his own page, partly for privacy, and partly to make it easy for their kids to keep up the research one day. A wee bit fanciful perhaps, but he'd always been a dreamer. He smiled.

He could hear Becca expressing her delight. His smile faded. Well, she'd gotten her wish. She wasn't one of those, those seal folk. No clouding of her lineage with odd, Selkie bloodlines.

Cameron spoke once again, assuring Becca that one day, when things calmed down, they would have to sail away to a Greek Island where they could really spend some time bonding and getting to know one another.

"There's something else I need to tell you, Becca."

"Yes?"

"I've opened an account for you at the Bank of Scotland on Somerled Square."

"That's my bank."

"Yes. So I've paid off your mortgage at Café Fish. You'll still have to work hard, but at least you won't have to worry aboot the stress of a mortgage payment through the rest of the pandemic and any recovery period that may follow."

Recovery period? Who was Cameron fooling? Scotland might never recover—along with every other country in the world who relied on fishing for part of its gross national product. Who knew what the long term effects on the environment might be?

Thankfully, by the time Rob finished his little rant to himself, Becca had quieted down and stopped gushing over Cameron.

"I've also deposited enough cash to renovate your kitchen and the dining area so it's all spruced up when you're allowed to reopen."

Rob listened to Becca say, "Thank you so much. It really needs it after the fire."

Which also wouldn't have happened if it weren't for Cameron. Robin seethed inside until he remembered what Becca had said about recovering her booths with woolens tweeds from the Isle of Harris. Poor kid. She deserved every penny Cameron was coughing up after all she'd been through. Hopefully, as the years went by, she could think of it that way—compensation of a sort, instead of blood money.

He listened with one ear as he scanned Becca's page on Ancestry, clicking absently on a green leaf to search a new clue. He read the notice that someone had been found who was an extremely close match – most probably a parent or a sibling. He looked at the chart, expecting to see Cameron Allanach's name. But that wasn't the name that was listed. He scanned the man's details. David Wilson. Too old to be a brother. He scanned the rest of the profile's information. David Wilson had to be Becca's father. So why on earth would Cameron claim to be Becca's father when he clearly wasn't?

His head started to throb as he scanned one clue after another, learning all he could about the man who was very probably Becca's father. Lord, how he prayed this David Wilson was a good man, morally upright, a truth teller. It appeared that he was married and had two sons. If Becca revealed herself, this could result in her finally finding the family she'd always longed for and never had. It could also be the start of an absolute nightmare for the poor man's family, and if they didn't react well, one more rejection for Becca.

His heart ached for her even as he listened to her desperate words to Cameron. Becca needed the love of a father. She'd said many times over that the love of her heavenly Father was all she needed to be happy on this earth, and maybe in one respect, it was. How he hoped and prayed that one day, she might know her earthly father as well.

He was glad he'd told Becca that he was adopted. She was the only other person who knew, besides his parents, and of course, James, with whom he shared just enough physical features to pass for a real brother. His family had lived on the Isle of Harris when they adopted him, an act of kindness after both of his parents had been killed in a boating accident. He was too little to remember much about his birth parents, so life had moved on with barely a glitch as he grew up. The only lingering turmoil had been caused by James' resentment and active dislike of him, which continued to this day.

He struggled to understand how Becca felt. Maybe he hadn't longed for his parents because he'd known they were dead, maybe because he'd had a replacement in the Murphy's. But Becca had also had a wonderful stepfather from the time she was old enough to remember. 'Twas a mystery to him.

He glanced down at his own family tree and saw a new clue had been added to his profile as well. Because he had limited time, he switched to his DNA matches. A new note beside a highlighted area of the Outer Hebrides read, *'You, and all the members of this community, are linked through shared ancestors. You probably have family who lived in this area for years— and maybe still do. The more specific places within this region where your family was likely from include Uist, where the legend of Clan MacColdrum tells of a union between the founder of the clan and a shapeshifting seal woman. The MacRoons (sons of the seal) are also very proud of their phocine origins. There is no shame in having a Selkie ancestor, and more and more are fascinated by the legends and DNA links that are now surfacing with advance testing.'*

So there it was. Proof of a sort that he was descended from Selkies. Not that he needed to be told what was by now obvious. He could hear Cameron's voice extolling his supposed virtue in cooperating with the police to bring Die Droge's heads to justice. Robin had no proof, but he knew instinctively that Cameron was lying. But Becca was eating it all up, praising him for his altruism and generosity.

Although it appeared that Becca's wish was coming true— that her father was not a Selkie—it remained to be seen what she would think of marrying someone with Selkie genes, not to mention bearing children of Selkie descent.

He sat for a moment and decided that as long as he was in a kirk, even if it had the misfortune of being James' kirk, he might as well pray.

Dear Lord. Please open Becca's eyes. Help her to recognize the truth and know lies when she hears them. And help me, too. I have a lot to learn about You and Your ways. Help me to help Becca, and please help her to realize that having Selkie genes is nothing to be ashamed of.

He opened his eyes and listened as Cameron reassured Becca one more time about how happy he was be her father. No surprise that he was lying, but why? What motivation did he have for letting Becca think their DNA was a match when it clearly wasn't?

CHAPTER 25

Becca listened to Cameron's reassurances that he had done nothing wrong and that he was in the process of providing Scotland Yard with information about Die Droge known only to him that was so exclusive and valuable that he was likely to be voted the Person of Year.

His voice was calm and composed. What he was saying was entirely believable. And then, she had a sudden revelation. Seriously. It was like a light bulb turned on in her brain.

Cameron was lying. Not just exaggerating or embellishing or inflating the truth, but outright lying. Why hadn't she seen it before? Why was she putting herself and Robin through this onslaught of falsehoods?

"So, the medicine that was given to my mother… It hasn't done any good as far as I can tell. So my first thought is, maybe they gave her a placebo just to make sure that Robin and I would keep our mouths shut until they finished their work and were hailed as heroes?"

"I'm not sure what you're getting at, Becca, but if you think I would do anything to harm your mother, then…"

Becca listened as Cameron sidestepped the issue. He had already hurt her mother. There was no reason to think he wouldn't do it again. Becca wanted to think that Cameron had changed, that he was older and wiser and out from under the influence of his father, and the allure of making more and more money. But there was no reason to indicate that it was anything but wishful thinking on her part.

"See, the thought that keeps going through my mind," she said, "is that if they gave my mother a fake drug to keep me beholden to them for a longer period of time, it would give them more time to bring the real cure to market and buy off the press before anyone was the wiser aboot what really happened or how the pandemic really came aboot."

Cameron looked at her with confusion etched in his eyes.

Well, he should be perplexed, the duplicitous slime ball. If she was right, the mainstream media sources had probably been blackmailed, told that if they ran anything but their manufactured story about Die Droge being the hero of the day for finding a cure, Die Droge would withhold the cure and millions more would die before someone else found a treatment that worked.

Aggie. Aggie was a complete brat, but she was at least honest, and so hungry to break a big story that she would tell all no matter what the ramifications. Because Aggie had guts. She was rude and absolutely not politically correct, and not beholden to anyone. Even if none of the big news networks would broadcast her story, there had to be smaller ones that would, local stations that would let people know the truth, which would then leak out on social media until the whole world knew.

And if she was wrong? All Becca knew was that she had to try. Cameron was lying. He was up to his neck in lies. He was still protecting Die Droge, and he was getting ready to fly— far, far away.

She wanted a father, and she wanted the money that Cameron had given her more than most anything in the world, but she had to tell the truth. She couldn't stand by and let Cameron buy her off with his fatherly gift.

"Keep the faith, Becca," Cameron was saying. "Your mother will be just fine. I feel it. And when she's well and the social distancing restrictions are lifted and the restaurants are open, I'll take the two of you out to dinner so we can celebrate her recovery. Robin, too, if you like. There's a 3-star Michelin rated restaurant on the road to Neist Point Lighthouse. I know you can probably cook just as good as their chef can, but wouldn't it be fun to let someone else prepare your dinner, serve you for a change? It'll be something normal—or should I say special—for all of us to look forward to."

"The Three Chimneys? I've always wanted to go there." She stood, gave Cameron the sign for hugs, and picked up her purse. "Walk me out?" She said everything she intended to say, and she didn't want Robin to be trapped in the chancel any longer than necessary. And, she had a good idea that Cameron didn't want to spend any more time in the kirk than he already had. His conscience might start to wear thin if he had to look at the cross any longer than he already had.

"Sure."

A few seconds later she was out in the fresh, albeit chilly air. She almost stumbled over a newspaper as they were exiting, and circled back around to verify what she'd seen as soon as Cameron had pulled his car away from the curb.

Really? Her face was plastered in obscene living color across the front page above a headline that read: CAFÉ FISH OWNER AND HER LOVER WITHHOLD CURE. The byline was Aggie's.

#

The second Becca reentered the sanctuary and motioned for Robin to come out from his hiding place, he pulled the velvet curtain aside and jumped over the railing of the chancel. At the same time, James entered from the far aisle.

"I should have known," James said. "My internet started fluctuating and I heard voices—NOT prayerful voices, mind you, but voices engaged in conversation."

"Ooh," Robin said in his best imitation of James' voice. "Heaven forbid people should engage in conversation in God's house. He's against conversation, isn't he? I mean, really!"

He only stopped because Becca looked embarrassed.

It took James a half a second to jump in and take over. "Conversation, no. Café Fish owner and her lover withholding a cure that could save billions of lives worldwide, yes."

"What?" Robin bored his eyes into James'.

"Don't look at me." James' haughty expression drove him crazy. "Your new lover knows what I'm talking aboot."

Robin had a sick feeling in the pit of his stomach. He turned slowly and looked at Becca. "What is going on?"

"I'm on the front page of the paper. Aggie strikes again."

"You're kidding."

"I'm not. I haven't had time to read the article, but it's not good." She thrust the newspaper in his direction and stepped a few feet closer to hand it off.

"Watch out," James said. "The law says two meters apart even for lovers—unless you're from the same household."

"Let it go, James." Robin turned to Becca. She looked gutted, but if he were to go to her and take her in his arms the way he wanted to, they'd only be giving James more grounds for his derisive comments.

He glared at James. Yes, he and Becca had declared their love—made love—in a unique setting, in a once in a lifetime situation after they'd both almost died. He saw nothing wrong with that. They'd get married soon enough, when he wasn't penniless, and they weren't fighting for their lives and trying to survive a pandemic.

Becca was old-fashioned. Having what she saw as an indiscretion plastered across the front page of the paper was the last thing he would have wished for her or their fledgling relationship. She'd intended to be a virgin on her wedding night. He got that. While he thought what they'd done was a beautiful thing, and the only bright spot in the whole pandemic, he respected her feelings.

"I need to get back to the Fish." Becca looked like she was trying not to cry.

"Thanks for your support, James. Your compassionate nature is such a blessing, and I appreciate the way you've so kindly welcomed Becca into our family. Yes, it's always nice to see you."

He took Becca's arm and led her from the sanctuary. So much for taking refuge in a safe place, a sanctuary filled with love and grace. He wanted to beat on James the way Die Droge had beat on Becca.

He stopped walking when they were down the street a ways from the kirk. "Tell me what happened in there. Before James made a mess of things."

"It wasn't James. It's Aggie who's causing trouble." She frowned.

"I mean with Cameron."

"Couldn't you hear what I said?"

"Yes. And I could tell that you had a change of heart. Saw the light."

She blushed. "You could?"

"I prayed that God would open your eyes to the truth."

"Oh, Robin." Her face flushed. "You did that for me? And God listened. And acted."

"It sure seemed that way to me."

"I need to speak to Aggie." She looked as determined as he'd ever seen her, but what was going through her mind, he had no clue. He hoped she wasn't planning to strangle the reporter.

"I had this idea. It came to me right aboot the time God opened my eyes to the real Cameron, so I think He planted the seed. God, not Cameron."

"Go on."

"This Scotland Yard investigation is going nowhere fast. Who knows what's going on with them? My guess is they're bound by all kinds of legal and ethical protocols which probably leaves their hands tied. And I think the mainstream news outlets are in on it, too. We bought into the whitewash job and the lies we've been told ourselves, until recently."

Sadly, she was right about that.

"If we go to a major press outlet at this point—well, first of all, Aggie's little story has ruined our credibility. And if a reputable source were to run anything but a manufactured story about Die Droge being the hero of the day and finding a cure, Die Droge would withhold the cure and millions more would die before someone else finds a vaccine."

"Right."

"But Aggie has their ears. Much as I hate this picture of me—this headline aboot us—she's captured their attention. You know how popular the rags are in Great Britain. Aggie is their kind of reporter. And, she has no scruples. She's so hungry to break the next big story that she would tell all no matter what the ramifications. She's just arrogant enough to run with the story. She's not beholden to anyone, and she could care less aboot who might get hurt. Even if none of the big news networks broadcast the story, local ones would pick it up. And once it hits the internet – this is so big, it would go viral in hours."

"I think you're right." The more he thought about it, the more he agreed that it was time to bring Die Droge down. And if Soren was right, and another group of scientists was killing seals to use in research to find a cure, then it was doubtful that Die Droge would hold off releasing their vaccine.

It occurred to him that it might be a good idea to check with Scotland Yard before they proceeded but they'd been there, done that, and it hadn't worked out all that well.

Becca started to walk. "So, what are we waiting for? Let's go find Aggie."

#

Becca motioned for Robin to wait. "I'm going to pretend I'm mad at her."

"That shouldn't be much of a stretch." Robin nodded at the headline of the Highland Journal she was holding.

"Exactly." She gathered her emotions about her like a shawl, drawing them in and intensifying them so they would burst loose with a frenzy when she let go.

"Thanks a lot, Aggie!" Becca waved the newspaper in Aggie's face and pretended she didn't see Aggie nod at the camera man to start rolling.

"Do you know what you've done? Not only have you severely jeopardized my business's chance of surviving the pandemic, you've endangered everyone who has the virus or is vulnerable to it."

Aggie primped and looked the part of a much aggrieved victim. "And why is that, Rebecca Ronan?"

"Listen, Aggie. As Robin and I have recently proved, the German company Die Droge Pharmaceuticals, led by Cameron Allanach of Skye, intentionally infected Scotland's fish population to start a second worldwide pandemic that they could then find a cure for, netting billions of pounds in profit."

"This is shocking news." Aggie didn't even try to disguise the fact that she was on tape. She looked directly at the camera and went on to repeat Becca's accusations in a loud, clear voice. "I see you're with local tour boat guide, Robin Murphy. Mr. Murphy, do you have anything to say aboot Ms. Ronan's accusations."

"Unfortunately, Die Droge's greed has cost millions of lives around the world. To the best of my knowledge, what appears to have happened is that the virus they created and released in Scotland's waters mutated, and the cure they planned to release in the earliest stages of the pandemic no longer worked. I'm sure they've been scrambling to come up with a new formula that does work, but I think it's time to shine a light on their deception and share what they know about this virus and the research they've already done, so other drug companies around the world can help to find a cure."

Becca was so proud of her 'lover' at that moment that she wanted to hug and kiss Robin senseless.

And then, Aggie asked Robin another question. "I've heard that Die Droge, and possibly other companies, have been focusing their research on the seal population in the Outer Hebrides Islands. My understanding is that, while the seals consume great quantities of infected fish, which is, in fact, the mainstay of their diet, they show no ill effects from eating the contaminated fish and seem to be immune to the virus. Given the natural antibodies seals appear to have to the virus, do you recommend further testing of seals and other marine mammals to determine if they can be helpful in finding a cure for the pandemic?"

Becca flicked on her new mobile, hit the camera app and pressed video, then record.

Robin turned a sickly shade of green and swayed. "No! I do not condone the killing of seals for any sort of research. Experimentation on any kind of animals has been banned in the UK for years. Why would that be reversed now? It's wrong to kill one species to save another. We all agree on that, or should!"

Aggie smiled in a condescending sort of way. "But surely, given what's at stake, the lives of a few seals is nothing in comparison to the billions of human lives that could be lost as a result of the pandemic."

Robin looked as though he'd been speared.

"Is it true," Aggie continued her assault on Robin, "that you and Ms. Ronan, your lover, and the owner of Café Fish, purposely withheld information from the police in order to save the seals, when bringing Die Droge's travesty to the immediate attention of the police might have saved countless lives?"

Becca pushed Robin to the side. "Right. You can try to blame this whole mess on Robin and me. Die Droge is the one who created this virus, for their own financial gain. No humans or seals would have died if it weren't for them and their devious plan. If you'd concentrate on bringing them to justice instead of trying to ruin my life, you'd be helping a lot of people and saving a lot of lives."

Aggie's bravado faded for a spilt second.

Becca was so mad she could barely breathe. "And that concludes our interview. Which, by the way, I never agreed to, and may not be used without my specific permission."

She was vaguely aware that Robin had taken her by the arm and was whisking her back to the Fish.

Robin slammed the door behind them to keep out the throng that had followed them from the harbor. "What happened back there?"

"Oh, Robin. I'm so sorry."

"It's not your fault."

"What are we going to do?"

"Well, Cameron certainly isn't going to help us."

"Neither is Aggie." Rob rolled his eyes. "I need to get out to the island. I mean, I don't want to leave you, but when Aggie's report breaks, they're going to need protection. I didn't even have the chance to warn them before the first slaughter began. This time, I can tell them what's coming so they can disappear or be prepared at the very least."

Becca sniffed the air. "You make it sound like they can understand you. How are you going to warn them? Bang a drum to warn them off the island?"

She smiled, but Robin just gave her a funny look and didn't say anything. She was just trying to lighten the mood.

"Well, I'd rather come to the island with you if you don't mind. It still stinks like smoke in here and I don't feel safe after what Aggie said aboot us."

"Sure," Robin said. "Let's leave as soon as we get some supplies together and refill the fresh water tanks. We need to call Scotland Yard before we're out of mobile range and tell them that Cameron is a flight risk."

"I'll do it. Robin? I know I've said it before, but I'm so sorry I dragged you into this whole mess."

"I would have been involved anyway. As long as there are seals being slaughtered, I'm bound to try to stop it."

She still didn't understand why Robin was so attached to the seals. It wasn't that she didn't think they were adorable creatures. They were. But Robin was completely obsessed with them. Or so it seemed to her. And really, she kind of agreed with Aggie about that, If it came down to rescuing a handful of seals or saving mankind, what choice did they have?

But of course, she knew better than to say that to Robin. "I need to call the hospital before we leave and get another update on my mom's condition. And I'd like to take a shower before we head out."

"Good idea. I'll do the same so we're leaving with a full tank. Let's try to be ready to leave in aboot two hours so we still have enough daylight to take us home."

Again, she was struck by the fact that Robin really saw the island and the seals that lived there as home – family.

Robin stepped forward and wrapped her in his arms. He felt rock hard, comforting, protective, and snuggly. "Becca? Getting to work with you has been my salvation, both figuratively and literally. Don't ever feel you need to apologize for anything that's happened between us."

CHAPTER 26

After Robin had showered and rinsed out his clothes, he went to his Ancestry page to follow up on what he'd learned earlier. It would take over an hour to refill the fresh water tank, and he intended to put the time to good use. He wouldn't have access to the internet while they were at the island, so he wanted to try to find out everything he could about Becca's probable father before they left.

He tried Googling David Wilson, but there were hundreds of thousands of people with that name. He narrowed his search to those with Scottish addresses, but it didn't help. It was quite common. Besides, who was to say that Emma didn't have a romp on the beach with a tourist from America or a business traveler from Denmark? The Isle of Skye swelled to three or four times its population in the summer months when Becca had been conceived. People from all over the world flocked to Skye in the tourist season.

After almost a year and a half of being shut down, with no tourists, no excursions, and pretty much no income, it was hard to remember how Portree had been when it was swarming with tourists, car parks clogged with buses and vans, restaurants and accommodations so full that people had to circle back to Inverness to find dinner and a room. But that was Skye in non-pandemic times. Becca's father could easily have been a David Wilson from anywhere in the world.

He went back to Ancestry and looked at The David Wilson's family tree. Thankfully, it was public. A shiver of fear ran down his spine. How he hoped, for Becca's sake, that David Wilson was a good man, an honest man – someone who would welcome her into his life and love her the way she deserved to be loved.

Curiosity surged through his veins. Becca's father could be a fisherman, a school teacher, a doctor, a farmer. He could be married. He could be single, a permanent beach bum; he could own a penthouse in New York City.

He thought about Becca's personality traits, the things he loved about her. She was hard working, gentle of spirit, and creative. She was a perfectionist, strong in her faith, loyal, and committed to the people and things she loved. Much as he appreciated Emma's finer qualities, he could honestly say that Becca and Emma didn't share a lot of similarities in their makeup. He knew the whole gambit about nature vs. nurture, that there was a distinction between genetic and cultural influences. But in his mind, if Becca hadn't inherited her predominant traits from Emma even though she had Emma's genes and had been raised in the environment designed by her mother, there was a good chance they'd come from her father.

He held his breath and started to search David Wilson's family tree. Okay. His parents were listed, so he could see that David was born in Wester Ross, and graduated from the culinary program at West Highland College in Portree, where Becca had also gone to college. He slid his mouse to the next tier of ancestors. Wilson's parents were both born in Applecross. Now that he knew where to look for the David Wilson he wanted to know about, he did a little searching on the internet.

David Wilson owned and operated an establishment in Lochcarron called Saelkie's Seafood Bistro. Hmm… Interesting name.

David's parents, Douglas and Melissa Wilson, owned a

garden shop and teahouse in nearby Applecross. At first glance, it seemed like the Wilson family was a group that Becca would fit right into.

He still had an hour and a half before Becca was due to meet him on the boat. He looked up Rod MacKenzie's mobile number and rang him. Rod would know what kind of a man David Wilson was. Maybe he was being a bit overprotective, but he was not about to plunk Becca down in the middle of another Cameron Allanach situation.

#

Becca spent the next half hour going through her cooler and throwing away rotten lettuce, dimpled tomatoes, and black, speckled mushrooms. She threw away three pounds of ground mince, some ham that had turned green, and a container of Mornay sauce that had bits of mold growing on the surface. It broke her heart to waste so much food. It equated to throwing money in the trash bin and she hated it.

While she was at it, she wiped another layer of soot off the glass and stainless doors, handles, and vents. She'd purposely left her shower until she'd finished dealing with the mess, and was she ever glad. Rob had offered to stay and help, but to be frank, she'd needed some time to herself.

She'd started a quick load of laundry before she tackled the cooler, so it was ready to pop in the clothes dryer before she stepped in the shower. She hung her clothes on the line at home, but there just wasn't the space or the time to do it at the Fish. There was so much to think about today, so much on her mind. She checked the mail, paid a handful of bills that needed to be posted before she left town again. No payroll, but she had to file a report assuring the government that she had no payroll taxes to report.

By the time she finished, there was about 60 pounds in her account, which was awful. She simply didn't have time to deal with it.

Almost an hour later, she finally stepped into the shower.

It felt amazing to feel the water rinsing the grime out of her hair. She used her best conditioner to make her hair feel silky and smooth, then buffed her heels and brushed her back. She hadn't felt so clean and fresh in days. Robin might feel just fine after a swim in the sea but she would take a nice hot shower any day, even if it was in the cramped bathroom at the Fish instead of her nicely tiled shower at home.

She didn't want to be a baby, and she appreciated everything that Robin was doing to help her, but she simply wasn't meant to be a boat dweller or to live off the land.

She gathered several tins from her pantry, the last of a pan of caramel shortbread she'd made a week ago, a cheesecake that would likely go bad before she reopened, and a hunk of Clootie Dumpling fudge from Kilted Fudge Company's fudge of the month club she'd signed up for earlier in the year.

She had the fondest, sweetest memories of the time she'd spent glamping with Robin on his secret island hideaway. The experience of making love with him for the first time, surrounded by beauty, under the brightest stars she'd ever seen overhead and the sound of the surf caressing the sand, rivaled her best ever memories. It couldn't have been more perfect. But was it her comfort zone? Her happy place? No. It was Robin's.

Try as she might, she couldn't help wishing they'd spent their first night together in a quaint B&B with a sea view, lush quilts and fluffy pillows, a cozy loveseat in front of the fireplace, and a kitchenette stocked with gourmet hot chocolates, a tin of biscuits, and a custom Charcuterie Board heaped tall with artisan cheeses, cured meats, antipasti, fruits, and other locally sourced delicacies.

She finally sat down to ring up hospital and see how Emma was doing. She knew if something horrible had happened, there would have been a message on her mobile when she returned to civilization, so there was that. But it got harder and harder to ring them again and again, only to hear the same discouraging, "So sorry, dear, but I'm afraid your mother's condition is unchanged."

Her mood plummeted. It was exactly what she'd expected, but she still felt gutted. For a second, she reconsidered her decision to go back to the island with Robin. Not that it would help. As long as she wasn't allowed to visit her in hospital, there was nothing she could do. The best thing she could do was to stay involved with the investigation to make sure a cure was found as quickly as possible.

"Can I talk to her?" Even she wasn't sure where the question came from. Silence. "I'm serious. If someone would be willing to hold the phone to her ear for a few minutes so I could just talk to her—encourage her a little bit—I would be so grateful."

A few minutes later, she was able to tell her mother that she loved her. She hoped it wasn't the last time she'd be able to say the words.

#

Robin glanced at the clock every few minutes. He didn't want Becca walking in on him when he was talking about David Wilson. A few seconds later, he connected to Rod MacKenzie.

"How is Sea Worthy doing? I suppose ye still have nae been out much."

"It's still very slow. I think on top of travel not being allowed, people's perceptions of the sea have changed. It's like they view it as being contaminated because that's where the virus came from."

"It breaks my heart," Rod said. "It's been pretty dire at Lachlan, too. We hosted one local wedding but they were only allowed to have 25 people. Half of their family members dinnae even get to attend. That's been it for the summer."

"I sure hope they come up with a cure soon, but even then, it may take people awhile to warm up to the idea of eating seafood or going on an expedition to enjoy the isles."

"Katelyn says the second the all clear is given, we're going to drive to Skye and have two of Rebecca's Fisherman's

Pies."

"I'm sure she'd be pleased to see you – assuming Café Fish is still open. It's been a rough time for her, too. Her mother is in hospital with the virus and has not been doing well."

"I'm sorry to hear that."

Robin took a deep breath. "Rod, I'm calling aboot something kind of personal—a question I'd like to ask of you, if you'll agree to keep it confidential."

"I'll help if I can."

"I'm calling aboot the owner of Saelkie's Seafood Bistro on the Main Street in Lochcarron. Just interested to know if he's a good guy, honest sort, personable chap, and so on. If you know him or have had any dealings with him, your opinion would be most welcome."

Rod hesitated. Robin hoped it was just curiosity that had his tongue tied in knots, and not some sordid tale he didn't want to impart.

"David Wilson? A heart of gold is what that one has. He's hardworking, honest, well-respected in his field, and very agreeable. I've never heard a word uttered against the man. Everyone seems to like him."

"Great. Thanks, Rod. That's just what I was hoping to hear."

"Once things are back to normal, give us a ring when ye have a free evening. Katelyn and I would love to treat ye and Rebecca to dinner at Saelkie's."

"We could pick you up at the castle and give you a ride into town on Sea Worthy."

Rod laughed in a pleased sort of way. "T'would be a great pleasure to see the grand lass again."

"Then we'll be sure to make it happen—hopefully soon."

He was set to call David Wilson as soon as he ended his call with Rod—strike while the iron was hot—but by the time he'd looked up the number for Saelkie's, Becca was rounding the corner with an overnight bag, ready to be on their way.

He took a second to glance at his own Ancestry Family

Tree while he waited for Becca to get to the boat. It looked like he had another clue or two. To save time, he switched to his DNA matches to see if there was anything new. He'd checked many times before, and he'd never had a single match.

His eyes opened wide. He blinked to make sure he wasn't dreaming, or on the wrong page, investigating somebody else's life. He read the words, Possible 2nd or 3rd cousin, and wanted to dance. He was actually related to someone else in the world!

Becca reached the edge of the dock, so he flipped out of the app and acted like something significant hadn't just happened. He would have loved to share his discovery with her and to find out what he could. He was dying to find out what he could. But he couldn't risk bringing up the topic of Ancestry for fear she would want to check her own matches.

So he kissed her. And he kept his mouth shut. He would tell her about David Wilson when the time was right.

#

Becca tried to relax and not think about how deep the water off the coast of Skye was. Whereas Robin was flying high now that he was back on the water, she'd rarely felt so tense. Maybe it was because she'd just come from the Fish, where she'd left a frustrating situation completely unresolved. She'd tried to cram a week's worth of paperwork and problem solving into two hours, and she'd succeeded in getting an amazing amount of work done in the short amount of time she'd had, but she needed to get back there as soon as possible and finish what she'd started.

Robin said they had another half hour to go before they arrived at 'his' island. Thirty long minutes to think about storms at sea and waves taller than the boat, and the Titanic.

"We'll be there before you know it," Robin said, looking happier than happy.

Lord, how could she be in love with a man who was so at

249

home on a ship when she was terrified of the wind and waves? She tried everything she could to calm down. She closed her eyes and imagined she was watching Jesus walking on the water, with Peter at his side. She imagined her Savior calming the seas on her behalf, while He said in a soft voice, "Do not be afraid." She tried to accentuate the positive, to think about the beauty of the sun reflecting off the water, the blue of the water and sky, the white froth of the trail of the wake, instead of the fact that the boat could go down at any time, leaving her and Robin to drown or be eaten alive by sharks.

"I wonder what's going on over there?" Robin pointed to a small island off to the left. They could see a boat hovering just offshore. He turned in the direction of the ruckus, and as they got closer, they could hear men yelling in a foreign language. Chinese?

"Please, Robin. Don't go any closer. Who knows what this is aboot? The last thing we need to do is to get involved in a—"

"Oh, I think we both know what this is aboot." Robin's eyes were focused on the scene unfolding in front of them. The boat was still at full speed even though they were getting closer and closer.

"No, Robin. Please! There are only two of us! There's no way we can combat—"

"We have no choice."

For a second, she thought she was going to be sick from fear of what Robin was going to do—and from the sight of seals being caught, clubbed, speared, and hauled on board the other ship. It was all in clear view.

"Stop it! Stop it immediately!" Robin screamed, pulling in so close that he could step from one ship to the other. "You have no right!"

Did he intend to board their ship? They were going to kill him. And then they'd have to kill her!

"Robin, please. No!" She clutched at his arm. He ignored her pleas. He was like a wild man. If she'd been scared when they were still at a safe distance, she couldn't begin to describe the emotions she felt when Robin started screaming at the men who were hurting the seals. He was absolutely frantic, driven to insanity, inconsolable.

He started emitting a high pitched squeal that she'd heard seals make. It sounded like a keening sound. It was absolutely unearthly. It scared her half to death. Who was this man? She felt like Robin was a stranger.

The Chinese men—Korean? Japanese?—stared at Robin and stopped what they were doing in shock.

"There's nothing we can do, Robin! Please! Let's get out of here while we can!"

"I'm not leaving until they stop attacking the seals. They have no right!"

The Chinese turned away from the seals and aimed their spears at them.

"They're – we're – we're going to die! Get us out of here before we get killed! You can't help the seals if you're dead!"

A spear zinged past Robin and landed on the deck. "They're just trying to intimidate me."

She knelt on the deck and prayed. She'd never been so scared. "You can't save the entire world! They're seals! Half of them are already dead. They're not worth risking our lives for!"

Robin picked up the spear that had landed on the deck and aimed it at the men on the other boat.

"I'm not backing down. Soren would risk his life for me if the tables were turned. I know he would."

"You need to back away, Robin. This is insane." What could she do except plead with him to understand? "They're already dead! Let them take what they came for or they'll just go somewhere else and kill more seals. The damage is done." She sobbed. "There's nothing we can do."

"I have to try. Why can't you understand?"

The foreign crew hauled the dead seals on board. It was horrible seeing their dead bodies dragged aboard the foreign vessel, their beautiful heads smashed and bleeding, broken and bloodied.

Robin eventually kneeled beside her and fell to the deck as though his strength was sapped. "I'm so sorry. So sorry."

Was he talking to her, or to the seals? She heard the engines of the other boat backing away from them, then leaving. She started to shake. They were both crashing after the adrenalin rush brought on by the attack. She was proud of Rob and she was furious with him. And the bigger problem was that she just didn't understand him. Not at all.

"What do you have against seals?" Robin's voice was shot. Torn, ragged, grief-stricken.

"I have nothing against seals." He was mad at her? He had risked her life—and for what? "I just happen to value my own safety and well-being over theirs. Is that a crime? I'm human. They are not."

Robin moved away from her, like he couldn't stand to be close to her. "Well, what if they were? Maybe they're Selkies. Maybe they're half human. They were being tortured and killed. Would that make you care?"

"Of course I care! I hated seeing them being hurt, dying. It's killing me inside. But I—I don't believe in Selkies."

"Well, I do."

Well, maybe he should go talk to her mother. "You and my mother," she muttered.

"Emma is awesome," Rob snapped. "You don't appreciate her enough. It wouldn't hurt you to take a few rules from her playbook every once in awhile."

Okay. Now she was mad. "What? You want me to go down to the beach every weekend and sleep with whatever man I meet up with, maybe even get pregnant by some fantastical creature that legends are made from?"

"So your mother told you your father was a Selkie. Is that why you hate them?"

"I do not hate Selkies. How can I hate something I don't believe in?"

"You believe in Fairies."

"Maybe. I don't know. I guess I'm open to the idea."

"And how is that different? Again, I'm asking you, what do you have against Selkies? Why can you open your imagination to the idea that there could be fairies, but not Selkies?"

"You really want to have this discussion now? Fine! Fairies are light and bright and airy. They're dreamy and magical. Seals are…dark…wet…slimy things that live in the sea - which terrifies me."

Robin looked completely disgusted.

"Listen. I'm fine with sharing the world with Selkies. They can live in the sea and frolic and play to their hearts content and I can stay on the land where I'm more comfortable."

"If they're not all dead by the time the pandemic is over," Robin said.

"Well, that's a concern we all share." She sighed. Her anger was evaporating, but her opinion was unchanged. "I just don't think they're important enough for you to risk your life, and mine, too. I'm sure they know how to take care of themselves, if they even exist."

CHAPTER 27

Later that afternoon, when they were settled on his island, Robin was still so mad at Becca that he could barely look at her. Well, maybe mad wasn't the word for what he felt. Disappointed? Upset? Sad? He felt a little of each. Becca was so kind and accepting of people, even those who were different than she was—well, with the sometimes exception of the rows she got into with Emma. Why couldn't she understand how he felt about seals? Why was she so flippant aboot Selkies?

It wouldn't be a problem if he wasn't related to the Selkies. He didn't know how many generations his Selkie heritage went back, but it was something he wanted to be proud of and celebrate. Happy as he was to share his beachside haven with Becca, he longed for the days when he had felt one with the Selkies in his dreams and woken up naked and soaking wet after swimming with them all night long. He hated the fact that he felt he had to hide his connection to Soren and Shelagh from Becca.

And there lay the crux of the problem. He couldn't believe that Becca would be repulsed by him, or reject him if she knew what he really was, but he was beginning to wonder.

"I said I was sorry," Becca said.

He refused to answer. Of course, she'd said it. Several

times. But did she mean it? Did she feel it in her heart?

He watched out of the corner of his eye as Becca huffed and walked away.

Part of him wished that Soren and Shelagh would come to them now, reveal themselves so Becca could meet them, experience them in their human form, and get to know them. If given the chance, how could she not love them like he did?

An hour or so later, his stomach started to rumble. They had planned to eat something out of the tins Becca had brought along, but the idea no longer seemed appealing. If she wasn't here, he could fish for his supper. Hopefully his Selkie blood would protect him. At this point, he was so hungry for fish that he didn't care.

"I just found two absolutely beautiful haddock swimming in a tide pool." Becca's voice called out from the other end of the beach. "They look healthy to me." Silence. "I'm willing to risk it – are you?"

He started to walk in her direction.

"We'll just sauté them a little longer than usual to make sure they're done." Becca's voice was relaxed and confident.

"Too bad you can't take them back to Café Fish and make something really splendid out of them." He could almost taste her creamy Haddock Mornay with mashed neeps and tatties.

Becca smiled. "Sometimes it's nice just to have a simple meal. Haddock is so flavorful that it's good on its own."

Five minutes later, his hands were busy cleaning and filleting the haddock, but his brain was still whirling with everything that had happened in the last twenty-four hours, including their run-ins with Aggie and her camera crew and the seals on the next island over.

He could feel Becca's eyes on him as he worked to remove the bones. He pushed his anger to the side. It felt good to be preparing a fish again. He couldn't wait to get a fire built and have a taste.

His hands slowed as Becca started to speak. "So all this Selkie business makes me wonder if every fish, every animal has some sort of sentient spirit—you know, like if a seal can turn into a Selkie, who's to say that a cod can't turn into a codkie. Yet you have no trouble slicing them open and eating them."

Yet again, his insides crumbled. How could she be so insensitive?

He tried to compose himself before he spoke. "First of all, fish aren't mammals."

"I know that, but cows are, and grunters are, and we eat them."

He rolled his eyes. "Can we not talk aboot this before we eat?"

Her silence said more than her words. Again, there was a lot he could have said, but for now, he guessed he wouldn't. He didn't want this to come between them any more than it already had. "Let's focus on the good news. There were no dead seals waiting for me on my island when we arrived, and hopefully, the Chinese crew that's harvesting seals won't drop in on them as long as Sea Worthy is docked here. Hopefully by the time we head back to Portree, they'll have left the area."

Becca's eyes were stony.

"Speaking of your mother," he said, well aware that he was getting in one last dig. "Has there been any change in her condition?" He almost wished he could tell her that he'd been trying to contact her real father, or talk about what he'd discovered at Ancestry, but he couldn't. Not now. As far as trying to defend how he felt about the seals – well, it seemed absolutely pointless at this stage. Hopefully, one day soon, once he told Becca everything, she would be a wee bit more supportive.

They ate their meal in silence. The fish tasted incredibly delicious, disproportionately so, like a first meal after a long fast. He felt full and content when they freshened up in a nearby stream, shook the sand out of their blankets, and got ready for bed.

The sliver of moon that lit the sky, the stars that sparkled above, the tent that gave them privacy was just as gauzy and romantic looking as it had been when they'd made love under its cover. But tonight, there was no snuggling, no whispered feelings, no gentle lovemaking. They lay in the confined space like two rigid surf boards, awkward and stiff.

But when he finally fell asleep, Soren and Shelagh were there. Shelagh was crying. Soren was holding her, telling her that it had to be done.

Soren sounded shaken. *What they need to cure the sickness is found in seals, but the seals' blood won't mix with humans'. My body is unique. My blood will end the sickness and save the humans.*

Shelagh groaned. Robin's heart sank. Soren was planning to sacrifice himself to save humankind.

"No! You can't. I won't let you!" Robin cried out.

You will. Soren sounded so sure. *Becca has the disease. It is growing in her lungs. It is in her blood.*

Robin's emotions spiraled downward in a vast vortex of anguish. Was he to lose all of them? Becca? Emma? Soren?

No. Soren's calm presence started to seep through Robin's panic.

"I can save her then. If I have Selkie blood, then I must also have the antibodies needed to save her."

It's not enough. Becca's body will not accept your gift. My blood is the only thing that will work.

"If all it takes to heal her is a blood transfusion, why do you have to die? Just go to hospital in your human form and let them draw your blood."

Like all of God's creatures, Selkies have a cycle of life. I can take human form but once a year.

"I danced with you and Shelagh on Midsummer's Eve."

Yes, but the day is past, and until it comes again, I can only appear as a seal.

Robin's brain raced ahead. "The virus Die Droge created is very virulent. Billions will die if it is not stopped before then." He could not accept that there wasn't another way. "But if you go in willingly and I help you communicate with the scientists, can't they get what they need without killing you?"

We all know what would happen to me.

Robin felt his mind, his body, his spirit, deflating. He knew awright. They might be able to withdraw the blood they needed to save Becca, and the seal that was Soren might be fine. But once they had a captive specimen, Soren would spend the rest of his life in a cage, subjected to experiment after experiment. And once they determined what he already seemed to know, they would kill him regardless. They would have to get at the tissue they would need to cultivate the vast quantities of antibodies required to save mankind.

A rush of love, gratitude and appreciation flowed from his heart to Soren's. "Please help me find another way."

There is no other.

He thought of Becca. He would do anything to save her if it came down to it. But what Soren was suggesting was unthinkable. "What can I do to help?"

The sooner we do what needs to be done, the better.

Evil forces were at work. It was about the money. It was always about the money.

Soren's thoughts floated to join with his. *I promise you, Robin, that evil will not prevail. No gain will come from their actions.*

Robin had to trust him. He had to believe. His mother had told him many times that plans born out of hatred and bitterness only harmed the ones who perpetuated them. They were destined to fail.

A solution born of love will conquer all and help many.

Rob sighed. He knew Soren was right, but his head felt like it was about to explode from trying to absorb it all.

Soren's tone was quiet but firm. *You must find someone knowledgeable who can be trusted. Show them this beach. The rest of the seals will be gone. You will know that the lone seal that remains is me. Until then, your life will be in danger.*

"I don't think I can do it." He felt sick. The weight of Soren's request was crushing his chest. He felt like he was rising from the water—a great depth of water—gasping for air.

It must be done as soon as possible so they can find a cure.

"What are you mumbling aboot?" Becca's voice cut through the fog.

You must do it—for me. Soren sounded scared but resolute. *You will do it to save the ones you love. It is what any good father would do.*

"Are you okay?" Becca was facing him, propped up on one elbow.

"I'm fine." He was panicked, sweating. "How are you feeling?"

"Now that you mention it, I do feel a little odd. Like I could—" Becca threw back the covers, leaped up and ran from the tent. He heard her retching from where he lay.

Robin looked at the cracks of sky peeking through the framework of the tent. "Oh, Lord. What have I done?"

Becca had been well and good when they left Portree. Was it the haddock? Had the adrenalin rush and subsequent crash ruined her immune system? She'd been fine when they went to bed. But now it was morning, and a whole different... His mind trailed off. It was morning – and Becca was sick.

#

Becca could see herself in the reflection of the tide pool where they'd found the haddock the night before. She looked—and felt—absolutely green. "I am so sorry, Robin."

"No problem. Can I get you anything?"

"Some peppermint essential oil from the nightstand by my bed?"

She watched as Robin's face fell.

"At least you still have your sense of humor. Is it just your stomach that's upset or do you feel any other symptoms?"

She assessed her body, thought about how she felt. "Well, my eyes are a little scratchy but I'm sure it's just the sand. It's a little chillier than it was yesterday. The breeze just moves the sand around, I suppose."

"You think it's chilly?" Robin asked.

"Yes. Why? Don't you?"

"Not really," Robin said.

"I wish I had brought a sweater." She knew better than to assume the weather would stay the same for longer than a half hour. Emma had never been one to chide her about wearing a jacket—just not that kind of mom, but still. She should have remembered to bring a wrap of some sort. She started to shiver a little.

"What's wrong?" Robin was watching her so closely that she felt like a rabbit about to be plucked off the ground by a sea eagle soaring overhead.

"I'm just a little chilly, that's all."

"Do you have a fever?"

"I don't think so. But I feel really..." She ran for the far side of the beach and threw up at the edge of the water.

She clutched her stomach and bent over. "I hurt all over all of the sudden. I feel like I just want to curl up in a ball and die."

"Don't say that!" Robin was close behind. He ran to her side and handed her a canteen with fresh water from the boat.

"I'm so thirsty." She drained the flask and still wanted more. "What's happening to me?"

"I'm not sure, but you're sick, and it's morning, and you know what that means. And just to be on the safe side, I wish we hadn't eaten the haddock."

"You're scaring me."

"You should be scared. You being sick changes everything."

"What does it change? If I'm sick, I'll get better. I'm young and healthy. It's probably just a 24-hour bug. I'll be fine." But even as she said the words, she could feel herself slipping into a fog. Was she dreaming? Had she passed out? Is this what unconsciousness felt like? Was her mother living in an otherworld, a dreamland, as she lay in hospital? Knowing Emma's colorful imagination and free spirit, she could almost envision the wild fantasies her mother was having.

She could hear Robin's voice, but as though it was coming from a great distance. Had he left her?

"I told Soren I wouldn't turn him over to the scientists. I can't do it! I don't care how much he wants me to. I can't. But a baby changes everything. How can I let you and our baby die? Soren is willing to make the sacrifice. Am I to let my stubbornness result in the death of everyone I love and care aboot?"

Wait a minute. There was a baby? Whose baby was he talking aboot? Did Robin have some Selkie child she didn't know about? Had he made love with a Selkie woman on the beach, only to have her bear him a child and then go back to the sea? That's what they did, didn't they? She had heard how beautiful they were, how alluring and irresistible. Who could blame Robin for falling under her spell? But what about her? Would Becca be expected to care for a baby that wasn't hers? How could she be a good mother to a child who was born of a creature she didn't believe existed?

"There's got to be another way." Robin's voice filtered through the mist.

The whole beach was drenched in a thick, impenetrable fog. She was covered in damp. Or was it sweat? It had gone from being chilly to being so warm and muggy that she felt like she was in a steam bath or a sauna.

"There's got to be a way to save Becca without killing you!" Robin's voice sounded completely anguished.

He was going to kill someone to save her? She tried to sit up. How had she ended up in a heap in the sand anyway? She tried again, struggling as though the weight of the world was holding her down. Well, of course it was! Robin was going to kill someone, kill someone for her – and the baby. How could she lie there and endure such a thing?

She can hear you, you know. A voice other than Robin's spoke. A woman's voice. It sounded closer than Robin's did, but she didn't understand how that could be? If Robin was on his mobile with someone using his speaker phone, the voices should be equally loud. But there was no service on the island. Had someone else come to the island, or had they left and gone somewhere else? It was so weird. Her brain felt as sharp as could be, but the rest of her couldn't comprehend anything. Her senses were altered, her perceptions were garbled. She hoped her mind was intact, and that she just wasn't imagining that.

"She won't understand what she's hearing. She doesn't believe in Selkies."

How ironic. The one thing that can save her and her mother and she doesn't believe it exists.

A deep shame washed over her as she listened. She didn't want anyone or anything to have to die on her account. Maybe Selkies were real. Or maybe she had a high fever and was delusional.

She gave up trying to listen and drifted off to la la land, where she could hear nothing but the soft sound of her own heartbeat.

CHAPTER 28

Robin called for an ambulance the second he had bars on his mobile. Becca was lying on the deck writhing with stomach pains and mumbling nonsense in her delirium. He'd been running the engine at full throttle and tending to her, too, but now that they were between Raasay and Skye, he had to be at the helm, watching for pleasure craft and steering clear of a few shallow areas where hidden rocks necessitated navigating. He sped by Kilt Rock and all the other places he usually stopped so his passengers could admire their beauty, keeping up as much speed as he could. He had to get Becca to hospital.

Soon enough—at least he hoped so—he was coming into Portree Harbor. He could see the flashing lights of the ambulance and pulled in as close as possible.

He glanced over his shoulder. Becca had been strangely quiet for the last few minutes, which in his opinion, was far more concerning than her moans of agony.

The paramedics rushed on board the second he lowered the plank, fully masked and gowned.

"Please be gentle with her."

They ignored him and worked quickly and efficiently. A crowd was gathering and they ignored them, too.

Someone yelled out. "I know them! It's the couple who

had a cure for the virus and kept it to themselves."

"Screw them!"

Robin stood tall and yelled back at them. "Eejits! If we had a cure for the virus, would we need an ambulance?"

Silence. Becca was on a backboard. "Robin, I'm so scared." Her eyes closed once again.

He took her hand. It was limp. "It's too early to tell, but I believe she is pregnant. Please don't do anything to her that might hurt the baby."

The paramedic in charge said, "There's no way an embryo that tiny can survive outside the mother's womb, so if a decision has to be made, we save the mother and hope she will conceive again."

A lump formed in Robin's throat. It couldn't come to that. It just couldn't. "I'm coming with her." He went to climb into the ambulance.

"I'm sorry. It's not allowed."

"I have reason to believe I have antibodies to the virus in my blood. If I'm tested and I'm right, it could save her life."

"And it could end yours."

"I've been with her the entire time. If I'm going to get it, I'm sure I'm already infected."

The paramedics exchanged veiled glances. The leader nodded.

Things were chaotic when they reached hospital, but they tested him without any argument. He was told he could wait in the waiting area. It was empty. No other family members or visitors were being allowed in.

"Sir?" A nurse entered the room.

"Is it Becca?" He jumped to his feet.

"Her condition is unchanged. But your test results are back and you do not have the virus. You do have antibodies. We assume it's because you've had a mild case."

Or because I'm a Selkie, he thought. But he said nothing.

"Would a blood transfusion help her?"

"It would if your blood types were compatible."

His mind flew to Soren, waiting on the beach, willing to

help, willing to sacrifice his own life to save Becca's and countless others.

"Aye." He crumpled back into his chair, his will defeated. But then, a spark of hope ignited deep inside his heart. "As long as I'm negative, and immune, could I please see Becca's mother, Emma Gibson?"

"I guess that would be awright."

A few minutes later, he was chatting with Emma. They hadn't been told she was doing better. She was still on oxygen and got winded very easily. And she was very distressed to learn that Becca was in hospital.

"I should be the one to die, not Becca." Tears streamed down Emma's face.

"She's not going to die, and neither are you." Robin told her about Soren and his offer, and that he couldn't bear the thought of Soren sacrificing himself for anyone, even Becca.

"But ye love her," Emma said. "If she's pregnant with yer child, ye must come to terms with what ye have to do."

"Of course I love Becca. But I love Soren and Shelagh, too. They're my friends. They're my brother and sister."

Emma clutched his hand. "Do you think I've developed antibodies? Would my blood be a match to Becca's? They wouldnae be magical Selkie, half-human, half-seal antibodies, and I know I'm nay completely well, but if I'm compatible, ye can hook me up and drain me dry!"

He squeezed her hand. "It would be worth a try if the doctors agree."

An hour later, Becca's situation was still deteriorating, but when Emma's blood was determined to have the antibodies Becca needed, a blood draw was scheduled, and then a transfusion.

"Please, Lord. Please let Becca and the baby be okay."

They were asking him to be patient. He was trying his best to remain positive. There was power in positivity, in faith, and he intended to use that power to its best advantage.

He paced the room, doing his best to pray. It was a new thing for him. He'd been fretting and worrying for decades. It was hard learning to do things differently, even when it involved a change for the better.

He paced and prayed for an hour – still no word. He needed something to do. Maybe it wasn't an ideal time to call David Wilson, but it was Wilson's daughter who was hovering between life and death, and the man probably had a right to know just in case Becca...

He dug David's number out of his wallet and dialed before he could think of any more dire outcomes. Have faith. Keep looking up! All things work together for good. Be thankful in all circumstances. He reminded himself of each of the little truisms Becca was fond of saying while he punched in David's number.

"Aye, this is David Wilson."

Dougal Wilson, the man who'd answered "Saelkie's Seafood Bistro" in a bright, upbeat voice, had taken a few seconds to bring his da to the phone.

He'd debated the issue of how to address the matter of Becca being Wilson's daughter hundreds of times. Chit chat until he found a way to ease into it gently? Blurt it out? Make up some reason why Wilson and Becca needed to meet, hope they liked each other, and then tell them the truth? Make reservations at the Bistro one night and hope Mr. Wilson had time to talk about something other than how good dinner tasted?

In different times, he might have handled things with more discretion, or a wee bit more finesse. The way things stood, he didn't see any point in holding back. "Mr. Wilson, you don't know me, but I'm a friend of Becca Ronan's. Becca recently showed up on your list of Ancestry matches as an extremely close DNA match. Because she's too young to be your sister, or a parent, there's every reason to believe you're her father. That's what I'd like to talk to you aboot."

Silence. The connection was so faint, the background so quiet, that he wondered for a second if the man had clicked off.

Then, quietly, "Give me a second." He heard shuffling

noises and the sound of a bell ringing as a door opened and closed.

"I'm outside where I can speak without being overheard." Silence. "Would ye please repeat what ye just said? I have nae been on Ancestry for some weeks so this is a wee bit of a shock to me."

Robin repeated what he had said.

"If this is an attempt to blackmail me, I willnae cooperate. I've never once been unfaithful to me wife, so if ye think ye—"

"Was there anyone else in your life before you were married? When you were young?"

Silence, as though he was sifting back through the wind and sands of years gone by. "Only once, with a beautiful creature whose name I dinnae even know."

"May I ask what year it was, and when it happened? Becca was born in the latter part of May, 1985." He didn't need to prove anything to the man—the DNA testing had already done that, but he needed to keep the man on his mobile long enough to come to grips with the idea and accept the truth of what had happened all those decades ago.

"Saints preserve us," Wilson said. "I have another bairn." He hesitated. "Is she there? May I speak to her?"

"I'm sorry to say she's in critical care in hospital. She has the virus. But she's been looking for her father for years now, and I'm sure she'll be ecstatic to learn that you've been found—especially since you're not a... you're not a Selkie are you?"

"Ye've made me laugh and cry in the same few sentences. Is she expected to recover?"

"We're all praying that she will."

"My wife is also in hospital with the virus, but I've nay been allowed to visit."

"I'm so sorry."

"Thank ye. It's been a difficult week, with that, and the bistro shut down again." Another silence. "Can I ask ye for your name and number, and my daughter's name and number so I can write it down and keep in touch with ye until such time as we can get together and sort things out?"

"Certainly. I'm Robin Murphy." He gave Wilson his number. "Becca's given name is Rebecca Gibson Ronan. She owns and operates Café Fish in Portree."

Silence. He didn't know what he'd expected – perhaps some show of interest that his daughter was in the same business as he, a comment that he'd heard nice things about the place, or maybe even been there, although restaurant owners were so notoriously busy at their own places that they rarely went out to eat at others. But nothing. Maybe someone had come outside to see what was keeping him? He tried to be patient.

"So ye're telling me that my daughter and ye are the ones who colluded with Die Droge to bring this scourge upon us all? The ones who have a cure, but withheld it from the rest of us until we were so desperate for it that we'd pay any amount to buy the cure that ye've conveniently developed just in time to make the maximum amount of profit? Because if that's who ye are, I want nothing to do with either of ye! I dinnae care what my DNA says! No daughter of mine would e'er do such a thing!"

"Da? Was the call aboot Mam? Is everything awright?" Robin heard a voice call from a distance.

"We are those people, but what you've heard is all distorted information conjured up by the media, in particular, a woman named Aggie who has a vendetta against Becca."

Wilson paused. Robin could almost hear the man's anger oozing through his mobile.

"Ye can say what ye will – that's what liars do. But this I know to be the truth – my wife is lying in hospital, and we know nay whether she'll live or die. There be a grain of truth in most stories, even when they be fiction. And I stick by my belief that nae daughter of mine would find herself in that position. Nae. I'll be sticking clear of the two of ye until things are sorted."

He heard a muffled voice in the background. "Da? Did

you hear what I said?"

Robin tried to say, "But, we—" but the connection had already been cut.

#

Becca wafted in and out of consciousness, at times able to hear as if from a distance, and other times, lost in a blinding fog. She thought she overheard Robin saying something about a seal they'd brought in. What was that about? Was she dreaming?

"Please forgive me, Soren."

Was that Robin speaking? Who was Soren? What was going on?

"So you'll call the scientist from Iceland?"

A voice that she didn't recognize said, "It's our only hope of saving either of them."

Another unfamiliar voice. "You mean both of them. Becca needs an antibody cocktail now, and Soren appears to be the only one who can give us what we need to prepare it."

Robin said, "But it's not right. There's got to be some way of saving her without sacrificing him."

What were they talking about? She tried to focus so she could hear the rest of the conversation, but her head was pounding and she needed to sleep.

When she came to again, she could still hear voices. Had she slept for five minutes, five hours, or a whole day? She tried to fight her way through the fog so she could hear what they were saying.

"At least Emma is responding to the infusion we gave her earlier. We hope the antibodies in your blood are enough to save her, but if we were to give Becca your blood, her body would treat it as a foreign invasion. Her immune system would attack your incompatible blood cells instead of incorporating them into her body."

She had no clue what they were talking about, but her mother was getting better! Her heart swelled with happiness.

Another voice she didn't recognize said, "Sorry to disappoint you, but I checked Emma's chart again before I came in. Sadly, the progress she made yesterday has all been – she's suffered another setback."

"Our hope is that if we can find a successful remedy for Emma, we can add any newly formed antibodies from her blood to the cocktail we're formulating for Becca."

She heard Robin say, "It would be pretty ironic if her mother's milk healed her so to speak."

"There's no way it will happen without Soren's contribution. The antibodies we need to cure the virus are found in seals, but their genetic make-up is incompatible with that of humans. For whatever reason, Soren's body seems to have unique features that we hope will allow those the seal antibodies to adapt, survive, and thrive in humans. You have the antibodies in your blood as well – enough to save Emma. But not enough for everyone.. Becca's blood is not compatible with yours. If you were to give her your blood, her body would treat it as a foreign invasion. Her immune system would attack your donated blood cells instead of incorporating them into her body. The fact that his blood has qualities similar to a human's O negative makes his contribution even more promising."

A woman with a thick accent—an accent unrecognizable to her—said, "This science is so new. I have no idea exactly what the end result is going to be, but Soren's blood may be the bridge we need to get Becca's body to accept the foreign antibodies."

All she could remember about the next few hours, days, whatever, was that she was being pulled down, down, down, lower and lower, by a vortex that was swirling so rapidly it couldn't be stopped. She was caught in a deep sea eddy with no end, a rip tide that kept her so far from shore that she wondered if she would ever make it home. Fever, chills, cramps, aches and hot flashes raged through her body. She prayed for the times when she was so out of it that she didn't know what was happening to her.

And then one day, she saw the sun shining through the window of her hospital room, and the blue sea beyond. And she knew she had walked through the valley of the shadow of death and survived.

"Robin, please tell me what's going on. How long have I been…Is my mother…?"

"Your mother is fine, she still tires easily and she may need oxygen for some time, but she's improving every day."

"What aboot The Fish?"

"Your mother told me who you use for your carpentry repairs and I asked him to start working on a new floor for the kitchen. He's prepping the sub-flooring and hoping you're up and aboot soon so you can sort out the tiles you'd like to use."

"Thank you." She owed him such a debt of gratitude. "And am I going to…?"

"A donor was found who had the needed antibodies to help you get better." Robin's voice should have reflected happiness, but he sounded so sad.

"But that's good news, isn't it?"

"Sure it is." Robin looked like he was going to cry.

"So why are you so sad?"

"These are tears of joy," Robin claimed.

But she knew him better than that.

"You can tell me aboot it—whatever's bothering you."

Robin didn't say anything for a minute or two. "I know you'll want to get Café Fish reopened as soon as possible. I wish there was more I could do to help. I'm actually a fair to passable cook but I don't have recipes for anything you normally make and I don't want to let your customers down. And Aggie's been sniffing around. It's been quite a week. I wanted to get back to the island and make sure the Chinese or whoever they were are leaving the seals alone, but there's only so much I can…"

"Please don't…I've been thinking, when I had my few lucid moments. All you have to do to help me is to set my mind at ease aboot the money Cameron left for me. I want your name to be on the bank account Cameron opened for me so if something happens to me, the money won't go to waste."

"Part of me feels so guilty aboot how the money was procured that I don't want to touch it." Robin looked even more depressed than he had a few minutes earlier.

"I've decided to use the money to repair the damage done to Café Fish. It was Die Droge that ruined my business and started a fire in the kitchen, so I feel justified in using their money to get the place cleaned up."

"Maybe we can still take that trip to Lewis and Harris to get that Harris Tweed you've been dreaming aboot to recover the seat cushions and booths."

"We'll see." She smiled. "It's sweet of you to remember."

"And what aboot the rest of the money? Cameron will have no need of it where he's going."

"Well, Cameron intended for me to use it to pay off my mortgage, and I would like to use it to cover my mortgage payments for the next, maybe six months, so I can concentrate on getting my strength back. But the rest I feel I should share with the other restaurant and hospitality businesses in the Western Isles to help them get back on their feet and compensate for the losses they've had."

Robin smiled. "Maybe in the form of some sort of a grant? I can help you get it set up if you like. Unfortunately, it's probably going to be awhile before my business picks up since tourists still aren't being allowed in the country without a lengthy quarantine."

"Thanks. I'd like that."

"I'm glad you're going to keep enough money to cover your mortgages for at least the next little bit. You need some time to recover physically, get your strength back and slowly ease into reopening the café. You also need to take into consideration the lawsuit against you that Aggie keeps threatening. That whole mess is what started this thing."

"I had almost forgotten." She winced. It felt like someone had slapped her. A wave of nausea swept through her midregion. "Did Aggie's mother die or recover? I think I knew at one point, but my mind is in such a fog that I don't know if I dreamed it or if it really happened."

"I'm sorry, Becca, but she didn't make it."

Her mind flooded with fresh worries. "Aggie's mother getting sick, whether from my restaurant or not, is one more thing that's entirely Die Droge's fault."

"Exactly. So you shouldn't feel guilty about using Cameron's money to get you out of that mess either."

"If we still gave Aggie an exclusive so she could break the news aboot the cure, with the stipulation that she would drop the case." Robin's look told her he did not approve that plan. "Or we could sell the story to one of the major news networks. I'm sure that would give us enough money to fight the lawsuit and still have money left over to give a boost to the tourism and hospitality industries in the Western Isles."

"No. Just no. I want to help the businesses, too, but I can't stomach the idea of profiting off—what happened."

What had happened? She still felt like Robin was not telling her the whole story.

Robin reached for her hand. "I know I'm changing the subject, but there's something else I need to tell you when you feel a little stronger. But for now, can you just trust me when I tell you to relax, forget aboot your troubles, and believe that there are good things to come?"

Did Robin not know that being in the dark would not only increase her stress levels by at least 50 percent, it would make her so jittery she wouldn't be able to sleep a wink all night?

CHAPTER 29

Rebecca dropped Robin's hand—first and foremost, because she was irritated with him, which was probably a sign that she was truly getting better—and tried to scoot over in her hospital bed, a feat she was too weak to have done with one hand.

She looked Robin square in the eye and tried to mentally warn him that now wasn't the time to mess with her. "I feel fine. Is this aboot Soren?"

"What do you know aboot him?" Robin's face changed from calm and hopeful to defensive and angry. He suddenly looked to be in a complete panic.

"I heard the name Soren mentioned several times when I was in and out of consciousness."

"Forget aboot it."

Was that bitterness she heard in his voice?

Robin started to pace the room. "What I need to talk to you aboot is your father. Your real father."

A hot flash zinged through her body. Was it a remnant from the virus, some residual from her fever, or the fear of hearing something she didn't want to know?

"So tell me. Did Cameron's test—he said he was my father."

"Yes. And I'm not sure why, because he's not. For

whatever reason, it's one more lie he told you."

She took a moment to digest the disappointment. "So someone else is claiming to be my father?"

"No, but he recently had his DNA tested and he is definitely your dad."

Wow. So she really did have a father. He was alive and well enough to care about tracing his ancestry.

"Just tell me. I'm fine with whatever you have to tell me aboot my father as long as you're not going to try to tell me he's a Selkie." She laughed. She was teasing of course. Because there was no such thing.

#

"Robin? Robin Murphy? I have to talk to you! This is important!"

"We know you're in there, and we're not going anywhere until you come out."

"Robin Murphy? Clark Kensington from the New York Times. I know business has been slow for a long time now. If you grant us exclusive rights..."

Yeah, yeah, yeah—if he just gave an interview to one of the major news networks, all his troubles would be over.

He ignored the voices. He couldn't stay below deck forever, but he could hope the throng of reporters would disperse in another hour or two. He had a meeting with the carpenter who was repairing Becca's subflooring so he could pick up some samples to show her. If he needed to, he'd fight his way through the media crowd to be there. There was no way he was going to let this whole insane frenzy result in more delays in getting Café Fish ready to reopen.

"You're a hero, Robin! We just want to honor you for exposing Die Droge's plot and helping Scotland Yard bring them down." He heard a loud cheer rising up from the cluster of reporters, and if he knew the town of Portree, probably a handful of locals, too.

If they knew the truth, they would understand why he was

nay hero. Traitor was more like it. Not that he wasn't relieved that Die Droge's research had been confiscated and other drug companies were continuing the effort—and making good progress. The fact that they now had the formula that was used to create the virus was key in finding a cure, although everyone said developing a vaccine would still take time.

He understood why everyone was so happy that Die Droge had been caught and brought to justice.

But it wasn't him who had made it all possible.

It was Soren. Soren's contribution was going to save the world, not his.

"We just want to talk to you about Murphy's Cocktail!" Another cheer rose up from the crowd.

All the major networks had reported that Robin was the one responsible for saving millions of lives by pointing a renowned Icelandic marine mammal scientist and a Danish epidemiologist in the direction of a unique species of seals that allowed them to develop an antibody cocktail doctors were calling Murphy's Cocktail.

"Your brother James said he would give us an interview if you won't."

That was it. He couldn't take it any longer. He flung the door open and burst through to the deck. Fresh air swept over him, filling his lungs, but doing nothing to wash away his perceived sins.

"Here's your story. I refuse to take any credit for the new treatment. I have asked specifically that my name NOT be used in the study the doctors will be releasing."

"Why? Why are you being so modest?"

"My involvement was minimal—and 'Murphy's Cocktail' sounds like something that should be on the menu at an Irish Pub. I'm sure they'll think of something more distinguished to call it if you give them time."

They laughed, like it was funny. Maybe the antidote should be called 'Selkie's Assortment.' But he couldn't say that.

Another reporter screamed, "It's said that the incentives

and rewards offered by the World Health Organization and other medical entities for coming up with a cure will make you a rich man. Will you keep operating your expedition boat once you're a millionaire?"

"I have not and will not be accepting any monetary compensation for my involvement."

"Gie it laldy," someone shouted with the same gusto they were complimenting him on. Had to be a local.

"But you are admitting that you were heavily involved in discovering a seal whose antibodies had the capability to reduce viral loads and save lives. Will you tell us what island the seal lived on?"

"Yes. Seal Island." Maybe that would get them off his back. Every island in the Outer Hebrides had seals living on it. Good luck sorting that out.

"A specific location? Latitude and Longitude?

That was when he panicked. What if they went looking and discovered the makeshift shelter he used to sleep in when he spent the night at the beach? Or the wispy tent that he and Becca had slept under when they'd made love, or even the remnants of the fire ring they'd used when they were glamping?

"This interview is over." Would he ever be able to go to his island again without fear of someone following him, or having planted a tracking device on his boat? How he hated this whole business!

He was all but blinded by the flash of their cameras a little later when he went to meet the tile layer who was doing Becca's floors. The same thing happened when he went to hospital, samples in hand. At least these days, he didn't have to put on a clergy shirt and pretend to be his brother to visit patients. He was, after all, The Robin of Robin Murphy's Cocktail. Every staff member knew him by name. That's the respect and special privileges you earned when you sold out a Selkie and became a hero.

Becca was awake and even more her old self when he found her new room.

When he asked her how she was feeling, she said, "Like my head's mince."

But she was out of isolation and not in need of the extra care or machines she'd been hooked up to. For that, he was thankful.

Becca was curious to know what he'd learned about David Wilson, so he told her the rest of what he knew and reassured her that although Wilson was a bit on the crusty side, he was not a Selkie.

She remembered less and less about the days she'd been gravely ill, but he explained to her about the antibody cocktail that the scientists had designed to reduce her viral load and save her life. He did not tell her about Soren sacrificing himself or that Selkies were real, or that he was part Selkie, or, that if she was indeed pregnant with his baby, then their child would be, too.

It was a lot for her to take in, even without the bits he kept from her.

"So is Cameron in jail?"

"The transmission rate is so high on the Isle of Skye that they didn't want to risk transferring him to Glasgow right now, so he's still here. He was under house arrest last I knew, with plans to jail him in Inverness."

"And the rest of his cronies from Die Droge?"

"Scotland Yard has taken in all of Die Droge's Scottish operatives thanks to my list. Others are being extradited from France to stand trial in London. I've given them all the evidence we had. They may want to interview you once you've recovered."

He could tell Becca's feelings were mixed, but she said, "Without you, they'd still be searching for the simplest of answers, and instead, they've found out who's responsible and are well on their way to being able to clean up the mess the virus made of the world."

"Please don't—I don't deserve—just stop."

Becca's face fell. But he just couldn't be gracious when he felt so undeserving.

Becca turned sad, sympathetic eyes on him, which in truth was the last thing he needed. "I know this has been hard on you, I know you were against this and I can only imagine how gutted you feel because seals had to be used in the research."

"You have no idea how I feel!" He did feel gutted, and angry with himself for feeling the way he did when Soren had actually been gutted—literally gutted. It was so wrong to feel sorry for himself when it was Soren who had paid the ultimate price.

"Well, I feel thankful that you did what had to be done to save my life – and mother's—and so many others. I'm proud of you, Robin."

He resented the hell out of Becca at that moment. How could he accept her accolades when he felt so horribly guilty? Would he ever be able to forgive himself?

His mind flew to Shelagh. Shelagh would understand how he felt. The question was, did she despise him for what he'd done to Soren, or did she feel enough devotion to him to help him heal?

#

Robin eased Sea Worthy into the narrow section of the Loch Carron that tapered to an end just a few kilometers past the town that it bordered. Lochcarron looked festively adorned, as it always did. He admired the people for maintaining and decorating their pretty little town with banners and strings of pendants just as they would have if there had been no pandemic. The triangular flags attached to the bunting fluttered in the wind, a welcome greeting to one of his favorite places.

Sea Worthy surged ahead even though they were going up against a stiff wind, as though she knew she was going home.

Becca looked scared to death, not of the wind and the waves, but of meeting her father—her birth father—for the first time. Robin grabbed her hand and held on tight until the wind gusted so strongly that he had to let go so he could hold onto the boat's wheel with both hands.

"It'll be fine." It was one of those days when he almost had to yell to be heard over the combined roar of the wind and the engines. "Katelyn and Rod both say he's a good man, very fair, and reasonable." He didn't tell her about his previous conversations with David, when her father had let loose with his frustration at Robin and Rebecca over Aggie's article. Better Becca didn't know about that quite yet. David had agreed not to mention it. Thankfully some people took the old adage of not discussing politics or religion over dinner seriously.

He pulled up to the shore and sidled up to the dock as gently as he could.

Becca waited patiently as he dropped anchor and secured the boat. "Is it just in my head, or is every eye in Lochcarron on us?" They disembarked and started walking down the lengthy main street to Saelkie's Seaside Bistro.

Becca gave a little shudder. "I feel like I'm on the set of a classic Old West cowboy movie – like the townspeople are all hiding behind their shutters and shades watching us – or is it just my imagination?"

"I think it feels dead for the same reason Skye does—because everybody's shut down. There are no tourists, and the locals are staying at home or quarantining just like they are in Portree."

"It's still eerie."

The sign for Saelkie's came into view – its ornate, nautical lettering was edged on either end with hand-painted seals, some dappled, some grey, all with big eyes rimmed with long lashes.

"Why would anyone name their restaurant Saelkie's? Does it mean he believes they're real?" Becca shook her head scornfully. "I certainly hope not."

Robin's heart shed a tear, but he decided he would give her a pass. She was upset and nervous. Now wasn't the time to confront her.

They were within a few yards of the Bistro. Becca stopped

and grabbed his shoulder. "I can't do this. My mother is still hovering between life and death, and Cameron, well, we went through so much with him, and now, this man is claiming to be my father. I just don't know how much more I can take."

He wrapped his arms around her and drew her close. "I have faith that Emma is going to pull through. Cameron is NOT your father. And David Wilson is not claiming to be your father. He is your father as proven by DNA testing. And I think it's a good sign that he wants to meet you and get to know you better. Relax."

"I'll try." Becca gulped.

"That's all any of us are asking." He pulled his mask and then hers aside and kissed her.

A few seconds later, he knocked on the door of Saelkie's.

David Wilson opened the door. He had on a mask. "Come on in if ye like. I'm alone. But I thought if we went outside and sat at one of the picnic tables down by the water, we could take our masks off and get to know each other properly."

Robin looked at Becca to gage her response. He'd marveled at the realization that her eyes were the exact same shape and color as David Wilson's when he'd first seen a picture of her father. Looking at both of them now, in quick sequence, he could see it even more clearly. He hoped she could, too.

David Wilson opened the door to the Bistro a little wider, but he said, "I think the wind is just strong enough that we shouldnae have to worry aboot midges. 'Tis as good a reason as any to spend a little time outdoors."

Robin knew Becca well enough to know she was smiling. The ice had been broken.

"Good idea," Becca said. "Midges love me. My mother always said it's because I'm so sweet. Of course, they never bother her at all."

David laughed. "My boys always liked going fishing with me because the midges flock to me and leave them completely alone."

They chitchatted and traded stories as they walked out to the table and sat down.

"How many children do you and your wife have?" Becca's voice sounded nervous.

"I have two sons. One works with me at Saelkie's, as head chef. The other is a fisherman, and supplies our restaurant and many others in the area with their seafood and Catch of the Day needs."

Becca looked like she was having one of those small world moments. "Is his name Duncan?"

"Aye. Duncan is my fisherman, and Dougal is my chef."

"Duncan was the one who told me that the seafood was infected. I really had to admire him for not trying to hoist one last load off on me since I hadn't checked my email and didn't know what was going on."

"He's a good lad."

"I hope he's been faring well," Robin said. "It's frustrating not to be able to do your job."

"Aye. He's been taking care of Dougal's children while he's at the Bistro and his wife is at work. She's a nurse and she's been working long hours as you might imagine."

"I'm sure it's a problem with all the daycare centers closed."

"It's been hard for everyone," David responded.

A brief silence ensued. Robin resisted the urge to start blathering about whatever.

"I understand you're the head cook at Café Fish," David said. "Your place has an excellent reputation. I've heard your Fisherman's Pies are the best in the west."

"Thanks. I really miss making them."

There was a brief silence, and then Becca blurted out, "So, do you remember my mother? And if you do, can you tell me aboot your relationship with her—what happened between the two of you? I brought a photo of her when she was in college."

A new silence stretched out, even longer than the first. Becca handed the photo to David.

"Aye, I remember her awright." He looked at the photo and smiled. There was more silence. "Becca, ye're a grown woman, so I'm going to speak to ye as such. I had nae relationship with yer mother at all. Ours was a one-time encounter."

"I understand if you don't want to talk aboot it."

"Nay. I owe ye that much." David pursed his lips. "I was scuba diving at the edge of a beach and strayed too far from the boat. I found myself in shallow waters, so I walked up the beach and took my mask off to breathe in the fresh air. Thankfully, I'd been diving in shallow waters all along so there was no issue with surfacing when I did."

His eyes took on a faraway look. "Yer mother was lying on the beach without a stitch of clothing on. There was something so alluring aboot her that it was magical. I'd ne'er seen such a beauty. There was a melancholy note in her eyes that I knew I had to satisfy.

"The whole thing was like a dream. I stripped off my wet suit—"

Robin looked at Becca to see how she was reacting. Had she heard what David just said? No wonder Emma thought Rebecca's father was a Selkie! She'd seen him rise out of the water, covered in what looked like seal skin, then removing it to reveal a man's body. Knowing Emma, and the times being as they were, he wouldn't be surprised if she'd taken a little something to enhance her mood as she lay sunbathing. It all made so much sense, especially if Emma had been high.

David went on to say that they made love on the beach, so hungry for each other, so lost in passion, that they never even exchanged names. Later, when David had seen his boat coming closer to shore, he'd decided to swim for it. That was the last time he'd ever seen or heard news of Emma.

"If I'd known we had a child, I would have found ye, lass. I promise ye I would have helped yer mother and been a part of yer life."

Becca sat so still, Robin thought she might have fainted, probably caught up in thoughts she couldn't begin to process.

Robin didn't want Becca to feel any pressure to speak until she was ready, so he said, "Thanks for your honesty, David."

"My wife is in hospital with the virus. I'm nay prepared to move forward with introductions or anything else until I've had a chance to speak with her." He drew in a deep breath. "Since you were conceived before I even met her, she shouldnae feel betrayed. But still, I hope ye'll respect my wishes so I can tell her aboot ye when she's back up and weill."

"I understand," Becca said. "I just appreciate you meeting me and explaining things."

"Can I ask ye one more thing?" David visibly relaxed. "Did ye attend a seminar by a guest lecturer whilst ye were a student at West Highland College entitled Pick-up Pastries for Parties?"

Becca's eyes opened wide. "I did. I loved that class! I still use several of the ideas my teacher suggested that day. Was that you?"

"Aye. Old, grey-haired men are nay anything memorable to a young college-aged lass."

Becca blushed. "Well, maybe not in that way, but I certainly appreciated the wisdom you shared with us." She smiled. "Can I ask you one more question?"

"Aye. Dinnae be shy."

"This may sound odd, but why is your bistro called Saelkie's?"

"Because for a long while, I believed yer mother to be a Selkie—a dream come to life. I've ne'er told anyone, but I lost my virginity to her. It was all so magical – she was so beautiful and enthralling that the thought of being with her lifts my mood a bit even to this day. And isn't that what the heart of a restaurant intends to do? To lift the spirits of all who enter in, and if by a little magic, so be it."

"I'm so thankful you told me that. I've always wished I was wanted, and I know I wasn't, but—"

"Now wait a minute, lass. You may nae have been planned, but ye cannae nae want something ye dinnae even know aboot."

Robin liked this man. He really did.

Becca said, "What I was going to stay is that it helps to know that at least I was created in a magical moment — instead of a drunken stupor or an assault or you know, a hurtful situation filled with a sea of regrets."

"My darling daughter." David said. "I'm delighted to welcome ye into my life. My only regret is that I dinnae know ye sooner."

Becca was crying tears that Robin hoped were happy ones. She was pure emotional these days.

She said, "I hope we can make up for lost time."

"Aye, lass. I promise ye we will."

CHAPTER 30

Becca could feel the tension in her shoulders evaporating as she and Robin motored their way past the town of Loch Carron and beyond. The mountains, the blue water and bluer skies were breathtaking. And it was all twice as beautiful because she finally knew who her father was. It was even better because he wasn't a conman or a crook. David Wilson had been warm and welcoming – and as an added bonus, he wasn't a Selkie.

She sighed. She hadn't felt so content in months. "I can't tell you how relieved I am that the whole Selkie myth has been put to rest once and for all." Becca felt happier than she had in years. "This nonsense aboot my father being a Selkie has followed me around my entire life. I can't begin to explain how unsettling it was to have to entertain the idea that I was descended from a bunch of slippery seals every time my mother made her ridiculous claim."

Robin smiled, but for some reason, he looked dubious. "I'm glad you feel good aboot finally finding your father – it's wonderful the way things worked out. David is a good man, and someone with whom you share a lot in common. Now that we've heard his explanation aboot being in a wet suit, and knowing your mother was probably a bit stoned at the time they hooked up, it's completely plausible to understand why she thought he was a Selkie."

"Exactly. I knew her story couldn't possibly be true the way she told it. I mean, really. What a ridiculous notion."

She assumed she and Robin would share a good laugh about the whole ludicrous idea of Emma having sex with an imaginary half man, half seal and file it on the shelf with other inside jokes they could tease each other about over fits of giggles in years to come.

And then, Robin said, "What I was going to say is that just because your father is not a Selkie doesn't mean that they're not real, that they're not out there."

She laughed. By herself. "Oh, fiddle faddle. First Emma, now, you."

"Your father, whom we both agree is a completely respectable, very knowledgeable man said he thought your mother was a Selkie when he found her on the beach. He obviously believes in them if he thought that were the case."

She shrugged, trying not to let Robin see how bugged she was by his refusal to drop the subject. "Don't get me wrong—I'm thrilled with my father and feel blessed to have found him. I really like David. But you heard the way he talks. Not that there's anything wrong with having a thick Scottish accent, but he's obviously pure folksy, just the type that you would expect to believe in the old legends."

Robin gave her an irritated look. "Most legends are based on facts."

Well, it might be news to Robin, but he wasn't the only one who was annoyed. She gave him a withering glance. "Of course they are. Ballads, stories, folklore fascinate us because they give us a chance to escape into an alternate universe. All you have to do is to look at what's going on in the world and it's easy to understand why people want to believe in a place where the laws of time and space don't apply and our imaginations can run wild, a fantasy world where we can be who we want to be when we want to be it. I mean, I like reading novels with shape shifters and werewolves and even vampires now and again—but it doesn't mean I believe they actually exist. I guess it's fun to let my desires run wild and imagine that I can literally do things I would never even consider doing in real life. But that doesn't mean I actually believe in the magical creatures I meet in the world of fantasy novels."

Robin sighed and stared off into the distance.

He was at the helm, so she couldn't look into his eyes and try to get him to smile. So she said, "Can we talk aboot something else? Please? I feel like we finally have our lives back. I have my health again, and it looks like my mom is going to make it, and the Fish will be up and running again before we know it, and you'll soon have tourists booking expeditions and we can start planning our wedding. There's so much to feel good aboot, Please? Can't we talk aboot something happy?

Robin didn't say a word.

The wind blew away her sigh while she waited. She listened to the hum of the engine, the sound of the surf, the splash of water drops against the hulls, the screeching of seagulls, the sounds of the wild and let the noises keep her company. It stayed that way until they were almost home.

Robin turned to face her. At first, she was happy that Robin was talking to her again, but only a few seconds into his speech, she knew something was wrong.

"I can't marry you, Becca. I'm sorry, because I know you didn't want to make love with a man until you were married, and now, we've made love and I can't marry you. We can't undo what we did, and I will always love you, but I can't ask you to be my wife."

"Why not? I don't understand." Was he saying he wanted them to live together instead of marrying? Or was he saying he wanted to break up? Her body started to stiffen as she waited for reassuring words about the timing being wrong, or them not being able to afford a wedding, or Rob needing to get his business back in the black before he could think about anything else.

But nothing came. No explanation. Not anything to hold

on to. No words of comfort. Nothing.

"You've got to explain this to me, Robin. You owe me that much."

"If it turns out that you're pregnant, and I do believe that's probably the case, please know that I'll help with the baby. I won't turn my back on my child or its mother."

She almost choked on the tears streaming down her cheeks. "If you think that helps… This isn't aboot my virginity or a baby that may or may not exist, it's aboot loving you and wanting to spend the rest of my life with you and not understanding why you've gone from feeling the same way aboot it that I do, to suddenly walking away from me. From us. Please tell me what happened to change your mind, because I have no clue what is going on."

"No. You don't have a clue."

The words he spoke were so faint that she barely heard him over the sound of the boat rumbling its way toward the dock. What on earth did he mean by that?

She saw tears running down Robin's cheeks, too, and his completely forlorn, gut-wrenching expression. Her first instinct was to run to him, to comfort him, to kiss his tears away.

But of course, she couldn't. And she knew she shouldn't, because Rob thought she was clueless, yet she couldn't argue with him because she had no idea what he was talking about.

#

Becca celebrated her next day of freedom from hospital by stopping by Café Fish to see how the new flooring looked. But instead of finding a gleaming new tile floor, she opened the door to find a commercial cleaning crew hosing down her kitchen with some sort of product especially made for ridding surfaces of smoke damage. The walls were streaked with black soot and the water funneling down through the drain in the floor was black. The technicians applying the treatment each wore a facial apparatus that looked like a gas mask. They wouldn't let her in even though she was wearing her mask.

A few minutes later, when she was heading back to check on her house, she was glad she hadn't pressed the cleaning crew to enter the Fish because her doctor called to confirm what she and Robin had both suspected. She was pregnant.

The doctor's estimate of how far along she was jived with the one and only time period she and Robin had been together sexually. No surprise there. But she was relieved when the doctor assured her that her illness and treatments hadn't seemed to cause any harm to the baby, that he or she appeared to be thriving.

Her first instinct was to run to Robin to share the good news. But then, she had no idea how he would view the situation now that they were no longer together. The only other person she could think to turn to was Emma. While her mother wasn't known for her expertise in being understanding or comforting, Becca thought she would at least be able to relate to the dilemma Becca was soon going to find herself in – being a single mother, just like Emma had been.

Then again…

"I'm sorry, Rebecca, but ye are such a dolt."

It wasn't the first time her mother had called her a stupid jerk, but good grief. She'd just found out she was pregnant, Robin wasn't speaking to her, and her entire life was a mess. A little support might have been nice.

Emma didn't look chagrinned in the slightest. In fact, she was very vocal in continuing her assault. "Ye're a fool, Becca. I know ye're my daughter, but honestly, ye're being ridiculous."

"I'm being ridiculous? Robin is the one who walked out on me without even telling me why!"

"Have ye tried to find out what's wrong?"

"He wouldn't say anything except that he couldn't marry me."

"Did he say he loved ye?"

"Yes, but what difference does it make if he won't talk to

me or tell me what's wrong? How can I fix something if I don't know what the problem is?"

Her mother glared at her. "I hope this isn't aboot the Selkies."

"I thought we were over that, Mother. David Wilson was in a wet suit. He stripped out of it when he saw you on the beach. He was not a Selkie. You just thought he was because you were drunk, or high, or whatever."

"And ye're judging me after having yer own little rendezvous on the beach and getting yerself pregnant? At least I can blame my indiscretions on being high. You have no excuse."

"Robin loves me!"

"Well, where is he then?"

She started to cry. Why she hadn't let her mother waste away in hospital, she had no idea. This was not what she needed. Her mother couldn't just comfort her and give her a little support every once in awhile?

"And Cameron loved me, too!" Emma huffed and didn't let up even though Becca was in tears. "Robin believes there are Selkies. He's met them personally. He's had relationships with them. If ye continue to refuse to accept that there are Selkies in the world, ye'll continue to alienate him. Yer rejection of the Selkies – Robin's friends, aye, his family – is tantamount to a rejection of him personally."

She had a sudden, terrifying revelation. Robin had been so sad when the scientists had developed the cocktail that saved her life. He should have been happy. He'd been devastated that a seal had to be sacrificed to find a cure for the virus – even though it had saved her life and many others. Why hadn't he been able to see that a seal's life was – well, a seal's life. And then, when…

Oh, Lord. What if the seal whose life had been taken to save hers was one of the seals that Robin considered to be his friends? Her mind started to whirl. She wasn't ready to concede that Selkies really existed, but if there was something special about the antibodies from this particular seal that had worked when all the other seals that they'd tested had not...

Her stomach turned at the thought that Robin had had to deal with the knowledge that a being he considered a pet, or a friend, or whatever – had died on her behalf.

Lord, what had she done?

If what she suspected was true...

"Mother?" She shared her suspicions.

Her mother looked at her for a long time without saying anything. She took her hand in hers. Tears started to stream down her face.

"I dinnae know this for sure, sweetheart, but have ye thought aboot the fact that the reason Robin has such an affinity for seals, such a heart for their well-being, is that he has a wee bit of Selkie blood himself?"

"No. I –" Her mind leapt from one conversation to another – the horrid, cynical, insensitive things she'd said. How could she have been so selfish? She didn't want to say anything in front of her mother, but for the most part, her disgust for the whole Selkie concept was a calculated attempt to be nothing like her mother. She'd never even stopped to consider how her uncharitable attitude had made Rob feel.

So she would adapt, adjust her attitude. Maybe, eons ago, a seal-like man-creature had existed. Maybe that's why the Selkie legends were so embedded in Scottish culture and literature. It didn't mean such a creature still existed today, but it could explain ancient traces of their blood and certain antibodies being found in modern day people – even seals. She did not believe Darwin's Theory of Evolution – the world and its inhabitants were much too intricately designed for it to have come about by chance – but it was a proven fact that there was evolution within species, and that humans shared quite a bit of DNA with other species. Since Selkies came from the sea, where life was considered to have begun, maybe there was some credence in the Selkie theory.

"Tell me everything you know aboot them."

Her mother's face registered disbelief, then doubt, then joy. "I'd be happy to."

Becca jumped in. "I've always heard that the original stories about seal folk came aboot because of explorers who wore heavy furs and visited places like Orkney – real people who the primitive islanders only imagined to be Selkies. You know, kind of like David coming out of the sea in a wet suit. A very understandable misconception."

He mother gave her a look.

She tried again. "Another theory I've heard is they're the reincarnations of people lost at sea, or humans trapped in the form of seals. When I was in secondary school, one of my teachers told us there is a Biblically inspired view that seals are fallen angels who landed in the sea while angels that fell on the land became fairies."

Her mother smiled. "Ye're wrong, but I'm aware that those sorts of ideas have been floating aboot for years. I once had a Sunday School teacher tell me that when God parted the waters of the Red Sea, and Pharaoh and his men were pursuing Moses and the Children of Israel, the Egyptians became seals when the waters came together and they were drowned. She said that if we listened closely to the seals barking, we could hear the sound of the soldiers calling 'Pharaoh'. Of course, she was an Icelander, so who knows where the story came from."

Becca sighed. "Remember when I was in primary school and I had that friend whose Dad was lost at sea?"

"Wasn't he a fisherman?"

"Yes. I think his ship went down in a storm."

"Probably a hurricane," her mother said. "Back then, they didn't have the means to forecast them with such pinpoint accuracy or so far in advance the way they do now."

"Well, one day she told me that the reason her da's body was never found was that when he realized there was no way he could make it home to be with her and her mam, he joined the seal people and became one of them."

"Oh my. What did ye say to her? I hope ye dinnae—"

"I told my teacher what she'd said, and my teacher told me that everyone deals with grief differently, and if it brought her comfort or made my friend feel better to think of her da living on as a seal, then we should just let her think that."

"Poor girl. She's probably out at sea every chance she gets even today, combing the beaches and rocky outcroppings, hoping she'll catch a glimpse of her da." Her mother's eyes took on a special gleam. "Or maybe she already has."

"You can't possibly believe that—"

"Who am I to say that one legend is true and another isn't? That's what I'm trying to tell ye, Rebecca. You have to open your heart to a whole big world full of possibilities. Read 'The Hobbit' by Tolkien and tell me ye don't believe in hobbits and elfish folk by the time you're done."

"Not the same. It's a work of fiction."

"So read or watch 'The Little Mermaid', or 'Peter Pan'."

"Fairy tale, fiction."

"Or are they?" Emma asked the question with all seriousness. "All I'm saying is that, if ye limit yerself to the few things ye've experienced directly and tangibly, in yer corporeal form, ye miss out on so much. Ye should know this, Becca, being a person of faith."

Of course she should. She couldn't reach out and touch God with her hands or hold him in her arms, but she could see Him with her heart and feel Him with her soul. She nodded.

Emma took her opening. "So here are a few things I believe to be true aboot Selkies. Of course, I've only ever met males of the species."

"Of course." Becca rolled her eyes, although this time, she tried to be subtle about it.

"Selkie males are much freer than their female counterparts. And they can only mate with human women."

"Lucky for you," Becca said, trying her best not to be sarcastic.

Emma ignored her. "Some say males can roam at will on both land and sea, but others believe they can only appear in their human form once a year, on Mid-Summers Night Eve. Some say they appear as humans only once every seven years.

They seem to be fairly well-meaning creatures who have a sense of family responsibility and an affection for their human wives and offspring."

"Kind of difficult if they're only around one night a year, or once every seven years."

"Right. Well that's why I passed along that belief to ye when ye were little. I dinnae want ye to have the expectation that yer father was suddenly going to come home and live with us."

"Right. You told me that was the reason my real daddy couldn't come to visit us."

"I didn't want ye to think he dinnae care. The truth is, neither the male nor female Selkies form lasting relationships, even with their offspring. They constantly struggle with how to manage their dual existence, and always return to the sea after a brief period on land. Their sea identity always predominates. Given the opportunity, they will always return to their seal form, even though they know it may be a year – or even seven – before they can return to see their loved ones on land."

Becca sighed. As far as she was concerned, her mother had messed her up for life when she told her that her father was a Selkie. "You couldn't have just told me my father died in a tragic auto accident and let that be the end of it?"

"I told ye what I believed to be true. Ye would really prefer that I had lied to you?"

Another sigh. "I guess not. But we digress. I need to find a way to make it up to Robin, to accept him as he is no matter what my true beliefs."

"Oh, Becca." Her mother looked a bit gob smacked, a rare thing for Emma. It took a lot to rattle her. "I find it very concerning that yer highest goal is to come up with a plan to convince Robin that ye can tolerate his feelings – ye cannae just believe?"

Becca thought long and hard before she answered. "I don't know." Maybe she could. Maybe she couldn't. She honestly didn't know.

CHAPTER 31

All Robin wanted to do was to sail off into the sunset to see if he could find Shelagh. But he didn't dare chance it. Reporters followed him 24 by 7, hoping to get the story of the decade. They seemed to know that there was more to the story than he was telling them and that whatever he was hiding was somehow connected to the seals.

He could see a storm brewing to the west as nightfall came to Skye. Lightning etched the sky in lacey designs over Raasay when he finally went below deck. The waves jostled Sea Worthy as it strained away from the anchor and bucked against the dock. When the waves came into Portree Harbor this strong, it could only mean one thing – a storm approaching from the northwest, sliding between the islands. It promised to be a rough night.

He was almost ready to bunk down when his mobile rang. Aggie. Just what he needed before he tried to sleep through a stormy night – some good, old-fashioned mental agitation in addition to the bucking waves.

He answered. Better to get it over with than to fret about it all night long.

Aggie's opener was. "You gave me your word."

He should have managed a quick comeback, but he was tired and dispirited. "Listen, Aggie. We promised you an exclusive interview. You promised not to leak the story until we had proof. Things turned out a lot differently than either of us thought they would. We can start over and move on from here, or we can hurl insults and threaten each other until hell freezes over, which, judging by the way things are going in the world, may not be far off."

"Then I'd better hurry up and file my lawsuit against Café Fish to make sure I get my hefty cash settlement before the world ends."

"I can't speak for Becca, but it's going to be hard to convince a judge that a sympathetic hero like Becca purposely tried to harm your mother." His attempts at making peace didn't get him very far with Aggie, but he tried.

"But I have hospital bills, and loss of income."

"Doesn't everybody? I don't see how Becca and I can be held responsible for something that was entirely Die Droge's fault, especially given that the judge will know that the crisis would still be ongoing if it weren't for us."

"But my mother is dead. Her last few weeks on this earth were a living hell, and because of it, I'm emotionally damaged. And it happened at Café Fish."

"You're going to have to speak to Becca aboot that. Maybe she'll give you a month's worth of her Fisherman's Pie to compensate you for your trauma. But I don't know. I can't speak for her."

Although he was truly sorry Aggie had lost her mother, it was almost fun sparring with her. In the end, she gave up, but she promised it wouldn't be the last time they heard from her.

He'd already showered, so he plugged in his mobile to recharge while he slept, then slipped under his blanket.

The waves were getting stronger by the minute. The up and down sensations might have rocked him to sleep if he hadn't known worse was coming.

His mobile rang again. He sat up, disconnected the phone from the charger and lay back down. It was Becca. He'd never thought he'd be even less excited to hear from her than he had been Aggie, but there he was.

"Sorry to bother you." Becca sounded hesitant.

"No worries. I'm still awake."

"I probably shouldn't be telling you over the phone, but since you kind of already know…"

"We're having a baby?" He couldn't help himself. It was such happy news, even though he and Becca were not together.

"I've been doing some thinking and I have a few things to say." Becca's voice shook with emotion. "You loved me even when you thought my father was a Selkie."

"Why wouldn't I, Becca? I know you haven't had the pleasure of knowing them like I do, but Selkies are beautiful creatures. They're kind and intelligent, gentle and loving. Even in the old days, they were legendary for being lovers of music and song, for giving barren women children, and for changing the tears of heartbreak to joy."

"You make them sound so real, and like people – is that what I should call them? Like someone – something – some folks I'd like to get to know?"

"I'm glad you feel that way. Because you already know one."

"I do?"

He wanted to say, yes, and the baby in your womb has Selkie blood, too, and the crux of the problem is that you have to believe in order to come to terms with what that means. But he wanted her to feel comfortable. He didn't want to force the truth on her before she was ready.

And then, it must have hit her head on. "But that would mean that our baby…"

"Yes."

"And that's because you're part Selkie, and that I'm alive because the seals – the Selkies – who saved my life have special antibodies that transcend their species and ours. Well, mine."

"I'm not a different species than you are, Becca. I just have a wee bit of Selkie blood in my genes."

"What is it like, being part Selkie? Please help me to

understand."

He so wished she was on the boat with him, and not just a voice on his mobile. But the storm was kicking up pretty hard now, and well, maybe this was better. Maybe it was just his generation, but sometimes it was easier to say certain things over a mobile than in person, easier still in a text or chat.

"My Selkie blood is the reason I have antibodies. I can eat all the fish I want and never get sick. That's why my antibodies were used in the cocktail along with Soren's to develop a cure."

"So Soren is a Selkie?"

"Yes."

"When you first met him, how could you tell he was a Selkie? Does he look different than the other seals? Does he know our language or is there some sort of Selkie language that you use to communicate?"

"Selkies look the same as other seals when they're in seal form – well, maybe their eyes and facial features are a little more expressive. I'm not sure anyone would notice it but another Selkie. But the thing that makes them unique is that they're sentient. I can hear them speaking in my mind. Sometimes they come to me in my dreams, but not always. I don't know how else to explain it, Becca. It's like nothing else I've ever experienced."

"I wish I could—I mean—could you be happy being with me even though I can't share—or even fully understand that part of you?"

"I love you, Becca, but I know I can't expect you to love me. I understand how you feel aboot seals. I get that the whole Selkie thing must be pretty mind boggling."

"I've done some research and checked Ancestry. It is mind-boggling, and I can't say that I understand it all, but I promise you that I love you just the way you are. You know what they say aboot Selkies. It's probably the Selkie part of you that makes you so lovable."

"That's really how you feel?"

"Please forgive me, Robin. I'm asking for a second chance.

I promise I won't disappoint you."

"Of course. I love you, Becca." If they'd been together, he'd have shown her just how much he loved her.

"Robin?"

A wave hit the boat with such force that his head hit the end of his bunk.

"Did Soren give his life so that I could live?"

"Yes." The word came out as a whisper. Part of him didn't want to talk about it now, or ever. But it was important that she knew. It was important that Soren's legacy live on – in Becca, in their child, in the story of their lives.

"Please tell me. Tell me everything."

And so, he told her – about Soren, and Shelagh, and the others with whom he'd danced and swam and awakened naked on the beach. While the wind and the waves battered his boat, his memories of Soren both bruised his heart, and lifted his soul to new heights.

And when the story was done, and he could feel that she believed, and not just with his mind, but in the pure core of his being, in the place he felt the Selkies, he asked her, "Can you be here at dawn's light?"

"Yes." Becca's voice was a whisper. It was as if they both knew something extraordinary was about to happen. Or maybe it already had.

#

Robin squeezed Becca's hand as they left the protection of Portree Harbor – and the reporters who had been hounding him every day from mid-morning to dusk.

"Leaving at dawn was the only way I could think to give them the slip. Thankfully, none of them seems the early bird type."

"I hope none of them has taken a room overlooking the harbor or they might have heard the boat start up. Of course, they'd still need a boat to follow us."

"I've heard rumors that one or two of my competitors

have been put on standby so the second I take off, the reporter whose got them on retainer could board and pursue me." Robin opened the boat to full throttle now that they'd cleared the boats that were docked along the fringes of the harbor.

"And I'm sure they're all so hungry for business that they'd do it for the right price."

"Can't blame them." He let go of Becca's hand to turn the wheel with both hands.

"No," Becca said. "But I can make sure I don't give them a tourism grant when it comes time to divvy up Cameron's money."

Becca was definitely getting her spunk back. He turned hard to the left. He planned to stick close to the coast today instead of heading toward Raasay, which was the quickest route to open sea. Mix things up a bit in case anyone did try to follow.

Becca grabbed a hold to steady herself. "Well, I bet none of the other excursion boat captains sleep on their boat, so you'd still have the advantage."

"Yes, but some of them have faster boats. And I wouldn't put it past the reporters from the BBC or CNN to hire a sea plane. I guess you can do whatever you want if your budget is big enough."

Becca huffed her disapproval. "They should respect people's privacy when they're asked to stand down."

"I'm sure if I had a high priced attorney, I could make them go away, but we both know that's not happening anytime soon."

Becca sighed. "I know sharing the money Cameron gave me is the right thing to do, but sometimes I'm tempted to use it all for us – just make our problems all go away – maybe buy a restaurant on the Isle of Lewis or somewhere in the Highlands now that I've learned to cook dishes without seafood."

He laughed. They'd all had to adjust, that was for sure.

"So what's the plan?"

"I need to see Shelagh. She's Soren's sister, and she was devastated when Soren was taken."

Becca's voice was soft and respectful. "Did she approve of his decision to give himself up? I'm not sure I would have if I was in her position."

"She was against the idea, and very upset. I'm not sure what kind of reception we'll get, but I have to try."

"I understand."

"I'm taking a different route than usual, and I don't plan on going anywhere near the island until I'm dead certain we haven't been followed. Even then, we won't stay for long, just in case. Although while we're there, I need to destroy the makeshift shelter I built, the tent where we slept when we were on the island together, our fire rings, and any other evidence of our being there. If someone were to spot signs of life, it wouldn't take long to put two and two together."

"So the seals aren't put at risk."

"Exactly. No one has used the word Selkie in all this time, but they know there is something different and special aboot these certain seal. The legends have fascinated Scots for centuries. I'm afraid of what they would do to get proof that they really do exist."

"Or to be able to do more research." Becca winced as though it hurt her to think about it. "Were any of the seals that were randomly slaughtered at the beginning of the pandemic Selkies?"

"I assume not. If they had caught a Selkie by accident, they would have had tissue that gave them what they needed for a cure, and Soren wouldn't have had to give himself up."

Becca leaned against the rail and stared at the ripples fanning out from Sea Worthy's wake. "It's just so sad. I feel guilty for getting sick and being one of the people Soren had to save."

"He didn't have to do anything. He chose to do it." Robin adjusted his setting and put the ship on autopilot. The waters were as smooth as glass, at least near shore. Quite a switch from last night.

"Still, it's sad he had to die," Becca said, sounding as blue as the water and sky surrounding them. "When I was a teenager, a little boy I used to babysit lived on a farm. The family had a handful of chickens, cows and pigs, and his da had told him to say thank you to one of the grunters because later that day, he was going to take him to the locker so they could have bacon to eat over the winter. After his da left, he asked me how they got the bacon out of a grunter. Well, I didn't want to be the one to tell him, so I asked him what he thought. He said, they probably opened up the pig and took the bacon out, and then stitched the pig up so he could come home."

"Well, the kid was certainly a thinker."

"Yeah. I always wished his theory was true."

"I wonder what his da said to him when he got home. I hope he didn't laugh."

"I hope not, too." Becca took his hand. "Have we hit upon a sore spot?"

"Well, having heard the dynamics between James and me, you can probably imagine that I was teased more than a bit whilst I was growing up. I always thought it was because I was adopted, but my mates at school said their families made fun of them, too. Why, I can't imagine. Some sort of an attempt to make sure your kid has thick skin when he's grown?"

"Emma still mocks me for no other reason than I'm so different than she is." Becca stared out at the sea. "I've asked you before, but has everything that's happened to you recently made you want to search for your birth parents?"

He adjusted his setting to the new curve of the land. "When I was last on Ancestry, a couple of matches indicated I might have some distant cousins out there somewhere. I haven't had time to follow up."

"That's wonderful!" Becca took his hand. "What did your family tease you aboot? I assume it wasn't aboot your Selkie blood, since you only just found out."

"Right. But even then, I loved stories about magical or

mythological characters – C.S. Lewis' *Chronicles of Narnia*, Swift's *Gulliver's Travels*, Tolkien's *The Hobbit* and *Lord of the Rings*. When I was little, *Peter Pan* was my favorite storybook. When I tried to talk aboot the books I was reading, they were critical of my choices and kept asking me what I'd been smoking or what kind of fairyland I was living in. My mother liked memoir type, family saga books that were entirely based in reality. Her favorite series was Laura Ingalls Wilder's *Little House on the Prairie*."

Unfortunately, she could relate. "Emma second guessed or flat out disagreed with every choice I made as a kid. She thought I was weird, and always said that if she didn't remember the exact moment she pushed me out of her belly, she'd swear I wasn't her bairn. One time, she even said the nurses at hospital had to have switched me at birth, because I couldn't possibly be hers."

"Ouch. Don't parents realize what damage they do to us when they say things like that?"

"I know Emma loves me, but… well… evidently not."

"Yeah. I was always the odd one out. My mother named me Robin because I evidently looked like a little ragamuffin when they adopted me – disheveled ill-cut hair sticking up from my head, and clothes that were raggedy and nearly threadbare. My straggly appearance evidently reminded my mother of the jagged, uneven petals of a ragged robin, which happened to be one of her favorite flowers, so she called me Robin." He sighed. "I think she intended it as some sort of an endearment, but all it did is to act as a constant reminder of how different I am."

He looked up and scanned the open waters for boats. "I keep checking… The only boats likely to be out this early in the day are fishing boats, and no one's fishing."

"And probably won't be for a very long time. How are they ever going to decontaminate the marine population? Has anyone proposed a plan?"

"Not that I've heard," Robin said.

"I hope they figure it out soon, or I'll have to change the

restaurant's name to Café Coo."

They both laughed, but Becca's face looked pure serious.

"Maybe that's what we should use Cameron's money for."

"To restore marine life?"

"Yes!" She looked more excited than he'd seen her since before she got sick. "We could create a seal sanctuary, and make sure they're protected from this sort of thing ever happening again, Someone needs to address the healing of our fish supply."

"I love that idea!" A rush of warmth coursed though his body. Lord, he loved this woman. She wasn't perfect, but she had a big heart that was bursting with good intentions, and he loved her so much.

They talked about ideas for their seal sanctuary until they started to near the island.

Suddenly, his instincts revved into a state of high alert, as though someone had yelled "Don't come any closer!" in his ear. He could only assume that Shelagh was very close by.

CHAPTER 32

Robin's heart sank. He'd wanted to find Shelagh and he'd found her. Was she so mad at him that she wasn't going to allow him to visit the one place in the world that he loved the most?

Go south until you see a large rock protruding from the sea. There is a small beach on the far side. We will meet you there.

His mind whirled with possibilities as he turned the ship to the south. What had the voice meant by "we?" He'd heard that it was hard for people to adjust to saying "I" or "me" instead of "we" or "us" after a death of a spouse or family member. His heart went out to Shelagh. He hoped seals were able to help each other through times of grief the way humans did. He knew dogs were sensitive to loss and grieved when their master of another family pet died, so he assumed that seals were capable of the same emotions. He regretted that he'd never tried to find out more about Shelagh and Soren's family. He'd never even thought to ask.

He scanned the horizon. As far as he could tell, they still had the waters to themselves. He thought he knew the rock in question – he had never stopped because no seals inhabited the island. Seals liked to cluster in colonies and this beach wasn't big enough.

He motioned for Becca to keep quiet. What was going on?

Do not fear, Robin. We are only trying to protect the other seals.

This time, the voice he heard wasn't Shelagh's or even that of a woman. What they were communicating to him made sense. He didn't think he'd been followed, but even he couldn't rule out the possibility that someone had attached a tracer to Sea Worthy. Pretty sad when seals exhibited more common sense than mankind.

Do you not recognize me, my friend?

If he hadn't known better, he could have sworn it was Soren. The cadence of the voice – the resemblance was uncanny.

"Soren?" He said aloud, feeling like he was in shock and confused.

Becca's eyes met his, asking, what?

"Soren? You're alive? How can that be?"

Becca looked like she was about to cry.

He looked down and saw a large, familiar-looking seal circling the boat. His heart felt like it was going to burst.

What happened was only possible because the Icelander you called in was part Selkie. I was able to communicate with him.

Robin's brain whirled with joy. He tried to tell Becca what he could imagine of the scenario. "The Icelandic marine mammal scientist I asked to come to Skye so Soren would be treated more humanely must have come up with a way to do the impossible. At one point he was talking aboot using an untried surgical technique to remove the tissue they needed for experimentation along with part of Soren's colon, which they could then use to coax the antibodies to grow and reproduce." Robin's head was spinning. "When I never heard any more aboot it, I assumed they weren't able to proceed, or that they had tried and failed."

Becca looked as relieved as he had ever seen her. "So instead of killing Soren, they performed surgery and stitched him back together again so he could return to his natural environment?"

"Just like your grunter story." Robin turned and kissed her.

Becca smiled. "Can Soren hear me if I speak to him?"

"I'm not sure."

She moved to the runnels and started to speak. "Soren, I never thought I would be able to thank you for saving my life. I'm so happy you survived, and so humbled to have the chance to show my appreciation to you for being willing to give your life so that I could live mine."

"Anyone would have done the same," Robin said, after hearing Soren's voice speak to him.

"I wouldn't have." Becca's voice was small and reluctant. "I feel so ashamed because I know I wouldn't have done the same for you, or any other seal. Robin would have. But I... I..." She started to shiver. Robin drew her close.

"Soren? Shelagh?" Robin spoke out loud so Becca could hear what he was about to say. "I don't know how to thank you enough. We owe our lives to you."

Soren's voice sang in the recesses of his mind. *Celebrate the things that make us unique.*

Rob whispered the words to Becca and she squeezed his arm. "You have a gift for understanding others."

"Right, because I've always felt so misunderstood."

"You can thank James for that one." Becca laughed.

"And Cameron. I'll never understand how he could do what he did."

She sighed. "We can work on that one together. Except I'll be trying to appreciate my mother in spite of our differences."

Rob felt an outpouring of emotion from Soren and tried to put the thoughts into words that Becca could understand. "Becca, you never felt truly loved or accepted, but because of it, you have a tender heart, much wisdom, and the gift of being able to recognize and appreciate true love when it is given to you."

Becca wiped tears from her eyes. "Aye. That's me. I never want to be accused of being normal. Like it says in I Corinthians – But God has placed the parts of the body, every one of them, just as he wanted them to be."

The breeze was drying his tears before they could be seen, but he felt the love – the gratefulness – just the same. "We're all essential parts of the body. We all have gifts that we can use to help each other."

There was a ripple of motion in the water around the ship. Sunlight sparkled in the droplets flying into the air.

Becca nuzzled against him. "All things bright and beautiful, all creatures great and small, all things wise and wonderful, the Lord God made them all."

"Praise the Lord from the earth, you great sea creatures of the ocean depths." Robin had no idea where or who the words came from. He must have learned them long ago in Sunday School and forgotten about them until now.

Becca spoke quietly, as if she stood in great awe of the universe. "Here is the sea, vast and spacious, teeming with life of every kind, living things both great and small – I think it's from somewhere in the Psalms."

"You believe." Robin looked at Becca watching the waves, the seals frolicking in the sea, and knew that he had finally found a place where he was truly accepted for exactly who and what he was. "You really believe."

Becca reached for his hand, looking surprised with herself. "I do! I believe in Selkies."

"And I believe in God," Robin added.

Becca twirled around him, her arms open and accepting. "It's a mystery that I don't begin to understand."

"But you believe."

"I do. And I believe in love."

"And I believe I've finally found a family." Robin heard Soren and Shelagh frolicking in the water. Just as he could sense Becca's understanding and support, he could feel Soren and Shelagh's joy.

And then, a ripple in the water, the swish of a tail, and his Selkie friends were gone. He turned away from the sea and wrapped his arms around Becca. It was time to return to Portree and rebuild their lives. But he knew it would go swimmingly, because Becca was with him, and she believed.

ABOUT THE AUTHOR

Thirty years ago, Sherrie rescued a dilapidated Victorian from the bulldozer's grips and turned it into a B&B and teahouse, the Blue Belle Inn. After 12 years of writing romance novels, Sherrie married her real-life hero, Mark Decker, a pastor. They share two houses, 85 miles apart, and Sherrie writes on the run whenever she has a spare minute. Sherrie enjoys playing the piano, painting, photography, writing murder mysteries and planning her next European adventure. Sherrie's highly-acclaimed contemporary romantic suspense novels and mysteries include her popular Wildflowers of Scotland novels, PLUM TART IRIS, a mystery set in old Bohemia, SEASIDE DAISY, a mystery set in Ireland, LOVE NOTES, set in Northern Minnesota, and DAYBREAK, the long-awaited sequel to Sherrie's début novel, NIGHT & DAY, where it's midnight in Minnesota and daybreak in Denmark.

Reviews are appreciated! You will find Sherrie at Amazon.com, Goodreads.com, and BookBub.com

Follow Sherrie at
https://www.facebook.com/SherrieHansenAuthor

Follow Sherrie's blog at

www.Sherriehansen.wordpress.com

Made in the USA
Columbia, SC
29 June 2021